Contents

Books by William Saroyan

Stories

The Daring Young Man on the
  Flying Trapeze
Inhale and Exhale
Three Times, Three
Little Children
Love, Here is My Hat
The Trouble with Tigers
Peace, It's Wonderful
My Name is Aram
Saroyan's Fables
Dear Baby
The Saroyan Special
The Assyrian
The Whole Voyald
The William Saroyan Reader
My Kind of Crazy Wonderful People
The Man with the Heart in the
  Highlands
My Name is Saroyan

Novels

The Human Comedy
The Adventures of Wesley Jackson
Rock Wagram
Tracy's Tiger
The Laughing Matter
Mama I Love You
Papa You're Crazy
Boys and Girls Together
One Day in the Afternoon of the
  World

Memoirs and General

The Bicycle Rider in Beverly Hills
Not Dying
Here Comes There Goes You Know
  Who

After Thirty Years:
  The Daring Young Man on the
  Flying Trapeze
Short Drive Sweet Chariot
I Used to Believe I Had Forever,
  Now I'm Not So Sure
Letters from 74 Rue Taitbout
Days of Life and Death and Escape to
  the Moon
Places Where I've Done Time
Sons Come and Go, Mothers Hang
  in Forever
Chance Meetings
Obituaries
Births

Plays

My Heart's in the Highlands
The Time of Your Life
Love's Old Sweet Song
The Beautiful People
Across the Board on Tomorrow
  Morning
Sweeney in the Trees
Talking to You
Hello Out There
Get Away Old Man
Razzle Dazzle
Jim Dandy
Don't Go Away Mad
Sam Ego's House
A Decent Birth a Happy Funeral
The Cave Dwellers
The Paris Comedy
Sam, the Highest Jumper of Them
  All
Two Short Summertime Plays of
  1974

SAROYAN
THE NEW SAROYAN READER

*A Connoisseur's
Anthology of the
Writings of
William Saroyan*

Donald S. Ellis · Publisher · San Francisco

Creative Arts Book Company
833 Bancroft Way
Berkeley, California 94710

PUBLISHER'S NOTE

Each piece in this book was typeset from the original text. The inconsistencies in punctuation are due to stylistic changes in Saroyan's writings.

For information:
Donald S. Ellis
Creative Arts Book Company
833 Bancroft Way, Berkeley, California 94710.

ISBN 0-916870-80-4 (clothbound)
     0-916870-81-2 (paperback)

Library of Congress Catalog Card No. 83-73533

Acknowledgments

I am most grateful to the William Saroyan Literary Foundation for kindly permitting material from the following books by William Saroyan to be reprinted: *Inhale and Exhale; Three Times Three; Love, Here is My Hat; The Trouble with Tigers; Peace, It's Wonderful; The Adventures of Wesley Jackson; The Assyrian and Other Stories; Rock Wagram; The Whole Voyald; After Thirty Years: The Daring Young Man on the Flying Trapeze; I Used to Believe I Had Forever, Now I'm Not So Sure; Letters from 74 rue Taitbout, or, Don't Go But If You Must Say Hello to Everybody; Places Where I've Done Time* and *Sons Come & Go, Mothers Hang in Forever*.

Two chapters from *Not Dying* are reprinted by permission of Harcourt Brace Jovanovich, Inc.; four chapters from *Here Comes, There Goes, You Know Who* by permission of Simon & Schuster; extracts from *Days of Life and Death and Escape to the Moon* by permission of the William Morris Agency, Inc.; selections from *Chance Meetings* by permission of W. W. Norton & Company; and one chapter from *Obituaries* by permission of Creative Arts Book Company. Acknowledgement is also made to Hairenik Publications, Boston, for the use of four items published in their journals.

I also wish personally to thank William Saroyan's Literary Executor, Gerald Pollinger, for his support and assistance through a long and difficult gestation period, and my friend Brian Glover for his patient searching of the New York second-hand bookstores for out-of-print Saroyan titles, and for sending me a number of new works as they appeared in the United States, plus reviews and other valuable information. I must mention, too, Jack Trevor Story, without whose early encouragement the project might not have been undertaken.

B.D.

For Carol, Rebecca and Suzanne,
with love—

B.D.

William Saroyan

*A Biographical Sketch
Based Largely On His
Own Writings*

*A*rmenak Saroyan journeyed from the old Armenian city of
Bitlis to America ahead of his family in 1905, establishing
himself in New York, where he worked to raise the money that
would be needed when they joined him. He expected that they would
wish to remain in New York, but soon after their arrival he found himself
obliged to abandon the beginnings of a career as a preacher and travel on
with them to California, a land said to resemble Armenia itself, where
many other Armenians (refugees from the Turkish troubles) were
settling. His fourth child and second son William (the only one to be
born in the New World) was born in Fresno on the last day of August,
1908. Armenak died from peritonitis at San Jose only three years later, at
the early age of thirty-six, a failing fruit farmer, far from home in body
and spirit. He was to remain in William's mind as a very dim memory,
but also as an enduring source of motivation and encouragement, for
Armenak had also been a writer, an unpublished one. The son meant to
succeed where the father, in impossible circumstances, had failed.

Following their father's death, William, his brother Henry and his
sisters Zabel and Cosette spent several years at the Fred Finch Orphanage
in Oakland, while Armenak's young widow Takoohi took up menial
work in nearby San Francisco. The family was eventually reunited back
in Fresno, in the San Joaquin Valley, and William Saroyan's formidable
maternal grandmother Lucy (also widowed), who was to be a strong
influence on him, joined the household. As he grew up there, an
American boy also becoming part of the exiled Armenian tribe he
assimilated the raw material for many of his later stories.

It is not surprising that young William Saroyan, who was destined
to be a writer strongly in the American unschooled tradition, had an
undistinguished academic career. He left school early—the school work
was too slow and predictable and there was constant friction, caused by

boredom and by frequent reminders that he was the son of an immigrant. He was urged to go to college, but college was not in his plans. When he was twelve years old, little Saroyan read, by chance, the Guy de Maupassant story "The Bell," and the secret ambition to be a writer started to form. He became, then, a frequent visitor to Fresno's public library and he learned to touch-type at the Technical School.

While still at school he had sold newspapers in his spare time to earn money badly needed by his family, who were living in what he describes, in *My Name is Aram*, as "the most amazing and comical poverty in the world." Later he became a messenger with a postal-telegraph company, acquiring a reputation for high-speed deliveries.

By the time William was eighteen Fresno was too small for him and the urge to leave town and seek his fortune grew strong. His first attempt to leave took him only—and by mistake—as far as Los Angeles, where in a moment of desperation he joined the National Guard, though this unsuitable employment lasted only for two weeks. He had a story accepted by *The Overland Monthly*, a western magazine which in its day had published the work of such famous writers as Jack London and Ambrose Bierce, but it couldn't pay anything. Then, a year or so after he'd left Fresno, Saroyan took a Greyhound Bus to New York. Things started badly when he discovered on arrival that his suitcase containing nearly all his money had been sent in error to New Orleans. His luck didn't improve much and in less than six months the adventure was over. The hoped-for major literary breakthrough hadn't come and William was homesick. He returned to California wiser, more sober, embarrassed, yet glad to be rid of the absurd expectation that he would suddenly write something so irresistible that it would bring him instant fame.

It was becoming clear that his literary apprenticeship was going to be a lengthy affair. He moved to San Francisco, working when he could at a variety of uninspiring jobs (one was with a funeral establishment). On a number of occasions he sought more congenial work on newspapers and in bookstores, but always without success. The Saroyan scowl (as he later termed it) may have been a problem. With the coming of the Great Depression he was more committed to writing than ever, and gave up all pretense of following seriously any other career. Occasional winnings from gambling supplemented the scant living he earned, at this time, by working on Saturday market stalls selling vegetables. Although the prospect for an unknown young writer specialising in his own unorthodox brand of short stories was bleak indeed, during this difficult period he refused to compromise his literary integrity. He continued instead to work in defiance of what was commercially acceptable—a hard and lonely path but the only choice for a writer of true originality.

An Armenian journal, *Hairenik*, began to publish his work in 1933[1], but he was growing tired of rejection elsewhere and was almost ready to stop sending stories to "idiot editors of insignificant magazines." Late in the same year, though, he sent to *Story*, a national magazine, "The Daring Young Man on the Flying Trapeze," a story, part experimental, about a young writer who starves to death, with dignity. The editors of *Story*, Whit Burnett and Martha Foley, were on the lookout for new writing talent; Saroyan's story was accepted and he was paid fifteen dollars.

The young writer, now in his middle twenties and feeling that time was running out for him, decided on an act of boldness to convert this piece of good fortune into a decisive breakthrough. In *After Thirty Years: The Daring Young Man on the Flying Trapeze* (1964) he tells us that he wrote to the editors of *Story*—without invitation, and not knowing how they would react—informing them that for the whole of the month of January 1934 he would send them one newly written story each day.

This he proceeded systematically to do, still full of the usual doubts that harrass the unestablished writer, but determined to carry through the ambitious work program in as positive a frame of mind as possible. He began with no firm ideas as to what the stories would be about—no plots or characters in mind—but this didn't matter because his basic working method of choosing a starting point more or less at random and taking it from there—at speed—was already well established. Midway through the month a telegram, both expected and unexpected, arrived from the editors with the message he needed: yes, the stories were being received with great interest—keep them coming! This was the decisive moment of acceptance, marking the end of his long apprenticeship. Many years afterwards he was to write that the only success that means anything to a writer happens when he becomes accepted as a writer at all. The rest is beside the point.

More of these pieces were printed in *Story* in later months, and as word spread of this new and exciting literary find stories were soon appearing in such magazines as *The American Mercury, Harper's, The*

---

[1] James H Tashjian, in his preface to his *My Name is Saroyan* collection (Coward-McCann Inc, New York, 1983), emphasises that the appearance of Saroyan's work in *Hairenik Daily* in 1933 (under the pseudonym Sirak Goryan) was important in launching his career. Saroyan evidently sent copies of his *Hairenik* stories to Whit Burnett and Martha Foley at *Story*, and to Edward J O'Brien. The result was his near simultaneous discovery by Burnett and Foley, who asked for something fresh and got "The Daring Young Man on the Flying Trapeze," and O'Brien, who selected a *Hairenik* story called "The Broken Wheel" for his *Best American Stories of 1934*.

Yale Review, Scribner's and *The Atlantic Monthly*. By October 1934 Random House was ready to publish *The Daring Young Man on the Flying Trapeze, and Other Stories*. Surprisingly, for a collection of short stories, the book was a best-seller. William Saroyan—or Saroyan, as he now became—had arrived on the literary scene with a bang.

Naturally, there were those who resented this sudden leap to fame and fortune of an unschooled writer from the slums, who broke or disregarded the rules to an unprecedented degree, and one who already had a reputation as a self-proclaimed genius. He was attacked in *Esquire* by Ernest Hemingway, in petulant mood, while James Thurber was inclined to dismiss him as just another proletarian writer who couldn't write anyway and tried to make a virtue of the fact. It was a controversial beginning, but Saroyan was unimpressed either way. Soon he was planning a trip to Europe, and to the land of his forebears.

Judging by the number of references to it in his later writings, this first journey to foreign parts was to remain the most important and deeply meaningful of his life. He didn't quite reach his father's city, Bitlis, however. That was in part of the old country finally annexed by Armenia's ancient enemy Turkey. His travels, taking in London, Edinburgh, Paris, Vienna and Moscow, could extend only as far as Erivan, in Soviet Armenia, some two hundred miles short. Saroyan opposes nationalistic ideas in his writings while exhibiting a strong emotional attachment to Armenia, and this inconsistency—or dilemma—is nowhere more apparent than in his short story *Antranik of Armenia*, written shortly after this first visit to the scene of the racial effacement of his own people. In Moscow he met the Armenian poet Yeghishe Charentz, and was promised an interview with the great Russian writer Maxim Gorky, though this offer was later withdrawn because he had written unflatteringly that Russia under Communism had disappointed his hopes for the emergence of a new civilized order based on the ideals of the common man. Passing through Finland before returning to America he paid the composer Sibelius an unplanned visit, which he recorded in energetic style in *Finlandia*, a piece written the same evening in his hotel room.

More collections of short stories (*Inhale and Exhale; Three Times Three; Little Children; Love, Here is My Hat; The Trouble with Tigers; Peace, It's Wonderful*) followed against the continuing background of the Depression. Written in a variety of styles and moods, though with the Saroyan voice always clearly in evidence, these early stories established his reputation, as a writer with staying power, and provided the foundation for the rest of his career. Despite thinking of himself as a "world writer," he could not avoid being a writer of his time and place—America in the years of the Depression—and many of the stories are intimately bound up with the poverty and hardship of the time. In fact, his most successful early collection was *My Name is Aram* (1940), a book presenting in a poetical light the Armenians of his home town in the days of his boyhood. Having known such conditions himself from an early age he did not see the situation as greatly abnormal, and this in combination with youthful exuberance and the strong poetic streak always present in his work helped lift his stories of the Depression well above the level of mere realism or mere criticism of wealth and privilege.

Saroyan's career as a playwright began in earnest with *My Heart's in the Highlands* in 1939, a play adapted from one of his best short stories "The Man with the Heart in the Highlands" (written some years earlier in a condition close to fever just prior to an operation for appendicitis which saved his life). The play was well received, most importantly by George Jean Nathan, and was swiftly followed by his greatest theatrical success, *The Time of Your Life*. This American classic earned for the new playwright the New York Drama Critics' Circle Award and the Pulitzer Prize (it was the first play to win both), though the latter he declined because of his strong feelings about commerce patronising the arts. After returning from a last short visit to Europe before the now inevitable war broke out he had been inadvertently tipped off by a cousin that the play was in difficulties. Saroyan flew to Boston to take personal charge against a very tight schedule. This action, as well as his assertion that he had written the first draft of the play in six days added to his reputation for arrogance, despite the great success which followed on Broadway (where the cast included the young Gene Kelly). *The Time of Your Life* was followed by a series of Broadway productions (*Love's Old Sweet Song, The Beautiful People, Across the Board on Tomorrow Morning, Talking to You, Hello Out There*), and for a period in 1941 he established a Saroyan Theatre at the Belasco. Suspicious of the New York theatrical establishment, he preferred to finance and direct his own work.

Late in 1941 he took time off from his theatre activities to write a film scenario in Hollywood, *The Human Comedy*. He sold the script to M.G.M. for sixty thousand dollars, but then offered to buy it back for a larger sum when his demand to produce and direct the film himself was refused. A trade paper denounced the studio when it declined. The film, starring Mickey Rooney, was a hit, but was hardly to Saroyan's liking. He turned the script into a novel, which became his most successful book—and ironically the one he was, later on, least happy with because of the patriotic note he had introduced towards the end.

Marriage and World War II now intervened. In October 1942 he allowed himself to be drafted into the army, despite his pacifist opinions, and early in the following year he married Carol Marcus, a young society girl, and a friend of Oona O'Neill (who was to marry Charlie Chaplin). After the birth of their son Aram, Saroyan was posted to England. In London in 1944 (with the Signal Corps) he was allowed time off to write a novel to promote Anglo-American relations. Working in the Savoy Hotel (at his own expense) he produced in just a few weeks *The Adventures of Wesley Jackson*. His reward was supposed to be leave to visit his new family in New York; but the novel failed to please (publication was in fact delayed until after the war) and the deal was forgotten. Instead the possibility of a court-martial was talked about, for the book was strongly anti-war at a time when such sentiments were unthinkable. Discharged at last in September 1945, he later said that he had fought the army for three years—and won.

But the late nineteen forties were to be very difficult years for William Saroyan. He had lovingly dedicated a 1944 collection of short stories, *Dear Baby*, to his wife, but after the birth of daughter Lucy in 1946 the marriage began to fail.[2] And at the same time his literary career went into steep decline. He had already ceased offering plays to Broadway producers because of his intense dissatisfactions with the system (in particular, he was appalled by the growing practice of arranging a private viewing of a play before potential backers, which put Art directly on trial before Money); and the critics disliked *Wesley Jackson* when it finally appeared in 1947. Fashions had changed, hastened by the impact of the war, and Saroyan was suddenly almost old hat. Responding to this challenge would be difficult enough, but he was now in earnest pursuit of the "fantasy of founding a family," which in his view meant satisfying the social ambitions of his wife and mother-in-law. He was in poor condition for dealing with such demands. He was drinking and gambling heavily, and these were no doubt contributory factors in the marriage breakdown. When things finally came to a head in 1949, however, he felt sufficiently the aggrieved party to walk out and leave immediately for Europe.

In Paris, in a mood of despair, he wrote *The Assyrian*. This long story about a dying writer, en route to the homeland to which he feels drawn, became the basis of a new collection. On his return to America, noting that his wife was having a "grand time," he went to Reno for a divorce, spending time in Las Vegas, gambling, while he established the necessary residence period in Nevada. This particular gambling spree

---

[2] Aram Saroyan has published a very different view of his parents' marriage from the one put out over the years by William Saroyan, and offered an unusual interpretation of his father's evidently painful emotional problems. (*Last Rites*, William Morrow and Company, Inc, New York, 1982)

was financed in part by an advance of 36,000 dollars on three as yet unplanned books—an indication that his career had not yet touched rock bottom. The books were eventually produced in a single month: two novels, *Rock Wagram* and *The Laughing Matter*, in both of which marriage breakdown is a major theme; and a shorter fantasy work, and something of a personal favourite, *Tracy's Tiger*. None was commercially successful, but soon afterwards he had a surprising world-wide hit with a pop song, "C'mon-a My House," sung by Rosemary Clooney.

Saroyan's divorce from Carol Marcus lasted only until 1951, when they were remarried—a seemingly disastrous move, for it soon led to fresh divorce proceedings, and this time his wife was represented by the celebrated Hollywood lawyer Jerry Giesler, a deeply despised adversary. Carol was given custody of the children, and once they were satisfactorily housed, Saroyan began looking for a place for himself. He finally settled into a modest but instantly loved house on the beach at Malibu, where he began trying to pick up the pieces. The marriage, especially in its final stages, had been a costly and killing experience, and he was now head-over-heels in debt to the Tax Collector.

Saroyan probably never recovered fully from the twin psychic blows of his unhappy marriage and the three wasted years in the army (to these could be added the fact and character of the war itself), but at Malibu in the fifties he regained his soul sufficiently to arrest the alarming decline of his literary fortunes. In 1952 he published *The Bicycle Rider in Beverly Hills*, the first of his several book-length experiments in autobiography. This book was followed by a warm-hearted novel of the theatre (written for his daughter and serialised in the *Saturday Evening Post*), *Mama, I Love You*; a new collection of short stories, *The Whole Voyald*; and a book for his son, *Papa, You're Crazy*. He had another play on Broadway, *The Cave Dwellers*, in 1957, and there were a number of television productions and adaptations of his works. Meantime he was publishing short stories and articles in the usual wide variety of magazines and newspapers. During the six years at Malibu he earned (on later estimate) around a quarter of a million dollars—an accomplishment involving no serious concessions to commercial pressures despite his desperate need of money in those days. But these earnings did nothing to improve his tax situation; the debt remained (roughly fifty thousand dollars in 1958) and there seemed little prospect of ever paying it off.

He left Malibu in 1958 and headed for Europe, with no clear plan, only the vague thought that he would buy a vineyard and perhaps even forget about writing. His typewriter stayed in its case for a period. But gambling losses used up the vineyard money and at length he found himself in Paris, faced once more with the unwelcome prospect of trying to work himself out of debt. (His book *Not Dying* is mainly concerned with this period.) He contacted the film producer Darryl Zanuck, who was based in Paris at the time, and uncharacteristically agreed to write a play for money. This was by no means a complete sell-out because Saroyan had never learned how to write specifically for money, so that anything he wrote was bound to be at least partly authentic. In this particular case he was asked to do a film scenario, but elected instead to write a play, for which he was paid sixty thousand dollars. *The Paris Comedy, or the Secret of Lily* was a hit in German translation in Vienna, and later in Berlin, and more work of the same lucrative though somewhat distasteful kind followed for a time. Typically, though, the money earned was not used for the careful paying off of debts. "I certainly didn't gamble away every penny," he wrote in a memoir, in a flippant mood. "I drank some of it away, and I bought a raincoat."

Gambling was only the most uncontrollable manifestation of his compulsion to get rid of money as fast as he earned it. He was also an insatiable traveller, and as a matter of course would seek out the best and most expensive hotel in a new town or city. And in his day he had given away vast amounts. But gambling was the worst of it; and yet he needed to gamble. It was central, he claimed, to his approach to writing, and to life. He often justified it by saying that it helped his work, and many of his best stories and plays were apparently written in the aftermath of a bad gambling experience. He despised the whole business of money-making—or The Money, as he sometimes put it ("Had The Money not revealed itself as a stupid thief, I might have lingered a year or two longer in the Business World")—and gambling provided the perfect opportunity to demonstrate his contempt for the stuff.

But throwing it away on lavish scale clearly couldn't go on if he was ever to get the Tax Collector off his back. He had always been able to earn money when he needed it; now he had to learn how to hold onto it, even if that meant according it a grudging respect. He set up home and a working base in a fifth-floor walk-up apartment in a none too prosperous district of Paris, and the fight back to solvency began in a serious way, if not exactly in earnest.

He was invited to write an autobiography and, believing it would pay his debts, he produced his most complete and conventionally arranged autobiographical work, *Here Comes, There Goes, You Know Who*. But on his own admission the book did rather poorly, and in any case he had made a bad deal through his customary habit of not bothering to study the small print. Amongst his other activities in the early sixties, he created *Sam, the Highest Jumper of Them All* with Joan Littlewood's Theatre Workshop in London, after admiring its production of Brendan Behan's *The Hostage*. Two novels followed, *Boys* and *Girls Together* and *One Day in the Afternoon of the World*; then in 1964, thirty years after the publication of his first book, he repeated his early effort of writing a new story or piece each day for a whole month, keeping at the same time a daily journal in which he discussed his present life and work in relation to January 1934. This was published alongside the original stories as *After Thirty Years: The Daring Young Man on the Flying Trapeze*. Meanwhile his plays were being taken up with enthusiasm in eastern Europe, notably in Czechoslovakia.

Gradually he brought his gambling and drinking under reasonable control, though there were lapses. During a three months stay in London in 1966, for instance (occupying a flat with his son and daughter, now both young adults), he managed to get through twenty thousand dollars. But by 1967 he was able to declare in *Days of Life and Death and Escape to the Moon*: "I'm free . . . . I've paid all debts, I'm earning a living." He had acquired a second home in Fresno (though he hated what the developers had done to the city over the years), and it became his habit to spend part of the year in each location, when he wasn't on the move.

In the late sixties he finally got around to sifting through some of the mass of stuff he had written through the years which had appeared only in magazines or newspapers, or in some cases hadn't been published at all. The result was an entertaining collection of articles, essays, short stories, memoirs, poems and short plays, each with a specially written introduction. Indulging his fondness for long titles to the full, he called the collection *I Used to Believe I Had Forever, Now I'm Not So Sure* (actually the title of one of the plays). In his last book of the sixties he used the autobiographical device of writing a series of "letters" to various people, eminent and otherwise and most now dead, who had either influenced him or remained in his memory for some important reason. A number of these pieces were first published in the *Saturday Evening Post*. He called the book, *Letters from 74 rue Taitbout, or, Don't Go But If You Must Say Hello to Everybody*.

These autobiographical books were turning into a series. Next came *Places Where I've Done Time* (1972), in which, with no regard to chronology, he used the theme of places that had figured importantly in his life. But a note of rancour and vindictiveness was creeping in as the series progressed. As a matter of principle, he had always tried to write about people with the "largest possible sympathy," but now he was beginning to see them in a wholly realistic way. This trend continued in *Sons Come and Go, Mothers Hang in Forever* (1976); though *Chance Meetings* (1978), with its delicious memories of some of the more obscure people he had met, is something of an exception.

He had always produced a great deal of material that he never got around to publishing (throughout his fiftieth year, for example, he had worked on a book called *Fifty-Fifty*, which on completion he immediately set aside as being too long and beyond salvaging); and in the seventies, perhaps because the money pressures had eased so much, it seems likely that a significant part of his output remained unprinted. His work was still very much in demand in Europe, however, as his career approached its end, with stage and television productions of his plays in recent years in Czechoslovakia, Romania, Finland, Spain, Germany and Poland. *The Cave Dwellers* continues to be a particular favorite.

With the gradual intrusion of a bitter tone in his memoirs went a growing preoccupation with death, as is indicated by some of the titles alone. This preoccupation reached its fullest expression in his last published book,[3] *Obituaries* (1979). Finding that he had known a good number of them personally, he used *Variety's* list of the show-business dead of 1976 to spark off his memories, thoughts, feelings and fears. Though scarcely a happy book, *Obituaries* must be counted a *tour-de-force*—Saroyan in totally free mood, pushing expression and meaning to the limits of language. Latterly the critics were finding much to admire in his work, and *Obituaries* was accorded generous attention in *The New York Times Book Review*.

William Saroyan once said that to write was for him simply to stay alive in an interesting way. In a career lasting nearly half a century he remained through the good times and the bad a writer in the purist sense, writing almost invariably out of himself (as he put it), in the manner of a poet, with only surface commitment to the orthodox literary forms. He sought in his fictional work to dispense with the device of emotionality, or spurious excitement. Nor was he much interested in creating strong, memorable characters—another phony device. Speaking of a novel sent to him by a publisher, he said it wasn't bad, but it was about specific people in that peculiarly specific way that makes a novel meaningless. He cultivated a simple style of writing that was nevertheless sophisticated in its poetic depth and complexity and that was utterly devoid of clichés. He saw little value in what he termed safe writing, and was most pleased by the accidental element in his own work.

Having the peasant's mistrust of doctors, Saroyan seldom consulted them. He saw the fight against illness and death as a personal struggle with God (the Witness), Fate or Bad Luck. When he visited Europe for the last time in 1980, however, cancer had already been diagnosed. Five days before he died in May 1981, at the Veterans Hospital in Fresno, he

---

[3] *Births*, a short sequel to *Obituaries*, written in Paris in June-July 1979, has been published posthumously. (Creative Arts Book Company, Berkeley, 1983.)

telephoned a posthumous statement to the Associated Press: "Everybody has got to die, but I have always believed an exception would be made in my case. Now what?"

In a generous tribute *The New York Times*, accounting for his genius, described him as "an orphan hurt by a sense of rejection, craving love and bursting with talent." The *Times* in London felt that his reputation might come to rest on his later experiments with autobiography. And *Time* magazine (an old enemy) said that "the ease and charm of many of his stories will continue to inspire young writers. It is a legacy beyond criticism."

Brian Darwent
Frodsham, England
November 1983

THE NEW SAROYAN READER

Antranik
of Armenia

I didn't learn to speak Armenian until my grandmother came to our
house and every morning sang about Antranik the soldier until I
knew he was an Armenian, a mountain peasant on a black horse
who with only a handful of men was fighting the enemy. That was in
1915, the year of physical pain and spiritual disintegration for the
people of my country, and the people of the world, but I was seven and I
didn't know. From my own meaningless grief I could imagine something was wrong in the world, but I didn't know what. My grandmother
sang in a way that made me begin to find out, singing mournfully and
with great anger, in a strong voice, while she worked in the house. I
picked up the language in no time because it was in me in the first place
and all I needed to do was fit the words to the remembrance. I was an
Armenian. God damn the bastards who were making the trouble. (That
is the way it is when you are an Armenian, and it is wrong. There are no
bastards. The bitter feeling of the Armenian is also the bitter feeling of
the Turk. It is all absurd, but I did not know. I did not know the Turk is a
simple, amiable, helpless man who does what he is forced to do. I did not
know that hating him was the same as hating the Armenian since they
were the same. My grandmother didn't know either, and still does not
know. I know now, but I don't know what good it is going to do me
because there is still idiocy in the world and by idiocy I mean everything
lousy, like ignorance and, what is still worse, wilful blindness. Everybody in the world knows there is no such thing as nationality, but look at
them. Look at Germany, Italy, France, England. Look at Russia even.
Look at Poland. Just look at all the crazy maniacs. I can't figure out why
they won't open their eyes and see that it is all idiocy. I can't figure out
why they won't learn to use their strength for life instead of death, but it
looks as if they won't. My grandmother is too old to learn, but how about
all the people in the world who were born less than thirty years ago?

How about all those people? Are they too young to learn? Or is it proper to work only for death?)

In 1915 General Antranik was part of the cause of the trouble in the world, but it wasn't his fault. There was no other way out for him and he was doing only what he had to do. The Turks were killing Armenians and General Antranik and his soldiers were killing Turks. He was killing fine, simple, amiable Turks, but he wasn't destroying any real criminal because every real criminal was far from the scene of fighting. An eye for an eye, but always the wrong eye. And my grandmother prayed for the triumph and safety of General Antranik, although she knew Turks were good people. She herself said they were.

General Antranik had the same job in Armenia and Turkey that Lawrence of Arabia had in Arabia: to harass the Turkish Army and keep it from being a menace to the armies of Italy and France and England. General Antranik was a simple Armenian peasant who believed the governments of England and France and Italy when these governments told him his people would be given their freedom for making trouble for the Turkish Army. He was not an adventurous and restless English writer who was trying to come to terms with himself as to what was valid in the world for him, and unlike Lawrence of Arabia, General Antranik did not know that what he was doing was stupid and futile because after the trouble the governments of England and France and Italy would betray him. He did not know a strong government needs and seeks the friendship of another strong government, and after the war there was nothing in the world for him or the people of Armenia. The strong governments talked about doing something for Armenia, but they never did anything. And the war was over and General Antranik was only a soldier, not a soldier and a diplomat and a writer. He was only an Armenian. He didn't fight the Turkish Army because it would give him something to write about. He didn't write two words about the whole war. He fought the Turkish Army because he was an Armenian. When the war ended and the fine diplomatic negotiating began General Antranik was lost. The Turkish government looked upon him as a criminal and offered a large sum of money for his capture, dead or alive. General Antranik escaped to Bulgaria, but Turkish patriots followed him to Bulgaria, so he came to America.

General Antranik came to my home town. It looked as if all the Armenians in California were at the Southern Pacific depot the day he arrived. I climbed a telephone pole and saw him when he got off the train. He was a man of about fifty in a neat American suit of clothes. He was a little under six feet tall, very solid and very strong. He had an old-style Armenian moustache that was white. The expression of his face was both ferocious and kindly. The people swallowed him up and a committee got him into a big Cadillac and drove away with him.

I got down from the telephone pole and ran all the way to my uncle's office. That was in 1919 or 1920, and I was eleven or twelve. Maybe it was a year or two later. It doesn't make any difference. Anyway, I was working in my uncle's as office boy. All I used to do was go out and get him a cold water-melon once in a while which he used to cut in the office, right on his desk. He used to eat the big half and I used to eat the little half. If a client came to see him while he was eating water-melon, I would tell the client my uncle was very busy and ask him to wait in the reception room or come back in an hour. Those were the days for me and my uncle. He was a lawyer with a good practice and I was his nephew, his sister's son, as well as a reader of books. We used to talk in Armenian and English and spit the seeds into the cuspidor.

My uncle was sitting at his desk, all excited, smoking a cigarette.

Did you see Antranik? he said in Armenian.

In Armenian we never called him General Antranik, only in English.

I saw him, I said.

My uncle was very excited. Here, he said. Here's a quarter. Go and get a big cold water-melon.

When I came back with the water-melon there were four men in the office, the editor of the *Asbarez*, another lawyer, and two clients, farmers. They were all smoking cigarettes and talking about Antranik. My uncle gave me a dollar and told me to go and get as many more water-melons as I could carry. I came back with a big water-melon under each arm and my uncle cut each melon in half and each of us had half a melon to eat. There were only two big spoons and one butter knife, so the two farmers ate with their fingers, and so did I.

My uncle represented one of the farmers, and the other lawyer represented the other. My uncle's client said he had loaned two hundred dollars to the other farmer three years ago but had neglected to get a note, and the other farmer said he had never borrowed a penny from anybody. That was the argument, but nobody was bothering about it now. We were all eating water-melon and being happy about Antranik. At last the other attorney said, About this little matter?

My uncle squirted some water-melon seeds from his mouth into the cuspidor and turned to the other lawyer's client.

Did Hovsep lend you two hundred dollars three years ago? he said.

Yes, that is true, said the other farmer.

He dug out a big chunk of the heart of the water-melon with his fingers and pushed it into his mouth.

But yesterday, said the other lawyer, you told me he didn't lend you a penny.

That was yesterday, said the farmer. To-day I saw Antranik. I have no money now, but I will pay him just as soon as I sell my crop.

Brother, said the farmer named Hovsep to the other farmer, that's all I wanted to know. I loaned you two hundred dollars because you needed the money, and I wanted you to pay me so people wouldn't laugh at me for being a fool. Now it is different. I don't want you to pay me. It is a gift to you. I don't need the money.

No, brother, said the other farmer, a debt is a debt. I insist upon paying.

My uncle swallowed water-melon, listening to the two farmers.

I don't want the money, said the farmer named Hovsep.

I borrowed two hundred dollars from you, didn't I? said the other farmer.

Yes.

Then I must pay you back.

No, brother, I will not accept the money.

But you must.

No.

The other farmer turned to his lawyer bitterly. Can we take the case to court and make him take the money? he said.

The other lawyer looked at my uncle whose mouth was full of water-melon. He looked at my uncle in a way that was altogether comical and Armenian, meaning, well, what the hell do you call this? and my uncle almost choked with laughter and water-melon and seeds.

Then all of us busted out laughing, even the two farmers.

Countrymen, said my uncle. Go home. Forget this unimportant matter. This is a great day for us. Our hero Antranik has come to us from Hairenik, our native land. Go home and be happy.

The two farmers went away, talking together about the great event.

Every Armenian in California was happy about the arrival of Antranik from the old country.

One day six or seven months later Antranik came to my uncle's office when I was there. I knew he had visited my uncle many times while I was away from the office, in school, but this was the first time I had seen him so closely, he himself, the man, our great national hero General Antranik, in the very room where I sat with my uncle. I felt very angry and sad because I could see how bewildered and bitter and disappointed he was. Where was the glorious new Armenia he had dreamed of winning for his people? Where was the magnificent resurrection of the ancient race?

He came into the office quietly, almost shyly, as only a great man can be quiet and shy, and my uncle jumped up from his desk, loving him more than he loved any other man in the world, and through him loving the lost nation, the multitude dead, and the multitude living in every alien corner of the world. And I with my uncle, jumping up and loving him the same way, but him only, Antranik, the great man fallen to nothing, the soldier helpless in a world now full of cheap and false peace, he himself betrayed and his people betrayed, and Armenia only a memory.

He talked quietly for about an hour and then went away, and when I looked at my uncle I saw that tears were in his eyes and his mouth was twisting with agony like the mouth of a small boy who is in great pain but will not let himself cry.

That was what came of our little part in the bad business of 1915, and it will be the same with other nations, great and small, for many years to come because that way is the bad way, the wasteful way, and even if your nation is strong enough to win the war, death of one sort or another is the only ultimate consequence, death, not life, is the only end, and it is always people, not nations, because it is all one nation, the living, so why won't they change the way? Why do they want to go on fooling themselves? They know there are a lot of finer ways to be strong than to be strong in numbers, in war, so why don't they cut it out? What do they want to do to all the fine, amiable, simple people of every nation in the world? The Turk is the brother of the Armenian and they know it. The German and the Frenchman, the Russian and the Pole, the Japanese and the Chinese. They are all brothers. They are all small tragic entities of mortality. Why do they want them to kill one another? What good does it do anybody?

I like the swell exhilaration that comes from having one's body and mind in opposition to some strong force, but why should that force be one's own brothers instead of something less subject to the agonies of mortality? Why can't the God damn war be a nobler kind of war? Is every noble problem of man solved? Is there nothing more to do but kill? Everybody knows there are other things to do, so why won't they cut out the monkey buisness?

The governments of strong nations betrayed Antranik and Armenia after the war, but the soldiers of Armenia refused to betray themselves. It was no joke with them. It would be better to be dead, they said, than to be betrayed by their own intelligence into new submission. To fight was to be impractical, but not to fight was to be racially nullified. They knew it would be suicide because they had no friend in the world. The governments of strong nations were busy with complex diplomatic problems of their own. Their war was ended and the time had come for conversation. For the soldiers of Armenia the time had come for death or great good fortune, and the Armenian is too wise to believe in great good fortune.

These were the Nationalists, the *Tashnaks*, and they fought for Armenia, for the nation Armenia, because it was the only way they knew how to fight for life and dignity and race. The world had no other way. It was with guns only. The diplomats had no time for Armenia. It was the bad way, the God damn lousy way, but these men were great men and they did what they had to do, and any Armenian who despises these men is either ignorant or a traitor to his race. These men were dead wrong. I know they were dead wrong, but it was the only way. Well, they won the war. (No war is ever won: that is a technical term, used solely to save space and time.) Somehow or other the whole race was not annihilated. The people of Armenia were cold and hungry and ill, but these soldiers won their war and Armenia was a nation with a government, a political party, the *Tashnaks.* (That is so sad, that is so pathetic when you think of the thousands who were killed, but I honour the soldiers, those who died and those who still live. These I honour and love, and all who compromised I only love.) It was a ghastly mistake, but it was a noble mistake, and Armenia was Armenia. It was a very small nation of course, a very unimportant nation, surrounded on all sides by enemies, but for two years Armenia was Armenia, and the capital was Erivan. For the first time in thousands of years Armenia was Armenia.

I know how silly it is to be proud, but I cannot help it, I am proud.

The war was with the Turks of course. The other enemies were less active than the Turks, but watchful. When the time came one of these, in the name of love, not hate, accomplished in no time at all what the Turks, who were more honest, whose hatred was unconcealed, could not accomplish in hundreds of years. These were the Russians. The new ones. They were actually the old ones, but they had a new theory and they said their idea was brotherhood on earth. They made a brother of Armenia at the point of a gun, but even so, if brotherhood was really their idea, that's all right. They killed all the leaders of the Armenian soldiers, but nobody will hold that against them either. Very few of the Armenians of Armenia wanted to be brothers to the new Russians, but each of them was hungry and weary of the war and consequently the revolt against the new enemy was brief and tragic. It ended in no time at all. It looked like the world simply wouldn't let the Armenians have their own country, even after thousands of years, even after more than half of the Armenians of Asia Minor had been killed. They just didn't want the Armenians to have their nation. So it turned out that the leaders of the Armenian soldiers were criminals, so they were shot. That's all. The Russian brothers just shot them. Then they told the Armenians not to be afraid, the Turks wouldn't bother them any more. The brotherly Russian soldiers marched through the streets of the cities of Armenia and told everybody not to be afraid. Every soldier had a gun. There was a feeling of great brotherliness in Armenia.

Away out in California I sat in my uncle's office. To hell with it, I said. It's all over. We can begin to forget Armenia now. Antranik is dead. The nation is lost. The strong nations of the world are jumping with new problems. To hell with the whole God damn mess, I said. I'm no Armenian. I'm an American.

Well, the truth is I am both and neither. I love Armenia and I love America and I belong to both, but I am only this: an inhabitant of the earth, and so are you, whoever you are.

I tried to forget Armenia but I couldn't do it. My birthplace was California, but I couldn't forget Armenia, so what is one's country? Is it land of the earth, in a specific place? Rivers there? Lakes? The sky there? The way the moon comes up there? And the sun? Is one's country the trees, the vineyards, the grass, the birds, the rocks, the hills and mountains and valleys? Is it the temperature of the place in spring and summer and winter? Is it the animal rhythm of the living there? The huts and houses, the streets of cities, the tables and chairs, and the drinking of tea and talking? Is it the peach ripening in summer heat on the bough? Is it the dead in the earth there? The unborn of love beginning? Is it the sound of the spoken language in all the places of that country under the sky? The printed word of that language? The picture painted there? The song of that throat and heart? That dance? Is one's country their prayers of thanks for air and water and earth and fire and life? Is it their eyes? Their lips smiling? The grief?

Well, I do not know for sure, but I know it is all these things as remembrance in the blood. It is all these things within one's self, because I have been there, I have been to Armenia and I have seen with my own eyes, and I know. I have been to the place. Armenia. There is no nation there, but that is all the better. But I have been to that place, and I know this: that there is no nation in the world, no England and France and Italy, and no nation whatsoever. And I know that each who lives upon the earth is no more than a tragic entity of mortality, let him be king or beggar. I would like to see them awaken to this truth and stop killing one another because I believe there are other and finer ways to be great and brave and exhilarated. I believe there are ways whose ends are life instead of death. What difference does it make what the nation is or what political theory governs it? Does that in any way decrease for its subjects the pain and sorrow of mortality? Or in any way increase the strength and delight?

I went to see. To find out. To breathe that air. To be in that place.

The grapes of the Armenian vineyards were not yet ripe, but there were fresh green leaves, and the vines were exactly like the vines of California, and the faces of the Armenians of Armenia were exactly like the faces of the Armenians of California. The rivers Arax and Kura moved slowly through the fertile earth of Armenia in the same way that the rivers Kings and San Joaquin moved through the valley of my birthplace. And the sun was warm and kindly, no less than the sun of California.

And it was nowhere and everywhere. It was different and exactly the same, word for word, pebble for pebble, leaf for leaf, eye for eye and tooth for tooth. It was neither Armenia nor Russia. It was people alive in that place, and not people only, but all things alive there, animate and inanimate: the vines, the trees, the rocks, the rivers, the streets, the buildings, the whole place, urban and rural, nowhere and everywhere. The earth again. And it was sad. The automobile bounced over the dirt road to the ancient Armenian church at Aitchmiadzin, and the peasants, men and women and children, stood in bare feet on the ancient stone floor, looking up at the cross, bowing their heads, and believing. And the Armenian students of Marx laughed humbly and a little shamefully at the innocent unwisdom and foolish faith of their brothers. And the sadness of Armenia, my country, was so great in me that, sitting in the automobile, returning to Erivan, the only thing I could remember about Armenia was the quiet way General Antranik talked with my uncle many years ago and the tears in my uncle's eyes when he was gone, and the painful way my uncle's lips were twisting.

Inhale and Exhale, 1936

The Horses
and the Sea

Drinking beer in *The Kentucky* on Third Street, I met a fellow
named Drew, father English, mother Italian, and he said he
had just got off the boat, straight from Australia, assistant
engineer. He was a tall dark half-breed with a solid chin and a long
horsey face. Like most seamen ashore he seemed to be in a daze, and
although he'd hear something I'd say, he wouldn't understand the
meaning immediately. It would take him thirty seconds or maybe a little
longer to make out what I was talking about. It looked as if he had
something important on his mind, but in reality he was only becoming
adjusted to land, to the city, and what was going on. In reality he still
had the sea in him and it was taking him time to get the land back into
his brain. He wasn't liking it either: it wasn't pleasing him very much.
He had gone to sea when he was fourteen and, on and off, man and boy,
he had been to sea ever since. He was nearing his fortieth year, but
appeared to be in his middle twenties: it is like this with some seamen:
they lead a hard life, they drink, they go away in ships, they walk in the
streets of alien cities, they do a lot of swift living, and yet they keep
young. Drew was one of these men, and we were drinking beer together,
talking.

We got to be friends casually, the way it happens in saloons, and
Drew began to talk about himself, how it had been with him from the
beginning, feeling restless, dreaming of cities, wanting to walk in them,
and all that. Regular Joseph Conrad stuff, a young fellow from inland
longing for the sea. I said I had an idea how it had been with him. I
myself had gone off with a circus when I was fifteen, but with me it had
been something different, the grace of the lady who stood on the horses
and went around in a ring. Something like that. Boyish adoration for
something hard to define, part woman, part horse. But in the end I went
back home and forgot all about it. A horse is a horse, and a woman—

well, a boy is apt to learn in a circus. So I went back home and got a job in a grocery store. The inside of a circus tent may appear to be the universe while the circus is going on, but when the show is over and the tent is taken down it is not so wonderful: everybody in a hurry, wagons rolling, poles falling, canvas coming down, elephants walking to the trains: it is not so fine, taking the universe to pieces every other day. Everything gets to have too much impermanence, and after a while the ferocious restlessness of the jungle animals becomes frightening. Either this, or I wasn't cut out to be a circus man.

Anyway, I said I had an idea how it had been with Drew. We drank another beer and all of a sudden he said, Do you understand horses? I want to gamble a little because I haven't much money and winter is coming.

You could have knocked me over with a feather, as they say. The things we had been talking about, and all of a sudden this sort of talk.

I don't know a thing about horses, I said.

But Mac winked at Drew and said, Don't believe it. He's the best handicapper on Third Street.

Drew wasn't very alert mentally, as I've said, and he wanted to know if I ever played the horses. It seemed he hadn't quite understood what Mac had said. I told him I had been playing the horses regularly for over seven years and that all in all I was about eleven dollars and sixty-five cents ahead of the game.

Drew said, I'm feeling lucky to-day. I'd like to make a little bet.

We went around to Number One Opera Alley, through *The Kentucky* to the alley. It was Belmont that day, Arlington Park in Chicago, and Tia Juana, across the border. I began to look over the racing sheets to get a line on distances, odds, weights, and jockeys, and it looked like a bad day at every track. Not one race looked like a business proposition: everything was even-stephen, three horses in every race that might win, and these kind of races are no good. I want a horse to be there to win alone, by two lengths at least, at good odds. My object is not to make the bookies rich, but Drew came up with the name *Sea Bird*.

That horse, he said, sounds good.

What do you mean, good? I said.

The name, he said. *Sea Bird*.

I had to laugh: it was damn funny. I happened to know. *Sea Bird* was a no-good worthless piece of female horse-flesh. She hadn't won a race since she had gone to the barrier two years ago. I liked her name myself but horses with fancy names don't win races. Names have nothing to do with it, although once in a long while a man may win a few dollars by following name hunches. It isn't often though. I told Drew to lay off the horse.

Nevertheless, he liked the name so much he bet a half dollar on her across the board, dollar and a half in all, four bits to win, four bits to place, and four bits to show, and *Sea Bird* ran eighth in a nine-horse race. If she had won, Drew would have got a potful of money. He made the remark himself. If she had won, etc.

Then he said, She sounded good to me. Too bad a horse with a name like that has to be so slow.

I said she was probably a very handsome horse, but not of the running breed, the fast running, the nervous, hysterical kind, the kind that know a race is a race and like to win.

Drew was holding a dollar in his hand and looking bewildered. All those names. It was confusing. What horse do you like up there? he asked.

I said that I didn't like any horse that day. Not one race looked O.K. to me. I told him I wasn't betting.

Well, said Drew, make a suggestion.

I asked if he had money and he told me he had about twelve dollars. He had been in town four days and he had bought a suit of clothes, a pair of shoes, and a few other things: he had been drinking a little and now all he had was twelve dollars. I suggested he ought to hang on to it and forget the horses for the time being, but no, he wanted to make another bet, at least one more.

I named the horse *Unencumbered*.

Then Drew gave me the surprise of my life. What's it mean? he asked. That word?

It means, I said, why, it means *un* encumbered. Do you know what encumbered means?

Drew said he did not.

Well, I asked him what the hell difference it made what the word meant. The horse was pretty good. It ought to win. It would win, if the race was on the up and up, if it wasn't a dope-race.

The odds were six to one. I told him to bet a half dollar to win and quit whether the horse won or not.

Drew bet two dollars on *Unencumbered* to win: he was a gambler, I could see that. He said, You like this horse. I think she'll win.

Now I am sorry I ever suggested the horse because it did win and it sort of made a tramp of Drew. We left the joint and he was full of gratitude. Now, he kept saying, if we could only make one bet a day like this, he would be able to get through the winter in good style. He said, Will you meet me every noon at *The Kentucky?*

I told him I would, but that it wouldn't be wise for him to have too much confidence in the horses. It didn't always work out so nicely. Sometimes you didn't win a bet in a week, sometimes two weeks.

The next day he had very good luck. I gave him a horse that won, and Pete, the unemployed Southern Pacific engineer, gave him a horse that won, and Drew himself bet only two of his own hunches that lost, so that at the end of the day, he was three dollars to the good.

I could tell he was going haywire because he bought a copy of *The Racing Form* and said he was going to go at the thing scientifically, and the next day when I saw him he said, I've got this racket all figured out. I've got eight winners for to-day.

It isn't impossible to pick eight winners in one day, but I never knew anybody who ever bet eight horses that won, and didn't bet any others.

I didn't say anything and Drew bet his eight horses and two of them won, and the two that won paid very little, and at the end of the day he was out seven dollars.

Afterwards he took it easier and made only one or two bets a day, and one day, about two weeks later, he was broke and I lent him a dollar.

I'm waiting for a boat, he said.

What happened to your boat? I said.

It went back to Australia, he said. Five days ago. I lost my job. They got another assistant engineer.

I didn't see him again for a month. Then he came tearing into Number One Opera Alley in a way that made me know he had money.

I been painting houses, he said. Making six, seven dollars a day.

He had on a brand-new suit and there was a smell of paint with him.

Giving up the sea? I said.

Sure, he said. Seven dollars a day is a lot of money.

He made three swift bets, the kind guys with lots of money and lots of faith in luck make, and lost.

He felt pretty good, though.

I thought I'd lose, he said. I just wanted to find out.

That was funny. How much was it? I said.

Seventeen dollars, he said.

He went away in a hurry.

When I saw him again, about six weeks later, I knew he wasn't painting houses any more and didn't have much money, maybe five or six dollars.

He wasn't wearing a brand-new suit and he wasn't acting game. He was being very cautious about everything. He was looking at the form charts in a way that meant he didn't want to make a bet just to find out if he was right in believing he would lose, he wanted to make a bet and win, although he was pretty sure no matter what horse he bet on he would lose, and he couldn't afford to lose, and looking at the form charts this way he was looking bewildered and confused and worried. Too many things could happen. He could bet on *Will Colinet* at two to one that ought to win, and it would lose; and *Bright Star* at six to one, that ought to come seventh would win: or he could bet on *Bright Star*, and *Will Colinet* would win, and no matter which horse he played he would lose, and he kept looking at the form chart and trying to make up his mind.

Then he walked away from the form chart and we bumped into each other.

Any luck? I said, but I didn't mean horses.

Haven't made a bet yet, he said. Can't make up my mind.

He stayed around till the races were over and didn't make a bet, and I knew he had very little money.

So many things could happen, it was beginning to scare him because he believed only one thing could happen so far as he was concerned: he would lose all his money.

The next day he was busy all day studying the form charts and looking up the past performances of the various horses, but at the end of the day he hadn't made a bet. After each race he would be amazed that he didn't have sense enough to bet on the winner. And at the end of the day his senselessness in not having bet on every winner and become rich disgusting was to him, and he was all bawled up and couldn't make a bet, not even a small half dollar one.

And it was the same the next day. All the races were run, and all the winners came in, and he didn't pay out or collect a nickel, because he couldn't make up his mind to accept the challenge of possibility and win or go broke, although one or the other would be better than trying to get along everyday on forty or fifty cents, two lousy meals, and one lousy room to sleep in.

And it was like this for five or six days, and I knew it was getting worse and worse with him: afraid to make up his mind, and all his money being spent carefully for things he needed, and now hardly anything left, so I took him to an Italian restaurant for a big dinner.

My ship is three days out of Frisco, he said.

I knew how he felt. He felt lousy. Here he was in the stinking city, in the stinking places of the city, doing no work, fretting about the comparative nervousness of horses, fretting about the infinite pos-sibilities of a single event, a horse race, and three days out of Frisco, on the Pacific, was his ship, and on the ship were the men, working, doing the simple things that would bring the ship to port, doing the things that would bring about the happening of only one event, not a horse race, but a ship crossing an ocean from one city on one continent to another city on another continent, and no two ways about it, and all around the ship the clean sea, and above the ship the clean sky, and the simplicity of day, and the certainty of deep sleep at night because he had worked and because the sea could be heard, even when it was very silent, and no confusion in his mind.

The next day he told me frankly he was broke, and I told him I would lend him as much money as he needed each day, and I did, and in a couple of days *The Texan* came to port, and he went down and talked to the Captain and the Chief Engineer, and got his job back. They told him he had missed one of the best voyages of the ship, and when he came uptown to Number One Opera Alley to pay me the money I had loaned him, he said, This voyage I missed because I stayed in the city, painting houses and betting horses, was one of the finest *The Texan* ever made. Four days out of Sydney they hit a big storm and the ship rolled all over the place. Everybody ate standing and the coffee would spill out of your cup while you were drinking it, and nobody could stay in his bunk to sleep, and then they hit the calmest sea anybody had ever seen, sunshine and warm breezes, and the tables steady as tables in restaurants.

And then I knew how it was. It was the *kind* of challenge that he didn't like: it was a manufactured kind. It was fake. It didn't need to be one way or another in the first place, and that was why he couldn't figure it out. They dared you to pick one horse out of six or seven or eight or nine or ten or eleven or twleve, and if you did, you were a fool, even if you picked the right one, and if you didn't but were interested you were a greater fool, and the whole thing was goofy. Who cared about a horse race, anyway? And what if you did win? What if you got rich? It was the same. And the challenge wasn't worth accepting in the first place. But with the sea, with the ship, it was different. There was danger, but it was reasonable. There could be a storm and the ship could sink and everybody could drown, but there was sense to it because you were working to get a cargo to port and when the sea got rough and tried to leap over the ship you could know it was dangerous and still go on drinking coffee out of a half-empty cup and go on sleeping and the ship would go on moving, and you liked it even when it was dangerous because it was clean, the sea was clean, the job of getting the ship to port was a clean job, and there was a lot of sense to it and even if the ship sank and everybody was drowned it was all right because it was clean and the idea was a clean idea.

Inhale and Exhale, 1936

Our Little
Brown
Brothers the
Filipinos

*I*don't suppose you ever saw a two-hundred-and-fifty-pound Filipino. They don't come that size very often, but when they do, brother, look out. It's as bad as an earthquake or a hurricane. I guess I was just about the best friend Ramon Internationale had in the world, but do you think I could ever figure out what that crazy baboon was liable to do, especially in a wrestling match? I never could figure out anything. I used to sit in the little office on Columbus Avenue and worry about him all the time. He just wouldn't lose. He was the biggest and toughest and wildest gorilla that ever got out of the jungle into the world. The only difference between him and something goofy in a cage was that he could talk, and boy how he could talk. Perfect English. You know nothing, he used to say; you do not know anything.

Ramon Internationale? I said. Never heard of him.

Never heard of him? he said. Ever hear of Jimmy Londos, Strangler Lewis? Ever hear of Dempsey? Well, this baby was all of those guys in one large package. Not to mention Firpo. Where the hell were you two years ago?

I was right here in Frisco, I said.

Well, so was Internationale, he said. What were you doing, hiding? Didn't you ever read the papers? Don't you remember seeing his picture on the front page of every newspaper the day after he wrestled six policemen, one referee, two timekeepers, three reporters, and me?

No, I said. I don't remember. Who won the match?

Who won the match? Who else? Internationale won the match. The ligaments of my left leg were in a knot three weeks after that trouble. His heart was broken about that. He claimed he didn't know it was me. He said he thought it was some enemy of his people. He figured everybody in Frisco hated his people. Tom, he said, why didn't you stay out of that trouble? Who told you to jump in there when I was angry? I told him I had to do it to keep him from going to jail.

How come? I said.

I was his manager. That's how come. I couldn't let him mangle all them citizens without trying to quiet him down. The crowd thought it was the best wrestling match in the history of the game. That was the only thing that kept him from going to jail. The crowd was tickled to death because he knocked everybody out of the ring and then refused to move. He stood right in the middle of the ring and refused to move. The crowd was tickled to death. It was like some crazy giant challenging the whole world, and that's something that always goes over big with people who go to wrestling matches.

What started the trouble in the first place? I said.

What? he said. You don't mean what. You mean *who*. It wasn't *anything*. It was Internationale. He was supposed to lose a match to Vasili Ivanovitch, the Russian rock crusher, so Vasili wouldn't look like a punk. Vasili looked like a real tough guy, but Internationale could floor him in three minutes any day in the week. I agreed with Vasili's manager that Internationale should throw the match, but I didn't know very much about Internationale at the time. He didn't like the idea of losing to Vasili. He just didn't like the idea of losing at all. He couldn't understand such a thing. I had got five matches for him and he had won each of them easily because they weren't framed. This was his first big match, so of course it was framed. Well, he moped in the office four days in a row before the match. Tom, he said, I don't want to wrestle this Russian if I got to lose to him. I can floor that fellow in three minutes. I knew that. He didn't have to tell me, but the game has rules and if you don't want to starve you've got to play the game according to the rules. Internationale could floor any man in the world in three minutes, but that's no business. There's got to be a contest. The crowd likes it better when a strong man loses. I argued with him four days in a row and even then I didn't know for sure what he would do. I guess he himself didn't know. I guess he wanted to wait until he got into the ring with the Russian rock crusher before making up his mind. He was supposed to let Vasili floor him after eleven minutes the first time, and after seven minutes the second. Well, he let Vasili floor him the first time after fifty-seven minutes. He nearly killed that poor Russian in them fifty-seven minutes. Then he laid down in the middle of the ring, flat on his back, and Vasili sprawled all over him, trying to act tough. That was the first fall. It was two out of three.

Well, when they started the next one Vasili got a little careless with his facial expression, figuring he was going to win anyway, and he got Internationale sore, and Internationale floored the Russian in seven minutes. I was scared stiff and when I went to Internationle in the dressing room I knew it was all over.

He was smoking a cigar. Tom, he said, you know nothing; you do not know anything.

What's the matter? I said.

That Russian fool thinks he's tough, he said. He thinks he can have fun with me.

No, I said. You're wrong, Ramon. He knows you can floor him in three minutes.

You know nothing, he said. You do not know how it is with me in the ring. It is not like out here, talking. When he starts thinking he is better than I am I got to show him he's wrong. I got to lay him out.

Don't be like that, Internationale, I said. Lose this match, so we can get a return match at more money.

I don't want more money, he said.

Listen, Internationale, I said. Who was it took you out of the pea fields down in Salinas and brought you up to Frisco and made a great wrestler out of you? It was me, wasn't it? Well, you got to play ball. You got to do me this little favour. You got to lose this match to Vasili Ivanovitch because if you win, you and me both are just about through in this game. No manager in the country will give us another match.

Why? he said. I can floor any of their wrestlers. Why do I have to lay down for them?

Well, I said, that's the way the game is played, and we've got to play the game according to the rules.

So it was time to go back to the ring. The crowd was yelling for more, especially all the little Filipinos, not one of them more than a hundred ten pounds in weight, but every one of them dressed in purple and red and green clothes, every one of them smoking a long panetela cigar. There must have been a thousand of them, but it looked more like a million. Every one of them had bet money on Internationale to win, and me and Vasili's manager and a couple of cops and the referee and the timekeepers and the three newspaper reporters had bet on him to lose.

First Internationale took to throwing Vasili out of the ring, and Vasili kept rubbing his bruises and groaning and looking around at everybody to see why everything was going wrong. Internationale threw him out of the ring three times, and then Diamond Gates the referee figured he'd stop all the nonsense. Vasili was horsing around a little and Internationale fell on his back. He was getting up, holding Vasili by the nose, eyes, ears and hair with one hand, and both feet with the other, all primed to throw him out of the ring again, when Diamond Gates patted Vasili on the back and called him the winner. Of course that was the only thing to do, but it was a mistake. Internationale threw Vasili out of the ring, and then he threw Diamond Gates out, and then the three reporters, who had been drinking a little, jumped into the ring and Internationale threw them out, and then the cops jumped in, and the ones he didn't get to throw out, he knocked out, and then I jumped in. Less than ten seconds later I was sitting in Harry White's lap, away back in the tenth row. By the time my head cleared Internationale was standing alone in the centre of the ring challenging the world. The crowd was tickled to death.

Didn't you ever read about that in the papers? he said.

No, I said. I guess I missed that. But what happened? How did it end?

Well, he said, Internationale kept waving at Vasili to come back into the ring like a man and finish the match, but Vasili wouldn't think of it. Then Internationale asked the cops to come back, and the timekeepers, and the reporters, but nobody would come back, and then he made a speech. Boy, that was the craziest speech I ever heard. Everybody in Dreamland was yelling and laughing and whistling, but everybody heard what Internationale said in his little speech. There were two ladies in the crowd and Internationale said, Ladies and gentlemen, you know nothing; you do not know anything. The referee says I am the loser of this match, but you know nothing. I am the winner. I challenge Vasili Ivanovitch, the Russian rock crusher, to return to this ring, and I challenge anybody else in this audience to enter this ring, and I will not leave this ring until the referee declares that I am the winner.

The crowd cheered louder than ever, because Internationale *was* the winner.

From a safe distance Diamond Gates shouted, The winner of this match is Vasili Ivanovitch. The bout is over. Everybody go home.

Well, nobody got up and left the building, not one solitary soul. Then somebody ordered the lights to be turned out. That was a crazy mistake. The little Filipinos thought it was a plot, so in the darkness they started hitting people on the heads with pop bottles, and when the lights went on, everybody in the crowd was slugging somebody else, including the two ladies. And Internationale was still in the centre of the ring, alone.

He wouldn't budge. About two hundred police arrived with sawed-off shotguns, tear-gas bombs, clubs, and horses. The horse cops rode right into Dreamland on their horses, because they were afraid to get off. They ordered everybody to get out of the building, and after a half hour or so the building was empty except for two hundred cops, fifty of them on horses, the three reporters, Diamond Gates, Vasili Ivanovitch, his manager Pat Connor, the two timekeepers, and me. The cops pointed shotguns at Internationale and told him to get out of the ring or they would shoot. I was scared stiff. I know the cops wouldn't really shoot, but I was afraid one of them might get nervous and kill him accidently. I didn't want anybody to hurt Ramon Internationale because I knew he was right. So I ran up to the ring and begged him to get out. He said he wouldn't leave the ring until he was declared the winner, or at least until Vasili returned and went on with the match. Vasili returned from the shower room dressed in his street clothes, smoking a cigar.

It was the worst affair I ever saw. Little by little the little Filipinos started coming back into the auditorium to see the finish of the fight, and the horse cops would turn their horses around and run them out, and five minutes later they would come back in, anxious to learn the final result of the match. Their countryman Ramon Internationale was still in the centre of the ring and still alive, and they wanted to know how the match was going to turn out. About fifty of them sneaked up to the balcony where the horse cops couldn't go, and they locked the doors, so the other cops couldn't reach them. It was the craziest thing I ever saw. Then they started to cheer Internationale. The cops pointed sawed-off shotguns at them and threatened to mow them down, but these fifty little Filipinos wouldn't move. They were as stubborn as their hero Internationale. And then somebody fired into the ceiling, and one of the little Filipinos fainted. This made the other forty-nine Filipinos sore, so they started throwing pop bottles at the cops. A couple of horses got scared and busted loose, falling all over seats and crying out with pain. And Internationale wouldn't budge.

I almost cried, begging him to get out of the ring. You known nothing, he shouted at me; you do not know anything.

Outside, people from all over San Francisco were rushing to Dreamland in automobiles, by street car, and by foot, and although we didn't know it, there was a crowd of over three thousand people in the streets, and more arriving every minute. People love to see one man, especially someone dark-complexioned, challenging the whole world, and nine times out of ten they are for him. This crowd was certainly on Internationale's side. Most of the people hadn't seen the match, but from what they found out about it from people who had seen it, they were sure Internationale was the winner. They started guessing how long he'd be able to hold out against the police, and wondered how the police would finally get him out of the ring. They believed he would die before he'd get out, unless they declared him the winner. Even people who had never before heard of Internationale. They just knew he would stand there in the middle of the ring and let them kill him because that's exactly what they themselves would do if they were as big as he was, and as crazy. The part that bothered every one of them was his being a Filipino. They couldn't understand how a Filipino could grow to be two-hundred and-fifty-pounds in weight, but everybody was glad it had happened.

You know how happy the world was about the successful birth of the quintuplets.

They had to get the chief of police out of bed at midnight to ask him what they should do, and, boy, was he sore? It took them over twenty minutes to explain just what had happened and what was going on, and even then he didn't know for sure. Finally, he got out of bed and put on his clothes and came down to Dreamland in a red automobile travelling sixty miles an hour through heavy traffic, with a half dozen motorcycle cops in front and a half dozen behind. I remember how amazed he was when he walked into the auditorium and saw all the horse cops riding up and down the aisles, and Internationale in the middle of the ring, and the fifty little Filipinos in the balcony, throwing pop bottles. One of the bottles busted on the cement floor right beside him, and that's when he turned around and saw the little Filipinos up there. He was scared to death.

What the hell are all the well-dressed Filipinos doing up there? he said.

Ha ha, said the reporter from the *News*. They've locked themselves in, and they're throwing pop bottles. So let's see you get them out. Go ahead, you're chief of police. Get them out. Let's see you get Internationale out of the ring, too. You're a brave man. Go in there and throw him out.

The chief took one good look at Internationale and decided to argue it out. He said they wouldn't put Internationale in jail if he got out of the ring peacefully and went home, but if he refused to do so, they would gas him out and put him in jail for ten years. Internationale said, You know nothing; you do not know anything, and one of the little Filipinos in the balcony threw a pop bottle that hit another horse and the horse jumped from the sixth row into the ring. The cop on the horse took one big leap and landed in the fourth row because Internationale was moving toward him. The horse, however, was too stunned to move, so Internationale got into the saddle. It was the craziest thing in the history of wrestling. I was afraid he was going to throw the horse out of the ring, too, but Internationale was too kind-hearted to do a dirty trick like that. He loved dumb animals.

Every once in a while we could hear the crowd outside booing, and we knew why, but the chief didn't. What the hell are they booing about? he said.

No cop would tell him, so the reporter from the *News* told him. Ha ha, he said, they're booing you and the cops, that's who. Every man, woman, and child out there is one hundred per cent for Internationale.

So the chief came over to me. He was disgusted.

You his manager? he said, and I said I was.

All right, he said. Get him out of there.

So I began begging Internationale to get out of the ring again. Well, this time that crazy frightened horse neighed at me. I nearly fell over. I guess the horse didn't want to get out of the ring either. Internationale said the same thing as before. You know nothing, he started to say, and I said, I know, I know, don't tell me again. I do not know anything. But for the love of Mike, Ramon, get the hell out of that ring.

He wouldn't budge.

So the chief and Vasili Ivanovitch and Vasili's manager and the referee and the timekeepers and the reporters and two dozen cops held a little meeting. They decided to send Vasili back into the ring to finish the match, but he wouldn't hear of it. He began to stamp his feet like a baby, pointing at the horse, but that was only an alibi. He was scared to death. He said he had been declared the winner once and that was enough. Then the chief sat down and started to groan. He would be disgraced. The whole city would laugh at him.

He jumped up, looking furious. Gas him out, he said. He looked up at the fifty little Filipinos in the balcony. Gas them all out, he said. Our little brown brothers the Filipinos, he said. Gas them all out.

How about the horse? somebody asked.

Gas the horse out, too, said the chief.

Then he heard the crowd outside booing, and he changed his mind.

Wait a minute, he said. Aren't there fifty able-bodied men among you who are willing to go into that ring and arrest him?

There wasn't one, let alone fifty.

The chief was disgusted. He telephoned the mayor, and the mayor swore at him for five minutes. Then the mayor told him to leave the Filipino wrestler on the horse in the ring, and the fifty little ones in the balcony, and clear the streets and let the Filipinos stay in the auditorium until they got sleepy or hungry and went home. The chief thought this was a great idea until he found out the people in the streets wouldn't go away and kept rushing into the auditorium and sitting down and cheering, at least five thousand of them. It was a clear night in August and everybody was feeling great and didn't want to go home.

The chief was panic-stricken. This was worse than a strike. It was ten times worse.

He telephoned the mayor again and talked a long time. Then he told Diamond Gates to go into the ring and declare Internationale the winner.

I can't do that, Diamond Gates said, and the chief said, Like hell you can't. You go on in there and declare that crazy Filipino the winner or there won't be any more wrestling matches in Frisco.

So Diamond Gates tried to get into the ring. Every time he ducked under the lower rope the frightened horse would stand on its hind legs and neigh very mournfully and Diamond Gates would run half way up the aisle, sweating and shivering. Finally he stood on a seat and declared Ramon Internationale the winner. Everybody in Dreamland cheered, especially the fifty little Filipinos in the balcony, and gradually the auditorium emptied. Then Internationale got off the horse and left the ring.

I never did find out how the horse got out of the ring. It was scared to death.

Inhale and Exhale, 1936

The Black
Tartars

*I*n 1926 there were only twelve Black Tartars in Russia, and now, in 1935, there are only ten because of the deep love of Mago the soldier for Komi the daughter of Moyskan.

In 1926 Mago was nineteen years old. I met his brother and his brother's wife on the train from Kiev to Kharkov. Mago's brother Karachi is no soldier and he doesn't care if Black Tartars vanish from the world altogether because he believes it is wiser to live quietly than to live greatly and foolishly, and he would rather be a Russian, anyway. But Mago, no. He would live greatly.

Karachi spoke in Russian to the Jewish girl on her way to Tiflis and the Jewish girl translated his words to me. Karachi's wife was a Ukrainian girl. Karachi didn't care to marry a Black Tartar and preserve the race and the culture of the race. All he wanted was to live and have a girl near him when he didn't feel so good.

The Jewish girl translated and Karachi's wife smiled and moved closer to the young Black Tartar.

Moyskan, said Karachi in Russian to the Jewish girl and the girl in English to me, was an excellent singer. He not only sang the older Black Tartar songs but made new ones, especially when he was drunk. After beating his wife, his songs were full of lamentations and he would call on God to destroy him, and the next day he would complain bitterly to his friends, What can I do if God wills me to live?

Moyskan had five sons and one daughter. Three of the sons were killed in small wars or in banditry, one was in Siberia for no reason in the world, and the other was a worker in a Moscow tractor factory. Moyskan's daughter Komi was the most beautiful girl in the world, said Karachi. I fell in love with Komi, he said, my brother Mago fell in love with her, and all the officers and men of the Soviet Azerbaijan Army fell in love with her. Any man who saw Komi fell in love with her, he said.

He lit a Russian cigarette, inhaled deeply, and glanced impatiently at his wife and at the Jewish girl, and then said very politely, Komi was not like these, God forgive my crazy brother, wherever he may be. She was all beautiful things of the earth. Her heart was a dark sea. A black deep endless sea, and my brother wanted her for his wife.

Moyskan said *yes* with a new song. He sang the wedding of my brother Mago and his daughter Komi three days and three nights without stopping, except to drink.

Komi said to my brother Mago, said the young Black Tartar, I do not wish to love you.

My brother Mago stole a horse and brought it to her and again she spoke the same words.

It was a fine horse and any other girl would have loved my brother for stealing such a horse for her, but not Komi.

My poor brother stole a dress for Komi, and again she said she did not wish to love him. He stole a cow for her and Moyskan slaughtered it and ate it, and he stole a table for her, and still she did not wish to love him and he said he would steal an American automobile, for her, only he did not know how to drive an automobile.

I am a year younger than my brother Mago, said Karachi. An older brother speaks to a younger brother. A younger brother does not say to an older brother, You must not do this, you must do *this*.

It is not this way with Black Tartars only, he said. It is the same with many people. Is it so with Americans?

In a way, yes, I said.

My brother, said Karachi, wished to steal an American automobile for Komi because he loved her so much. I loved Komi, too, but when a sea is dark and wild only a great man will wish to swim across the sea, or a crazy man, or a man who is not afraid to die, or who wishes to die, and did not wish to die. My brother was not sleeping at night and he was not sleeping during the day, and I could see in his eyes that he could destroy the world in order to love Komi, that he could kill her so that no other man could love her, that he could do *anything*. It is foolishness, said Karachi, but it is greatness, too. Only my brother Mago is a real Black Tartar. Only he is a fool and not ashamed to be a fool. Only he would steal an American automobile for Komi. The officers of the Army would not do it and the soldiers would not do it. They knew fear. To steal an American automobile that belongs to the government is to die.

Mago stole a Cadillac and drove it into a hotel, said Karachi.

He wished to take Komi an American automobile, but he did not know how to drive, and he drove into the New Europe Hotel on Malygin Street, in Baku.

Karachi got up from the bench and shook his head slowly and sadly.

My brother, he said. My crazy brother. My poor crazy brother Mago.
To love so deeply.

He sat down again and remained silent for some time, remembering
his brother, looking at the floor sullenly.

Ahkh ahkh ahkh ahkh, he whispered.

Do you understand such a thing in America? he asked.

Ask the American, he said to the Jewish girl, if they understand such
a thing in America.

He wants to know if you can understand such a thing in America,
said the Jewish girl.

Tell him yes, I said to the Jewish girl. Tell him it is the same
everywhere. Tell him it has nothing to do with the form of government,
Capitalist, Fascist, or proletarian, it is the same everywhere.

The Jewish girl translated what I said, and the young Black Tartar
said in Russian to me, Da, da.

My brother, said Karachi, drove the American automobile through
the door of the New Europe Hotel on Malygin Street in Baku. He broke
the door down. He broke the glass window to a thousand pieces. He
frightened all the people in the hotel. He arrived in the lobby of the hotel
in the American automobile with his head bloody from pieces of broken
glass. My brother Mago sat in the automobile and smoked a cigarette and
everywhere around him ran a hundred people, shouting and screaming,
and then two hundred people, and then came Moyskan, and then Komi.

My brother said, Komi, is there another soldier in the Azerbaijan
Army who would do this for you? Is there another man in all the world
who would do this for you?

This was in 1926, said Karachi. The years go by, he sighed. The
landscape of life changes. (He says, said the Jewish girl, the landscape of
life changes. I do not know how to translate his words.) The dead are
forgotten by the living. My poor crazy brother killed Komi. My brother
who loved her more than any other man in the whole Azerbaijan Army.
My poor brother who is now in Irak or Afghanistan or dead. Ahkh ahkh.

Everybody said my brother would be shot in the morning. To steal
an American automobile. To steal from the government.

To the New Europe Hotel they sent one officer of the Army and one
hundred soldiers.

The officer said to Mago, What are you doing in this automobile?

I am sitting in this automobile, said Mago.

The officer said, Where did you get this automobile?

My brother said, I got this automobile on Narimanovskaya Street,
in front of the building of the People's Commissars.

The officer said, You know this automobile belongs to the Central
Executive Committee?

Yes, I know, said my crazy brother.

You stole this automobile? said the officer.

Yes, said Mago, I stole it.

My brother was brave and crazy, said Karachi.

Do you know what is the punishment for such a crime? said the officer.

Yes, I know, said my brother. It is death.

Ahkh, Mago, Mago, Mago, said Karachi.

He turned bitterly to the Jewish girl and asked many questions. I knew they were questions from the intonations of his voice and from the expression on his face.

What is he asking? I asked the Jewish girl.

He is asking if I am translating every word, said the Jewish girl. He wants to know if you understand the deep love of his brother. He does not believe any man who has not seen Komi can understand why his brother stole the American automobile and drove it into the New Europe Hotel.

Tell him I understand, I said.

Da? he asked me. Yes? You understand?

Yes, I said.

Everybody, he said, is listening carefully to the officer and my brother, and when my brother says the punishment is death, everybody is talking out loud and saying, Listen, listen to him, did you hear? the punishment is death, he knows, he is not afraid.

Then why did you steal this automobile? said the officer.

Because I love Komi, said my brother.

Then everybody is being very quiet, only one man is speaking. This man is a man with a hunchback. He is saying, The whole world is in love with Komi, even I. And somebody is putting a hand over his mouth because it is true and the people are ashamed. They are ashamed to love a girl so beautiful and they are proud that my brother Mago is not ashamed to love such a girl and to steal an American automobile for her and drive it into the New Europe Hotel.

The officer was in love with Komi too, said Karachi.

The officer did not make any reply. He understood.

So they took my brother Mago to the military jail in Baku. In the morning they began to ask him many questions. To every question he answered the truth.

They said, Did you steal a horse?

And my brother said, Yes, I stole a horse.

Did you steal a dress? Did you steal a cow? Did you steal a table? Yes. Yes. Yes.

Why did you steal these things?

I stole them for Komi.

The military Judge was a big Captain. He was an old man with a big moustache.

Who is Komi? said this man.

She is a Black Tartar girl, said Mago. She is the most beautiful girl in the world. I am a Black Tartar. I love Komi and I want to live in the same house with her. There are not many Black Tartars in the world. I do not wish to see the tribe of Black Tartars to end in the world. I wish to love Komi.

You do not look very black, said the Judge.

I have not been in the sun very much lately, said my brother. I am in the Azerbaijan Army and I work where it is shady, in the stable. A month in the sun and I am as black as Komi herself. It is the shade of the stable that has given me this sickly white colour. In times of war I ride in the cavalry, but in times of peace I work in the stable.

I never heard of Black Tartars, said the Judge. I have seen many white Tartars. Who are the Black Tartars?

They are the ones who are black, said my brother.

Ah, said the Judge. How many Black Tartars are there in the world?

In the world I do not know, said my brother. In Baku there are only nine or ten. Thirty years ago a Black Tartar named Kotova went to America. He is now an American and his children are not black any longer and they live in Pittsburgh.

What language do you speak? said the Judge.

Mostly other languages, said my brother. Arabic, Kurdish, Turkish, and lately Russian.

Have you any language? said the Judge.

Yes, we have a language, said my brother.

Is it a written language? said the Judge.

Of course, said my brother. Only there is no Black Tartar in the world who can read or write in our language or in any other language.

Ah, said the Judge. What is your word for *sun*?

We have no word for *sun* in our language, said my brother.

Have you any words at all in your language? asked the Judge.

Oh, yes, said my brother. We have many words. They are Arabic and Kurdish and Turkish and Russian, only we speak these words in our own language, as Black Tartars.

How is that? asked the Judge.

We speak as Black Tartars, said my brother. We *are* Black Tartars and any words we use are in our language.

And you stole the official automobile of the Central Executive Committee in order to give it as a gift to this Black Tartar girl you love. Is that so? asked the Judge.

Yes, it is so, said my brother.

Please bring this girl to me, said the Judge.

In the afternoon of the same day they brought Komi to the room where they were asking my brother questions. The Judge was looking at papers when she entered the room. Then he began to read aloud, opening the trial. He was reading aloud when he lifted his eyes and saw Komi. He stopped reading and stared at her.

Is this the girl? he said.

Yes, said my brother. This is Komi.

Give her a chair, said the Judge. He looked very excited. Why are you fools standing around? he said. Give her a chair.

After a while Komi stood before the Judge and he asked her some questions.

Do you understand what has happened? he asked.

No, said Komi.

This foolish young soldier, said the Judge, is in love with you. He has stolen a horse for you, a dress, a cow, a table, and finally the official automobile of the Central Executive Committee. Do you understand?

No, said Komi. Mago is my cousin.

Komi, said Mago. That is not so. I am not your cousin.

Silence, said the Judge. Do you realize you are on trial for your life?

I am not her cousin, said Mago. You can ask any Black Tartar in Baku.

Silence, said the Judge.

He turned to Komi, bending away over his desk in order to be closer to her.

Do you love this foolish young soldier? he said.

No, said Komi.

Now then, said the Judge, and he leaned way back in his chair.

Now then, he said, let me see.

You have stolen the official automobile of the Central Executive Committee, he said.

Yes, said Mago.

You were in love at the time, said the Judge.

Yes, said Mago. I am still in love, I shall always be in love with Komi.

Silence, said the Judge.

By law the punishment for such a monstrous crime, said the Judge, is immediate death.

He is my cousin, said Komi. You are not going to kill him, are you?

I am not afraid to die, said Mago.

Silence, said the Judge.

He turned to Komi again, leaning forward.

We shall do everything in our power to forgive this sorrowful misconduct of your cousin, he said. We shall examine his record and if he has murdered no man during the last five years, we shall return him to the ranks of the Army where his behaviour will be closely watched.

Four days later, said Karachi, they returned Mago to the Army. Everybody in Baku was happy about this.

One evening my brother Mago saw Komi in an automobile with the Judge. The Judge was crowding over Komi, and Komi was laughing at him. The Judge was an old man and his children were older than Mago.

My brother Mago was very angry. First, he said, he would kill the Judge, then he would kill the Judge's wife, then each of his five children, the oldest first, the next oldest next, and so on down the line until all of them were killed.

Then he said he would not kill the Judge, he would steal two good horses, and tie Komi to one of the horses and take her into the hills where he would keep her until each of them died, either of old age, or starvation, or from loving one another too much and not wanting to be alive.

My brother Mago went to Komi and said. Why are you going around with this rotten old man?

Because I want to, said Komi.

He is not a Black Tartar, said Mago. If I see you with him again, I will kill him.

He saved your life, said Komi.

I will kill him, anyway, said Mago. You are a Black Tartar and you must love a Black Tartar.

I do not know what I am, said Komi. Maybe I am not a Black Tartar.

You are a Black Tartar, said Mago. I want you to live in the same house with me.

I do not wish to love you, said Komi.

You will love me, said Mago. You are a Black Tartar and I am a Black Tartar and you will love me.

Ahkh, ahkh, said Karachi. There are so many girls in the world. But my poor brother would not look at another girl as long as Komi was alive. Maybe you will understand this, but my poor crazy brother killed Komi and went away to Irak or Afghanistan, or maybe he killed himself, too. We do not know.

She would not love him, said Karachi. He was the one man in the world for her, and she would not love him. He drove the American automobile into the lobby of the New Europe Hotel for her and still she would not love him.

One morning before daybreak my brother Mago went to Moyskan's house with two of the finest horses from the stables of the Azerbaijan Army. He entered the house and tied Komi's arms and legs, kissing her lips and hands and hair. Moyskan helped him because he did not think it was good for Komi to go around with an old man, but Moyskan's wife cried and screamed until Moyskan knocked her down. Then my brother Mago tied Komi to one of the horses and took her with him into the hills.

Nobody knows what happened there, said Karachi.

No man in all the world loved a girl as deeply as my brother Mago loved Komi, he said.

They sent soldiers on horses into the hills. First ten soldiers, then twenty, then fifty, then a hundred, then the whole Azerbaijan Army. The old Captain was very angry. He said, Shoot that foolish young soldier, but bring back the young girl unharmed. But the soldiers did not find my brother or Komi.

One morning they found Komi dead. My brother Mago had held her under the water of a shallow stream. He did not want her to live if she would not love him.

In America, said Karachi, does a man love a woman so deeply?

I don't think so, I said.

He turned to the Jewish girl again and began to talk to her very rapidly.

He is saying, said the Jewish girl, that he wants you to understand it was not a crime. It was not hate, it was love. You have never seen Komi, he is saying. He wants you to know his brother was a great man. He was a man who wanted to live greatly. That is why he did all those foolish things.

Tell him I know how it was, I said.

And the Jewish girl told him.

He did not speak for many minutes.

Then he said, Ahkh, Mago, Mago, Mago. And many other words in Russian which I did not understand.

What is he saying? I asked the Jewish girl.

He is saying, To kill such a girl as Komi, To kill her. To end the life of such a one as Komi. A man must love deeply to do such a thing.

Kharkov, Russia. June, 1935

Inhale and Exhale, 1936

Finlandia

I was walking down Annankatu Street in Helsingfors when I saw two horns, a cello, a violin, and a picture of Beethoven in a store window, and remembered music. You go out into the world and all you see is telegraph poles and city streets, and all you hear is the train moving and automobile horns. You see multitudes of people trying to do all sorts of things, and in restaurants and in the streets you hear them talking anxiously. You forget music, and then all of a sudden you remember music.

Jesus Christ, you say. There is nothing else. After the train stops and you get off, or the ship docks and you walk down the gangplank, or the airplane comes down to the earth and lets you put your feet where they belong, there is nothing. You have arrived and you are nowhere. The name of the city is on the map. It is in big letters on the railway station. And the name of the country is on the new coins which buy bread, but you are nowhere and the more places you reach the more you understand that there is no geographical destination for man.

To hell with this, you say. London, and nothing. Paris, and nowhere. Vienna, and nothing. Moscow. The same. Dialectical materialism. Class consciousness. Revolution. Comrades. Baloney.

Nothing. Nowhere.

There is no place to go in that direction. And it breaks your heart. Jesus, you say. This is the world. These are the places of the world. What's the matter? Everything is haywire. And in the streets of every new city you feel again the world's dumb agony.

In Helsingfors it is not so bad, although there is private ownership of property in Finland. People own small objects. In the market those who own fish, sell fish, those who own tomatoes, sell tomatoes. Maybe it is Capitalism, but even so you can't find anything wrong with the people.

When I saw the cornet and the trombone and the cello and the violin and the picture of Beethoven, I felt very mournful. The shape of the cornet is no small triumph, and even a tin violin is a poem of an idea.

I went into the store and asked the girl in English if I could listen to some phonograph records of Finnish music. The girls of Finland are quiet, healthy, beautiful. Their mothers and fathers are Lutherans and believe in God. The girls look as if they also believe, but even if they don't, they probably go to church every Sunday and sing and it amounts to the same thing. They aren't fanatics, but they probably go to church because it is all right. It is rather nice. Everybody is there, and the old Sunday mood of the world quiets the harsh noises and irritations of week days, and by the time the sermon is over everybody feels less important than on week days and there are no hard feelings. You own the bank. Good. Keep it. I have a bicycle. You are the mayor. Good. I am a clerk in an office. No hard feelings, and the Sunday sun is bright.

In Russia, though, there is no such thing as Sunday. The girls of Russia burst into false laughter every time a movie puts over a little anti-religious propaganda because they know it is not true, there were never any saints, religion is the opium of the people. Karl Marx is the closest thing to a saint the world has ever known. Trotsky is a rat, Lenin was almost the second coming of Jesus, and Comrade Stalin is something amazing. As a result the girls of Russia don't look very good. They are so wise it has spoiled their complexions. All the same, Russia is at least a thousand years ahead of Finland. Look at the things they are doing. Building cities. Creating a classless society. Calling everybody Comrade. Years and years ahead. The girls look pretty bad, though.

The girl in the music store in Helsingfors was very old-fashioned. She was polite. She didn't know anything about creating a classless society, so she had time enough to do one small thing at a time, instead of doing nothing at all, and that loudly, the way it is in Russia. Not all the time of course. There are some girls in Russia who are almost like the girls of Finland, but these are the ones who are not militant. It's Dictatorship of the Proletariat, so it's Dictatorship of the Proletariat, and they go on living their private lives. These kind will never be leaders. They will never elevate the lives of the peasants. They are very unimportant. But most of the girls in Russia a traveller meets smell dialectical. It's something like the smell of a weed you know is poison.

Jean Sibelius, I said to the girl in the music store. *Finlandia.*

Two months ago Helsingfors was very far from where I was. I was in a room in the Great Northern Hotel in Manhattan, 517, with bath. Helsingfors? Where's that, anyway? Now I am in Helsingfors, and the only thing I know about the location of Manhattan is that you get into a boat and after six days, if the boat is fast, you see the skyline of Manhattan, and there you are. It is the same with Helsingfors or anywhere else. You are so many feet and so many inches off the cement pavement. The sky is over you. The sun comes up in the morning. In

Manhattan, of course, it gets darker in the summer than it does in Helsingfors in the summer. It never gets very dark in the summer in Helsingfors. At midnight it is still pretty light, and a couple of hours later the sun comes up again.

And it is fine. It is tremendous. It is the crazy world. The urban corners of what is affectionately known as civilization. A cornet, a trombone, a cello, and a violin in a store window. And of course music is the most effective opium of the people there is, unless it is composed by a dialectical materialist. Then nobody knows what it is. But if it is good, then the boy who did the job is fooling somebody, maybe Marx.

All I wanted was music. No dialectics. Just the simple old-fashioned fury of one man alone, fighting it out alone, wrestling with God, or with the whole confounded universe, throwing himself into silence and time, and after sweating away seven pounds of substance, coming out of the small room with something detached, of itself, alive, timeless, crazy, magnificent, delirious, blasphemous, pious, furious, kindly, not the man, not all men, but a thing by itself, incredibly complete, an incision of silence and emptiness, and then sound and the shapes of things without substance. Music. A symphony.

Finlandia, I said. The word was strong and good, and I was there. I am in Finland, I thought. This store is on Annankatu Street in Helsingfors. Jean Sibelius lives in Finland. It was here that he composed *Finlandia*, and in America five years ago I heard *Finlandia*, and I have been hearing it ever since, and the ear of man will never cease hearing it.

It is no small thing to hear *Finlandia* in Helsingfors.

The girl was very pious, changing the needle, letting it touch the record, winding the phonograph. She went away six paces and stood humbly listening. After the silence the music began to leap out into the world again. Finland.

O Jesus Christ, there is no geographic destination for man. And the music charged into the chaos of the world, smashing hell out of error, ignoring waste, and creating a classless society. Last year in England the king listened and knew the truth, and to-morrow in Nebraska a child will listen and know the truth, and it will be the same with kings and children a hundred years from now, or a thousand.

I smoked four cigarettes, and then this great work of Jean Sibelius ended. The silence that had existed before the music began came into existence again, and now it was no longer *Finlandia* but Finland, Helsingfors. The girl could not speak English, but she also could not say anything in Finnish. She smiled, almost weeping. Then she hurried away and returned with an album containing the records of a whole symphony by Sibelius.

No, I said. It was very kind of you to let me hear *Finlandia* in

Helsingfors. I cannot buy. I am only here on my way back to America. I am sailing to-morrow for Stockholm.

I brought some marks from my pocket and asked if I could pay for hearing *Finlandia*.

This, the appearance of money, spoiled everything. Now the girl not only did not understand what I was saying, she did not understand the *meaning* of what I was saying. She could not understand how I felt. With the music she knew and she didn't need to understand the words.

She wanted to give me something for the money.

No, I said. This money is for hearing *Finlandia*.

This was too much. She went away and returned with a girl who spoke English.

I explained everything, and the girl who knew English interpreted to the girl who did not, and we all laughed.

No no, said the girl who spoke English. Would you like to hear some more of Sibelius?

No, I said. I want to remember *Finlandia* in Helsingfors. Do you know Jean Sibelius?

Yes, of course, said the girl.

The other girl stood by watching our faces.

What sort of a man is he? I said.

Big, said the girl. He is very big. He comes to this store very often. He lives in Helsingfors?

Yes.

Look, I said. I am in Helsingfors to-day and I may never be here again. To-morrow I am going to Stockholm. I am an American, and I am supposed to be a writer. Do you think Jean Sibelius would see me?

But wait a minute. Let me explain.

The first time I heard *Finlandia*, five years ago in America, I got up from the chair, pushed over the table, knocked some plaster out of the wall, and said, Jesus Christ, who is this man? Now, it was almost the same. It is not every day that I am in Helsingfors, and it is not every century that Jean Sibelius is in Helsingfors the same day.

Yes, said the girl. Wait a moment, please. I will get the number.

And she went upstairs. She returned running.

Jean Sibelius is in Jarvenpaa, she said.

How far is that from Helsingfors? I said.

One hour, said the girl.

I wrote the name of the place on an envelope and hurried away. The two Finnish girls walked all the way to the door with me. They were almost as excited as I was. From America, and he has heard *Finlandia*. Music is international. (And it is. Even the word music is. If you say bread in English, many people will not know what you mean, but if you say music, they will know.)

I thought I would send a telegram. I tried to write one but it sounded lousy. It doesn't mean a thing in a telegram.

I asked the hotel clerk if I could reach Jean Sibelius by telephone. I felt like a fool. Such a thing is ridiculous.

Of course, he said.

And before I knew it I was talking to him over the telephone.

I am from America, I said. Everybody in America likes your music.

I am at this place in the country, he said in English. Come at seven.

It was half past four, and it took an hour to get to Jarvenpaa, so that left me about an hour in which to try to figure out what the hell was going on. Who am I to see Jean Sibelius? What can I say to the man who composed *Finlandia*, and what will he have to say to me? He is seventy years old and I am twenty-seven. I was born in America. I am a punk writer, and he is a great composer, Jesus Christ.

But that's music for you. I didn't know what I was doing.

It is *Finlandia*. And it was Finland. The girls were beautiful and very quiet and very polite. It is a writer's job to try to find out how these things happen: that music, and the clean innocent faces of the girls of Finland.

I went up to my room at the Torni Hotel and tried to think of some questions to ask Jean Sibelius, but nothing is more disgusting than a question, and the ones I wrote were the worst questions anybody every thought of asking anybody else. They were long involved questions, asking if perhaps it is true that all art forms are inherent in nature and all the artist can do is reveal these forms, and what effect does the world of man, the world of cities, trains, ships, skyscrapers, factories, machines, noises, have on a composer, and if music should have a function, and what is the quality which most nearly makes a competent composer a great composer, his spiritual heritage, his race, the experiences and remembrances of his race, his own personal experiences, or simply much energy, some anger, and the will or impluse to declare his mortality at a certain time and thus to be immortal?

Jesus Christ.

And God forgive me I actually asked the questions.

It was an old Buick going like a bat out of hell through the clean landscape of Finland, and along the roads were boys on bicycles, girls walking, and farmers going home on carts. Clean air. Fresh green growing things. Clean sky. Cool clean lakes. Cool trees. Grass. The place of *Finlandia*.

It is not easy to explain. It is not only these things, but something more. Maybe it is because there is hardly any night at all during the summer. Maybe it is because they are Lutherans, and have a church, and believe. Maybe it is because Finland is north. Cool. Quiet. Blond. Blue eyes. I don't know what the hell it is.

It was a country house in this landscape. The cabdriver stopped the car in the country and asked three young girls where was the road to the house of Jean Sibelius. The girls told him he had travelled too far. It was about a quarter of a kilometre back. In Finland everybody knows about Jean Sibelius and many people in and around Helsingfors have spoken with him.

Don't get this wrong. I mean something. Don't get the idea I mean it is remarkable that many people have spoken with Jean Sibelius or that it is splendid of him to know so many people. I mean it is all the same. These are the people of Finland. Jean Sibelius is the big man who makes music, and the others are the others, and it is the same. They are all alive in Finland.

I went into the house all mixed up. The maid was waiting for me and welcomed me in Finnish. He was seated, talking to a young man, an American-Finn from California, and he got up, and then it was the thing I was after, *Finlandia*, Jean Sibelius, seventy years old, and timeless, and a child, the smile, the fury of politeness, *yes yes yes*, the strong hand, the introduction to his friend, the strong gesture, the energy, sit down, and Jesus Christ, what about those crazy questions? I couldn't talk, I had to say my piece and scram and I wanted to do so, so I began to explain about the questions, stumbling, a very big man, and I don't mean bulk alone, and I was from America, eleven hours in Helsingfors.

He answered the God damn questions, and it was great. Yes, yes, silence. Silence is everything. (He jumped up, his big hands trembling and got a can of cigars. Cigar? And then he shouted for whisky, and in a moment the maid came into the room with whisky.) Music is like life. It begins and ends in silence. He made a wild gesture, every nerve of his body alive. Drink whisky, he said. I didn't know what to do. I poured a drink for his young friend, and another for myself, and we drank.

The world of cities, I said. Trains, ships, skyscrapers, subways, airplanes, factories, machines, noises, what effect?

I felt like a fool.

He was furious and began to speak in his native tongue.

He cannot answer, said the young man. Music speaks for him. It is all in the music.

I am sorry about these questions, I said. I'll leave out some of them.

He spoke in Finnish, and the young man interpreted: Beauty and truth, but he does not like the words. Not the words. It is something different in music. Everybody says beauty and truth. He is no prophet. Only a composer.

And the angry-kindly smile in the ferociously stark face.

Drink whisky, he said in English.

I went on to the one about what is it that makes the man great.

No, he said in English. You cannot talk about such a thing.

It was swell. It was the real thing. It was too silly to talk. He was too wise to fool with words. He put it down in music. I felt swell because he was so young, so much a boy, so excited, nervous, energetic, impatient, so amazingly innocent, and on the way back to Helsingfors I began to see in the landscape of Finland the clean clear music of *Finlandia*.

Helsingfors, Finland. July, 1935.

Inhale and Exhale, 1936

Lucy
Garoghlanian

*M*y grandmother came into the room and stared bitterly at everything, grumbling to herself and lifting a book off the table, opening it, studying the strange print and closing it with an angry and impatient bang, as if nothing in the world could be more ridiculous than a book.

I knew she wanted to talk, so I pretended to be asleep.

My grandmother is a greater lady than any lady I have ever had the honour of meeting, and she may even be the greatest lady alive in the past-seventy class for all I know, but I always say there is a time and place for everything. They are always having baby contests in this crazy country, but I never heard of a grandmother contest. My old grandmother would walk away with every silver loving cup and gold or blue ribbon in the world in a grandmother contest, and I like her very much, but I wanted to sleep. She can't read or write, but what of it? She knows more about life than John Dewey and George Santayana put together, and that's plenty. You could ask her what's two times two and she'd fly off the handle and tell you not to irritate her with childish questions, but she's a genius just the same.

Forty years ago, she said, they asked this silly woman Oskan to tell about her visit to the village of Gultik and she got up and said, They have chickens there, and in calling the chickens they say, *Chik chik chik*. They have cows also, and very often the cows holler, *Moo moo moo*.

She was very angry about these remarks of the silly woman. She was remembering the old country and the old life, and I knew she would take up the story of her husband Melik in no time and begin to shout, so I sat up and smiled at her.

Is that all she had to say? I said. *Chik chik chik* and *moo moo moo*?

She was foolish, said my grandmother. I guess that's why they sent her to school and taught her to read and write. Finally she married a man who was crippled in the left leg. One cripple deserves another, she said. Why aren't you walking in the park on a day like this?

I thought I'd have a little afternoon nap, I said.

For the love of God, said my grandmother, my husband Melik was a man who rode a black horse through the hills and forests all day and half the night, drinking and singing. When the townspeople saw him coming they would run and hide. The wild Kourds of the desert trembled in his presence. I am ashamed of you, she said, lolling around among these silly books.

She lifted the first book that came to her hand, opened it, and stared with disgust at the print.

What is all this language here? she said.

That's a very great book by a very great man, I said. Dostoyevsky he was called. He was a Russian.

Don't tell me about the Russians, said my grandmother. What tricks they played on us. What does he say here?

Everything, I said. He says we must love our neighbours and be kind to the weak.

More lies, said my grandmother. Which tribe of the earth was kind to our tribe? In the dead of winter he went to Stamboul.

Who? I said.

Melik, she shouted. My own husband, she said bitterly. Who else? Who else would dare to go that far in the dead of winter? I will bring you a bright shawl from Stamboul, he said. I will bring you a bracelet and a necklace. He was drunk of course, but he was my husband. I bore him seven children before he was killed. There would have been more if he hadn't been killed, she groaned.

I have heard he was a cruel man, I said.

Who said such an unkind thing about my husband? said my grandmother. He was impatient with fools and weaklings, she said. You should try to be like this man.

I could use a horse all right, I said. I like drinking and singing too.

In this country? said my grandmother. Where could you go with a horse in this country?

I could go to the public library with a horse, I said.

And they'd lock you in jail, she said. Where would you tie the horse?

I would tie the horse to a tree, I said. There are six small trees in front of the public library.

Ride a horse in this country, she said, and they will put you down for a maniac.

They have already, I said. The libel is spreading like wildfire.

You don't care? she said.

Not at all, I said. Why should I?

Is it true, perhaps? she said.

It is a foul lie, I said.

It is healthful to be disliked, said my grandmother. My husband Melik was hated by friend and enemy alike. *Bitterly* hated, and he knew it, and yet everybody pretended to like him. They were afraid of him, so they pretended to like him. Will you play a game of *scambile*? I have the cards.

She was lonely again, like a young girl.

I got up and sat across the table from her and lit a cigarette for her and one for myself. She shuffled and dealt three cards to me and three to herself and turned over the next card, and the game began.

Ten cents? she said.

Ten or fifteen, I said.

Fifteen then, but I play a much better game than you, she said.

I may be lucky, I said.

I do not believe in luck, she said, not even in card games. I believe in thinking and knowing what you are doing.

We talked and played and I lost three games to my grandmother. I paid her, only I gave her a half-dollar.

Is that what it comes to? she said.

It comes to a little less, I said.

You are not lying? she said.

I never lie, I said. It comes to forty-five cents. You owe me five cents.

Five pennies? she said.

Or one nickel, I said.

I have three pennies, she said. I will pay you three pennies now and owe you two.

Your arithmetic is improving, I said.

American money confuses me, she said, but you never heard of anyone cheating me, did you?

Never, I admitted.

They don't dare, she said. I count the money piece by piece, and if someone is near by I have him count it for me too. There was this thief of a grocer in Hanford, she said. Dikranian. Three cents more he took. Six pounds of cheese. I had five different people count for me. Three cents more he has taken, they said. I waited a week and then went to his store again. For those three cents I took three packages of cigarettes. From a thief thieve and God will smile on you. I never enjoyed cigarettes as much as those I took from Dikranian. Five people counted for me. He thought I was an old woman. He thought he could do such a thing. I went back to the store and said not a word. Good morning, good morning. Lovely day, lovely day. A pound of rice, a pound of rice. He turned to get the rice, I took three packages of cigarettes.

Ha ha, said my grandmother. From thief thieve, and from above God will smile.

But you took too much, I said. You took fifteen times too much.

Fifteen times too much? said my grandmother. He took three pennies, I took three packages of cigarettes, no more, no less.

Well, I said, it probably comes to the same thing anyway, but you don't really believe God smiles when you steal from a thief, do you?

Of course I believe, said my grandmother. Isn't it said in three different languages, Armenian, Kourdish, and Turkish?

She said the words in Kourdish and Turkish.

I wish I knew how to talk those languages, I said.

Kourdish, said my grandmother, is the language of the heart. Turkish is music. Turkish flows like a stream of wine, smooth and sweet and bright in colour. Our tongue, she shouted, is a tongue of bitterness. We have tasted much of death and our tongue is heavy with hatred and anger. I have heard only one man who could speak our language as if it were the tongue of a God-like people.

Who was that man? I asked.

Melik, said my grandmother. My husband Melik. If he was sober, he spoke quietly, his voice rich and deep and gentle, and if he was drunk, he roared like a lion and you'd think God in Heaven was crying lamentations and oaths upon the tribes of the earth. No other man have I heard who could speak in this way, drunk or sober, not one, here or in the old country.

And when he laughed? I said.

When Melik laughed, said my grandmother, it was like an ocean of clear water leaping at the moon with delight.

I tell you, my grandmother would walk away with every silver loving cup and gold ribbon in the world.

Now she was angry, ferocious with the tragic poetry of her race.

And not one of you *opegh-tsapegh* brats are like him, she shouted. Only my son Vahan is a little like him, and after Vahan all the rest of you are strangers to me. This is my greatest grief.

Opegh-tsapegh is untranslatable. It means, somewhat, *very haphazardly assembled*, and when said of someone, it means he is no particular credit to the race of man. On the contrary, only another fool, someone to include in the census and forget. In short, everybody.

And when he cried? I said.

My husband was never known to weep, said my grandmother. When other men hid themselves in their houses and frightened their wives and children by weeping, my husband rode into the hills, drunk and cursing. If he wept in the hills, he wept alone, with only God to witness his weakness. He always came back, though, swearing louder than ever, and then I would put him to bed and sit over him, watching his face.

She sat down with a sigh and again stared bitterly around the room.

These books, she said. I don't know what you expect to learn from books. What is in them? What do you expect to learn from reading?

I myself sometimes wonder, I said.

You have read them all? she said.

Some twice, some three times, I said. Some only a page here and there.

And what is their message?

Nothing much, I said. Sometimes there is brightness and laughter, or maybe the opposite, gloom and anger. Not often, though.

Well, said my grandmother, the ones who were taught to read and write were always the silliest and they made the worst wives. This soft-brained Oskan went to school, and when she got up to speak all she could say was, They have chickens there, and in calling the chickens they say, *Chik chik chik.* Is that wisdom?

That's innocence, I said in English.

I cannot understand such an absurd language, she said.

It is a splendid language, I said.

That is because you were born here and can speak no other language, no Turkish, no Kourdish, not one word of Arabic.

No, I said, it is because this is the language Shakespeare spoke and wrote.

Shakespeare? said my grandmother. Who is he?

He is the greatest poet the world has ever known, I said.

Nonsense, said my grandmother. There was a travelling minstrel who came to our city when I was a girl of twelve. This man was as ugly as Satan, but he could recite poetry in six different languages, all day and all night, and not one word of it written, not one word of it memorized, every line of it made up while he stood before the people, reciting. They called him Crazy Markos and people gave him small coins for reciting and the more coins they gave him the drunker he got and the drunker he got the more beautiful the poems he recited.

Well, I said, each country and race and time has its own kind of poet and its own understanding of poetry. The English poets wrote and your poets recited.

But if they were poets, said my grandmother, why did they write? A poet lives to sing. Were they afraid a good thing would be lost and forgotten? Why do they write each of their thoughts? Are they afraid something will be lost?

I guess so, I said.

Do you want something to eat? said my grandmother. I have cabbage soup and bread.

I'm not hungry, I said.

Are you going out again to-night? she said.

Yes, I said. There is an important meeting of philosophers in the city to-night. I have been invited to listen and learn.

Why don't you stop all this nonsense? she said.

This isn't nonsense, I said. These philosophers are going to explain how we can make this world a better place, a heaven on earth.

It *is* nonsense, said my grandmother. This place is the same place all men have known, and it is anything you like.

That's bourgeois talk, I said in English.

These philosophers, I said in Armenian, are worrying about the poor. They want the wealth of the rich to be shared with the poor. That way they claim everything will be straightened out and everybody will be happy.

Everybody is poor, said my grandmother. The richest man in the world is no less poor than the poorest. All over the world there is poverty of spirit. I never saw such miserliness in people. Give them all the money in the world and they'll still be poor. That's something between themselves and God.

They don't believe in God, I said.

Whether they believe or not, said my grandmother, it is still a matter between themselves and God. I don't believe in evil, but does that mean evil does not exist?

Well, I said, I'm going anyway, just to hear what they have to say.

Then I must be in the house alone? she said.

Go to a movie, I said. You know how to get to the neighbourhood theatre. It's not far. There is a nice picture to-night.

Alone? said my grandmother. I wouldn't think of it.

To-morrow, I said, we will go together. To-night you can listen to the radio. I will come home early.

Have you no books with pictures?

Of course, I said.

I handed her a book called *The Life of Queen Victoria*, full of pictures of that nice old lady.

You will like this lady, I said. She was Queen of England, but she is now dead. The book is full of pictures, from birth to death.

Ah, said my grandmother looking at an early picture of the Queen. She was a beautiful girl. Ahkh, ahkh, alas, alas, for the good who are dead, and my grandmother went down the hall to the kitchen.

I got out of my old clothes and jumped under a warm shower. The water was refreshing to the skin and I began to sing.

I put on fresh clothes and a dark suit. I went into the kitchen and kissed my grandmother's hand, then left the house. She stood at the front window, looking down at me.

Then she lifted the window and stuck her head out.

Boy, she shouted. Don't be so serious. Get a little drunk.

O.K., I said.

Part II of 'The Living and the Dead'
Three Times Three, 1936

Gus the
Gambler

*I*t will do you a world of good to know about my friend, Gus the gambler, Jim said, because, although Gus is dead, his memory will linger on and on.

Jim was a little drunk of course, and the reason he figured it would do me a world of good to know about his friend Gus was that he wanted to tell me about Gus. It seems Gus was a man one inch under seven feet, broad as a barrel, gentle as a lamb, courteous to the point of nausea and in every particular a genius. Although married five times, he did not murder one of his wives. He left them. Deserted them. He did this courteously, Jim argued, bowing deeply, waving his hat in front of him, and uttering only one or two of the milder words of profanity of the English language. He deserted his wives out of politeness and consideration, in order not to be compelled to murder them and suffer much personal inconvenience.

My dear, Gus used to say to a wife he was about to leave, if you are ever in need of ten cents for coffee and doughnuts, or for that matter fifteen cents for a hamburger and coffee, I shall be deeply hurt and offended if you do not call on me.

And mind you, Jim said, wagging his head in drunken insinuation, Gus was the kind of man who normally knocked down anyone he disliked and commented about it later.

I floored Hollywood Pete this afternoon, Gus used to say mournfully to a group of horsebettors. I'm afraid I hurt the feelings of that lousy gambler.

Well, said Jim, Gus died at the age of ninety in a beer parlour on Powell Street, at a quarter past two in the morning.

They didn't find out that Gus was dead for two days and two nights because he seemed to be asleep and nobody had guts enough to go over and try to wake him up.

Gus was a heavy sleeper. One winter in Chicago, Jim said, Gus was so unhappy, he slept two months in a row, in a suite of rooms at the Revere House. Every other night they used to send up a girl to get in bed with Gus, and a barber every three days to give him a shave. He could tell it was still winter by the touch of their hands.

My God, he used to groan, get in here where it's warm. God Almighty, is there no kindness in the world?

He was almost seventy at the time, Jim said.

One night Gus took hold of a small hand that was very warm, and he thought winter was over. He jumped up out of bed and put on a light sport suit. When he stepped out of the hotel, he saw streets white with snow, and he hopped right back in again. It seems the girl was running a fever. When Gus got back to his room, he was very polite.

He took off his hat, bowed very low, and said, My dear young lady, I should be very grateful to you if in the future you would not mislead me as regards the weather and time of year. From the warmth of your hand I was led to believe winter was ended and summer was coming in. Is it possible that you are ill? If so, leave this room immediately.

There was a gentleman, Jim said.

A man of intelligence, Jim said, yet he had no public schooling worth mentioning.

What the hell was his last name? I said.

Nobody knows, Jim said. A number of low-minded gamblers at one time concocted a foul theory that Gus was the illegitimate son of a king of Austria and a travelling musical comedy girl from America. Another school of thought, Jim said, argued that Gus was the son of a Salvation Army corporal and a girl of the streets. In all probability, however, Gus was a descendant of New England church-people, for to his dying day he was a man of faith.

Faith in what? I said.

Faith in anything, Jim said. He was a pious man. When the whole world turned against a horse you probably don't remember, a lovely trotter of thirty years ago named Miss Rebecca, and the odds on this horse rose to a hundred to one, Gus, always a man of faith, bet one thousand dollars on Miss Rebecca to win, and she won.

How did that happen? I said.

The other trotters were the unfortunate victims of an accident, Jim said.

What sort of an accident? I said.

An unfortunate accident, Jim said. It seems eight trotters a quarter of a mile ahead of Miss Rebecca stumbled one upon another and were badly hurt, and Miss Rebecca, going to the outside of the track, trotted in alone, breaking the world's record for the slowest time for the mile.

What made the other trotters stumble and fall? I said.

Providence, said Jim, although a number of low-minded gamblers invented the theory that Gus caused them to stumble and fall by means of one of two things.

One of two things? I said.

One group claimed Gus hired a hypnotist to destroy the balance and equilibrium in Kansas City, the trotter most heavily backed by wise money, said Jim, and another group claimed Gus hired eight hypnotists to destroy this same balance and this same equilibrium in each of the eight trotters. Both theories, I need not point out, I am sure, were false.

Well, what the hell made them stumble then? I said.

An act of God, Jim said. Gus was one of the most pious gambling men of his day, if not *the* foremost. I was at his side when he appealed to God in language impossible, utterly, to repeat; language so poetic and eloquent that it caused me, a young man of seventeen at the time, to burst into tears.

I can't believe it, I said. Do you mean to say you actually burst into tears?

I do, Jim said.

How much had *you* bet on Miss Rebecca? I said.

Ten dollars, Jim said.

Well, why did you cry? I said.

For having such little faith in the power of prayer, Jim said. If I had been a believer as Gus was a believer I would have bet thirty dollars.

Is that all the money you had? I said.

No, I had forty, Jim said.

Wouldn't you have bet all forty? I said.

No, Jim said. Only thirty.

Why?

Because I was not a believer as Gus was, Jim said. If I was dead sure the horse was going to win, I still would have bet only thirty.

That's funny, I said, I would have bet every penny I could get hold of.

Your faith, Jim said, is comparable to that of Gus himself.

Faith nothing, I said. If I figure a horse is going to win, I'm going to bet him for all I'm worth.

Your parents, in all probability, said Jim, are New England church-people.

They ain't, I said.

There's much of the pious man in you, nonetheless, said Jim.

I wish you could remember the prayer Gus said the day Miss Rebecca came in, I said.

I remember only its most ineloquent passages, Jim said.

And what were those passages? I said.

Language of the street, Jim said. Language which in my mouth or your mouth or the mouth of Curley the bartender or any other man alive would be offensive, and yet language which in the mouth of Gus could offend no one.

Well, what did he say? I said.

Stumble, you bastards, stumble, he said.

That don't sound like a prayer, I said.

The difference, said Jim, is in the mouth that utters the words. In the mouth of my dead and noble friend, Gus the gambler, it sounded very much like a prayer.

I wish I had met Gus, I said.

He would have spoken to you as a father to a son, Jim said. He would have given you three winners for the next day, informed you as regards the tricks of black-jack and poker dealers, and how to win the friendship of such men, and he would have furnished you with the addresses of many charming ladies.

Gee, I said.

In the absence of Gus, said Jim, I, hardly his equal in stature, nobility, or faith, can give you only one winner for to-morrow, and suggest that, rather than seek the friendship of card-dealers, to enter no game at all, and furnish you with only one address.

Even so, I said, I am very grateful.

Jim named the horse and wrote down the address.

In his later years, Jim said, Gus developed an interest in Christian Science which for thoroughness and eagerness could not possibly have been exceeded by Mary Baker Eddy herself.

I never heard of the horse, I said.

There's never been a horse named Mary Baker Eddy, said Jim. That is the name of a Boston lady, a lady, I might say, of the greatest charm, not to say daring, who, in a fit of inspiration, stumbled one night on the theory that pain is imaginary.

Sounds like a fluky theory to me, I said.

On the contrary, said Jim, it is not completely without truth, though there is an element of the far-fetched in it, as Gus himself finally admitted.

He did? I said. How come?

He hurt his fist in a fight with a gambler from Mobile, Alabama, said Jim.

What happened? I said.

It was a coloured gambler with a straight-edge razor in one hand and a chair in the other, said Jim. Gus knocked the chair out of one hand, and the razor out of the other, and then the coloured gentleman, who had a large mouth, bit Gus's hand, and Gus howled like a baby.

Gus kicked the coloured gentleman in the pit of the stomach and, said Jim, I'm afraid this sect of the Christian religion is founded on something closely akin to folk-lore or fantasy.

Jim, I said, I got to go now, but if I see you again soon, I hope you'll tell me more about your friend Gus.

Jim called Curley over to him and started to tell Curley it would do him a world of good to know a little more about Gus the gambler, and Curley, who knew everything there was to know about Gus the gambler, and Jim, and everybody else in the world, just told Jim to keep it till to-morrow.

Love, Here is My Hat and Other Short Romances, 1938

The La Salle
Hotel in Chicago

*T*he philosophers were standing around the steps of the Public Library, talking about everything. It was a clear dreamy April day and the men were glad. There was much goodwill among them and no hard feelings. The soapboxers were not supercilious towards the uninformed ones as they ordinarily were. The Slovak whose face was always smoothly shaven and whose teeth were very bad and who was usually loud and bitter and always in favour of revolution, riot and fire and cruelty and justice, spoke very quietly with a melancholy and gentle intonation, his bitterness and sadness still valid, but gaiety valid too.

I don't know, he said with an accent. Sometimes I see them in their big cars and instead of hating them I feel sorry for them. They got money and big houses and servants, but sometimes when I see them, all that stuff don't mean anything, and I don't hate them.

The listeners listened and smiled. The eccentric one, who was religious in an extraordinary way, and old, who hated three kinds of people of the world, Catholics, Irishmen, and Italians, scratched his beard and didn't make an argument. He hated Catholics because he had once been a Catholic; he hated Irishmen because Irishmen were cops and cops had hit him over the head with clubs several times and pushed him around and knocked him down and taken him to jail; and he hated Italians because Mussolini was an Italian and because an Italian in New York had cheated him thirty years ago.

Now he listened to the Slovak and didn't make an argument.

The young men, who were always present but never joined the meetings, stood among the old men and smoked cigarettes. One of them, who was in love with a waitress and wanted to get married, said to the small anarchist who was violently opposed to everything in the world, A lot of people that are married—both of them work.

The anarchist was usually high-strung, impatient, and sarcastic, but on this day he did not mock the young man or laugh out loud in the peculiar way he had that was neither natural nor artificial.

That's true, he said. And the young man was glad to have someone to talk to.

The anarchist was a man of forty-five or so. He had a well-shaped head, thick brown hair, and his teeth were good. He thought Communists were dopes. You God damn day-dreamers, he said to them one day. I know all about your Karl Marx. What was he? He was a lousy Jew who was scared to death by the world. (The anarchist himself was a Jew, but his love of Jews was so great that it had turned to hate and mockery.) You think you've got a chance, he said, but you've got no more chance than anybody else. Nobody's got a chance. Even after you have your lousy revolution you won't have a chance. What will you do? Do you think anything will be different?

Then he became very vulgar and the Slovak said, What's the use talking to you? You've got your mind made up.

On this day, though, the anarchist was very kindly and allowed the young man who was in love to tell his story.

I only had a quarter, the young man said, so I walked into that cheap hamburger joint—Pete's on Mason Street, right around the corner from the Day and Night Bank—because I figured I could get a lot for my money. It was around midnight and I hadn't had anything to eat since breakfast. That was last week, Friday. I ain't been working lately and on top of everything else I got kicked out of my room. The landlady kept my stuff because I owed her two dollars. I got the quarter from a rummy-player on Third Street who'd been lucky. Well, my insides were groaning and I felt sick, but all I wanted was a big sandwich and a cup of coffee. It's funny the way things go. I didn't have any place to sleep either, and when I sat down on the stool at the counter and she came up to take my order I didn't even look at her. She put a glass of water down and I said, A hamburger with onions and everything else and a cup of coffee. The Greek started to make the hamburger and she brought the coffee. I took two sips and looked up. I had been looking down at the spoon and fork and knife. She was standing to one side looking at me and when I looked up she smiled, only it was different. It looked like she had known me all her life and I had known her all my life and we hadn't seen one another for maybe ten or fifteen years. I guess I fell in love. We started talking and I didn't try to make her or anything because I was so hungry and tired, I guess, and maybe that's why she liked me. Any other time I guess I would have tried to make her and just have a little fun. She took me up to her room that night and I been staying there ever since, five nights now.

Here the young man began to be confused. The anarchist was very kind, however, and the young man explained.

I haven't touched her or anything, but I really love her and she really loves me. I kissed her last night because she looked so tired and beautiful, and she cried. She's a girl from Oklahoma. I guess she's had a few men, but it's different now. It's different with me too. I used to do office work, but I ain't got a job any more. I been going around to the agencies, but it don't look very good. If I could get a job we could get married and move into a small comfortable apartment.

A lot of people that are married—both of them work, he said. But I ain't got a job. When one of them works, he said, it's usually the man. I don't know what to do.

That's true, the anarchist said. Maybe you'll get a job to-morrow.

Where? the young man said. I wish I knew where. Everything's different with me now. My clothes are all worn out. I saw some swell shirts in the window of a store on Market Street for sixty-five cents; I saw a blue serge suit for twelve fifty; and I know where I can get a good pair of shoes for three dollars. I'd like to throw away these old clothes and begin all over again. I'd like to marry her and get rid of everything old and move into a small comfortable apartment.

The anarchist was very sympathetic. He didn't care about the young man himself, who was miserable-looking and worried and under-nourished and yet rather handsome becaue of this new thing in his life, this love of the waitress. He was delighted with the abstract purity and holiness of the event itself, in the crazy world, the boy starving and going into the dump for a hamburger and running headlong into love.

Maybe you'll get a job to-morrow, the anarchist said. Why don't you try a hotel?

The young man didn't quite understand.

No, he said, I don't think we'd care to live in a hotel. What we'd like to get is a small comfortable apartment with a bathroom and a little kitchen. We'd like to have a neat little place with some good chairs and a table and a bathroom and a little kitchen. I don't like these rooms that ain't got no bath in them, and you've got to go down the hall to take a bath and nine times out of ten there ain't no hot water. I'd like to fill a tub with warm water and sit in it a long time and then clean off all the dirt and get out and put on new clothes.

I don't mean to live in, the anarchist said. I mean to get a job at. I was thinking of these fine hotels that I'm accustomed to visiting the lobbies of.

Oh, the young man said. You mean to go to the hotels and ask for work?

Sure, the anarchist said. If you could get a job they'd give you a regular weekly salary and on top of that you'd make a little on tips.

I ain't had no experience being a bell-boy, the young man said.

That don't make no difference, the anarchist said.

Some of his old impatience began to return to him and he believed nothing in the world should stop this boy from getting a job in a hotel and earning a regular weekly salary and making a little more on tips and marrying the waitress and moving into a small comfortable apartment with a bath and filling the tub with warm water and cleaning off all the dirt and getting out and putting on new clothes, the sixty-five cent shirts and the twelve fifty blue serge suit.

That don't make a God damn bit of difference, the anarchist said. What does a bell-boy have to know? If they ask you have you had any experience, tell them sure, you were bell-boy at the La Salle Hotel in Chicago five years.

The La Salle Hotel in Chicago? the young man said.

Sure, the anarchist shouted. Why the hell not?

Maybe they'll be able to tell I ain't had no experience being a bell-boy, the young man said. Suppose they find out I ain't never been in Chicago?

Listen, the anarchist said. What if they do find out you ain't never been in Chicago? Do you think the world will end? (The anarchist himself was beginning to think the world would end if the young man didn't go out and get a job and move into an apartment with the girl.) Do you have to tell the truth, he said, when it doesn't make any difference one way or another if you've had any experience as a bell-boy or not or if you've ever been in Chicago or not, except that they *won't* give you a job if you *do* tell the truth and *might* if you don't?

The young man was a little bewildered and couldn't speak. The anarchist was so angry with the world and so delighted about this remarkable love affair that he himself didn't know what to say, or how to put what he meant.

He became a little unreasonable.

How the hell do you *know* you've never been in Chicago? he shouted.

The Slovak heard him shouting and stopped talking to listen. The eccentric one, the man of God, whose God was unlike anybody else's, moved closer to the anarchist and the young man, and little by little all the men gathered around the two.

What? said the gentleman.

He was beginning to wake up, and at the same time he was beginning to be embarrassed. He had been telling secrets, and now everybody was near him, near the secret, and everybody was listening and wanting to know what it was all about; why, on such a day as this, when everybody was glad and without ill will, and quiet, the anarchist was shouting.

How the hell do you know it? the anarchist shouted. Catch on? he said. You were *born* in Chicago. You lived there all your life until three months ago. Your father was born in Chicago. Your mother was born in Chicago. Your father worked in the La Salle Hotel in Chicago. *You* worked in the La Salle Hotel in Chicago.

The listeners didn't understand. They looked around at one another, smiling and asking what it was all about, and then they looked again at the anarchist who was suddenly so different and yet so much the same, and then they looked at the young man. It was all very confusing. But they knew it would be dangerous to interrupt the anarchist and ask a question or say something witty. They listened religiously.

There are a lot of good hotels in this town, the anarchist said. Begin at the beginning and go right on down the line and don't stop until they give you a job. Get up in the morning and shave cleanly and go down and talk to them and don't be afraid. Them hotels are full of people that got plenty of money and not one of them in the whole city has got better use for a little lousy money than you have. Not a lousy one of them, he shouted. What the hell makes you think you ain't never been in Chicago? Start with the St. Francis Hotel on Powell Street. Then the Palace on Market Street. Then the Mark Hopkins. Then the Clift. Then the Fairmont. What the hell do you mean you ain't been in Chicago? What the hell kind of talk do you call that?

Now the young man was completely awake, as the anarchist was awake. He seemed to understand what the anarchist was trying to tell him and he was ashamed because the men were near him and could feel, even though they didn't *know* what it was all about, what it was all about.

The anarchist took the man by the arm. His grip was very strong and the young man felt as if the man might be an elder brother or a father.

You understand what I'm telling you, don't you? he said.

Yes, the young man said.

He moved to go.

Thanks, he said.

He hurried down the street, and the anarchist stamped into the Public Library.

The men were very silent. Then one of them said, What the hell was he shouting about anyway? What the hell was all that stuff about the La Salle Hotel in Chicago? What *about* the La Salle Hotel in Chicago?

Love, Here is My Hat and Other Short Romances, 1938

Citizens of the Third Grade

om Lucca was incredible. Only eight years old, he was perhaps the brightest pupil in the third grade, certainly the most alert, the most intellectually savage, and yet the most humane. Still, his attitude seemed sometimes vicious, as when Aduwa was taken and he came to class leering with pride, the morning newspaper in his pants pocket, as evidence, no doubt, and during recess made the Fascist salute and asked the coloured Jefferson twins, Cain and Abel, what they thought of old King Haile Selassie now.

Same as before, Miss Gavit heard Abel say, You got no right to go into Africa.

And Tom, who wouldn't think of getting himself into a fist-fight since he was too intelligent, too neat and good-looking, laughed in that incredible Italian way that meant he knew everything, and said, We'll take Addis Ababa day after to-morrow.

Of course this was only a gag, one of Tom Lucca's frequent and generally innocent outbursts, but both Abel and Cain didn't like it, and Miss Gavit was sure there would be trouble pretty soon no matter what happened.

If General Bono *did* take Addis Ababa and Tom Lucca forgot himself and irritated Cain and Abel, there would surely be trouble between the coloured boys in the Third Grade and the Italian boys, less brilliant perhaps than Tom Lucca, but more apt to accept trouble, and fight about it; Pat Ravenna, Willy Trentino, Carlo Gaeta, and the others. Enough of them certainly. And then there were the other grades. The older boys.

On the other hand, if Ras Desta Demtu, the son-in-law of Emperor Haile Selassie, turned back the Italian forces at Harar, Cain and Abel, somewhat sullenly, would be triumphant without saying a word, as when Joe Louis, the Brown Bomber of Detroit, knocked out and humiliated poor Maxie Baer, and Cain and Abel came to class whistling softly to themselves. Everybody, who normally didn't dislike the boys, quiet and easy-going as they were, deeply resented them that morning.

No matter what happened, Miss Gavit believed, there would be trouble at Cosmos Public School, and it seemed very strange that this should be so, since these events were taking place thousands of miles away from the school and did not concern her class of schoolchildren, each of whom was having a sad time with the new studies, fractions and English grammar.

Tom Lucca was impossible. He had no idea how dangerously his nervous and joyous behaviour was getting to be. It was beginning to irritate Miss Gavit herself who, if anything, was in favour of having the ten million Ethiopians of Abyssinia under Italian care, which would do them much less harm than good and probably furnish some of the high government officials with shoes and perhaps European garments.

It was really amazing that many of the leaders of Abyssinia performed their duties bare-footed. How could anybody be serious without shoes on his feet, and five toes of each foot visible? And when they walked no important sound of moving about, as when Americans with shoes on their feet moved about.

Of course she hated the idea of going into an innocent and peaceful country and bombing little cities and killing all kinds of helpless people. she didn't like all the talk about poison gases and machine-guns and liquid fire. She thought it was very cruel of the Italians to think of killing people in order to gain a little extra land in which to expand, as Mussolini said.

Miss Gavit just bet ten cents the Italians could do all the expanding they needed to do right at home, in the 119,000 square miles of Italy. She just bet ten cents with anybody that Mussolini didn't really need more land, all he wanted to do was show off and be a hero. It was dreadful the way some people wanted to be great, no matter how many people they killed. It wasn't as if the people of Abyssinia were pagans; they were Christians, just like the Italians: their church was the Christian Church, and they worshipped Jesus, the same as Pope Pius.

The Pope, though, was a man Miss Gavit didn't like. She saw him in a Paramount News Reel, and she didn't like his face. He looked sly for a holy man. She didn't think he was really holy. She thought he looked more like a scheming politician than like a man who was humble and good and would rather accept pain for himself than have it inflicted upon others. He was small and old and cautious. First he prayed for peace, and then Italy went right ahead and invaded Abyssinia. Then Pope Pius prayed for peace again, but it was war just the same. Who did he think he was fooling?

She guessed every important man in the world was afraid, the same as the Pope. Poor loud-mouthed Huey got his, and for what? What did poor Huey want for the people except a million dollars for every family? What was wrong with that? Why did they have to kill a man like that, who really had the heart of a child, even if he did shout over the radio and irritate President Roosevelt by hinting that he, Huey Long of Louisiana, would be the next President of the United States? What did they want to invent guns for in the first place? What good did guns do the people of the world, except teach them to kill one another? First they worried about wild animals, and then Indians, and then they began worrying about one another, France worrying about Germany, Germany worrying about France and England and Russia, and Russia worrying about Japan, and Japan worrying about China.

Miss Gavit didn't know. She couldn't quite understand the continuous mess of the world. When it was the World War she was a little girl in grammar school who thought she would be a nun in a convent, and then a little later, a singer in opera: that was after the San Carlo opera troupe came to town and gave a performance of *La Bohème* at the Hippodrome Theatre and Miss Gavit went home crying about poor consumptive Mimi. Then the war ended and the parades ended and she began to forget her wilder dreams, like the dream of some day meeting a fine man like William Farnum and being his wife, or the still more fantastic dream of suddenly learning from authoritative sources that she was the true descendant of some royal European family, a princess, and all the other wild dreams of sudden wealth and ease and fame and importance, sudden surpassing loveliness, and most beloved young lady of the world. And sobering with the years, with the small knowledge of each succeeding grade at school, she chose teaching as her profession, and finally, after much lonely studying, full of sudden clear-weather dreaming of love, she graduated from the normal school, twenty-two years old, and was a teacher, if she could get a job.

She was very lucky, and for the past five years had been at Cosmos Public School, in the foreign section of the city, west of the Southern Pacific tracks, where she herself was born and lived. Her father was very happy about this good luck. The money she earned helped buy new furniture, a radio, and later on a Ford, and send her little sister Ethel to the University of California. But she didn't know. So many things were happening all over the world she was afraid something dangerous would happen, and very often, walking home from school, late in the afternoon, she would suddenly feel the nearness of this danger with such force that she would unconsciously begin to walk faster and look about to see if anything were changed, and at the same time remember poignantly all the little boys and girls who had passed through her class and gone on to the higher grades, as if these young people were in terrible danger, as if their lives might suddenly end, with terrific physical pain.

And now, with this trouble between Italy and Abyssinia, Benito Mussolini, Dictator of Italy, and Haile Selassie, the Lion of Judah, Miss Gavit began, as Tom Lucca's joyousness increased, to feel great inward alarm about the little boy because she knew truthfully that he was very kind-hearted, and only intellectually mischievous. How many times had she seen him hugging Mrs. Amadio's little twenty-month-old daughter, chattering to the baby in the most energetic Italian, kissing it, shouting at Mrs. Amadio, and Mrs. Amadio guffawing in the loudest and most delightful manner imaginable, since Tom was such a wit, so full of innocent outspokenness, sometimes to the extent even of being almost vulgar. The Italians, that's the way they were, and it was not evil, it was a virtue. They were just innocent. They chattered about love and passion and child-birth and family quarrels as if it were nothing, just part of the day's experience. And how many times had she seen Tom Lucca giving sandwiches from his lunch to Johnny Budge whose father had no job and no money? And not doing it in a way that was self-righteous. She remembered the way Tom would say, Honest, Johnny, I can't eat another bite. Go ahead, I don't want this sandwich. I already ate three. I'll throw it away if you don't take it. And Johnny Budge would say, All right, Tom, if you're sure you don't want it. That was the strange part of it, the same little Italian boy being fine like that, giving away his lunch, and at the same time so crazy-proud about the taking of Aduwa, as if that little mud-city in Africa had anything to do with him, coming to class with the morning paper and leering at everybody, stirring the savage instincts of the Negro twins, Cain and Abel Jefferson.

Miss Gavit believed she would do something to stop all the nonsense. She wouldn't sit back and see something foolish and ugly happen right under her nose. She knew what she would do. She would keep Tom Lucca after school.

When the last pupil left the room and the door was closing automatically and slowly, Miss Gavit began to feel how uneasy Tom was, sitting still but seeming to be moving about, looking up at her, and then at the clock, and then rolling his pencil on the desk. When the door clicked shut, she remembered all the little boys she had kept in after school during the five years at Cosmos and how it was the same with each of them, resentment at accusation, actual or implied, and dreadful impatience, agonized longing to be free, even if, as she knew, many of them really liked her, did not hate her as many pupils often hated many teachers, only wanting to be out of the atmosphere of petty crime and offense, wanting to be restored to innocence, the dozens and dozens of them. She wondered how she would be able to tell Tom why she had kept him after school and explain how she wanted his behaviour, which was always subtle, to change, not in energy, but in impulse. How would she be able to tell him not to be so proud about what Mussolini was doing? Just be calm about the whole business until Italy annexed Abyssinia and everything became normal in the world again, at least more or less normal, and Cain and Abel Jefferson didn't go about the school grounds apart from everybody, letting their resentment grow in them.

What's the matter now? Tom said. He spoke very politely, though, the inflexion being humble, implying that it was *he* who was at fault: he was ready to admit this, and if this offence could be named he would try to be better. He didn't want any trouble.

Nothing's the matter, Miss Gavit said. I want to talk to you about the war, that's all.

Yes, ma'am, he said.

Well, said Miss Gavit, you've got to be careful about hurting the feelings of Cain and Abel Jefferson.

Hurting their feelings? he thought. Who the hell's hurting whose feelings? What kind of feelings get hurt so easily? What the hell did I ever say? The whole world is against the Italians and *our* feelings ain't hurt. They want to see them wild Africans kick hell out of our poor soft soldiers, two pairs of shoes each. How about our feelings? Everybody hates Mussolini. What for? Why don't they hate somebody else for a change?

He was really embarrassed, really troubled. He didn't understand, and Miss Gavit noticed how he began to tap the pencil on the desk.

I don't know, he began to say, and then began tapping the pencil swifter than before.

He gestured in a way that was very saddening to Miss Gavit and then looked up at her.

You are an American, said Miss Gavit, and so are Cain and Abel Jefferson. We are all Americans. This sort of quarrelling will lead nowhere.

What quarrelling? he thought. Everybody in the world hates us. Everybody calls us names. I guess Italians don't like that either.

He could think of nothing to say to Miss Gavit. He knew she was all right, a nice teacher, but he didn't know how to explain about everybody hating the Italians, because this feeling was in Italian and he couldn't translate it. At home it was different. Pa came home from the winery and sat at the table for supper and asked Mike, Tom's big brother in high school, what the afternoon paper said, and Ma listened carefully, and Mike told them exactly what was going on, about England and the ships in the Red Sea, and France, and the League of Nations, and Pa swallowed a lot of spaghetti and got up and spit in the sink, clearing his throat, and said in Italian, All right, all right, all right, let them try to murder Italy, them bastards, and Ma poured more wine in his cup and Pa said in

American, God damn it, and Tom knew how the whole world was against Italy and he was glad about the good luck of the army in Africa, taking Aduwa, and all the rest of it, but now, at school, talking with Miss Gavit, he didn't know what to say.

Yes, ma'am, he said.

Miss Gavit thought it was wonderful the way he understood everything, and she laughed cheerfully, feeling that now nothing would happen.

All right, Tom, she said. Just be careful about what you say.

You may go now.

Jesus Christ, he thought. To hell with everybody.

He got up and walked to the door. Then he began walking home, talking to himself in Italian and cussing in American because everybody was against them.

Tom was very quiet at the supper table, but when Pa asked Mike how it was going in Abyssinia and Mike told him the Italians were moving forward very nicely and it looked like everything would turn out all right before the League would be able to clamp down on Italy, Tom said in Italian, We'll show them bastards. His father wondered what was eating the boy.

What's the matter, Tom? he said in American.

Aw, Tom said, they kept me in after school just because I talked about taking Aduwa. They don't like it.

His father laughed and spit in the sink and then became very serious.

They don't like it, hey? he said in Italian. They are sorry the Italian army isn't slaughtered? They hate us, don't they? Well, you talk all you like about the army. You tell them every day what the army is doing. Don't be afraid.

The next day Cain Jefferson swung at Tom Lucca and almost hit him in the eye. Willy Trentino then challenged Cain Jefferson to a fight after school, and on her way home Miss Gavit saw the gang of Italian and coloured and Russian boys in the empty lot behind Gregg's Bakery. She knew for sure it was a fight about the war. She stood in the street staring at the boys, listening to their shouting, and all she could think was, This is terrible; they've got no right to make these little boys fight this way. What did they want to invent guns for in the first place?

She ran to the crowd of boys, trembling with anger. Everybody stopped shouting when Miss Gavit pushed to the centre of the crowd where Willy Trentino and Cain Jefferson were fighting. Willy's face was bloody and Cain was so tired he could barely breathe or lift his arms. Miss Gavit clapped her hands as she did in class when she was angry and the two boys stopped fighting. They turned and stared at her, relieved and ashamed.

Stop this nonsense, she said, panting for breath from excitement and anger. I am ashamed of you, Willy. And you, Cain. What do you think you are fighting about?

Miss Gavit, said Cain Jefferson, they been laughing at us about the Ethiopians. All of them, teasing us every day.

How about you? said Willy. How about when Joe Louis knocked out Max Baer? How about when it looked like Abyssinia was going to win the war?

Then three or four Italian boys began to talk at once, and Miss Gavit didn't know what to think or do. She remembered a college movie in which two football players who loved the same girl and were fighting about her were asked to shake hands and make up by the girl herself, and Miss Gavit said, I want you boys to shake hands and be friends and go home and never fight again.

Miss Gavit was amazed when neither Willy Trentino nor Cain Jefferson offered to shake hands and make up, and she began to feel that this vicious war in Abyssinia, thousands of miles away, was going to bring about something very foolish and dangerous in the foreign section. In the crowd she saw Abel Jefferson, brooding sullenly and not speaking, a profound hate growing in him, and she saw Tom Lucca, his eyes blazing with excitement and delight, and she knew it was all very horrible because, after all, these were only little boys.

And then, instead of shaking hands and making up as she had asked them to do, Willy Trentino and Cain Jefferson, and all the other boys, began to move away, at first walking, and then, overcome with a sense of guilt, running, leaving the poor teacher standing in the empty lot, bewildered and amazed, tearing her handkerchief and crying. They hadn't shaken hands and made up. They hadn't obeyed her. They had run away. She cried bitterly, but not even one small tear fell from her eyes. When old Paul Gregg stepped from the bakery into the lot and said, What's the trouble, Miss Gavit? the little teacher said, Nothing, Mr. Gregg. I want a loaf of bread. I thought I would come in through the back way.

When she got home she took the loaf of white bread out of the brown paper bag and placed it on the red and blue checkered table-cloth of the kitchen table and stared at it for a long time, thinking of a thousand things at one time and not knowing what it was she was thinking about, feeling very sorrowful, deeply hurt, angry with every-body in the world, the Italians, the Pope, Mussolini, the Ethiopians, the Lion of Judah, and England.

She remembered the faces of the boys who were fighting, and the boys who were watching. She breathed in the smell of the bread, and wondered what it was all about everywhere in the world, little Tom Lucca kissing Mrs. Amadio's baby and giving Johnny Budge his sandwich and leering at everybody because of the taking of Aduwa, the Negro twins joyous about Joe Louis and sullen about Abyssinia. The bread smelled delicious but sad and sickening, and Abel Jefferson watching his brother fighting Willy Trentino, and the *Morning Chronicle* with news of crime everywhere, and the *Evening Bee* with the same news, and the holy Pope coming out on the high balcony and making a holy sign and looking sly, and somebody shooting poor Huey Long, and none of her pupils being able to understand about English grammar and fractions, and her wild dreams of supreme loveliness, and her little sister at the University of California, and the day ending. She folded her arms on the table and hid her head. With her eyes closed she said to herself, They killed those boys, they killed them, and she knew they were killing everybody everywhere, and with her eyes shut the smell of the fresh loaf of bread was sickening and tragic, and she couldn't understand anything.

The Trouble with Tigers, 1938

The Dale
Carnegie
Friend

The minute he smiled the way that was supposed to be sincere, and, in the voice that was intended to be winning, said, What line of work are you in, Mr. Sloan? I knew he was one who'd read that book and wanted to make friends and influence people, so I thought I'd let him practice his instructions while I amused myself in my own anti-social way.

Nothing in particular, I said, although I used to dabble around in pin games.

Pin games? he said.

Marble machines, I explained. You know. Nickel-in-the-slot, five marbles, eight, ten, or even as many as fifteen. Strictly games of skill.

That's very interesting, he said.

He was kind of interesting himself, but essentially in the category of those who get everything they get secondhand, from the outside, try hard all their lives in small and insignificant places, and wind up at the end of their lives with two dozen memories of luke-warm and ineffectual experiences. He was about thirty-four, a graduate of Stanford, and a natural-born half-wit with none of the charm of the true, uneducated, and unambitious half-wit; the kind who naturally fall into their places, behind soda fountains, in gasoline stations, in garages, on farms, in pool rooms, and places like that. The great tribe of half-wits is not a boring tribe until it gets ambition as it so often does in a country where all anybody needs to do in order to be somebody is read a book and make up his mind to get results.

Anyhow, he was probably all right from the start, but hadn't followed the path destiny had plainly marked for him, so now, after all the years of weary studying at school, he was eager to be a tenth-rater in a first-rate region, instead of a first-rater in a first-rate but different region. The only trouble was he was ambitious. He had everything but that instinctive understanding of himself which usually keeps the world's half-wits pleasantly preserved in good health for two or three centuries until they are naturally in line for promotion. Now, he wanted to put himself over by pretending interest in what I might be interested in, so I mentioned pin games, which I am, on and off, interested in. You meet an average of three people like him at every party you go to. They used to be all right, but that book is wreaking terrible havoc on them all over the place.

I'd been sitting near the shelf of books, just loafing around waiting for the evening to get along, glad to have Scotch to drink and nothing to do, and I wasn't paying any attention to the people who were having fun in their own way, talking and laughing and so on, and I guess he figured I was being ignored or something, so he came over to be my friend and do me the little favour of giving me his company. What he did was interrupt some pleasant dreaming, so I decided to kind of mosey along with him and, without hurting his feelings, to have a little fun myself. I have been told by thoughtful friends to watch out for such and such a person because he's an awful bore, but I haven't yet met anybody who could bore me, if I preferred not to be bored. Only bores get bored. The others get interrupted now and then.

Oh, yes, I said, when prohibition went out I was out of a job, so I had to figure out something legitimate to do, so I got to thinking and after a while I said, What are people more often than not? Bored, that's what. Then I said, If a smart guy like me can invent something to cash in on the boredom, at a nickel a cashing, he could clean up, and sure enough I did. I cleaned up a small fortune before they sent me to San Quentin.

For making pin games? he said.

No, I said. One thing led to another. I did a few other things, too.

But of course you're not really a criminal, he offered sympathetically. I could see him running through the book, trying to find the place that would help him with a friend from San Quentin.

Oh, yes, I said. Just as much a criminal as any of the other boys up there. I'm not there now, though, I notice. (I looked around for the law, kind of challenging the law to get me.) I bribed my way out. I was only there a year and a month. I was sentenced to from twenty years to life. That gave me a big laugh.

Well, he said. You certainly don't look any worse for the experience. You certainly look all right. You look as if you're in the very best of health. I don't see why anybody has to go to jail for making pin games.

It wasn't for making pin games, I said. It would take me at least three hours to explain just what happened. After the trial I myself didn't know for sure. All I know is they claimed I killed three people.

They were probably trying to frame you, he said.

No, I said, I confessed and everything, but my lawyer got to talking to me and the first thing I knew I denied everything. Nobody knows who killed them now, not even me.

Well, he said, I guess they were the kind of people who are better off dead. Like Dillinger.

These weren't guys like Dillinger, I said. (The more ridiculous the story got the more I tried to let him know I was only having fun, but he didn't get it.) These were just ordinary people, I said. Tax-payers. They had jobs in the bank, but I'd rather not go into detail. After the trial I've never been able to understand exactly what happened.

Well, he said, I didn't mean to bring up something unpleasant. Are you back in the pin game business again?

No, I said. Ever since I got out I've been kind of just taking things easy on the money. I don't have to work any more as long as I live.

You're certainly lucky, he said, to have all that money.

It isn't much, I said. The doctors don't give me more than a year to live. I've got a little over six hundred dollars.

He became sincerely sympathetic about this, and genuinely bewildered. For a moment I watched him trying to imagine what he ought to say next. At last he said cheerfully, It's not how long you live, so much; it's what you do.

It certainly is, I said. Sometimes I cry, but usually I don't mind. After all, what is life?

For a moment he seemed to wonder what, after all, life is. He must have dismissed six or seven platitudes on the subject before he spoke again.

Life is, he began to say.

Miss Avery, whose party it was, joined us at this point and took over the situation.

You two, she said. I've been noticing you out of the corner of my eye. Away over to one side, philosophizing about life and everything. Come along now.

She took the young man's arm and said, I'm sorry to drive you back to the fold, but back you go.

The young man turned away and melted into the central group of revellers, as they are sometimes called.

Miss Avery watched him a moment. Then she came out of her trance, and turned to me.

He's so brilliant, isn't he?

He certainly is, I said.

What in the world have you two been talking about all this time? she said.

He's been telling me about recent advances in the control and elevation of mass behaviour, I said.

Oh, you brilliant young men, Miss Avery said. Come along now, you must meet everybody.

The Trouble with Tigers, 1938

The People,
Yes, and then
again, No

They wonder what comes over people to make them disagreeable and unfriendly, unkempt and ill-mannered, sullen and brutish, stupid and vicious. Well lack of food and sleep does wonders to the human body, and *the people* inhabit bodies. That's the worst of it. If they could only get the people to inhabit mechanical equivalents of the human body, or maybe wax dummies; the economic problems of the wealthy would be over, and everything would be all right in the world. What is needed obviously is a sturdier kind of man, completely devoid of sense, although without ego, and yet an efficient and willing worker. Death through peace-time war or war-time war can no longer be regarded as a satisfactory solution to the problem of the wealthy; for war-time wars end, and statistics appear on paper: so many dead, so many wounded, on one side of the page, and so much money, wasted or invested, on the other; as well as the same land of the earth momentarily reidentified and newly nationalized. With oratory, most likely; and music. And marching. That is no longer a solution, since the undead, the viciously undying, return again to be the people, to be the object and subject of oratory. What is to be done about them again? They would still eat. They would still be clothed. They would still live. And when there is no military war, when the war is only the relatively joyous and comical war of the body against time and exposure, *enough of them* do not die.

In this war the skin dries; ages. Every surface inch of flesh becomes clogged. The vision blurs, multiplies, and the reality of the world is a triple reality; there are three and four truths to everything visible and invisible. The holy universe expands to unholiness. The senses are impaired. The body breathes poorly because the nostrils and lungs are clogged with world-dirt, time-dirt, flesh-dirt. The mouth and throat grow sticky with nothing. The teeth stretch deeply into ache, and the body is aware of the bottom of things, the ultimate; emptiness and death. The private parts itch; swell. The muscles lose suppleness; tremble. The brain is witless. Hearing is bad. The hair of the head is coarse, dry, deathly. And they wonder why the people are impossible. They do not know how the guts gurgle in their own rot and in the decay of bad food; how the juices of the body turn foul; how the blood stagnates.

What is needed is the sturdier and less mortal kind of man. What is needed is the contraption that will do the work and ask no more than a little oil now and then and certain minor repairs to certain minor parts.

Since they have decided that this world is not for the people, except in oratory, what is needed is the racially pure piece of machinery as man. The gentle and kindly machine. Since the people will not die, and will suffer, and will show themselves in the world, yet will not *have* the world, which is theirs, which they *made*, which they *own*, and which still, after centuries, they will not *take*, what is needed first is the noble war-time war, with the noble guns and gases, and the noble death for the people, and after the people have become absent from the scene, what is needed is the perfect mechanical unit of passivity; docility. The worker. The world-maker. The kingly slave, perfected and patented. The machine, unmortal, mindless, heartless, bloodless, safe and industrious. By God, they've got it coming. The wealthy deserve every consideration of the people, for they have won that war, they have clung nobly and fearlessly to their statistics. In the hills they have fought the living and won. One of them against a million of man. They are the heroes of our time.

Only this. Let them not say that it is *for* the people; *they* are not the people. And when they groan about money, about expenses, about losses, let someone in the world ask, What expenses? What losses? What the hell are you talking about? What can the mortal lose but flesh? If you spend every cent of that phony stuff, what the hell of it? Whose is it anyway? Isn't it the earth's and life's and man's? Was it ever intended to be a thing by itself? How can it be wasted?

One way or another will be all right with me, only let each side speak out honestly. This is your world and it is my world, and it is not real estate, and not nations, and not governments; it is this accidental place of mortality; it is this pause in time and space. It is this chance to breathe, to walk, to see, to eat, to sleep, to love, to laugh. It is not financial statistics. It belongs to this mangled tribe, this still unborn God, man.

But if they don't want the body ever to be born, I suggest that they trot out the mechanical man, the mechanical body, and let the other body be destroyed, and say no more about it.

The Trouble with Tigers, 1938

The Europa
Club

*I*n 1918 one of the gambling joints I used to loaf around in,
pretending to be selling papers, was The Europa Club on Tulare
Street, across the Southern Pacific tracks, near China Alley, in
Chinatown.

The Europa Club was supposed to be a gambling joint, but actually
it was nothing more than a place where men with no money sat around
and talked, and during the War I used to walk over to Chinatown and
visit this place. The ugliest men in the world were loafing in The
Europa Club in 1918. Italians, Greeks, Negroes, Chinese, Japs, Hindus,
Russians, and Americans. Every kind of American, from big dumb
Indians and sad-eyed Mexicans to old white-trash gamblers from Texas.

The place was full of tables and chairs and spittoons. There was a
player-piano in a corner, a bar along the back wall, and over the mirror
was an oil painting of a man who looked a little like Woodrow Wilson. It
was a great big painting, the work, no doubt, of a loafer who had painted
it for drinks.

The place stank. The air was polluted with the wasted hours of
many men, and every time I went into the place with a dozen papers
under my arm I used to try to figure out what kept them going. I used to
figure maybe it was the silent player-piano in the corner. Maybe they
were waiting for some spendthrift to show up and drop a nickel in the
slot. Maybe the men were waiting for music. Or maybe it was the big
painting of Woodrow Wilson, the great man of the bad years. Maybe it
was the dumb force within themselves, centuries old, demanding to
grow centuries older. Maybe it was nothing.

One day the little Jap called Suki swallowed a big fly.

He was a very melancholy-looking man. Any Jap who is loafing is a
melancholy-looking man because it's not in that race to loaf. He was
disgusted with everything, and nobody would be his friend. He tried to

get along with his countrymen who were loafing in the dump, but they wouldn't have anything to do with him. He tried to laugh with the Negroes, but he couldn't laugh that way, and they didn't like the disharmony of his giggle mingling with their guffaws. They bawled him out every time he tried to laugh with them. He tried to be friendly with the Indians and the Mexicans. But *nobody* wanted to be friendly with him, so he gave it up and just sat in a corner.

One day in August Suki noticed that everybody in the room was aware of the flies. Not bothered; just aware. It was very hot and very still in the room and the big flies were flying around and lighting on noses and making noise flies make. Suki got up from his chair and waved at a couple of them and didn't catch one. Everybody noticed him. He waved at another group of flies and this time caught one. The fly was furious and tried to get away, buzzing loudly, but Suki held it by its wings.

Then he swallowed it.

His countrymen went over to him and spoke in Japanese with great dignity and great seriousness. It seemed they wished to know why he had swallowed the fly. He told them he had swallowed the fly because he was going crazy, from loafing. His countrymen were very upset and at the same time very proud. They thought at first that he was showing off. He had no labor to perform in the world, he said sadly. They asked what labor he wished to perform, and he said he wished to plant and care for strawberries. They told him the season for the growing of strawberries was ended long ago. He said he knew that.

His countrymen told the other loafers why Suki had swallowed the fly.

For weeks during the last days of the War the loafers at The Europa Club talked about Suki and the fly he swallowed. Part of the time they looked upon him as a fool and part of the time as a hero.

Before the War ended, Suki swallowed four flies. I saw him swallow the first one and the last one. The Negroes told me about the others. They said he liked flies. They roared with laughter about Suki and the flies.

He was a very melancholy-looking man.

The loafers waited patiently, and at last the War ended.

When the soldiers of our town came back from the War, The Europa Club was sold to a soldier who kicked out the loafers and put the place in order. The soldier himself dropped nickels into the slot of the pianola and every time I walked into the place I heard music. Men were at the tables, really gambling, for money. At the bar were men who were drinking. It was all illegal and all that, but the soldier was a hard guy and he knew all the ropes. His best friends were cops.

One afternoon in February while I was in The Europa Club I saw Suki come in and buy a drink. He was disgusted, and after he swallowed the drink, he caught a fly and swallowed it. The soldier almost went out of his head when he saw Suki swallow the fly. He took Suki by the neck with his left hand and by the seat of the pants with his right hand and lifted him out into the street.

The little Jap walked away without turning around.

The soldier came back in and dropped another nickel into the slot. Then he turned around and saw me.

I want you to get the hell out of this place, and stay out, he said.

Peace, It's Wonderful, 1939

1924 Cadillac
For Sale

*A*ny time you think you can go out and pull something over on somebody, like selling them a bad used car, you're kidding yourself because people don't believe lies any more unless they've get their heart set on having the used car anyway. I used to sell an average of two used cars a week five years ago, but nowadays I'm lucky if I don't sell two a day. People who buy used cars these days would kill anybody who tried to stop them from buying. They just naturally want a used car. I used to try to argue them into believing they *ought* to have a used car, but that was before I found out I was wasting my time. That was before I found out people don't like to be fooled any more.

All I do now is hang around this used car lot and wait for people to come around and start asking questions about the jalopies we're showing.

I tell them the truth.

I let them know exactly what they're getting, but it don't seem to stop them any when they've got their hearts set on going for a ride in an automobile. They just naturally insist on making a down payment and driving away. It used to make me feel real proud and smart to sell a used car in the old days, but nowadays I feel a little hurt every time somebody comes up and forces me to sell him one of these out-of-date broken-down heaps. I feel kind of useless and unnecessary, because I know I ain't selling anybody *anything*. I'm just letting the tide of humanity rush where it pleases or must.

They come here by the hundreds every day, men, women, and children, wanting a used car, and all I do is let them have their way. I don't put up any kind of an argument, because it's no use. An old lady who doesn't know how to drive a car wants to buy an old Hupmobile because it's green, so why should I interfere with her wishes? I let her know the truth about the old heap, but she buys it anyway, and the next day I see her going down the street forty-three miles an hour. She's in sports clothes, and the radio's going full blast, with a crooner hollering: *Deep in the heart of me.*

My God, it's beautiful and awful.

And then again a small boy, no more than twelve, comes in here with eleven dollars he's saved up, and he wants to know how much is the cheapest car on the lot; and I show him a 1922 Chevrolet we've been offering for fifteen dollars for seven years now, and he hops in, holds the wheel and says he'll go home and get the other four dollars. He comes back with his big brother, who signs the papers for him, and the next thing I know they've got the hood lifted and they're repairing the motor. In my opinion the old heap's got no more chance of moving than a bronze horse in a park; but three hours later something happens, and the whole lot is full of smoke and noise.

It's the old Chevrolet.

By the time the smoke clears I can see them walloping down the street, and I know deep in the heart of me, as the song goes, that either the people of this country are natural-born heroes or that the average used car, for all any of us knows, is part human and will respond to tender loving care, just as anything else will.

There was a young Filipino came in here last April who'd been doing farm work down around Bakersfield, and he'd saved up a small amount of money which, he said, I wish to purchase a sports model Packard touring car with. Well, I had that great big battleship of a Packard that had been abandoned in the middle of the desert just south of Pixley about seven years ago, and I didn't want to see the boy gypped, so I told him I didn't have a sports model Packard touring car except one old one that had something fundamentally wrong with the motor and wouldn't run.

You wouldn't be interested in that car, I said.

I would appreciate it very much if you would allow me to look at it, the Filipino said.

His name was Vernon. I'm telling you this because I remember how amazed I was when he signed the papers. Vernon Roxas. The older boys who sat in the car with him when he drove out of the lot had names that were even worse. One of the boys was called Thorpe; another was named Scott, and another Avery. My God, them ain't names you ever see attached to people, native or alien, and me hearing them little men calling each other names like that made me stop in my tracks and wonder what the world was coming to. I mean I felt awful proud of them young citizens. I like people just so they're sensible and honest and sincere, and I like Filipinos as much as I like any other kind of people. I was just profoundly impressed by their superb adaptability. Them boys had not only adjusted themselves to our world: they'd fitted themselves out in the best style of our clothes, and they'd taken over our most impressive names. I felt awful proud of that condition in America among the boys from the Island.

Of course I was a little worried about their wanting that old Packard.

I showed the car to this boy Vernon Roxas, and he began crawling all over the car, trying out everything but the motor.

What is the price? he said.

Well, there was no price. I'd never bothered to give it a price because I was satisfied to have it in the lot as a sort of decoy, just to take space. I figured I'd do the boy a favor and name a big price so he wouldn't buy it.

Well, I said, it's pretty expensive. That'll run you about $75.

You mean $75 dollars is the first payment? the boy asked.

Well, right there I guess I could have swindled him, and for a moment I was tempted to do it; but I just couldn't go through with the idea.

No, I said; $75 is the total cost.

I'll take it, the boy said.

He brought all kinds of money from his pockets, and we counted. He had a little over $75. I drew up the papers, and he signed. He said he would come back later that afternoon with several of his friends. He'd take the car then.

He came back in two hours with eleven well-dressed Filipinos named Thorpe, Scott, Avery, and other names like that. Each of them was carrying a satchel containing tools and other stuff. Well, they took off their coats and rolled up their sleeves and went to work. One of them started working on the motor, and the others started working on other parts of the car. In less than two hours they had that old warship looking like the car the Governor rides around in when there's a parade. And they had smoke coming out of it too.

I mean they'd fought their battle and won.

I stood in the lot with my mouth open, because never before in my life had I seen such beautiful co-operation and strategy. They just naturally fell on that pile of junk and tightened and cleaned and greased and oiled until it looked like a five-thousand-dollar job. Then they all got into the car and slowly drove out of the lot with the motor barely making any sound at all, like the motor of a car just out of the factory.

I couldn't believe my eyes. Or my ears, either.

I walked beside the boy at the wheel, Vernon Roxas, while the car moved out of the lot.

Vernon, I said, you boys have just taught me the greatest lesson any man can learn.

It is our opinion, Vernon said, that this Packard will travel fifty thousand miles before its usefulness is exhausted.

Well, I said, I don't doubt it the least. I'm more or less convinced that it will keep moving as long as you boys want it to.

And don't ever think it's the car. Don't ever think its machinery. It's people. It's America, the awful energy of the people. It's not machinery, it's faith in yourself. Them boys from the Island went to work and changed that worthless heap of junk into a beautiful and powerful automobile with a motor that hummed.

When they drove out of this lot in that magnificent Packard my heart cheered this great country. People with no money having the polite impudence to want class and get it at no expense and to insist on getting it no matter how run-down and useless it might seem at first glance.

I don't *sell* used cars any more.

I just stand around in this lot and admire the will of the people, men, women, and children, as they take over a bankrupt and exhausted piece of machinery and breathe new and joyous life into it. I just stay here and admire this great and crazy race of adventure-loving people who can't be stopped by truth or expense. I just watch them throw themselves into a cause and come out with a roaring motor that five minutes ago was a piece of dead and rusted junk.

You're the first man who's come to this lot in six months and not *forced* me to sell him a car. I want to shake your hand. Like yourself I'm an honest man, and I believe as you do that every car in this lot is worthless, useless, and incapable of moving. I believe as you do that anybody who buys one of these cars is a fool and ought to have his head examined. It's my job to let the people have what they want, but I believe as you do that the most they can find here is junk, so naturally I admire somebody who agrees with me. This old 1924 Cadillac you've been looking at, in my opinion, isn't worth five cents, but we're asking sixty dollars for it. I don't think you're the type of man who could bring this car to life; and I wouldn't care to see you try, because if you failed I'd feel unhappy and maybe lose my faith in people.

But if you *want* to give it a try after all I've told you, well, that's your affair. I won't try to stop you. I'm telling you in all sincerity that this car is no good, but if you think you can fall on it like the others who buy cars here every day, and make it go, why go ahead. Nothing can amaze me any more, and if you've got your heart set on driving a Cadillac, well, here's a Cadillac, and good luck to you.

Peace, It's Wonderful, 1939

A Number
of the Poor

*O*ne summer I worked two months in a grocery store. I worked
from four in the afternoon till midnight, but after eight
o'clock there wouldn't be any business to speak of and all I'd
do was look out the window or go around the store and keep things in
order. It was a little store on Grove Street, in the slums. The people who
came to the store were all interesting and poor.

Only two or three of them didn't steal things, not counting little
children. Almost all the others stole more than they bought. It was just
that they needed the stuff and didn't have enough money to buy it.
They'd put a package of chewing gum in a pocket when my back was
turned, or a small cake, or a can of tomato soup. I knew all about it, but I
never let on. They were all good people, just poor.

Once in August a lady tried to hide a cantaloupe in her waist. That
was one of the saddest things I ever saw. She was a woman of fifty or so. It
was obvious that she had a lot more under her waist than herself and I
guess she just had to have a cantaloupe. That evening she didn't buy
anything. I guess she was broke. She spent about five minutes in the
store, asking about the prices of a lot of things, and tasting apricots and
peaches and figs. I'd tell her figs were ten cents a dozen and very good and
she'd say they looked good but were they really? Then I'd tell her to taste
one. She'd hesitate a little and then lift a very big one out of the crate, peel
it and very thoughtfully swallow it in three bites, tasting it carefully. She
was always a lady. With a little money to go with her charm I believe she
would have cut an impressive figure in a grocery store, but she never
seemed to have any. I thought it was wonderful the way she got the
cantaloupe without losing her dignity.

One of the few who came to the store and never stole anything was a
little Spaniard named Casal. You had to know which stole and which
didn't. Casal was one of those small men with big heads and sad faces

that you notice right away and wonder about. He used to come to the store almost every night at ten and stay for a half hour or so to talk. He was quiet-spoken and solemn and dignified. If you're no bigger than a boy of eleven, and weigh about ninety-two pounds, it's no cinch to be dignified.

I always had a lot of respect for Casal. He didn't seem to know anything. I don't suppose he'd read a newspaper in ten years. He had no ideas and no complaints about anything. He was just a very small man who had managed to stay alive forty-eight years. Little by little I came to know why he was so dignified and had no need to complain about anything.

It was because he was a father. He had a son of sixteen. This boy was six feet tall and very handsome. He was Casal's boy all right; there was no getting around that. He had his father's head. Casal was very proud of him; that's what kept him going. One evening he said: You know my boy? He is a fine boy. So big and good. Do you know what? Every night when I come home from work my boy says, Pa, get on my shoulders. I get on his shoulders and he carries me all around the house. Then we sit down and eat.

What can you make of something like that? That small father and that great son, the boy carrying the father around on his shoulders? There's something there, I think.

Another night Casal said, I'll tell you why my boy is such a good boy. His mother died when he was born. That's the reason. He never knew his mother. He was always alone. Even when he was a baby. I used to go home in my lunch hour to see how he was. Sometimes he'd be crying. Sometimes he'd be through crying and he'd be all alone waiting. He stopped crying when he was just a little baby. He learned to know how it was. After he was two years old it was a lot easier for him and for me too. You should have seen the way he grew. Do you like him?

I think he's a fine boy, I said.

Well, I'll tell you, Casal said. Do you know what? He wants me to stop working. He wants to work for me now. He says I've worked enough. He's good with machines. He can get a job as a mechanic in a repair shop. You know what I told him? I told him no. I told him, Joe, you're going to college. He gets along fine everywhere. He's a good boy. I'm going to send him through college. He's got a right. I like to work for him.

Sure, I said.

Casal was one of the fine ones who came to that store when I worked there.

There was a little red-head, about twelve, who was another. Her name was Maggie. She was very powerful, the way some kids of the poor are, and full of the swellest laughter in the world.

She used to come into the store and bust out laughing, right out of a clear sky, no preliminaries, no explanations or anything. She'd just come in and laugh. That always pleased me, but I'd never let her know it. So she'd laugh some more.

All right, I'd say. What do you want?

You know, she'd say.

Laughter.

A loaf of bread?

Bread! she'd say.

Well, what *do* you want?

Out of the corner of her eye, a glance.

What have you got?

There wouldn't be anything else to do with somebody like that, so I'd toss her a peach which she would catch and eat very daintily. Spoofing, though, of course, with her little finger extended.

They say I look like Ginger Rogers, she'd say.

They're liars.

I do, she'd say. You know I do. Do you like her?

She's swell, I'd say.

I look just like her, she'd say.

Twelve years old.

The country's full of them too, and it's no use worrying about them. They're all in the big movie.

Another was the little boy who never had a penny but always came to look. About four years old. I used to call him Callaghan. He was great. He'd spend an hour looking at the penny candies and never say a word, except maybe to himself. People would stumble over him but he'd stick to his spot and keep looking.

One evening the lady who stole the cantaloupe patted him on the head.

Your son? she said.

Yes, I said.

A fine boy, she said. He resembles you. How much are figs today?

Ten cents a dozen, I said.

Are they really good?

Yes, they are. I ate one five minutes ago. Please try one.

She did; and tried also a peach and an apricot.

She didn't buy anything that night either. She stayed ten minutes and I know she wanted to ask if she might borrow twenty-five cents till tomorrow, but didn't dare. At last she said, We're lucky to be living in California, aren't we?

I've never been out of the state, I said. I've never been out of this city. Is it different in other places?

Oh terribly, she said. Why, there are places you can hardly breathe in in the summertime. Chicago. And look how wonderful it is here.

She was at the open door and waved her arm gently outward at the sky.

The *air* is so fine here, she said.

When she was gone I called Callaghan. He came over immediately.

Would you like a licorice strap?

No answer.

He would, of course, but he wouldn't say so.

Come over here and take what you like, I said.

He came over behind the candy case but didn't reach to take anything.

Take anything you like, I said.

He looked at me, a little uncertain.

Sure, I said. You can have anything you like.

He couldn't believe it and was a little scared.

It's all right, I said.

He reached out and took a licorice strap.

Take something else, I said.

He put back the licorice strap and reached for a wax dog.

No, I said. Keep the licorice strap, too.

In all he took four different kinds of penny candies, but it took a lot of encouragement from me to get him to do it.

Okay, Callaghan, I said. Now go home and eat them. Take them with you.

Without a word, but still amazed, he went away.

The next day when he came back he said very quietly, the best is the licorice strap.

In that case, I said, I'll try one myself.

So I got him one and one for myself and together we ate them.

It was a good job while it lasted because of the fine, funny, tragic, little poor people who came there for things to eat or somebody to talk to.

Peace, It's Wonderful, 1939

Johnny the Dreamer, Mary the Model at Magnin's and Plato the Democrat

*T*he bar was crowded, the tables were all taken, and the place was full of smoke and noise. The best I could do was share a small table with a young man who'd been drinking for some time. Although he was alone, he was talking when I sat down. I had a half hour to kill, so I sat down and listened to him.

I drowned my sorrows with a girl named Mary once who used to be a model at Magnin's, he said. Ten years ago. I used to have to drown my sorrows every season in those days. When I say seasons I don't mean just the seasons of the year, I mean the fishing season, the football season, the opera season, and all the other seasons. I remember the terrible sorrow I had to drown once during the society season. It wasn't the easiest thing to do because of the pronunciation, which was embarrassing for me to listen to and more embarrassing for me to try to approximate, as it were. Ghastly is a simple word for me during the fishing season, but during the society season it's *ghastly*. Of course I can pronounce ghastly in the society manner as well as the next man. Interesting is another word I can pronounce the society way. I learned quiet a few of them. Ghastly, interesting, divine, chambertin, ecstatic, *élan*, André Gide, *bon mot*, and dozens of others.

The society season began for me that year in September, in the lobby of the De Luxe Hotel on Grant Avenue near Broadway, where I had a suite of one room and bath down the hall, and ended four days later in the Sky Room or the Starlight Room or some name like that of The Empire Hotel. There I finally sent the sorrows down for the third time, drowned them, and was carried out of the building by three friends, college men and each of them all-around good fellows.

Mary was in the swim of things with me during that time of sorrow and always held up my spirits when it seemed like the weight of my grief was too much for me to carry alone. My tragedy during the sorrow of the society season was the consequence of a stretch of bad luck at gambling, with disappearance of much-needed money. Money I needed, I must say, for the barest necessities of life. Bread and water and a pinch of salt. At last the tragedy was just too much. It suddenly became a matter of either the tragedy or myself. One of us had to go. The war was waged fair and square and I won. That is, Mary won. She did all the quarreling with the tragedy, squared off beautifully, jockeyed into contention, and fired away like mad—after which the tragedy got dressed, packed a bag and went in search of a cousin of mine named Nick who had a smile that could melt a heart of stone.

Mary was always glad to do it. Johnny, she always used to say, I've got all the faith in the world in you and any time things look gloomy, you just come to me and we'll sit down and straighten everything out. She used to say dozens and dozens of other nice things, too.

We were the most platonic friends in the world. You hear a lot of talk about platonic friendships, but probably no more than one platonic friendship out of a hundred is the real thing. With a bottle on the floor, a fire roaring in the fireplace and the phonograph playing Debussy, Mary used to read Plato to me for hours. I can remember lying back in the deepest sorrow and just listening to Mary reading, *Next then, I suppose, we must examine Democracy and find out how it arises and what it is like, so that we may know what the democratic man is like and estimate his value.*

I used to lie back and dream about what the democratic man is like, and then I'd just move back an inch or two more, and estimate his value. He would be like a fellow I knew once named Luke who always said all he knew was that he was a Democrat and wanted no trouble with nobody, just so they'd leave him alone. I estimated his value at ten cents a pound. He was a small man, and all told came to about $14.35 with his clothes on.

Plato was a real sweetheart to both of us in those days. Mary was improving her mind all the time because of the type of people she was meeting at Magnin's, who imagined themselves superior to Mary, not only in breeding but in education.

As a matter of fact, if the truth were known, Mary was always the best-bred of the lot, and for my money the best-educated. She was built like a Debussy daydream in a 1924 custom-built Stutz. But the debutantes and their mothers who came to Magnin's for their clothes hurt Mary's feelings, so she went and bought the collected works of Plato.

Every once in a while after I got through dreaming about what the democratic man is like, I would wonder what *Plato* himself was like and what his first name was.

What's his first name, Mary? I used to say.

First name? Mary used to say. Why, I don't know. They just called him Plato.

What was he, anyhow?

He was a philosopher. All this stuff I'm reading is philosophy.

Is that what it is?

Of course.

Well, I guess lots of stuff is philosophy and nobody stops to notice. This is all *Plato's* philosophy.

It sure is nice to know, I used to say. Read some more.

So Mary used to go back to the book and read.

But the money-makers fix their eyes on the ground and pretend not to see; instead they go on poisoning with their wealth any of the other citizens who give up the struggle, and increase the number of drones and beggars in the city. While, as for themselves and their own sons, their young men are luxurious and useless both in mind and body, lazy and too soft to endure pain or resist pleasure.

She used to read, *When the ruling class and the ruled meet one another in the streets or at public meetings, at festivals or in the army, when they serve side by side either on board ship or in the ranks and see one another facing danger, the poor will not be despised by the rich. On the contrary, often a poor man, strong and brown, stands in the ranks next to a rich man, who has lived an indoor life and is far too fat; and, seeing his shortness of breath and general discomfort, will surely think that such men as these are rich simply because the poorer classes are cowards. And whenever he meets his friends the word will get passed around. We can do what we like with these men; they are good for nothing.*

And my God I used to lie back on the floor at Mary's and just listen and listen to all that wonderful stuff that was philosophy.

I am quite sure, Mary would go on reading, *that they will.*

Now wait a minute, Mary, I used to say. Just let me get that straight. Will *what?*

Why, they will do what they like with the rich men, Mary would say.

Well, I used to say, what do you suppose they want to do with them?

Well, I'll read and find out, Mary used to say.

Well then, I suppose, she'd go on reading, *democracy comes into existence when the poor have conquered the rich, killing some, banishing others, and sharing citizenship and office with the rest.*

I see, I used to say. Good. Read some more.

So Mary used to go on.

That is how democracy is established, whether it be through armed force or whether the opposite side give in at once through fear.

That would make me jump to my feet and say, Well, by God, how long has this been going on?

This is all ancient stuff, Mary used to say. This was written before Chirst.

No fooling?

Of course.

Well, that's different, I used to say. Just so they don't come around and try to scare *me* with their armed force.

Scare *you?* Mary used to say. Why, Johnny, you're not rich.

That doesn't make any difference. Suppose I get rich some day?

Well, all right, Mary used to say. Just rest, and let me go on reading.

O.K.

Well, now Mary used to go on reading, *how will they live and what kind of a government will theirs be? First, of course, they are free, and the city is full of freedom and free speech and every one may do whatever he wishes.*

And where everyone may do as he wishes it is quite clear that each man will order his own life in the way that pleases him best.

So, I imagine, under this government we shall find men of all sorts and kinds.

Certainly.

Then this is likely to be a very beautiful form of government.

Along about this time I'd swim off to sleep and wake up just in time to come in on, *Is not this a gloriously pleasant kind of life for the moment?*

Perhaps for the moment.

And how considerate such a city is. No nonsense there about trifles.

It is wonderful.

It seems to be a pleasant form of government, varied and without rulers, dealing out of its own special brand of equality to equal and unequal alike.

Mary used to read Plato to me all the time in those days of sorrow. She wanted to improve her mind so she could talk down to the society riff-raff that was always trying to make her feel cheap.

Finally one day in the Geranium Room or something like that at the Harry Hopkins Hotel or some place like that, at the bar, Mary put a young loafer in his place who thought he could get away with etching-talk with a girl like her, brought up platonically. He was one of them boys who even before Christ were too lazy and too soft to endure pain or resist pleasure, and he passed a few intimate remarks to Mary who listened carefully, reflected on what the democratic man is like, weighed his value, considered the sum involved, and then said, You can talk that way to your society friends, my good fellow, but you can't talk that way to *me*—a model at Magnin's.

She was a sweetheart of a girl.

The drinker stopped a moment to remember what a sweetheart of a girl Mary was. Then he said, I remember the sorrow I drowned with her during the Horse Show season . . . .

Wait a minute, I said. It was time for me to go and I wanted to know more about Mary herself. Let's not rush into the sorrow you drowned with her during the Horse Show season. Tell me about Mary herself. What was her last name?

What? he said.

Her last name? I said.

Who's last name?

Mary's.

Mary who?

Your friend, the model at Magnin's, I said. The girl you used to drown your sorrow with.

What are you talking about, he said?

You were telling me about a girl named Mary that you used to drown your sorrow with, I said.

I've been quoting Plato, he said.

O.K., I said. It doesn't matter. It's been nice drinking with you.

You call yourself a drinker? he said. I used to pal around with a guy named Felix like you once in Boston. He was an Austrian on his father's side and an American on his mother's side. Claimed he was a child prodigy. Said he'd studied ten years. He was twenty-one but looked younger because he shaved every day. He always carried a violin around with him. Not in a case. Out in the open. The violin in one hand and the bow in the other. He used to wear short pants. I never could figure out why he wanted to be a child prodigy. I met his son, too. He was a nice-looking little boy, five years old, and he had his own little violin, right out in the open, too, and his own bow. When I saw the boy I told the father to sit down and put the lousy violin away for a minute and have a drink, but he wouldn't do it. He claimed he had to keep up with his studies if he ever intended to get anywhere in the world.

I'm sorry, I said. I've got to go now. I'd like to hear the whole story about Felix, but I'm late.

What's the matter? he said.

I've been sick, I said. I can't have more than seven without feeling a little confused. So long.

So long, he said.

He went right on talking—to God, most likely, who is a better listener than I am.

Peace, It's Wonderful, 1939

Romance

Would you rather sit on this side or would you rather sit on the other side? the red-cap said.

Hmm? the young man said.

This side all right? the red-cap said.

Oh, the young man said. Sure.

He gave the red-cap a dime. The red-cap accepted the small thin coin and folded the young man's coat and placed it on the seat.

Some people like one side, he said, and some like the other.

What? the young man said.

The red-cap didn't know if he ought to go into detail, about some people being used to and preferring certain things in the landscape looking out of the train from one side, and others wanting to get both sides of the landscape all the way down and back, preferring one side going down, usually the shady side, but in some cases the opposite, where a lady liked sunlight or had read it was healthy, and the other side coming up, but he imagined it would take too long to explain everything, especially in view of the fact that he wasn't feeling real well and all morning hadn't been able to give that impression of being on excellent terms with everybody which pleased him so much.

I mean, he said, it's no more than what anybody wants, I guess.

The red-cap figured the young man was a clerk who was going to have a little Sunday holiday, riding in a train from a big city to a little one, going and coming the same day, but what he didn't understand was why the young man seemed so lost, or, as the saying is, dead to the world. The boy was young, not perhaps a college graduate, more likely a boy who'd gone through high school and gotten a job in an office somewhere, maybe twenty-three years old, and perhaps in love. Anyhow, the red-cap thought, the young man looked to be somebody who might at any moment fall in love, without much urging. He had that sad or dreamy look of the potential adorer of something in soft and colorful cloth with long hair and smooth skin.

The young man came to an almost violent awakening which very nearly upset the red-cap.

Oh, he said, I've been sort of day-dreaming.

He wiggled the fingers of his right hand near his head or where people imagined one day-dreamed.

Have I given you a tip? he said.

The red-cap felt embarrassed.

Yes, sir, he said.

The young man wiggled the fingers of his left hand before his face.

I very often forget what I'm doing, he said, until long afterwards—sometimes years. May I ask how much I gave you?

The red-cap couldn't figure it out at all. If the young man was being funny or trying to work some sort of a racket, it was just too bad because the red-cap wasn't born yesterday. The young man had given him a dime and if the young man came out with the argument that he had given the red-cap some such ridiculous coin as a five-dollar gold piece the red-cap would simply hold his ground and say, This is all you gave me—this dime.

You gave me a dime, he said.

I'm sorry, the young man said. Here.

He gave the red-cap another dime.

Thank you, sir, the red-cap said.

Were you saying something while we were coming down the aisle? the young man said.

Nothing important, the red-cap said. I was only saying how some folks like to sit on one side and others on the other.

Oh, the young man said. Is this side all right?

Yes it is, the red-cap said. Unless of course you prefer not getting the sunshine.

No, the young man said, I kind of like sunshine.

It's a fine day too, the red-cap said.

The young man looked out the window as if at the day. There was nothing but trains to see, but he looked out the window as if he were looking to see how fine a day it was.

The sun don't get in here where it's covered up, the red-cap said, but no sooner than you get out of here into the open you'll be running into a lot of sunshine. Most California folks get tired of it and get over on the other side. You from New York?

There was nothing about the young man to suggest that he was from New York or for that matter from anywhere else either, but the red-cap wondered where the young man was from, so he asked.

No, the young man said, I've never been out of California.

The red-cap was in no hurry, although there was considerable activity everywhere, people piling into the car, other red-caps rushing about, helping with bags, and hurrying away. Nevertheless, he lingered and carried on a conversation. There was a girl across the aisle who was listening to the conversation and the red-cap fancied he and the young man were cutting quite a figure with her, one way or another. It was charming conversation, in the best of spirits, and, although between men in different stations of life, full of that fraternal feeling which is characteristic of westerners and Americans.

I've never been out of California myself, the red-cap said.

You'd think you'd be the sort of man to travel a good deal, the young man said.

Yes you would at that, the red-cap said. Working on trains, or leastaways near them, on and off most of my life since I was eighteen, which was thirty years ago, but it's true, I haven't set foot outside the boundary lines of this state.

I've met a lot of travelers though, he added.

I wouldn't mind getting to New York some day, the young man said.

I don't blame a young man like you for wanting to get to New York, the red-cap said. New York sure must be an interesting place down around in there.

Biggest city in the world, the young man said.

It sure is, the red-cap said, and then he made as if to go, dragging himself away as it were, going away with tremendous regret.

Well, he said, have a pleasant journey.

Thanks, the young man said.

The red-cap left the car. The young man looked out the window and then turned just in time to notice that the girl across the aisle was looking at him and was swiftly turning her head away, and he himself, so as not to embarrass her, swiftly continued turning his head so that something almost happened to his neck. Almost instantly he brought his head all the way back to where it had been, near the window, looking out, and felt an awful eagerness to look at the girl again and at the same time a wonderful sense of at last beginning to go places, in more ways than one, such as meeting people like her and marrying one of them and settling down somewhere in a house somewhere with, more likely than not after time enough, two or three offspring.

He didn't look at the girl again, though, for some time, but kept wanting to very eagerly, so that finally when he did look at her he was embarrassed and blushed and gulped and tried very hard to smile but just couldn't quite make it. The girl just couldn't quite make it either.

That happened after they'd been moving along for more than ten minutes, the train rolling out among the hills and rattling pleasantly and making everything everywhere seem pleasant and full of wonderful potentialities, such as romance and a good deal of good humor and easy-going naturalness, especially insofar as meeting her and being friendly and pleasant and little by little getting to know her and falling in love.

They saw one another again after about seven minutes more, and then again after four minutes, and then they saw one another more steadily by pretending to be looking at the landscape on the other side, and finally they just kept seeing one another steadily for a long time, watching the landscape.

At last the young man said, Are you from New York?

He didn't know what he was saying. He felt foolish and unlike young men in movies who do such things on trains.

Yes, I am, the girl said.

What? the young man said.

Didn't you ask if I was from New York? the girl said.

Oh, the young man said. Yes, I did.

Well, the girl said, I am.

I didn't know you were from New York, the young man said.

I know you didn't, the girl said.

The young man tried very hard to smile the way they smiled in pictures.

How did you know? he said.

Oh I don't know, the girl said. Are you going to Sacramento?

Yes, I am, the young man said. Are you?

Yes, I am, the girl said.

What are you doing so far from home? the young man said.

New York isn't my home, the girl said. I was born there but I've been living in San Francisco most of my life.

So have I most of mine, the young man said. In fact all of it.

I've lived in San Francisco practically all of my life too, the girl said, with the possible exception of them few months in New York.

Is that all the time you lived in New York? the young man said.

Yes, the girl said, only them first five months right after I was born in New York.

I was born in San Francisco, the young man said. There's lots of room on these two seats, he said with great effort. Wouldn't you like to sit over here and get the sun?

All right, the girl said.

She stepped across the aisle and sat across from the young man.

I just thought I'd go down to Sacramento on the special Sunday rate, the young man said.

I've been to Sacramento three times, the girl said.

The young man began to feel very happy. The sun was strong and warm and the girl was wonderful. Unless he was badly mistaken, or unless he got fired Monday morning, or unless America got into a war and he had to become a soldier and go away and get himself killed for no good reason, he had a hunch some day he would go to work and get acquainted with the girl and marry her and settle down.

He sat back in the sunlight while the train rattled along and smiled romantically at the girl, getting ready for the romance.

Peace, It's Wonderful, 1939

The Art of War

I think Harry Cook's a funny fellow, though.

One evening I was sitting on the pile of timber in front of our barracks reading around in a book I'd found in town called *The Art of War*, and Harry was over at the other end of the pile of timber lying on his back. The timber was a good place to sit or stretch out, but what it was for nobody ever knew. From the color it had turned you could see it had been there a long time. Well, Harry kept saying just loud enough for me to hear, "Private Cook reporting as ordered, sir. You can take the Army, Colonel, and I think you know what you can do with it."

So after a while I said:

"Who you talking to?"

"I'm talking to the Colonel," Harry said. "The son of a bitch."

"What?"

"You heard me."

"You can get court-martialed for that."

"You heard me," Harry said again.

"What have you got against the Colonel?"

"He used to be the credit manager of a department store."

"How do you know?"

"His stenographer told me. She looked it up."

"What did you have to see him for?"

"The Captain sent me."

"Why?"

"The Lieutenant."

"What'd you do?"

"The Sargeant told the Lieutenant I had made derogatory remarks about the Army."

"What'd the Colonel say?"

"Said I ought to be ashamed of myself. Said the only reason he wasn't having me court-martialed was that he didn't want to give the Post a bad name. So I gave him a bad name, and you know what it is."

Harry rolled down onto the next layer of timber, out of sight, so I went back to the book I was reading, but just then I saw a handful of Army men with one civilian among them come around the corner from the Post Exchange, headed straight for the timber. From the way they moved, I could tell they were important. You can tell an officer from a Private from the way he walks. It's not that the officer walks any better than the Private, it's something else. Even from a distance you can see that an officer feels he is being watched, either by superior officers or by the rank and file, and you can see that he thinks he is a pretty important man in this man's world, as he puts it—not as important as a Captain if he's a Lieutenant, but more important than the great majority of men in the Army, or in the world for that matter. I didn't have to see the tin chicken on the shoulder of the Colonel to know he was a big man, I knew it from the way he occupied his space among the other men in the group. He occupied his space a little more importantly than the Major beside him did, and the Major occupied his space a little more importantly than the two Captains beside him occupied theirs. The First Lieutenant was just a little trashy in that company, but the man who was most important of all was the civilian. He was the youngest of the lot too, probably no more than twenty-six or twenty-seven.

I got a little panic-stricken when I saw so many important men because I was out there in the open where I could be seen. I didn't like saluting in those days and I didn't like needing to think about it all the time, but nowadays it doesn't bother me at all because I go according to the way I feel. If I see a little old Colonel coming down the street who seems to be lonely and confused, almost as if he were no better than a Private, well, I catch his eye and give him a smart salute and move on down the street. But if I see some rollicking young fool charging up the street, on the verge of changing the history of the world from something sad to something hideous, I just naturally get lost in thought, or turn to look into a shop window, or lift my eyes to the sky, and move past the imbecile. I'll salute if the spirit moves me. I've saluted old beggars, children in the streets, beautiful girls, drunkards hanging onto lampposts, elevator operators in uniform, and all the fellows in the Army I like, regardless of rank, but I didn't like the group coming down the company street, so I ducked down, around, and out of sight. I crawled over to Harry Cook.

"What's the matter with *you?*" Harry said.

"The Colonel," I whispered. "Four other officers and a civilian."

We heard their voices now, and Harry made a face.

"Let's listen to 'em," I said.

But they didn't say anything worth listening to, so I started reading again, and Harry started singing very softly *If I had my way, dear, you'd never grow old.* I knew he was thinking of the Colonel.

The men were very cheery with one another in that special way that Army men have, but at the same time they were very careful too—not so much of what they said as of the tone of voice they permitted themselves to use. Every once in a while I'd hear the Major talking too brilliantly for his rank, and then I'd hear him change his tone of voice out of deference to the Colonel. It was that way with every one of them excepting the Colonel himself and the civilian. The Colonel was quite brilliant for a man who had only recently left the credit department of a big department store, but the stuff he said sounded pretty silly to me. I gathered that the civilian was a newspaperman who'd been sent by his paper to write a series of stories on how men in the Army live. Then I heard him say:

"Colonel Remington, I wonder if I might have a word with one or two of your men—anybody at all."

Then I heard the Colonel say:

"By all means, Jim. Lieutenant Coburn, will you fetch our friend Jim here a couple of our men? Use your own judgment, Lieutenant."

I heard the Lieutenant make the usual reply and hurry away. The men went back to being cheery, but of course not too cheery. Pretty soon the voices got too close to be comfortable and the first thing I knew the whole bunch of them were all the way around the pile of timber, right where they could see Harry Cook and me. Before I could decide what to do, they saw us! Every one of them saw us, but the Colonel especially. Harry pretended that he didn't know they were there and began to sing louder than he needed to in order to sound as if he didn't know somebody was near by. So it was up to me to do the right thing, only I didn't know what the right thing was. I jumped to my feet and discovered that I was standing a little over the heads of the men which made me feel foolish. Even so, I took the book from my right hand, so I'd be free to salute, and I saluted. Everybody excepting the civilian returned the salute, and the Colonel said, "At ease, son," so I knew he wanted to impress the newspaperman. He wanted the newspaperman to get the impression that he was a regular fellow. So, noticing the book, he said, "Catching up on your home-work?"

By this time Harry had stopped singing. He had spent some time looking up at me and then around at the group. He got to his feet, and when it was absolutely silly to do so, he saluted, but he did it as if he had all the time in the world. Well, there was an awful awkward moment there because Harry had saluted so slowly that the automatic reaction that takes place in Army men when they see a smart salute was upset. Nobody moved to return Harry's salute, and Harry wouldn't give in. He just stood there on the timber and held the salute. After a lot of fidgeting the Colonel returned the salute in a very irritated way, and all the other officers followed his example. By now they were all rattled and wished they hadn't run into us, I guess. It was so long since the Colonel had asked me if I was catching up on my home-work I didn't think a reply was in order, so I just stood there too. The newspaperman broke the tension by saying, "Colonel Remington, have I your permission to speak to these men?"

This time the Colonel didn't feel so cheery.

"I want you to speak to any man you please," he said. "Any man at all."

The newspaperman looked at Harry, smiled, and said, "How do you like the Army, Mac?"

Harry didn't smile.

"I don't like it," he said, "and my name's not Mac, it's Harry."

"What's your last name?"

"Cook."

Harry stepped down from the timber. I thought he was going to stand with the newspaperman and the officers and answer some more questions, but without another word he turned and walked away. I guess he went to the Post Exchange or to the movie. So that left me. I could see the Colonel was sore as hell at Harry for saying what he'd said and for doing what he'd done, so I decided to try to improve matters a little—first for Harry, and then for the Colonel himself, because I hate to see a man upset that way, no matter who he is.

"Harry got a letter from his father this afternoon," I said. "His mother's very sick, and his father thinks she's going to die. He's been crying all afternoon."

I got down from the timber as I spoke. I kept my eye on the Colonel to see how he was taking it, and sure enough he was taking it the right way. He was relieved, for one thing, and I got the feeling that he was thankful to me for getting him out of a tough spot. Newspapermen are a nuisance to Army men. They can make a lot of trouble for a Colonel who's bucking for a B.G. Men out of uniform, especially newspaper-men, take Colonels and even Generals with a grain of salt—their hero is the little man. The Colonel was smart enough to see that his best chance to keep the good name of the Post, and his own good name, was to be unhappy about Harry's unhappiness. But at the same time I could see how happy he was that Harry's mother was about to die because that meant that Harry didn't really dislike the Army, he didn't like the idea of his mother dying, which was something else again.

"Yes," the Colonel said looking at the newspaperman, "I thought that poor boy was going through some sort of emotional crisis. Major Goldring, will you please see that Private Cook is given a special furlough home? I want that boy to get on the next train out of town and go home for a few days. I want every man on this Post to understand that we—the Commanding Officers—are their friends. Get Private Cook home immediately, Major."

"Yes, sir," the Major said. "I'll attend to everything the first thing in the morning."

"The first thing in the morning be damned!" the Colonel said. "*Now!* Immediately!"

The Colonel turned to me.

"Where is Private Cook's home?" he said.

Well, I knew Harry's home was in the Sunset District of San Francisco, not far from where Pop and I used to live. But I didn't want to make any trouble because I knew there were two or three trains to San Francisco every night. I thought if I told the Colonel where Harry's home was, and the Major got Harry on the next train, pretty soon everybody would find out that Harry's mother wasn't sick at all, and Harry and me would both be in trouble. So I thought I'd say Harry's home was far away—so far away that the Colonel would drop the idea of getting Harry home on the next train and be satisfied to let him go on being unhappy.

"His home's in Alaska, sir," I said. I said that because when I saw the trouble coming I got to wishing I was somebody else instead of who I am, and that made me think of Eskimos, and Eskimos made me think of Alaska.

"Alaska?" the Colonel said.

"Yes, sir," I said. "He's an Alaskan."

I could see the Colonel had a problem on his hands now, and I was ready to believe the whole matter would be dropped and forgotten. Now, if the Lieutenant would only show up with two men his own judgment told him were appropriate for an interview with a newspaperman everything would be fine, and I'd go look for Harry. The Colonel looked over at the newspaperman, and if I ever saw a face you couldn't figure out it was the face of that newspaperman. It was a real honest-to-God poker face. The Colonel smiled at the newspaperman, but the newspaperman didn't change his expession, so the Colonel knew he was still on the spot.

"What city in Alaska?" he said.

"Fairbanks."

"Major Goldring," the Colonel said, "find out what planes are scheduled to go to Fairbanks, and get Private Cook on the next one—give him a special priority, and if he needs any money, attend to it for me personally."

"Yes, sir," the Major said and went off.

"Young man," the Colonel said to me, "go find your friend. He's going home."

"Yes, sir," I said and turned to go, but the newspaperman said, "Excuse me—what's that book you have?"

"*The Art of War*," I said. "By Clausewitz."

"May I ask how it happens that you are reading that book?" the newspaperman said.

"The intelligence of the average enlisted man in this Army," the Colonel began to say, but the newspaperman cut him short.

"Sherman said 'War is hell'," the newspaperman said. "Clausewitz says it's an art. What do you think it is?"

"I don't know very much about it," I said.

"What do you think of Clausewitz?"

"He's easy to read."

"What do you think of his ideas?"

"I think they stink."

"What's your name?"

"Wesley Jackson."

The newspaperman wrote my name on a little pad that he got out of his coat pocket. For a while the Colonel had been pleased with me, but when I got to talking freely—even though I didn't mean to—I saw that he didn't like it at all. It seemed to him that this fool newspaperman was going to go to work and write about a Private instead of about *him*.

"Where you from?" the newspaperman said.

"San Francisco."

"What'd you do as a civilian?"

"Nothing."

"Nothing?"

"I spent some time looking for work, I worked once in a while, but most of the time I loafed. My father was in the last War. He got a pension because he'd been wounded, so he and I always had enough to get by on."

"What's your father do?"

"Nothing."

"What's his trade or profession?"

"Hasn't got any. He was at college when he got drafted, but when he came back he didn't feel like studying any more."

"How do you know all that?"

"He told me. We were good pals until this War started."

"What happened then?"

"Well, Pop always liked to drink, but when they started drafting everybody again he didn't do anything *else*. He wouldn't even eat."

"What was your father's injury?"

"Gas, shrapnel, and shock. He's got some metal on the top of his head where some shrapnel almost scalped him."

"Do you like your father?"

"Sure."

"What'd you fight about?"

"We didn't fight. I tried to get him to stop drinking for a while, but he couldn't stop. He wanted to, but he couldn't. He'd go off on a drunk for three or four days, and when I'd ask him where he'd been he wouldn't be able to remember."

"If you didn't fight, how'd you happen to stop being pals?"

"He didn't come back."

"What'd you live on, then?"

"I found myself a Saturday job—three dollars. I lived on that."

"Where's your father now?"

"I don't know."

"Anybody else in the family?"

"My mother and my brother."

"Where are they?"

"They're in El Paso. My mother's brother—my uncle Neal—he's got a farm-implement business in El Paso, and my mother and my brother have been staying with him about ten years now, I guess."

"But you stayed with your father?"

"Yes. We've been together since I was nine."

Well, the newspaperman kept asking questions and I kept answering them, telling the truth every time and feeling more and more like a fool, hoping the Lieutenant would show up with the two men who would give the Post a good name instead of the miserable name Harry and I were giving it. But the Lieutenant didn't show up, and my hands kept sweating and I kept wishing I was an Eskimo, and the fellow kept hollering *Valencia!* because that was the song Pop used to sing when Mom first went off to El Paso with my brother Virgil, and Pop and me were dying of loneliness. After Pop and I got over the loneliness, Pop stopped singing *Valencia*, and I forgot all about it, but I remembered it again when Pop didn't come back, and by the time I was in the Army I kept hearing it all the time.

I thought I didn't like the newspaperman, but once we got to talking I could see he was straight, so I got over not liking him. For some reason the Colonel and the other officers just let us go on talking, but I'll be damned if I know why. Maybe they thought it was interesting.

"One more question," the newspaperman said. He looked at the Colonel out of the corner of his eye. Then he said, "How do you like the Army?"

Well, hell, there it was. Harry Cook had told him, so now he wanted me to tell him too. If I told him the truth the Colonel would be more unhappy than ever, and if I didn't tell him the truth I'd be a coward. I don't know why I didn't want the Colonel to be unhappy, considering I didn't like him any more than Harry did, but I know I didn't want the Colonel to be unhappy. It just seemed wrong to make the Colonel unhappy. I don't know how to explain this, but it seemed worse for me to make the Colonel unhappy than to be a coward. So then I got to thinking of the things I liked in the Army, but there were so few of them I knew I couldn't make a decision real soon, so I tried to seem cheerful and earnest at the same time and I said, "I like it fine."

Just then the Lieutenant came up with the two men he'd selected so I turned to go, but the newspaperman took me by the arm. The Lieutenant introduced the two men he'd selected. They were a couple of fellows who were permanently stationed at that Post. They did office work. I'd seen them around but I didn't know them. The newspaperman asked them how old they were and where they were from and what kind of work their fathers did, but he didn't write down any of the answers they made. The whole atmosphere got nicer and nicer, and the Colonel got to being cheery again, and then the Major came back and said, "There's a plane leaving for a field about a hundred miles from Fairbanks in three hours, sir. I've got Private Cook's furlough, travel orders, and money in this envelope."

I guess I must have looked pretty sick when I heard that, and I guess the newspaperman caught on to how I felt because he turned to the Colonel and said, "A fellow going all that distance on an airplane alone"—He turned to me. "Don't you think you ought to go along with your pal, considering his mother's so sick, and he's so unhappy?"

"I guess so," I said. "I guess I'd like to see Alaska all right."

By this time the two fellows who did office work were feeling cheery too, so one of them said, "Alaska? Who's going to Alaska?"

"Private Cook," the Major said. "We're sending him home. His mother's very sick."

Well, hell, I knew I was in for it now.

"Private Cook?" the office fellow said. "What Private Cook is that?"

"Private *Harry Cook*," the Major said.

Well, that newspaperman, he was O.K.

"Colonel," he said, "I'd like a word with you alone. Don't go anywhere, he said to me."

"By all means," the Colonel said to the newspaperman.

The Colonel and the newspaperman went around to the other side of the pile of timber and the rest of us stayed where we were and kept looking at one another. The two fellows from the offices knew something was fishy, but they didn't want to go too far with what they knew because in the Army they teach you not to go too far with anything no matter how right it is, just in case it might make trouble for somebody higher up because then he might thank you very much for informing him but after a week or two you might find yourself in some God-forsaken part of the country that you don't want to be in at all, so the fellows from the offices didn't say anything more about where Harry Cook's home was, even though they were sure it wasn't in Alaska.

The Major, he knew what was going on too, and every once in a while he'd sneak a look at me. I'd sort of smile at him, but he'd turn away quickly as if to say, "Steady now—don't weaken—don't say anything. The Colonel's in charge here. This is his show. Let's not embarrass the Colonel. He's talking to the newspaperman now. He'll make a decision for himself and give his orders. And we'll carry them out too."

The two Captains and the Lieutenant, they all got the idea too, so the only thing we could do was stand there and wait. We couldn't talk because if we did we might make a lot of trouble for the Colonel. Well, I wanted to go to Alaska all right, but I wasn't sure Harry Cook wanted to go. I wanted to go anywhere, just so I could get away from the Army for a while. I was fed-up with the Army, and if they flew Harry and me to Alaska that would be just fine because besides the change maybe I'd see an Eskimo at last.

Pretty soon the newspaperman and the Colonel came back. I could see they were on excellent terms now, so I felt pretty sure the newspaperman had promised to write a fine piece about the Colonel and help get him his B.G. Even though neither of them was smiling I knew everything was O.K., no matter where Harry Cook's home was, no matter who knew it.

The Colonel looked his men over, and they all acknowledged that he was Chief. Then he said, "Major Goldring, I want Private Jackson here to go along with Private Cook to Fairbanks, so please attend to the necessary details. Private Jackson will go as a courier." The Colonel turned to me and said, "Go find your friend and tell him the good news. Then I think the two of you had better hurry and pack your duffle bags. Lieutenant Coburn, will you arrange for transportation to the airfield?"

Everybody stood at attention and saluted the Colonel. He returned the salute, and the group broke up. I went straight to the barracks on the chance that Harry might be lying on his bunk, and sure enough he was. He was asleep. I shook him and when he opened his eyes I said, "Get up—you and I are going to Alaska in an airplane in three hours."

Harry said he and I were going to do something that I won't mention here. He turned over to go back to sleep. I was trying to get him to understand that what I was telling him was the truth when the newspaperman came into the barracks.

Lucky for Harry and me the only other fellow in the barracks was Victor Tosca and he was asleep on his bunk away over at the other end of the big room. The newspaperman looked at Harry and said, "I'm sorry I called you Mac. I didn't mean anything by it. How about shaking hands?"

"Sure," Harry said.

"Where's your home?" the newspaperman said, but I didn't care.

"San Francisco," Harry said. "I live in the Sunset District, just below Red Rock Hill."

"How's the family?"

"O.K."

"Any letters from home lately?"

"I got one this afternoon from my mother. She's made a cake and she's going to send it to me."

"Do you like cake?"

"Hell, yes—but this is a special cake," Harry said. "Dates and raisins and walnuts and rum and stuff like that in it. Don't you like cake?"

"I like cake too," the newspaperman said. "He looked at the two of us. I know *your* names, he said, so I think you ought to know mine. Jim Kirby. I write for U.P."

"Union Pacific?" Harry said.

"United Press," Jim said.

"What do you write?"

"Well, the boss wants me to write about soldiers. *You* fellows. Not the big shots, the *little* shots, you might say. I'm supposed to start out with a series of articles on life in Army Camps at home, and then move along with the mob."

Harry looked over at me and said, "Jackson claims we're going to take an airplane ride to Alaska in three hours."

"That's right," Jim said. "How do you like the idea?"

"I like it fine," Harry said. "Always did want to see the Klondike. But how come?"

"Well, your friend here," Jim said, "he and I went to work on the Colonel, and between the two of us we fixed it."

"No fooling?" Harry said.

"No fooling," Jim said. "And don't worry about anything. It's O.K. Well, you've got to pack your bags, so I'll say so long. Hope I'll be seeing you again."

We said so long to Jim Kirby and he turned and walked out of the barracks. Harry and I started packing our bags and Harry kept saying, "For God's sake, what did you tell the Colonel?"

It was a fine journey, going and coming, and it was a pretty nice place to be for a change, but the only Eskimo I saw worked in a saloon in Fairbanks. His name was Dan Collins, he was a Christian, and he looked more like an American than an Eskimo. I don't suppose the trip was a waste of time and money for the government because the Colonel had me carry some parcels and do a few things for him while we were up there. I went around to a half dozen Army Posts with the Colonel's stuff, and I took stuff back with me from every place I went to.

When Harry found out how and why we had got sent to Alaska he said, "Well, what do you know? The world sure is crooked, isn't it, Jackson?"

We were gone five days all told, and the minute we got back we went right on with our Basic Training, and every night Dominic Tosca and Lou Marriacci played games on Dominic's kid brother.

The Adventures of Wesley Jackson, 1946

The
Theological
Student

I began to meet the theological student about a quarter of a century ago in the plays of certain Russian writers. Tolstoy, Dostoyevsky, Chekhov, Andreyev and Gorki seldom wrote a play in which the theological student did not appear. The theological student seemed to be the playwright himself looking back at his youth with an amused but admiring eye. He was certainly a good man to have around—young; nervous; pale; often pimply; not the least bit handsome; ridiculous and pathetic; ill-clothed; ill-fed; eager for tea; full of the lore of heaven, hell and earth; and yet for all that a man who could be counted on to liven matters up considerably, for he was a devil at heart.

He was certainly always in the midst of a desperate struggle with sin, which appeared to be an overwhelming longing to kiss the girls, a longing that never failed to startle him and bewilder them. Some of the girls were women with children older than himself. These rather liked him, for he was clumsy, inexperienced, inept, and therefore amusing to them. More in charity than in passion they permitted him to breathe heavily in their arms, only to discover later in the afternoon that he was thinking of killing himself. His habit of coughing nervously in their faces made them cry out, "Oh, Alexander Alexandrovich!"—which he took for an expression of love. He disgraced himself in company by his ill-timed remarks and by his uncontrollable desire to escape being good.

He was useful to each playwright, however, in that it seemed perfectly natural for him to explain why humanity was unhappy.

In the plays of Tolstoy the theological student blamed man's unhappiness on women, and sometimes went so far as to mention certain physical parts of them to which men were so powerfully attracted that they could not give their undivided attention to God or farming;

and then, in another play, Tolstoy would have the theological student blaming something else.

Once, I believe it was the railroads, tempting men to run away. (From women of course, although the playwright mentioned only crying children and members of the local government who were forever greeting people in a most insincere manner.)

Another time the theological student, having had no stronger stimulant than a cup of tea, shouted that man is a beast because of his stomach; and went on to ask if anyone had recently noticed how frequently men sit down to eat, how much precious time is wasted in eating or in planning to do so, and what mischief attends the circumstance of a stomach full of meat, wheat, greens, cheese, wine and water.

Dostoyevsky's theological student claimed that man was unhappy because his very birth had been a nervous disorder.

Gorki's theological student was the best of the lot, though, for he hated everything which made life miserable, and everything made life miserable. The theological student proceeded quite logically to find fault with God, whereupon another side of Gorki, embodied in another character in the play—a notorious waster of sixty who had recently read a book from cover to cover—came forward with an attack on the government, blaming it for his present age and ill-health, and re-marking profoundly that he had once been thirty—no, even less than that—twenty! But now what? A ridiculous thing in a ridiculous black cloak! (Looking meaningfully across the room at Tatania Lvovna, age 18, and detecting in her the faintest trace of admiration.)

Having met the theological student and having found him an odd sort of fish—in no particular greatly different from anyone else I had met in the Russian plays—I began to wonder what it was that he was supposed to be studying. Whatever it was, did he study full-time or part-time? Did he study at school or at home? Or was he called a theological student simply because he was young? None of the play-wrights was very clear about any of this, other than to hint that what the theological student *wanted* was perfection.

At length I decided for myself that he studied theology books, and I decided to do so also.

A whole small mezzanine balcony with a floor of thick glass was devoted to books of theology at the Public Library in Fresno. Climbing the steep narrow stairway to this section of the library was like climbing upward on a small cramped ship. Once there, the feeling of sailing was very great, and the faces of the other readers seemed flushed by a mild fever, as if they were all a little seasick and were trying their best not to throw up. They were certainly dizzy from the height, the hot air, and the narrowness of the aislès between the shelves of books. I joined them and began to examine every book on the theology shelves.

Every book seemed depressing, but I was fearful of putting one of them back in its place until I was reasonably sure it was absurd and did not have hidden away in it somewhere what I was looking for.

What *was* I looking for? It did not occur to me at the time—nothing much occurs to anybody at the time and we might as well come right out and admit it—but whether I knew it in so many words or not I was very definitely looking for a theology which I myself might have written, or might one day write. That is to say, I was looking for what I believed was the only true theology. Robert Burns had already summed it up with Scotch economy, but one frequently forgets the remarks of poets. "A man's a man for all that" was right enough, and the implication of laughing about it was in the remark, but I imagined there would be a fuller recitation on the theme.

There wasn't, however.

The millions of words in the hundreds of books were little more than nonsense. Even so, I took home with me after each visit two or three of the theology books which I felt might not prove to be altogether senseless, and read around in them until I was convinced that the author was as ridiculous as any theological student in any Russian play.

No writer is more pathetic than the one whose passion is to complicate, and theology appeared to be a matter of complicating. If it was a matter of believing, why not believe and be done with it? Swedenborg sweated like a horse and wrote a couple of million words that must have had the effect of making it impossible for any reader ever again to smile, itself a kind of theological act, although uncomplicated and surely no more meaningless than Swedenborg's two million words.

All of which brings me to the plot of this story.

One evening on my way home from the Public Library I was met in the Santa Fe freight yards by a man who was profoundly complicated and desperately theological.

"Do you know," he called out from a distance of twenty yards, "that the world is going to end tonight?"

"What time?" I called back.

"Don't know the exact hour," the man said, "but it will be sometime tonight."

From his shoulders the man brushed dirt which had gotten there when he had leaped from a freight train and fallen.

"Did you just get to town?" I said.

"Yes, but I was born here twenty-seven years ago," the man said.

"Are you ready for the end of the world?" he went on, as he took to brushing dust from his pants.

"As ready as I am for anything else," I said. "Are *you* ready?"

"That's the trouble," the man said. "I'm not. I'm not at all."

Suddenly the man fell down.

"Do you know where the Emergency Hospital is?" I said. "It's at the back of the Police Station on Broadway, across from the Public Library, but if you don't want to go there, you can go to the County Hospital. It's across Ventura Boulevard at the Fair Grounds, but I suppose you know where these places are. I live on the way to the County Hospital and I'll go with you as far as my house. Maybe you can pick up a ride."

The man leaned on me and we stumbled in silence past Inderrieden's Dried Fruit Packing House. Crossing Ventura he fell again, and an automobile stopped. The driver of the automobile got out and came to the man and said, "What's the matter?"

"He ought to get to a doctor," I said. "He's hurt."

The driver of the automobile helped me get the man into the car. On the way to the County Hospital the injured man took one of the three books I had borrowed from the Public Library and opened it.

"*Either-Or*," he read. "By Sören Kierkegaard. Who's he?"

"I don't know," I said.

"A man ought to know who these people are," the man said.

He began to read the book. When we reached the hospital his grip was so tight on the book that I felt sure it would be damaged and the girl at the desk in the Public Library would examine the damage, and then me, and wonder how it had happened, but not say anything.

The driver of the car—a man who had remarked on the way to the hospital that his name was August Bockbell, a name I have never forgotten, perhaps because the driver—sensing that the other man was dying—gave an account of his *own* life, which included almost killing his elder brother over the ownership of a pocketknife—helped the injured man into the reception room, and then went off, apologizing that it was necessary for him to do so.

I did not go with him because the injured man was still reading the book I had borrowed from the Public Library, and it seemed to me that it would have been rude under the circumstances to ask him to return it. He was reading the book with incredible swiftness. When it was necessary for the injured man to go off with the nurse and a young man in a white coat who did not seem to be much of a doctor, I followed them down a hall to swinging doors, partly from anxiety about the man himself and partly from anxiety about the library book. At the swinging doors the nurse told me to return to the reception room. I wanted to ask her to please get my book for me, but instead I said, "He's going to be all right, isn't he?" The nurse gestured severely, as if to say, "No difficult questions at this difficult time, please."

I returned to the reception room and sat down.

When I examined the two remaining library books, I discovered that my library card with my name and address on it was in the book by Kierkegaard which the injured man had taken. My library card was as important to me as a passport is to a traveller. I had thought of waiting only ten or fifteen minutes for the book, but when I discovered that my library card was in it, I decided to wait two hours if necessary.

It was necessary to wait longer than that, however, during which time I grew very hungry—half-sick from it, in fact—and very angry, too. At first I was angry at the nurse who entered the reception room every ten or fifteen minutes in a state of confusion and excitement and refused to listen to what I had to tell her or to tell me about the condition of the injured man. After awhile I became angry about the man himself, whether he was to live or die—for he had most rudely taken off with a book I was charged on my honour to return to the Public Library in the same condition in which I had found it. Finally, I became angry about Kierkegaard, a man concerning whom I knew absolutely nothing except that he had written a book with the strange title of *Either-Or*.

After having waited more than three hours for the return of my book, the nurse came up to me in the reception room in a manner which revealed unmistakably that she meant to speak, and began by announcing a hopelessly garbled version of *my* name.

"Yes?" I said.

"He's dead," she went on. "Dr. Humpkit (at least that's what I *thought* she said) did everything possible for him, but it was just no use."

"I'm sorry. The thing I wanted to tell you was to please let me have my book."

"What book?"

"The book by Kierkegaard."

"He said it was *his* book. *His* library card with his *name* and *addresss* on it is in the book, at any rate."

"The card in the book is *my* card," I said. "Why do you get everything wrong? I was walking home from the Public Library with three books when I met the man in the Santa Fe freight yards. He had just jumped off a train and had hurt himself, so I helped him to Ventura Avenue where he fell down and a motorist stopped and brought him here. In the automobile he took one of the three books I had borrowed from the Public Library and kept it. Now he's dead, and just because my library card happened to be in the book, you've given *him* my name. Well, I'm sorry he's dead whoever he is, but I'd like to have my book back just the same."

"He himself told us his name," the nurse said. "I am entering it in the hospital records. We shall return the book to the Public Library for him."

"You've been to school," I said, because I was so angry and hungry, and then left the hospital and began walking home.

When I got there I found the street full of automobiles. The house was full of uncles and aunts and cousins from all over the city.

My uncle Khosrove was the first to see me, for he was sitting alone on the steps of the back porch smoking a cigarette.

He got up and shouted at the top of his voice into the house, "I told you it was a mistake. Here he is now, the same as ever, but very much in need of food."

Everybody inside the house came tumbling out, and then, after having seen me, they all hurried back in to set the table.

After I had had all the food I could get into my belly, my mother asked very sweetly, "Why did they come in an ambulance and say that you had died?"

"If I had known they were going to come in an ambulance," I said, "I would have come with them instead of walking three miles on an empty stomach at ten o'clock at night. They didn't tell me they were going to come in an ambulance."

"We've been terribly worried about you," my uncle Zorab said.

This was too much for my uncle Khosrove.

"We've been terribly worried about you!" he mocked. "When the man from the County Hospital told us you were dead, we were afraid you would not recover."

He turned to my uncle Zorab.

"Why do you talk nonsense?" he said. "Is it possible to worry about someone who is dead?"

My uncle Zorab cleared his throat nervously as he said, "Well, all I can say is, we worried, and here he is alive!"

"Man," my uncle Khosrove shouted, "will you never understand the very simplest sort of thing? There has been a mistake, as I said. Your worrying did not bring a dead man back to life. The boy's been involved in some sort of typical American complication. Unless you understand this now, there is no telling what terrible distortions will come into the telling of this family episode in years to come. Now that the boy has had his supper, let him tell us the whole story, and then one by one let us return to our own homes and our own lives. Whoever it was that died, we shall all join him soon enough, and it is quite all right. He turned to me. Now tell us what it was that happened which the people of the hospital reported to us as having been your death at the age of twenty-seven. I tried to tell these people that it was not you who had died, for you are not twenty-seven years old, but they replied that perhaps you had given twenty-seven as your age in a last attempt to be impressive. How old are you, and then tell us the story."

"I'm fourteen," I said.

And then I told the whole story, accurately, point by point.

My aunt Khatoon took to weeping softly for the young man who had died, claiming that he had died for *me*, so that I might go on living, a theory that made my mother angry; but my grandfather twisted his moustaches and said, "All very well and good, but who the devil is this man Kierkegaard to make such an ungodly fuss in this desolate and far-away village which is trying to pass for a city?"

"He is the man who wrote one of the three books I borrowed from the Public Library this afternoon, I said, but that's all I know about him."

"Well," my grandfather said, "that's fine. Now, all of you—get out of here. Go home where you belong. If it's for him you've been crying, there he is trying to get meat from between his teeth, so go home."

Everybody embraced lightly by way of celebrating my survival; there was kindly whispering among the women; the small boys took to wrestling in the living-room; and then at last everybody was gone excepting the Old Man and my uncle Khosrove. These two exchanged quarrelsome glances and then my uncle Khosrove said, "I know what you are going to ask him. Well, I'll give you the answer, to save him the trouble. You are going to ask him what he means by getting into complications of all sorts every other Friday, and I will answer for him that he doesn't mean anything at all by it. Some people come into this world asleep and go out of it asleep, and that is very thoughtful of them. A few others—like myself and this boy, my nephew Aram Garoghlanian— come into this world asleep, and then one fair Friday wake up and look around and notice what we are."

"What are we?" the Old Man asked politely.

"Armenians," my uncle Khosrove said quickly. "Could anything be more ridiculous? The Englishman has an empire to govern. The Frenchman has art to guide and measure. The German has an army to train and test. The Russian has a revolution to start. The Swiss have hotels to manage, the Mexicans mandolins to play, the Spaniards bulls to fight, the Austrians waltzes to dance to, and so on and so forth, but what have *we*?"

"Loud mouths to shut up?" the Old Man suggested.

"And the Irish," my uncle Khosrove went on. "The Irish have a whole island in which to be poverty-stricken; the Arabs a thousand tribes to bring together in the desert; the Jews child prodigies to send on concert tours; the Gypsies wagons and fortune-telling cards; the Americans chronic nervousness which they call freedom, but what have the Armenians?"

"Since you insist, tell me," said the Old Man. "What have the Armenians?"

"Manners," my uncle Khosrove said.

"Are you mad?" the Old Man said. "Nothing is so unnatural as a polite Armenian."

"I did not say *good* manners," my uncle Khosrove said. "I said manners. The good or bad of it I leave to others. Manners is what we have, and very little of anything else. You are going to ask this boy what he means by getting into complications of all sorts every other Friday. Your asking is manners. Well, go ahead and ask him. I'm going to the Arax Coffee House for a couple of hours of tavli. My going is more manners."

"Before you go," the Old Man said, "I think you ought to know I wished to ask the boy to report to me about the book by Kierkegaard, if he ever reads it. Now, I will go to the Coffee House *with* you."

The Old Man got up and yawned enormously. He yawned in three movements, after the fashion of symphonies, very slowly, wildly, and finally slowly and wildly by turns.

He went out of the house by the front door while my uncle Khosrove took the back. The screen doors slammed one-two, and I went looking for half a watermelon to eat, as I was very thirsty.

The following day I went out to the County Hospital and after a great deal of effort identified myself, retrieved my book, and took it home to read. The injured man had reached page 99, for he had folded the edge of that page over, so that he might easily find his place when next he took it up. After reading an hour and three-quarters I too reached page 99, and decided that I did not wish to read any farther. I took the book back to the Public Library and as I had expected the girl at the desk noticed the damage, examined it, examined me as I whistled softly, but did not say anything. I climbed the steep stairway to the mezzanine and continued my search for the book of theology that I hoped to find.

That evening I reported to my grandfather that Kierkegaard appeared to have been a Dane who had been born in 1813 and had died in 1855 after having spent the greater part of his time struggling with the devil, the church, and the complications of theology.

"Died at the age of forty-two," the Old Man said. "Struggling with the devil is most destructive, I see, but perhaps had he *not* struggled he would have lived only twenty-two years and left behind him not even the book he wrote. Have you read the book?"

"He wrote more than one book," I said. "I read the first 99 pages of one of them, and then I got tired of it."

"What did he say in the first 99 pages?"

"I'm not sure, but he *seemed* to say that everything is not enough."

"That is how it is with these fellows who are forever struggling with the devil," the Old Man said. "And the unfortunate man you met yesterday in the Santa Fe freight yards, what about him?"

"He died. Yesterday was the end of the world for him all right, just as he said."

"His real name?"

"Well," I said, "I have a name written down here from the book at the County Hospital which is *supposed* to be his name, but I am sure it is only another mistake. It's no mistake that he's dead, though. I suppose he might have lived had he not fallen into the hands of people so sure of themselves, and so quick to get things accurately wrong. I'm sure he didn't expect to die, for he turned down a page of the book, so that he might go on reading it. Here's the name I got from the Hospital book. Abo Mogabgab."

"How can that be?" the Old Man said. "Abo Mogabgab is the man from whom I buy my clothing, the Syrian with the shop on Mariposa Street, a man older than myself. Here, look into the lining of this coat at the label and read to me what is said there."

I looked at the label inside the coat and read aloud, "Abo Mogabgab."

"A magnificent example of American efficiency and theological accuracy," the Old Man said. "A man has been killed and a coat label has been given a funeral. And yet, here we are, all of us who are still alive, none the worse for the terrible efficiency or the fierce accuracy. Thank you for reporting to me on the gospel of Kierkegaard. I am still eager to learn, but I find that the farmer's gospel is still the best we have. Now, the vine is planted thus; and thus is it tended; and thus protected from rabbits; and thus are the grapes harvested; and thus are they made into wine; and thus dried by the sun into raisins; and in the winter thus it is that the branches of the vines are pruned; and in the spring thus it is that the vines are watered. What other gospel is half so pleasant, since it is all out in the weather? To hell with these stifling chambers in which poor men sit and confuse themselves. When they are all through for the day, don't they get up and go home and eat a bowl of stewed raisins with a piece of black bread, or drink a glass of wine with a lamb-chop, or eat a bunch of grapes with cheese and crackers?"

"I guess so," I said and went home.

When I got there I spent three hours in the backyard, working. My uncle Khosrove sat on the steps of the back porch and watched.

At last he got up and said, "For the love of God, what is it now? Why are you pestering the life out of that poor old Malaga vine? You have cleaned and repaired it until it looks like the ghost of a wretched old man, and only a moment ago it resembled a handsome, dreaming youth. Matter is beautiful only in its imperfections. Only blockheads seek perfection, which is death. Let perfection seek you. You needn't seek it.

Now, go inside the house and sit down and eat half a cold watermelon. You are not perfect, the vine is not perfect, but you can eat watermelon and pass water, so do so."

"What nonsense," I thought, but as I ate the watermelon I wondered if my uncle Khosrove was not just about the best theological student of them all.

The Assyrian and Other Stories, 1950

The Foreigner

Hawk Harrap, whose father came from somewhere in Asia Minor and used to sell vegetables and fruit from a wagon drawn by a horse, was of my time in Fresno, so I remember the days when he was a kid in overalls hustling *The Evening Herald* or sneaking in to the fights at the Civic Auditorium or playing hookey from Emerson School to sell soda pop at the County Fair and make a lot of money.

His father was Syrian but seldom spoke the language, as he had married a woman who was Scotch-Irish. Harrap was his name on all the school records, although his father's name was something that only *sounded a little* like Harrap. He was given the name Hawk by myself for being as swift as that bird or as swift as I imagined that bird was. By the time we were at Longfellow Junior High School together, the nickname was on the school records, too. Actually, his mother had named him Hugh after a dead brother.

The day I first met Hawk at Emerson School, in 1916, he took me to a boy named Roy Coulpa and insulted him by saying, "Roy, you're an *Italian!*" It did not seem to matter at all that Roy Coulpa *was* Italian. It was Hawk's tone of voice that was insulting. After making this painful and preposterous remark, Hawk shoved me into Roy with such force that we fell and began to wrestle. Roy was surprised and angry, and strong enough to make me exert myself. The school playground was Fresno dirt, so a lot of dust got kicked up as each of us broke free of all kinds of holds. The match stopped when the recess bell rang, and Roy and I got up and had a look at one another. We looked around for Hawk, too. We were not permitted to move until we heard the second bell, at which time we fell in at the entrance of the school. When a third bell rang we marched into our classrooms. Hawk was standing among the two dozen spectators. When I caught his eye he winked, and I wondered what the hell he meant.

After school he and Roy and I walked to California Playground, and there the three of us wrestled for the fun of it.

The point is, it was impossible to dislike him.

Hawk lived on O Street, so he and I walked home together when Roy set out for his house across the S.P. tracks on G Street, beyond Rosenberg's Packing House.

"What are you, anyway?" Hawk said as we walked home. "Even the teacher can't pronounce your name."

"I'm American," I said.

"The hell you are." Hawk said. "Roy's Italian, I'm Syrian, and I guess you're Armenian."

"Sure," I said. "I'm Armenian all right, but I'm American, too. I speak better English than I do Armenian."

"I can't talk Syrian at all," Hawk bragged, "but that's what I am. If anybody asks you what you are, for God's sake don't tell them you're American. Tell them you're Armenian."

"What's the difference?"

"What do you mean what's the difference? If you're Armenian and you say you're American everybody'll laugh at you. The teacher knows what you are. Everybody knows what you are."

"Aren't *you* American?"

"Don't make me laugh," Hawk said. "I'm a foreigner. My father sells vegetables from a wagon."

"Weren't you born in America?"

"I was born in Fresno. I was born in the house on O Street. What's that got to do with it?"

"Well, I'm American," I said. "And so are you."

"You must be looney," Hawk said. "But don't worry, you'll find out what you are soon enough."

One day months later, after lunch, Miss Clapping, our teacher, suddenly stopped teaching and said, "You Armenian boys who go home for lunch have got to stop eating things full of garlic. The smell is more than I can stand and I'm not going to put up with it any longer."

Hawk turned to see how I was taking the insult.

As a matter of fact lunch for me that day had been dried eggplant, okra and stringbeans made into a stew with chunks of shoulder of lamb, in which garlic was absolutely necessary.

The day wasn't so cold, however, that the windows of the room could not be opened or the radiator turned off. The classroom was air-tight and over-hot.

"Open the window," I said to Miss Clapping.

Hawk gave a hoot of amazement and Miss Clapping looked at me as if she had no intention not to finish my life immediately. The rest of the class stirred in their seats and waited for developments. I decided to kill

Miss Clapping and be done with it, but when I got to thinking how I might do it, the scheme seemed impractical. Miss Clapping went to he desk and studied her class book.

"Yes," she said at last. "Here is your name. I'm sure you know how to pronounce it. The Lord knows I don't."

Another insult!

She closed the book and looked at me again.

"Now," she said, "what did you say when I said you Armenian boys will have to stop eating garlic?"

"I said open the window."

"Perhaps I don't understand," Miss Clapping said, her lips beginning to tremble a little.

She put down the book she was holding and picked up a twelve-inch ruler. She stepped away from her desk and stood at the foot of the row in which my desk was the last one.

"Now, tell me," she said, "just *what* do you mean?"

"I mean," I said, "it would be stuffy in this room no matter what anybody ate for lunch. This room needs fresh air. It's easier to open the window than to ask people to cook stuff without garlic."

Hawk hooted again, and without any further discussion Miss Clapping moved down the row to my desk.

"Put out your right hand," she said.

"What for?"

"For being impertinent."

It happened that I had recently learned the meaning of that word.

"I haven't been impertinent," I said.

"You're being impertinent now," the teacher said. "Put out your right hand or I shall send you to the Principal, who will give you a thrashing."

"No, he won't," I said.

"Oh, he won't, won't he?" the teacher said. "We'll see about that. You're not going to make a fool out of me in *this* class. Put out your right hand."

Miss Clapping waited a full minute for me to put out my hand. So many things happened to her face, to her eyes and mouth, that I almost felt sorry for her. I certainly felt disgusted with myself, although I knew she was being ridiculous.

Finally she returned to her desk and with a shaking hand scribbled a note which she folded and handed to a little girl named Elvira Koot who took the note and left the room. The class sat in silence, the teacher tried to occupy herself looking into her book, and I wished I lived in a more civilized part of the country. At last the little girl returned to the room and handed the teacher a note which the teacher read. I was sure the Principal had considered the situation and had urged her to open the window; I was ready to apologize for having made so much trouble; but when I saw the evil smile on the teacher's face I went back to planning to kill her, for I knew I was headed for hard times.

"Report to the Principal in his office at once," Miss Clapping said.

I got up and left the room. In the hall I decided to kill the Principal too. I had seen him from a distance, the usual tall man around public schools; and I had heard about him; but I hadn't believed what I had heard. The report was that he was quite a rooster among the old hens who taught school and that he wouldn't think of giving you a chance to tell your side of a story. If one of the old hens said you deserved to be punished the rooster punished you. Instead of reporting to his office immediately, I left the school building and walked home.

My mother was in the kitchen cutting up half a dozen cabbages for sour cabbage soup.

"What are you doing here?" she said.

"I don't want to go to that school any more," I said.

I tried to explain as accurately as possible what had happened. My mother listened to my side of the story and cut up the cabbages and put them into a five-gallon crock and poured salt over them and put a piece of apple-box wood on top of the cabbage, and on top of the wood she put rocks the size of eggplants. She said nothing until I was finished, and then she said, "Go back to the school and mind the teacher. Hereafter when there is garlic in your lunch, eat a sprig of parsley. Do not be so eager to defend the honour of Armenian cooking."

This attitude infuriated me.

I went to my room and put some things together—a pair of socks, a sling shot, three pebbles, a key I had found, a magnifying glass, and a copy of The New Testament I had won at Sunday School—and tied them into a bundle, to run away. I walked two blocks and then went back to the house and threw the bundle on the front porch and went back to the school and reported to the Principal.

He gave me a strapping with a heavy leather belt. After this greatest insult of all, I dried my eyes and went back to my class and sat at my desk.

After school Hawk said, "See what I mean? You're a foreigner and don't ever forget it. A smart foreigner keeps his feelings to himself and his mouth shut. You can't change teachers. You can't change Principals. You can't change people. You can laugh at them, that's all. Americans make me laugh. I wouldn't fool with them if I were you. I just laugh at them."

What happens to a man like Hawk Harrap as the years go by?

Well, I had been out of the Army about a month when I decided to drive from San Francisco to my home town before summer ended, and try to find out. It was mid-October, and I wanted to eat some grapes and figs and melons and pomegranates and new raisins, anyway.

I reached Fresno early Saturday evening and telephoned Roy Coulpa and my second cousin Mug Muggerditchian and took them to dinner at El Rancho on Highway 99, just past Roeding Park.

It was 1945, and it was good to be breathing the air of the San Joaquin Valley again, and to be talking to fellows I had known most of my life, who had just come home from the war, too.

Mug mentioned two of his cousins who had been killed, and how it had affected their mothers and fathers; and Roy mentioned some Italian boys I had known long ago who had been killed, and a boy who was a mess from injuries to his head and spine, who probably wouldn't ever escape from the Army hospitals.

One thing led to another and then Roy Coulpa remembered Hawk Harrap.

"Hawk beat the draft," Roy said, "and as far as I'm concerned I'm glad he did. It would have been silly for a guy like Hawk to go through all that chicken, or get himself messed up by a lot of complicated injuries. He's got a half-interest in The Wink, a little bar on Broadway, but he's not there very much. He drives to Hollywood or Frisco or Reno or Las Vegas and has fun the same as ever. I ran into him in the bar about a month ago. Well, you know Hawk. He winks and takes care of himself. He was behind the bar but not in a white coat. He came out and sat down and we threw the bull a couple of hours. When I asked him how he had managed to beat the draft, a professional fighter three years, six feet one, two hundred pounds—well, maybe you remember the way he always was, even if you haven't seen him in ten or fifteen years. Swift and serious, but you always know he's laughing inside.

"'Roy,' Hawk said, 'you know the time to make money is when there's a war going on. That's no time to be saying yes sir and no sir.'

"Well, *somebody* made a lot of money out of the war," Roy went on. "I know Hawk didn't make it *all*, but I'm glad he made *some* of it."

Roy Coulpa told a half dozen stories about Hawk Harrap, and then he told this one which he got from Hawk himself:

Immediately after the war, Hawk took to walking around Hollywood with a cane, a discharge button in his lapel, and a gentle, thankful look in his eyes. He limped into the best places and reluctantly told stories to beautiful girls about his fighting in the Solomon Islands, in Casablanca, in Anzio, in Normandy—in the infantry, in the engineers, in the Navy, in the Marines.

Sometimes he would limp with his right leg, sometimes with his left. Sometimes he would shake all over and apologize and ask somebody for atabrine and accept another Scotch-over-ice instead and calm down and apologize some more and say he would be all right soon—sixty or seventy more attacks and he would be finished with malaria.

Sometimes he would have twitches in his face and ask a beautiful girl who had just mentioned her brother, named Jim, to please never, never mention that name in his presence again, and twitch some more and shake his head and shut up like a clam, trying to be mysterious; and then he would try to control himself enough to hint to her why he could not bear to hear that name, what had happened to his best pal, Jim Sooney, in the break-through at Bastogne.

Well, Jim Sooney and Hawk were old friends from O Street. Jim was Assyrian, not Syrian, but they were good friends just the same.

Jim and Hawk bought a hundred acres of good land in Reedley during the war and made a lot of money growing and shipping fruit and vegetables.

There was a pretty good farmhouse on the land to which Hawk sometimes invited friends for an all-night game of stud, and one Saturday night after the war he was there at sundown, waiting for the boys to arrive. All over the land watermelons were ripening, and he enjoyed seeing them. When it was night, around eight, Hawk was sitting in the rocking chair on the front porch of the farmhouse breathing the good air when three cars stopped on the road beside his watermelon patch, and out of the automobiles eleven boys and men fell on Hawk's watermelons. Hawk watched them a few minutes and then went into the shack and got the rifle off the wall. He strolled down the dirt road of his land and took everybody by surprise.

He said he was just back from Germany where he had almost lost his respect for mankind, and now that he'd come home and was trying to earn an honest dollar, here they were, showing their appreciation for all the private sacrifices he had made in helping to win the war and save civilization. Here they were, stealing his watermelons, taking bread out of the mouths of his children. He warned everybody to follow his instructions and not try to run, or he would shoot to kill. He had gone through a lot in Germany. He had been taught to kill, and he could easily kill every one of them. He counted the watermelon stealers over and over again, saying in a kind of madness, "One, two, three, four, five, six, seven, eight, nine, ten, eleven—almost a dozen. I killed twenty-seven Germans with a machine-gun once, and they hadn't done anything to me at all. Now, every one of you, lie down according to size, on this road."

A number of the watermelon stealers had recently been discharged from the Army and told Hawk so. He asked them not to provoke him. He hadn't made up his mind what he was going to do with them just yet, and he didn't want to be provoked into making an unfair decision.

Everybody stretched out in the road, and Hawk asked them to count off, which they did, or tried to do. The younger boys, twelve years old or so, were crying now.

Hawk said, "I wish I knew what to do. I must ask God for guidance. I don't want blood on my hands if it's not His will."

Somebody said, "It's not His will."

"We're not sure about that yet," Hawk said. "We're only poor ignorant misguided human beings. God brought me home from Germany. He will answer my prayer."

So then Hawk prayed.

"O God," he said, "these boys and men have come to steal my watermelons and I've caught them with their pants down. As you know, I served faithfully at Anzio, Normandy and Bastogne, suffering terrible embarrassment and being underpaid. Now that I have come home at last to my wife and five children, these men have come to take the bread out of their mouths. I have caught them, and I must do my duty. O God, please tell me what my duty is. Amen."

After a minute of silence Hawk said, "I thank you, O God."

A man lying on his belly in the dirt turned his head and said, "What did God say?"

"He said my duty is to kill every one of you, and I'm sorry, I must do my duty. I expect you to die like men and boys. Let the first volunteer stand at attention. I promise him a painless death."

Nobody moved to volunteer and the smaller boys wept harder than ever and begged for mercy. Finally, the boldest man got to his knees so that Hawk wouldn't take him for a volunteer and said, "For God's sake, man, I was at Bastogne myself. We'll pay for the watermelons, but don't do this crazy thing."

"Don't provoke me," Hawk said, "or I'll shoot you on your knees."

Now, Jim Sooney and four others stopped their car in the road and got out to see what foolishness Hawk was up to this time.

The man on his knees appealed to Jimmy Sooney and the others, but Hawk ordered the man to fall on his belly, which he did.

Hawk badgered the watermelon stealers a half hour, asking each of them to recite his name, his age, his address, his birthplace, his nearest of kin, his religion, blood type, race, amount of insurance carried, favourite movie actress, combat decorations, secret ambitions, and whether he liked apple pie for dessert better than jello. If a man said pie, Hawk said he was sorry for the man: if a man said jello, Hawk said he was afraid the man had made a poor choice. He asked the men to change their religions, and they were all glad to do it.

Finally, because he wanted to go in and start the poker game, Hawk struck a bargain with the watermelon stealers. He said he wanted to hear some good choral singing of hymns. If the group sang well enough to bring tears to his eyes, he would turn them free. He ordered everybody to kneel and sing, but the men couldn't think of one single hymn to sing.

At last one of the small boys began to sing, "Nearer, my God, to Thee," and the others tried to join in.

"It's not that the hymn isn't heartbreaking," Hawk said. "It's your lousy singing. Try another hymn."

The boy who seemed to know a hymn or two began to sing "I Love Life," but Hawk cut him short, saying that that was not a hymn at all but a dirty semi-classical number. The boy thought a moment and tried again. "When the Roll is Called Up Yonder," he sang, and the others tried to join in, but when the choral singing broke to pieces and the little boy tried to save them all by sobbing through the whole song alone and looked eagerly into Hawk's face, Hawk was still unmoved.

"One last chance," Hawk said. "I can give you only one last chance. I shall name a song and you must shout it out with all your might. If you hear me singing with you, then you shall know that I want you all to live. I want you all to go home and live decent, Christian lives. I want you all to sing 'Onward, Christian Soldiers'."

The watermelon stealers began to sing, but Hawk remained silent through three choruses.

At last Hawk began to sing, too, and the men and boys jumped up and ran off to their cars, slipping and falling and slamming doors and driving off.

Then Hawk Harrap and Jim Sooney and their friends went into the farmhouse and started the all-night poker game.

Nobody laughed while Roy Coulpa told the story, and there were tears in his eyes when he stopped talking.

"What's the matter?" Mug Muggerditchian said.

"Nothing," Roy said. "I just feel sorry for those guys."

"Hawk was only having a little fun," Mug said.

"I don't mean the watermelon stealers," Roy said. "I mean the guys in the war."

The Assyrian and Other Short Stories, 1950

The Cornet
Players

The town of Sanger, California, sits serenely around its Court House Park eleven miles east of the city of Fresno (population 65,000). Sanger's population is not great as populations go, a mere 5,332, but it is lively, and in one or two things unique. The town is noted among amateur observers, including the writer, for the alacrity, energy, and earnestness with which it creates and follows trends, for instance.

From 1919 to 1949 a rich variety of trends overwhelmed the population of Sanger, but the trend with which the writer is concerned is the trend of 1939.

This was the cornet-playing trend.

Early in that year a farmer named Khook Jenj gave his eighteen-year-old son a cornet for a birthday present, and this boy, named John, soon revealed that it was not impossible to learn to play the cornet without taking lessons. Of course John had received with the cornet a pamphlet entitled *Cornet Self-Taught* to which during the winter months he had applied himself assiduously, so that early in March his rendering of the song, "It's a Sin to Tell a Lie", was accepted by everyone who heard it, and everyone heard it, for John Jenj frequently stood alone in the Court House Park and played it. As it was well-known from his record at Sanger High School, and from his performances in other trends, that John Jenj was not an exceptional boy in any way, a thought occurred to a great many people of Sanger, and this thought was that they too could learn to play "It's a Sin to Tell a Lie" on the cornet.

Thus, the trend came into being.

One day in April as John stood in the Court House Park playing the song, he was joined by a boy of eleven playing the same song equally effectively on a second-hand cornet.

This boy's name was Peter Garifiola, although he was generally known as Pete or Petey Boy. John Jenj was a little scornful at first of Petey Boy's presumption, but after a while he condescended to chat with him about the art of playing the cornet, and a week later when Pete demonstrated unmistakably that he could do a thing or two on the horn that probably had never before been done by anybody in the world, John Jenj wisely decided to accept Pete as his partner.

They gave themselves the professional name of *Jenj and Garifiola, Cornetists Par Excellence, Suitable for Picnics, Weddings, and Funerals, Telephone Sanger 33 Ring 5.*

Sanger 33 ring 5 was the Jenj family telephone. Whenever John was at home and the telephone bell happened to ring five times he would lift the receiver and in a very business-like tone of voice say, *Jenj and Garifiola.* Now, it happened that the Garifiola family's telephone was on the same line, ring 7, so that if the ring happened to be either 5 or 7 and both boys happpened to be at home, both boys would get on the line. If the ring was 5, Petey Boy would listen to John Jenj, to see if it was a job to play at a wedding or a funeral, and if the ring was 7, John Jenj would listen to Pete. At the same time, everybody else on the line would listen, so that if it was actually an assignment very nearly the whole town would know about it.

Their fee to play was a dollar apiece, with refreshments provided by the client according to his personal inclination.

Jenj and Garifiola played "It's a Sin to Tell a Lie" at the wedding of Alice Mendoza to Ifton Slake, a part-Indian and they made the marriage more memorable than anyone had imagined might be likely. They played the song eleven times. They played it at the church with what they called "the religious feeling," and riding in the truck from the church to the house in which Ifton Slake lived on Sam Bogley's vineyard they played it with what they called "the rollicking, devil-may-care feeling." Jenj and Garifiola, in fact, had eleven accurately identified feelings with which they could play the song. After using up these eleven feelings, they reverted to a favourite feeling, or played the song with requested feelings.

They played the song with "the funeral march feeling," for instance, as they led the procession four blocks from the church to the graveyard when Eva Flange, aged three days, passed away, bringing the number of feelings up to a grand total of twelve.

In the meantime, the trend had acquired momentum, and competition was great. There had come into existence by the first of August a dozen more teams of cornetists, including a father and son, a mother and daughter, a husband and wife, a brother and sister, full brothers, stepbrothers, a full-blooded Tule Indian in costume and a real East Indian in turban, and two or three other odd combinations. Each team was in business in earnest. Each team handed out cards to the people in the streets or distributed descriptive pamphlets to every house in town as well as to a great many farm houses. Each team had at least one telephone number. And the free concerts in the Court House Park started early in the morning and continued late into the night.

Business for Jenj and Garifiola fell off a little with so much competition, but the boys were on their toes and they could always be counted on to offer—and what's more deliver—something extra, something no other team could offer. They were the avant garde of the cornet-playing trend, and the others were imitators. Still, some of the imitators were quick to pick up an innovation and perhaps improve or extend it, so that Jenj and Garifiola had to have a reserve of ideas.

The printing of new cards and pamphlets became so necessary a part of the business that they sent away to Chicago for a very simple press, and unlike their competitors did not limit their ink to black but used red and green as well, and finally blue. They also went in for pamphlets that told a story: how and when the team had come into being; how many hours per day they played; how many occasions they had played for; the names and addresses of satisfied customers; and the actual spoken or written remarks of many well-known people in Sanger who had heard them:

"You boys certainly brought something to Sanger nobody ever thought," Mr. Ed Hurling, assistant manager of Apperson's Notion Store, 909 Broadway.

"I could listen to Jenj and Garifiola the rest of my life," Mrs. Emma Stain, fancy laundry work, 307 Malaga Avenue, telehone 44 ring 4.

"Marvellous is the word for Jenj and Garifiola's cornet wizardry and musical statesmanship," Mr. Arthur F. Frogging, coloured, Ace Shoe Shine Parlour, next door to the Post Office, across the street from the Court House Park, the best shine in Sanger at any cost.

"I want Jenj and Garifiola to play at my funeral," Miss Constance Askler, plain housework at reasonable prices, cleaning, cooking, minor carpentry or gardening, families only, no bachelors, 411 Alberta Street, telephone 51, ring 2, make a note of it and put it by your telephone: 51 ring 2.

And so on.

Of course the boys solicited these testimonials in a friendly, co-operative manner, playing in front of the testifier's home or place of business, or directly in front of him or her in the street, and attracting a crowd.

Jenj and Garifiola, once they got going in earnest—which was early in May before the competition got tough—began to make a modest living through their art, earning frequently as much as eighteen dollars apiece a week; and one week during which there were a great many burials, weddings, and a wide variety of other occasions requiring cornet-playing they earned twenty-two dollars apiece. At the same time they kept learning more and more about what could be done in the cornet-playing business, and finally Peter Garifiola evolved what he generously called "The Jenj and Garifiola cornet-playing style."

This consisted of a rather tricky employment of John Jenj's cornet as any number of other instruments—the violin, the clarinet, the saxophone, the tuba, the flute, the drum, and so on—while Peter Garifiola exploited the melody. Still, not satisfied with this strange but effective innovation, the team worked out an even more clever idea: the employment of the human voice, generally in which might best be identified as the shout, as counterpoint to the melody. In this case, determined to be fair and square through and through, the partners agreed that John Jenj should play the melody and Peter Garifiola do the shouting.

This was very nearly their most magnificent achievement, and it impressed everybody in town the first time it was tried. That was in the middle of May, as the smell of summer was coming back to Sanger, and it happened at half past nine at night when everybody still alive somehow felt like shouting too. The song was still "It's a Sin to Tell a Lie", but Peter Garifiola's shouting was creative, so that a half dozen people gave the team a brand new idea by asking, "What's the name of *that* song?"

Without thinking, and knowing little about patent infringements or copyright laws, Peter Garifiola stopped shouting to say, "The Jenj and Garifiola Special."

"The Jenj and Garifiola Special" was frequently in demand thereafter, and one thing leading to another, John Jenj, with the full support and assistance of his partner of course—who had grown considerably in the meantime—took up composing, and in only three hours of a warm afternoon came forward with a ballad, "Sanger, Sanger, Heaven on Earth."

This song caught hold like wildfire and was soon being played and sung by the immitators. The melody was the melody of "It's a Sin to Tell a Lie" of course, rendered, however, in the Jenj and Garifiola style, but with something new added: *the hymn-quality*, for some of the words of the song had to do with a man's going away from Sanger, or *thinking* of doing so, and then feeling bitterly sorry that he ever did, or thought of doing, such a foolish thing.

The actual lines were:
> *When next you hear of me,*
> *In old New York I'll be,*
> *Alone and far from thee,*
> *Sanger, my heaven on earth.*

Children, who are deeply moved by these notions of far travel, upon hearing the song, invariably wept.

The beginning of World War II somewhat coincided with the cornet-playing business of Sanger when it was at its peak, but it was not the beginning of the war that put the business out of commission, it was the experience John Jenj had in concert, so to say, out of town, in Fresno, the evening of the first Sunday in October.

This came about as follows:

News of the cornet-playing fever spread from Sanger to the still smaller towns nearby, and then it reached the city of Fresno itself. *The Bee* decided to have a reporter pay a visit to Sanger and get to the bottom of the trend. This man, recently graduated from the College in Fresno and planning to write a novel at the next opportunity, had a touch of the poet in him. His name was Wallace Asfanasia, and he was nothing if not earnest in his ambition to find material for writing at home in Fresno rather than in the Latin Quarter of Paris. Wallace was a hard-working reporter but as he was paid by the line and as he was willing to work on speculation, the story of the Sanger cornet-playing trend was offered to him because it was cheaper that way. He would have to gamble on whether or not the managing editor of *The Bee* would want to use his story, and of course he would be required to pay his travelling and food expenses out of his own pocket. He was given carte blanche, however, to write the story any way that pleased him, and to make it as long as he cared to.

One entire day in Sanger was not enough for Wallace Asfanasia, however, so he went back to the town five days in a row, talking to John Jenj and Peter Garifiola, hearing them play, listening to Jenj's own ballad about Sanger, and asking them all kinds of questions. Some of these questions had to do with the cornet, with the cornet-playing business, with music in general, with the Jenj and Garifiola conception of music, and every now and then the questions had to do with what was happening in Europe. Jenj, older and more reserved than his partner, modestly answered the question about what was happening in Europe by admitting that he was not abreast of anything outside the musical world; but Peter Garifiola, younger and more confident about all things, said he didn't care what happened in Europe; Europe's affairs were Europe's affairs, and if the people of Europe would rather kill each other than take up art and music, well, that was no skin off his elbow.

"Do you think America will be drawn into the war?" Wallace Asfanasia asked the team, and Petey Boy said, "No. What the hell for?"

Two years later Wallace's conscription number was one of the first to come up, and the novel he was working on at the time was interrupted for five years. Hence, it may be presumed that he'd had a feeling all along that America was going to get into the war, and as it turned out his feeling was right.

After interviewing and listening to Jenj and Garifiola, the reporter moved on to their competitors, so that the trend would be thoroughly understood.

It was.

And Wallace Asfanasia made it perfectly clear in the brilliant story he wrote about it for *The Sunday Bee*. The piece was spread over two pages of the magazine section, and quite understandably concerned itself mainly with the creators of the trend, John Jenj and Peter Garifiola.

"In Europe," Wallace Asfanasia concluded his story, "the common people are not permitted by corrupt and selfish politicians and political systems to express themselves artistically, but in America they are. And only eleven miles from Fresno, the good people of Sanger—most of them from roots in Germany, Italy, France, Denmark, Finland, Greece, Syria, Armenia, Egypt, and Portugal, as well as a sprinkling of native American Indian stock—are a living demonstration of the power of democracy to guide the energies of the masses into expressive and creative channels. More power to you in the arts, Sanger! And more power to the leading lights of this musical renaissance, Jenj and Garifiola, the first a first-generation Syrian, the other a first-generation Italian! May our country never forget them, in war or peace!"

The story was a sensation and Wallace Asfanasia's name as a reporter with poetic undertones was instantaneously established. In addition to this, which was not his intention in the first place—largely he hoped America would not go to war and he felt his story might help America keep out of war—a great many Sunday pleasure-drivers motored out to Sanger that very Sunday, parked their cars, and got out to listen to Jenj and Garifiola, as well as to some of their imitators and competitors.

Among these travellers was the leader of the summer Sunday afternoon band concerts in Roeding Park, in Fresno, a Finn with a real musical education whose name was Lars Harling. This man immediately sought out the famous team and, having been deeply moved by the sweep of Asfanasia's story and believing it was the generous thing to do, invited the team to appear as soloists at the open-air concert the following Sunday.

"You boys will be paid five dollars apiece," Mr. Harling told the boys, "but you will be expected to take care of transportation, lodging and food."

Jenj and Garifiola accepted the offer and Mr. Harling drove back to Fresno just in time to lead that afternoon's band concert. *The Bee* was info. .ned by Mr. Harling himself of what he had done to encourage the Sanger cornet-players, and variations of the invitation appeared in every issue of the paper the following week.

Wallace Asfanasia wrote an inspiring editorial about Mr. Harling's act, but the managing editor could not break the rule of not having editorials run with a by-line. Still, a number of astute people guessed that the author of the editorial was Wallace, but he wasn't after glory. All he wanted was for this sort of thing to get the same kind of attention as embezzling, bribery, fire, rape and murder, and for America to stay out of the war. He did his share and then some, but of course it wasn't quite enough, and his sense of personal failure harassed him considerably all the years he spent in Australia and the Islands of the Pacific.

As for Sanger itself, the town was beside itself with pride, even though Sanger had been acclaimed for its illustrious sons at the height of the fruit-picking-and-packing season when ordinarly nobody had any time for anything except work. Time was somehow found by the people of Sanger to take pride in themselves, however, and everybody felt that this invitation for Jenj and Garifiola to appear with The Fresno Band was only the beginning of much greater things for them. Only a handful of people were going to be able to travel to Fresno and attend the concert, but the good wishes of everybody—busy working that Sunday in the vineyards and orchards and in the packing-houses—would go with the boys.

The excitement grew day by day, but no one's excitement equalled Peter Garifiola's. In the end it got out of hand and turned to pneumonia, and a serious problem arose.

Should John Jenj appear at the concert alone? Should he postpone the event until Peter Garifiola recuperated? Or should he select another partner from among the many other cornet stylists of Sanger?

Opinions varied of course, and Wallace Asfanasia, having gotten wind of Peter's illness, rushed to the boy's bedside and interviewed him. Sick as he was, Peter Garifiola said the people of Europe could kill each other all they wanted to; the American way of life was not like that.

The reporter then talked to John Jenj who was rather unreasonable about the whole thing, almost implying that Peter Garifiola had gotten cold feet and come down with pneumonia on purpose.

"I think I'll go it solo," John Jenj said, and this was mentioned in the reporter's Sunday morning story in *The Bee*.

"Unwilling to let Sanger down," Wallace Asfanasia wrote, "John Jenj stood as straight as he does when he plays the cornet, and he said, 'God willing, I'll do the best I can alone'."

By now the cornet-playing business of Sanger, California was swiftly deteriorating, although no one suspected it at the time.

The concert began on schedule at half-past two that Sunday afternoon with John Jenj occupying the guest soloist's chair on the bandstand, a cane and rattan chair of the same quality occupied by each of the other musicians. John was neatly dressed and reasonably calm. The concert had attracted an unusually large crowd which was spread out on the lawn, under the shade trees, most of them young men and women with nothing better to do than fool around. The day was hot, serene and peaceful, and to Wallace Asfanasia, sitting beside John Jenj on the bandstand, the war in Europe seemed far away indeed. The concert moved gracefully through the first three numbers, and then it was time at last for John Jenj to be introduced.

Wallace Asfanasia stepped to the front of the bandstand to introduce him. He said some things that brought tears to John's eyes, but these things didn't do anything like that to anybody stretched out on the lawn, or to any of the musicians on the bandstand. What it did to the musicians was make them bring funny papers out of their pockets which they began to read. What it did to the people lying around on the lawn was make them laugh out loud. But Wallace went right ahead with the speech he had prepared.

Some of the musicians began to whistle softly about some of Wallace's remarks about John Jenj. Still, Wallace knew he was right, so he went ahead fearlessly with his speech, talking better than he had talked when he had been valedictorian for the graduating class at Fresno High School in 1933, and still more tears came to John Jenj's eyes.

Now, however, a number of the young men who had nothing better to do than fool around on a Sunday afternoon at a serious band concert, began to make noises at Wallace Asfanasia, and John Jenj began to feel a little angry.

One thing about fellows from Sanger, they didn't take that kind of stuff from anybody anywhere, let alone an artist from Sanger who had been hired at considerable expense to apear with the band.

The next thing John Jenj knew almost every young man lying on the lawn was making vulgar noises, and they were making them loudly. As he talked on, Wallace Asfanasia reasoned that these noises were the direct consequence of the let-down of moral values in every part of the world when a major war begins. He felt sympathy rather than anger toward the makers of the noises. It was not their fault. Most of them probably felt, as he did, that pretty soon they *might* be in the army and in the war, and even if their apprehensions proved to be unfounded, as Wallace certainly felt at that time they would be, the young men could not be blamed for letting off a little steam. It was American to do that, and Wallace was all for it, in a way.

But John Jenj, about whom Wallace Asfanasia was now desperately trying to get an eloquent word in edgewise, did not feel so charitable about the rudeness of the young men and young women who were making the vulgar noies.

No fellow from Sanger took that kind of stuff from anybody anywhere, that's all.

Now, to make matters worse, the young men stopped making vulgar noises and began to *shout* at Wallace Asfanasia.

"Come on, come on, let the hick play his solo and sit down."

John Jenj heard this remark very clearly, and then he refused to take any more of it. He jumped to his feet and stepped forward. He was holding his cornet, and Lars Harling, who had been half-asleep in his chair, jumped to his feet, too, under the impression that John was ready to render his solo. He rattled his baton on the tin music stand and all the musicians in the band dropped their funny papers and got all set with their musical instruments, to be ready to go with "It's a Sin to Tell a Lie" when Lars gave them the sign.

But John Jenj didn't lift the horn to his lips. Instead he began to shout back at the young men and young women lying around on the lawn under the shade trees fooling around in the afternoon.

"We don't take that kind of stuff in Sanger," John shouted.

The young men and women laughed and shouted back at him.

"We just don't take that kind of stuff where I come from," John shouted.

Lars Harling rattled the tin music stand again, hoping to get John set for the solo, but John just didn't take that kind of stuff.

As the matter got out of hand, Wallace Asfanasia made his way to the edge of the platform, jumped down, and wandered off to a tree near which no one was lying, and from this point in the park he watched and listened to John Jenj and the people who had come to the band concert.

The worst of it was that even adults, husbands and wives with kids, were not in sympathy with John. Their kids weren't, either. Everybody was completely in accord with the young men and young women who were heckling John Jenj.

"People like you," John shouted, "ain't going to hear *me* play the cornet. I'll go back to Sanger where people appreciate music."

"Get going, get going!" the crowd shouted back at John Jenj.

Wallace Asfanasia decided to walk through the park and think about the novel he was going to start writing just as soon as he was sure he had gathered together enough material for something major rather than something minor. He walked swiftly for a young man with an ambition like that, and a fellow lying on the lawn remarked to his girl, "That guy looks like he's in a walking race, don't he?"

Wallace didn't know it at the time but he had literally turned his back on the people, and he had always believed that that was something he would never do. He had gone about two hundred yards when the shouting and laughing became louder than ever, and he believed he heard John Jenj's voice above all the others saying, "In Sanger we don't take that kind of stuff."

But now John's voice was more like a scream, and it occurred to

Wallace Asfanasia that in all probability John had leaped down from the bandstand and was using his cornet as a weapon, but probably not effectively.

Then the band began to play "It's a Sin to Tell a Lie," and without intending to do so Wallace Asfanasia began to say the words of the song to himself, although he was not by any means singing. Strange words they were, too, very strange indeed, and in some way connected with the war in Europe, no doubt.

Thus it was that the cornet-playing trend of Sanger came to an end, and was swiftly supplanted by a trend not nearly so local: a trend much more popular but not very much more reasonable than the cornet-playing one, but one the writer need not go into in detail, since so many others have already done so.

The Assyrian and Other Stories, 1950

Every Man is
a Good Man
in a Bad World
(Rock Wagram)

*E*very man is a good man in a bad world. No man changes the world. Every man himself changes from good to bad or from bad to good, back and forth, all his life, and then dies. But no matter how or why or when a man changes, he remains a good man in a bad world; as he himself knows. All his life a man fights death, and then at last loses the fight, always having known he would. Loneliness is every man's portion, and failure. The man who seeks to escape from loneliness is a lunatic. The man who does not know that all is failure is a fool. The man who does not laugh at these things is a bore. But the lunatic is a good man, and so is the fool, and so is the bore, as each of them knows. Every man is innocent, and in the end a lonely lunatic, a lonely fool, or a lonely bore.

But there is meaning to a man. There is meaning to the life every man lives. It is a secret meaning, and pathetic were it not for the lies of art, for which every man must be grateful, as he himself knows. For the lies tell him to wait. They tell him to hang on. The lies wink and tell him he is the one, and a man winks back, and goes about his business.

ᗡC

No man's life means more than another's, as each man himself knows. The luckiest man is the one who enjoys his portion, but no man is very lucky, for every man's portion is equally poor, and putting up with it is painful. Most of his experience cannot be enjoyed. Most of it hurts, and some of it kills, or inflicts the wound that stops him in his tracks.

Every man is an animal. He is the animal all men are, but after that he is also his own kind of animal. He is a small and lonely thing, not unlike all of his breed, all alive at the same time.

He is his own poor friend, his own proud stranger, his own cunning enemy, watching with sharp eyes his mother's own son, and he knows more than he is ever able to tell. Whatever the acts of his life, his own cunning friend and his own forgiving enemy watches and mocks or comforts him, and a man lives out his time in secret, leaving behind no word of what he was or did or knew. Or leaving half a word, mixed with laughter, or half an act of dancing mixed with love, in the warm light, along the bright floor of his own mother's kitchen when he was five and she was his girl, baking bread for him.

)C

A man lives his life in ignorance, never knowing the true meaning of any experience, never knowing the great truth about himself. He lives all of his life instantly every minute he is up and abroad, doing, or down and out of his bed, asleep, or turning in sleeplessness, or standing alone in nightmare. A man is suddenly instantaneously alive and out of touch with a secret. He is suddenly an instantaneous thing, and he does not stop being this thing until he is in touch again with the lost secret, and then it is that a man is dead. As long as he lives a man seeks the instantaneous woman, hoping to find in her the everlasting secret. But the man and the woman together do not find the secret. Even if they become father and mother of son and daughter, they do not find the secret, they are not healed of their loneliness, and they see their son instantaneously himself and alone, and their daughter also. A man's own are not his own, for a man himself does not belong to his own instantaneous self. His wife is not his own, nor is his son his own, nor his daughter.

In an instant a man is, in an instant he is not. He never knew who he was. The nearer he came to finding out, the more hopeless finding out became.

)C

No man cares about anyone but himself. No man loves anyone but himself. A woman is grateful to the man who plunges her into a passion for herself, and so it is with a man. Together they come to fine or ferocious feelings about themselves, and call it love. But it is only another way for them to forget for a moment the nagging truth that it is meaningless to live.

)C

Every man is a liar, a crook, a hoodlum, or a bore, and yet no man is any of these things on purpose, or eagerly, or especially, or to the exclusion of other and perhaps nicer things, and he is innocent. A man is a liar by accident. The more intense his search for truth the more apt he is to become a bigger liar than ever. He is a crook by accident, too, receiving, for instance, when he gives. He is a thief who does not know when he has stolen, or from whom, or what. His cheating is unknown to him, whether he cheats others or himself.

A man is a man by accident. He might have been an ape.

But a man hangs on to his illusion, living and dying a lie that must amuse worms. A man seizes his portion, however paltry it is, and jumps for joy.

Yes, he says, this is truly myself. I have all this hair and all these teeth. Yes, this is the one I am, and how unfortunate are the others with so much less.

But a man also laughs at his vanity, and winks at his death.

)C

A man is forever involved in a dream of cities, money, love, danger, oceans, ships, railroads, and highways. But in all of his sleep, in all of his travel, a man knows his true destination. He knows everywhere else he goes is a detour. But a man cherishes his detours, for they take time.

)C

A man and his friends are liars to one another. They are friends only of one another's best. Let one among them show his worst, and the e truth, friends are gone. Let one among them speak the truth, and and the the others are gone. Let one among them ask of another thothers will be gone. For a man lives for himself, and is righteous in this. The man who goes abroad to do good unto others also lives for himself, and is righteous in this, and a liar. So it is with the man who goes abroad to do mischief. He, too, is righteous, and a liar. A man is not a guilty thing, he is an innocent thing, as he himself knows.

)C

A man himself is junk, and all his life he clutters the earth with it. He carries junk around with him wherever he goes, and wherever he stops he accumulates it. He lives in it. He loves it. He worships it. He collects it and stands guard over it.

)C

All his life everything a man does he seems to have done before. He is forever kissing the same mouth, embracing the same woman, looking into the same eyes which will not yield their secret.

Is a man himself therefore or is he the race itself? Is every woman her own race, but never herself? Each woman the same but older now, or younger, weeping now and desolate, or laughing and contemptuous of desolation?

A man wears the same face all his life, but sees a stranger every time he shaves. He inhabits the same body all his life, but himself is never the same in it. Everywhere he goes is a place he knows and does not know, home and nowhere, his own place and nobody's at all.

He comes to birth and goes to death. He comes to desire and goes to despair. For every man is too much for himself. Every man is too many men to contain and control, as he himself knows.

✷

A man thinks he wants one thing but actually wants another, or wants both, or wants neither but can't think of something else to want, or is too young to stop wanting at all, or too old, or too far from a particular place he thinks he longs for, or his liver's enlarged, or his bile isn't flowing properly, or his intestines are clogged, or his heart is murmuring, or cancer's gotten a start somewhere, or the tissues of his brain are deteriorating, something else mysterious and unaccountable is happening to him.

He thinks he wants a watermelon to eat in the evening, but what he really wants is to feel as alive as he once felt when he ate a watermelon in the evening. He thinks he wants shoes, but what he really wants is to be admired. Or he thinks he doesn't want to be admired. He thinks he wants to be left alone, so he can keep his unhappiness to himself, but by the time he is alone, it's no longer to keep his unhappiness to himself, it's because he's gotten used to wanting to be alone and now wants to keep his happiness (which used to be his unhappiness) to himself.

He thinks he knows when he's happy and when he's not happy, but he never knows, because most of the time he's bored when he's happy and bored when he's unhappy, and he doesn't want to be bored. But if he stopped being bored and thought he wanted to be something else, he would be mistaken. He wouldn't want to be something else at all.

A man simply doesn't know. He doesn't know anything. A man simply does not live, he is *lived,* and not simply. He is lived foolishly and in everlasting indefiniteness and confusion. He is lived as a tiger is, or a shark, or a hawk, or he is lived as each thing that lives is lived, by turns, now a tiger, now a hawk. Still, he is always a man, a thing in shoes, a better worshipper of shoes than of God, a pale hairless thing of anxious ill-health, made of poisons and dreams, quivering fear and roistering delusions.

Ho for tomorrow! is the cry of his heart, or, Ah for yesterday! *Now* is always his time of pain, torment, and torture.

Today is the terrible time. This moment is hell. He is an

instantaneous thing which liveth in the insect's instant, an instant at a time until it is the last instant and the loneliest. Ho for tomorrow! but tomorrow never comes. Ah for yesterday! but yesterday is always gone and always a lie. He is a son of a bitch, whoever he is, and the name of his family is no help. He is a born crook, and the calling he follows is no help. But every one of him is innocent, as he himself knows. Everyone of him is alone in his innocence. Every one of him is righteous. For a moment at a time, every one of him is a comedian and maketh the others to laugh. That moment is the best he knows. The comic's moment is a man's greatest moment. When he maketh to laugh, a man is his own knows. and a hell of a fellow.

ᗄC

A man is nonsense all his life, the impractical joke of unknown enemies and beloved friends, a fraud who only now and then suspects. He *would* be different, but truth will not permit it. He feeds his soul on the smiles of other for themselves, which he believes are for himself. He decorates it with shoes, hats, ties, shirts, trousers, jackets. He comforts it with numbers: numbers of money, numbers of women loved, numbers of friends, good things done, good times known, schedules effectively kept, accidents with pleasure in them. He asks his soul to be thankful for him, for having provided it with so much, so much more than it might have received, so much more than any other man in the world ever gave his soul. He carries his gifts and his losses to his soul and asks that they be noticed, cherished, treasured. He goes into the arena where his soul lies like a tiger to amaze it with his fearlessness and love. He goes as a child, a boy, a man, astonishing and loving. Or he is rude to his soul, passing it in a crowd and not even nodding. He is a lifetime joke, his borrowed soul a patient witness, but *also* a joke. He is nonsense, as he himself knows. His soul is nonsense, as he himself knows.

ᗄC

Every man is afraid. He is afraid of many things or of everything, but in the end they are all himself, as he himself knows. A man is afraid all his life, for everyman is death given a face, eyes, ears, nose, mouth, body, and limbs, and every man is death given life, as he himself knows.

ᗄC

There is meaning to a man. There is meaning to the life every man lives. It is a secret meaning, but it is also simple and silly. It is something like this:

God knows I am nothing. Something winks and I am born. Something winks and I am dead.

A man builds a house and something winks. He finds a wife and something winks. A son is born to the man and his wife and something winks.

It is also something like this:

I didn't know any better, but I knew something was always winking. I never tried, but at the same time I never let things happen by themselves, either, and something always winked. When I did poorly, something winked, and when I did well, something winked. When I did nothing or thought I did nothing, something winked. When I winked, something winked backed. I winked every day and something winked back, I winked at my ignorance and something winked back. I winked at my hope and something winked back. I stopped winking and prayed, but still something winked back.

A man is meanings which come to nothing because something winks. A man who does not know that something is forever winking is a fool. A man who does not wink is a fool. But every man is a good man in a bad world, living his meaning alone, and winking, or being winked.

A man's secret meaning is something like this:

Last night I knew something I do not know this morning. This morning I knew something I do not know this afternoon. This afternoon I knew something I do not know tonight. Tonight I know nothing and something winks. Last year I knew something I do not know this year. The year before last I knew something I did not know last year. I do not know what it was I knew last night or last year, but I know I am dying, and I know something winks.

A man's secret is something like this:

I am mud that winks. I am weeds that wink. I am glue that winks.

A man's name is a wink. A man's fame is a wink. The life of a man is a circle made of winks. A wink is a smile going in a circle, from nothing to nothing. A wink swallows a man and his winking, his start and his finish. It swallows everything in the laughing circle. A wink is nothing. It is an eye circling around what it sees, bringing it to a laughing end. A man puts on his hat and the hat winks. It winks at the ceiling, the ceiling winks at the window, the window at the sun, the sun at the stars, the stars at one another. Time winks at space and space winks at light. The tree winks at the bird, the bird at the cat, the cat at the dog, the dog at the horse, the horse at the cow, the cow at the hen, the hen at the cock, the cock stamps on the hen and winks, then crows. The sand of the desert winks at the horned-toad, the horned-toad at the cactus blossom, the blossom at the sun, the sun at the moon, the moon at the vine, the vine at grapes, the grapes at wine. Numbers wink at symbols, symbols at measures, measures at music, music at statues, statues at men, and men at women. Art winks at art, language winks at lies, and lies wink at truth. The truth winks and weeps. It is the only wink that does not laugh. A wink is nothing, but a man is something. What is he?

He is a fool. He is a lunatic. He is a crook. He is a bore. He is a lie winking the truth which weeps. He is a tired lie which is tired of winking and sick of the truth which winks and weeps. A man is a sanitary thing. It is not often that syphillis winks in him. It is not often that rot in his brain winks at what he thinks. For all that, a man has fun winking and dying. He has a time.

⟆C

No man loves anyone but himself, but that is also a lie, as every man knows. Every man loves his own damned son, damned before he's born, damned to live a variation of his own damned father's life, damned to live a winking variation of the damned life every man lives. Every man loves his own damned winking daughter, winking in the eyes of her own damned mother. Every man loves his own damned winking daughter's mother. Every man loves his own damned mother and his daughter's mother and the damned nagging of them to get him to love them, notice them, remember them, and be their damned man.

⟆C

A man's mortality comes to him haphazardly in his mother's womb. His mortality is a disease. It is himself on schedule, in the beat of time. Whether it is pain a man knows or pleasure, his health is poor, for his illness is in him instantaneously and forever, and it is incurable, although every man is indestructible, as he himself knows.

⟆C

Why is a man nonsense all his life? Why is he the impractical joke of unknown enemies or beloved friends? Why is the fellow a fraud? Why does he smile? Why is he forever smiling and looking to be smiled at? Why doesn't he invent a philosophy? Why isn't he the Ambassador to Spain? Why doesn't he compose a symphony so astonishing that midway in it the musicians die of joy? That is a good thing. Why doesn't he evolve a tree that grows a new kind of peach? That would be an honourable thing. Why is he a fool? Why doesn't he go to the capitals of the world and say, One body, one soul, union, fraternity, friendship, accord, trust, and love? That would be a noble thing, would it not? Why is he a joke? Why doesn't he apply himself to his religion and be the salvation of mankind? Why doesn't he go about in his bare feet, his beard full, his eyes shining with love, his mouth and teeth making kind words, his voice as soft as a dove's, his hand a healing hand? Why doesn't he go among the sick and mad, and restore them? Why doesn't he give the old the youth they wasted? That would be better than being a joke, wouldn't it? Why is he smiling all the time, several of his side teeth gone? Wouldn't it be better to help out? Wouldn't it be better to show everybody the foolishness of hatred and cruelty? Wouldn't it be nice to teach everybody to love everybody? Why isn't a man big? Wouldn't it be better to be big? Why doesn't he make a name for himself? Why doesn't he make his name stand for something? Why does he permit his name to stand for nothing?

Why doesn't a man crawl into a cave and scratch the outline of a lion, a bear, or an elephant on the wall? Wouldn't it be nice to be remembered a thousand years for having scratched on the wall of a cave? Why doesn't a man open his mouth and sing, making up a song so comforting as to impel beggars to transfer money from one pocket to another, or businessmen from one bank account to another? Wouldn't that be lyrical? Woudn't it be practical and helpful? Why doesn't a man stop being nonsense and be something his mother can be proud of? Doesn't he love his mother? Why doesn't he say something his father can be happy about? Doesn't he love his father? Why does a man fall in with strangers whose sincerity is dubious? Doesn't he want to be something, make a name for himself in nuclear research, achieve the honour of a philanthropist, or the fame of an elder statesman? Why does he waste his precious time, annoy the hope everyone has put in him? Doesn't he know time lost can never be regained? Hasn't he heard? What's the matter with the boy? Will he never wake up? Will he never come to his senses? Why doesn't he get into high finance and help out that way? Why doesn't he sit down and work out a plan, based on common sense, whereby all people will have steady work in a factory? Why doesn't he think about the discrimination at expensive hotels against minorities? Would it hurt him to have strong feelings against intolerance and injustice? Couldn't he teach manners? Why does he have to be chasing his tail all the time?

Is it a world that dies in a man when a man dies, a world he never knew, never understood, never improved, never inhabited? Is a man, inside his small sack of skin, a whole world once he has fearlessly come out of the womb, fearlessly accepted his head, fearlessly accepted his schedule, winking fearlessly as he goes? Is a man a whirling dervish in his own whirling world and desert? Is he a man or a world? Is he good or is he bad? Is he true or is he false? After he has fearlessly stepped forward among the multitudes of his kind, is he fearlessly among friends and unalone, or is he fearlessly among enemies, incurably alone, but for ever innocent, and for ever indestructible? After he has fearlessly seized his woman and fearlessly loved her, loving mother and father, daughter and son, has he come to meaning? Or is this also nothing? After he has fearlessly loved life, world, beauty, and truth, is a man any closer to anything good than he ever was, than he was in the winking womb?

Every man is afraid of something, but most of all he is afraid of death and disgrace. There are a few moments in the life of any man in which there is no disgrace, and none in which there is no death. The nobler the man is the more aware he is of the disgrace in himself, the nagging absence of grace. The more alive the man is the more aware he is of the death in himself. Everything he is afraid of is himself, as he himself knows, going about his business, which is a business of deathly struggle all his life. But every man is fearless, too. He is afraid of nothing. Having fearlessly emerged from the womb, he is forever after fearless. Having fearlessly accepted his head, he can never again be afraid of anything. Having fearlessly gotten onto his feet and walked, he can go anywhere fearlessly. Having fearlessly looked into the eyes and face of his mother and father, he can for ever after look into the eyes and face of any man or animal. A man is a bold fellow. He is a game fellow. He is a fearless fellow.

ᕩC

A man is a born liar who cannot tell a lie. A man *can* be a decent animal. His friends are meaningless unless they are decent animals. But a man's friends are polite and lying animals, as a man himself knows. There is never a lie in the life of any animal that is worth being told, or any truth that is worth being concealed.

Thus, in the end, a man's best friend is his money, his tobacco, his whisky. A man's best friend is his feet, his hide, and his head. A man's best friend is his own time. His best friend is the sun, the very same which made light and heat for his father, and for his mother: the same that shined on him when he was no older than his son, on whom it shines now. A man is a born liar, born of liars, the father of them, and his best friend is his own animal which cannot lie, but may lie down in the heat of the afternoon, in the shade of a tree, and be there, be a friend there, be alive a moment there, half-asleep and half as if he had been there all the time. A man's own brother cannot be his friend, but a man can be the friend of his poor world and time. There is no truth for a man, there is no friendship for him except the truth of the sun, the friendship of time, his own personal sun, and his own personal time. There is nothing to say of these things. They are there and a man is there, and there's his truth, and there's his friendship.

ᕩC

The only thing a man does all his life is breathe. The instant he inhales he is alive, the instant he exhales but does not inhale he is dead. A man is very nearly everything the first time he inhales, he is very nearly nothing the last time he exhales, but between the first inhale and the last exhale a man is many things, and the things he does are many and strange. A man is a breathing thing. He breathes all the time. No matter what else a man does he also breathes. Breathing's what a man is. He is born to breathe. His life is a life of breathing. A man's appetite for air is everlasting. He stops breathing with violence. A man wants air to breathe, he wants the ability to breathe to stay with him, but in the end, in the time of his own end, every man is denied, he is denied the air he wishes to breathe, he is denied the ability to breathe, he stops breathing, he can laugh no more. Never again can he look at something and see it: at a face and see a face: at a tree and see a tree: at a sky and see a sky: at the sun and see the sun. Never again can he reach out to the things which are and touch them. Never again can he listen and hear: the crying of his infant son, the laughter of his infant daughter, the speech and song of both of them, the whispering at night of his woman. Let him be denied air to breathe and it is never again for him. Let the miracle of breathing be denied him, and though the earth be filled with the scent of water, grass, leaf, blossom, bee, and butterfly, it is never again for him. There will be no more dandruff from his head, no more junk for him to accumulate, no more gadgets to operate. He will make no more debris, he will be debris, he will be the original debris, silver and gold in his dead teeth. Never again will he be a man who could stand on a street corner, look around, and speak to somebody. Never again will he be a king, a commander in chief, a millionaire, a vice-president in charge of production, a philanthropist, a labour leader, a locomotive engineer, a poet, an actor, a convict, a warden, a preacher, a doctor, a dentist, a lawyer, a schoolboy, a son, a brother, a father, a good man, a bad man, a man of truth, a man of honour, a man of dignity, a crook, a deceiver, a sneak, a liar. If he can't breathe, he can't be anything but debris. If he can't breathe, he can't love anyone. He can't get into a car and drive, he can't take a train, he can't get into an airplane, he can't get aboard a ship, he can't ride a bicycle, he can't walk. He can't stand to walk. He can't sit. He can't lie down. He can't sleep, he can't sleep worth a damn any more. His memory fails him. He doesn't seem to remember anything any more. He has no taste for meat or bread or wine or water any more. He doesn't care which pair of shoes he puts on his feet. He doesn't even remember if he had feet. Didn't he go another way than on foot? Worst of all he can't laugh any more. He can't say cat. He can't talk with words and be saying at the same time other things, more loving things, kinder, gentler, more gently wicked than the violent wickedness of literalness. Somthing's happened. He's exhaled and he can't inhale any more. It is the end. It is the end of the world he was. It is the end of being out of touch. That which he knew would happen has happened. A man is dead, he is dirt, he is given a funeral, he is buried, he is no more, and never will he go there.

Rock Wagram, 1951

A Writer's Declaration

On 15th October 1934 my first book, *The Daring Young Man on the Flying Trapeze and Other Stories*, was published. The year 1934 seems quite near, but the fact remains that it was twenty years ago, as I write. Many things happened in those twenty years, several of them to me.

I didn't earn one dollar by any means other than writing. I wrote short stories, plays, novels, essays, poems, book reviews, miscellaneous comment, letters to editors, private letters, and songs.

Nothing that I wrote was written to order, on assignment, or for money, although a good deal of what I wrote happened to earn money. If an editor liked a story as I had written it, he could buy it. If he wanted parts of it written over, I did not do that work. Nobody did it. One editor took liberties with a short piece about Christmas, and the writer of a cook book to which I had written a free Preface added a few lines by way of making me out a soldier-patriot. I protested to the editor and to the writer of the cook book, but of course the damage had been done. During the Second World War I wrote no propaganda of any kind, although I was invited several times to do so. The point is that for twenty years I have been an American writer who has been entirely free and independent.

I consider the past twenty years the first half of my life as a published writer, and the next twenty I consider the second half. At that time I shall be sixty-six years old, which can be very old, or not. I expect to be more creative in the next twenty years than I was in the first twenty, even though I start with a number of handicaps. To begin with, I owe so much in back taxes that it is very nearly impossible arithmetically to even the score by writing, and I have acquired other personal, moral, and financial responsibilities.

I have never been subsidized, I have never accepted money connected with a literary prize or award, I have never been endowed, and I have never received a grant or fellowship. A year or two after my first book was published I was urged by friends to file an application for a Guggenheim Fellowship. Against my better judgment I filed an application, which was necessarily if not deliberately haphazard. How should I know what I wanted to write, for instance? I couldn't possibly describe it. My application was turned down and I began to breathe freely again.

I am head over heals in debt. I expect to get out of debt by writing, or not at all. I have no savings account, no stocks or bonds, no real estate, no insurance, no cash, and no real property that is convertible into anything like a sum of money that might be useful. I simply have got to hustle for a living. I mention these matters impersonally, as facts, and not to arouse sympathy. I don't want any.

Had my nature been practical I might at this time know financial security, as it is called. There is nothing wrong with such security, I suppose, but I prefer another kind. I prefer to recognize the truth that I *must* work, and to believe that I *can*.

I squandered a great deal of money that I earned as a writer and I lost a lot of it gambling. It seems to have been my nature to squander and to gamble, that's all. I gave some away, perhaps a great deal. I am not unaware of the possible meaning of the discomfort I have felt when I have had money, and the compulsion I have had to get rid of it somehow or other. I think I have felt the need to be only a writer, a writing writer, and not a success of any kind.

The ability or compulsion to hoard money has always seemed to me a complicated if not offensive thing. And yet I have always had sympathy for those who have been experts at hoarding, at legal means by which not to pay taxes, at timely thrusts into new and profitable areas of money-making, such as investments, real estate, inventions, oil, uranium, government contracts, the backing of plays, manufacturing, and marketing. The noticeable shrewdness of such people has always amused me, even when I myself have been the party to be outwitted.

When I was in the Army, for instance, in the snow of Ohio, in the dead of winter, a very capable money-man who was quite rich and young and not in the Army flew from New York to Ohio to discuss with me changes he felt I ought to make in one of my plays on which he had paid me a thousand dollars in advance. I met him whenever the Army regulations permitted me to, and I heard him out, which took a great deal of time I would have preferred to keep to myself. The man talked around and around, and it suddenly occurred to me that what he was really trying to say but couldn't was that he didn't feel the play would be a hit, and that he was helpless not to do something about the thousand dollars. This did not astonish me. I took a cheque for a thousand dollars to his hotel and left it at the desk, along with a short note. I wanted to see if my hunch was right. It was. We were supposed to meet the following night. We didn't. He flew back to New York with the cheque, cashed it, and I never heard from him again. There was no legal, or even moral, reason for me to return the thousand dollars. I simply couldn't bear to see him so upset about the small sum of money, all the while pretending that he was concerned only about art.

At one of the biggest moving-picture factories in Hollywood, when I discovered that I had been hoodwinked into making a poor deal, I met the executives who had done the brilliant hoodwinking, I established that they *had* done it, and I got into my car and drove to San Francisco. I was informed several years later that I had left behind wages due me under the terms of the hoodwinking agreement that amounted to something between five and fifteen thousand dollars. I never investigated the matter. The factory and its chief beneficiaries were hoarding profits by the millions, working diligently and profitably with the government on shabby propaganda films, and yet six or seven of the executives found it absolutely necessary to act in unison and to outwit the writer of a story they wanted desperately, from which they acquired three or four more millions of dollars. I have no idea what they have done with their money, but I am sure it has been something cautious and useless.

Before my first book was published I was not a drinker, but soon after it came out I discovered the wisdom of drinking, and I think this is something worth looking into for a moment.

In 1935 I drank moderately, and travelled to Europe for the first time, but the following nine years, until I was drafted into the Army, I drank as much as I liked, and I frequently drank steadily for nine or ten hours at a time.

I was seldom drunk, however. I enjoyed the fun of drinking and talking loudly with friends—writers, painters, sculptors, newspapermen, and the girls and women we knew in San Francisco.

Drinking with good companions can be a good thing for a writer, but let a writer heed this humble and perhaps unnecessary warning: stop drinking when drinking tends to be an end in itself, for that is a useless end. I believe I have learned a lot while I have been drinking with friends, just as most of us may say we have learned a lot in sleep. There is, however, a recognizable limit to what may be learned by means of drinking.

In the writing that I have done during the past twenty years, what do I regret?

Nothing. Not one word.

Did I write enough?

No. No writer ever writes enough.

Might I have written differently? More intelligently, for instance? No.

First, I always tried my best, as I understand trying. Second, I believe I was quite intelligent all the time.

Then, what about the theory of certain critics and readers that my writing is unrealistic and sentimental?

Well, I think they are mistaken. In writing that is *effective* I don't think *anything* is unrealistic. As for my own writing, I think it has always been profoundly realistic if not ever superficially so. I don't think my writing is sentimental either, although it is a very sentimental thing to be a human being.

As I write, I am back in San Francisco, where I lived when my first book was published, where I have not lived in six or seven years, and the day is the thirteenth of October. I drove up from Malibu two days ago for a visit of ten or eleven days while my house on the beach is being painted inside and out. I did not drive to San Francisco in order to be here on the twentieth anniversary of the publication of my first book, but I shall be here on that day nevertheless.

Already I have walked in the various neighborhoods of San Francisco I have known, to notice again the various houses in which I have lived: 348 Carl Street, 1707 Divisadero, 2378 Sutter, 123 Natoma: and the various places in which I worked before I had had a story published in a national magazine: various branch offices of the Postal Telegraph Company—on Market Street in the Palace Hotel Building, on Powell Street at Market, on Taylor at Market in the Golden Gate Theatre Building, and at 405 Brannan, near Third.

I was a clerk and teletype operator in the first three offices, but I was the manager of the office on Brannan. I have always been a little proud of that, for I was the youngest manager of a Postal Telegraph branch office in America, nineteen years old and without a high school diploma.

Yesterday I walked through the Crystal Palace Market and visited the stand at which I once hustled potatoes and tomatoes, the *Fiore d'Italia.*

I went into the building at Market and Sixth where the offices of the Cypress Lawn Cemetery Company are located. I worked there, too.

The vice-president said: "Do you intend to make Cypress Lawn your lifetime career?"

I said: "Yes, sir."

I got the job.

I quit a month later, but working there was a valuable experience. I remember the arrival of Christmas week and the vice-president's bitter complaint that owing to the absence of an epidemic of influenza the company's volume of business for December over the previous year had fallen 22 per cent.

I remarked: "But everybody will catch up eventually, won't they?"

The vice-president lifted his glasses from the bridge of his nose to his forehead in order to have another look at me.

"I'm a writer," I said. "Unpublished."

He asked me to look at some slogans he had composed for the company: *Inter here. A lot for your money.*

I said he had a flair.

I walked along the Embarcadero to the Dodd Warehouse, across from Pier 17, for I worked there a month, too. The trouble with that job was the floating crap games of the longshoremen every lunch hour in empty wagons or behind piles of lumber on the docks. My take-home pay every week was nothing, although I made a friend of the great Negro crapshooter and game manager who was called Doughbelly. The sunlight down there on the waterfront during those lunch-hour crap games was wonderful, and as I walked there yesterday I could almost see the huge old man calling the points of the game, and I had to remember that whenever he noticed I wasn't betting he correctly surmised that I was fresh out of funds and slipped me a silver dollar or two so that I might get back into the action.

Once, when I stayed away from the games for three days running in the hope of having a few dollars in my pocket for Saturday night, Doughbelly kept asking everybody: "Where's that Abyssinian boy?"

I was in the Dodd Warehouse eating sandwiches and reading Jack London, that's where I was.

It was at 348 Carl Street twenty years ago on this day, October 13th, that I opened a package from Random House and saw a copy of my first book. That was a hell of a moment. I was so excited I couldn't roll a Bull Durham cigarette. After three tries I finally made it, and began to inhale and exhale a little madly as I examined the preposterous and very nearly unbelievable object of art and merchandise. What a book, what a cover, what a title page, what words, what a photograph—now just watch the women swarm around. For a young writer *does* write in order to expect pretty women to swarm around.

Alas, the swarmers aren't often pretty. This is a mystery that continues to baffle me. Pretty women swarm around fat little men who own and operate small businesses. They swarm around chiropractors who are full of talk about some of their interesting cases and achievements. They swarm around young men who wear black shirts and have five buttons on the sleeves of their sport coats, who have no visible means of support, who spend hours chatting amiably about last night's preposterous trivia as if it were history.

Pretty women swarm around everybody but writers.

Plain, intelligent women *somewhat* swarm around writers.

But it wasn't only to have pretty women swarm around that I hustled my first book into print. It wasn't that alone by a long shot.

I also meant to revolutionize American writing.

In the early thirties the word revolutionize enjoyed popularity and was altogether respectable, but a special poll invented by a special statistician would be the only means today by which to measure my success in revolutionizing American writing. To pretend that my writing hasn't had any effect at all on American writing, however, would be inaccurate. The trouble is that for the most part my writing influenced unpublished writers who remained unpublished, and to measure that kind of an influence calls for a lot of imagination and daring. The good writers that my writing influenced were already published, some of them long published, but the truth is that my writing *did* influence their writing, too, for I began to notice the improvement almost immediately. And I didn't notice it in short stories alone, I noticed it in novels and plays, and even in movies.

What did my writing have that might be useful to writing in general?

Freedom.

I think I demonstrated that if you have a writer, you have writing, and that the writer himself is of greater importance than his writing— until he quits, or is dead.

Thus, if you *are* a writer, you do not have to kill yourself every time you write a story, a play, or a novel.

But why did I want to revolutionize American writing?

I had to, because I didn't like it, and wanted to.

And why, as a writer, was I unwilling to act solemn? Didn't I know that unless I acted solemn the big critics would be afraid to write about my writing? I knew. I refused to act solemn because I didn't feel solemn. I didn't feel I *ought* to feel solemn, or even dignified, because I knew acting dignified was only a shadow removed from being pompous. Some writers are naturally solemn, dignified, or pompous, but that doesn't mean that they are also naturally great, or even effective.

There simply isn't any mysterious connection between solemnity and great writing. Some great writers had great solemnity, but most of them had almost none. They had something else.

What is this other thing?

I think it is an obsession to get to the probable truth about man, nature, and art, straight through everything to the very core of *one's own* being.

What is this probable truth?

It changes from day to day, certainly from year to year. You can measure the change from decade to decade, and the reason you can measure it is that there have been writers (and others) who have been obsessed about it, too.

To become free is the compulsion of our time—free of everything that is useless and false, however deeply established in man's fable. But this hope of freedom, this need of it, does not for a moment mean that man is to go berserk. Quite the contrary, since freedom, real freedom, true freedom, carries the life and fable of man nearer and nearer to order, beauty, grace, and meaning—all of which must always remain correctable in details—revised, improved, refined, enlarged, extended.

Intelligence *is* arriving into the fable of life of man. It isn't necessarily welcome, though, certainly not in most quarters. In order to be a little less unwelcome it must be joined by humour, out of which the temporary best has always come. You simply cannot call the human race a dirty name unless you smile when you do so. The calling of the name may be necessary and the name itself may be temporarily accurate, but not to smile at the time is a blunder that nullifies usefulness, for without humour there is no hope, and man could no more live without hope than he could without the earth underfoot.

Life rules the world, impersonal and free life. The anonymous living tell their story every day, with the help of professional or amateur writers, but the greatest story-teller of all is time and change, or death. But death is not our doom and not our enemy. Next to birth it is our best gift, and next to truth it is our best friend.

I am back in San Francisco on the occasion of the twentieth anniversary of the publication of my first book—the beginning of my life as a writer, as a force in the life of my time, as a voting representative of my anonymous self and of any and all others whose aspirations parallel my own—to live creatively, to live honourably, to hurt no one in so far as possible, to enjoy mortality, to fear neither death nor immortality, to cherish fools and failures even more than wise men and saints since there are more of them, to believe, to hope, to work, and to do these things with humour.

To say yes, and not to say no.

What advice have I for the potential writer?

I have none, for anybody is a potential writer, and the writer who *is* a writer needs no advice and seeks none.

What about courses in writing in colleges and universities?

Useless, they are entirely useless.

The writer is a spiritual anarchist, as in the depth of his soul every man is. He is discontented with everything and everybody. The writer is everybody's best friend and only true enemy—the good and great enemy. He neither walks with the multitude nor cheers with them. The writer who is a writer is a rebel who never stops. He does not conform for the simple reason that there is nothing yet worth conforming to. When there is something half worth conforming to he will not conform to that, either, or half conform to it. He won't even rest or sleep as other people rest and sleep. When he's dead he'll probably be dead as others are dead, but while he is alive he is alive as no one else is, not even another writer. The writer who is a writer is also a fool. He is the easiest man in the world to belittle, ridicule, dismiss, and scorn: and that also is precisely as it should be. He is also mad, measurably so, but saner than all others, with the best sanity, the only sanity worth bothering about—the living, creative, vulnerable, valorous, unintimidated, and arrogant sanity of a free man.

I am a writer who is a writer, as I have been for twenty years, and expect to be for twenty more.

I am here to stay, and so is everybody else. No explosive is going to be employed by anybody on anybody. Knowing this, believing this, the writer who is a writer makes plans to watch his health casually, and to write his writing with more and more purposeful intelligence, humour, and love.

I am proud of my twenty years, undecorated as they may be. I am proud to be a writer, the writer I am, and I don't care what anybody else is proud of.

The Whole Voyald and Other Stories, 1956

The Rescue of
the Perishing

*T*here was a chicken hiding under a parked car on Van Ness Avenue, in the heart of town, on the first rainless day after eleven days and nights of storm, after the floods. And three cars farther down the street, there was a small dog hiding under another car.

He'd never have noticed them on his way home from the public library if they hadn't been so upset about something. The chicken, a big hen with mottled black-and-white feathers, was making noises that were for all the world almost human. And the little dog, a common lost dog not more than twice the size of a cat, was whimpering the same way, making almost the same appeal.

He'd passed up the chicken, astonished that it was there at all and half believing it must belong to the owners of the car, and then he came upon the dog.

It was after six, the streets were almost deserted, he was late for supper. He'd been to the library, examining the whole place—not one book, not one shelf of them, but the whole library, looking into one book after another, as if he were in search of something and knew what it was but just couldn't find it.

Whenever he was at the public library and got to searching that way he forgot time and supper and everything else, sometimes feeling glad about his luck, about drawing nearer to what he was looking for, and sometimes feeling miserable, believing his search was hopeless.

One afternoon during the eleven-day storm he rode out to Skaggs Bridge on his bicycle in answer to a radio appeal, riding six miles in heavy rain. There he got on a truck with twenty others, none of them under sixteen. He was twelve, and eager to prove that twelve years are enough to help in a flood. The truck travelled over muddy roads until it came to where the river was nearest flooding over. The men all smoked in the truck, and the boy took a cigarette when it was offered and tried his best to smoke it. He stayed with the men from five in the afternoon until one in the morning, and worked as hard as any of them. He stopped for coffee and sandwiches only when the others did, and together they put up a high bank.

But when the truck got back to the country store at Skaggs Bridge where he'd left his bike, the bike was gone.

He asked the old man at the store about the bike, telling where he'd put it and the kind it was. It was one he'd bought from Paul Saydak, who'd been rebuilding bikes for twenty years, working in the barn behind his house on Oleander Avenue. It was a lean bike and strong. Paul Saydak had let him have it for $27.50, although Paul had said it was worth $35.

The old man in the store, at half-past one in the morning, hardly knew what the boy was talking about, but he understood that the boy's bike had been swiped, and he couldn't help feeling upset about it. He didn't understand the part about Paul Saydak, but he went outside and let the boy point out to him where he had put the bike. Then he told the boy he hadn't been at the store at five in the afternoon, so he hadn't seen the bike at all. He said he would ask about it though. He went to the driver of the truck and asked him to get the boy home.

The next day the boy took a bus to school, and the next afternoon he hitchhiked to Skaggs Bridge to ask at the store about his bike. But nobody knew what he was talking about, and he himself felt he was making quite a lot of a $27.50 bike in weather like that, the river free in a dozen different places and millions of dollars lost in damages of all kinds. The bike was gone, that's all. And there wasn't a great deal of interest in the fact that it *was* gone, or in the circumstances under which he had given somebody the best chance in the world to take off with it. He'd listened to the radio appeal for help, he'd got on his bike, he'd gone as fast as he could go to where they'd asked him to go, and there somebody had swiped his bike.

"The radio appeal wasn't to *you*," his father said the night after the bike had been stolen.

"I thought it was," the boy said.

"No," his father said, "it was to *me*, and I didn't go. You might have known they'd steal your bike."

"I didn't think they would."

"Well, they did. And since they did, and since they had no right to, no right even to be *tempted* to steal it—anybody at the store should have taken it inside and put it away somewhere—well, I'm going to buy you a new bike. Any kind you want. Any time you want it. Tomorrow. You pick it out and I'll buy it."

"That's not it," the boy said. "I don't want a new bike."

"Well, you've lost the old one," the man said. "Pick out the one you want and I'll buy it."

"I liked my bike because I'd bought it with money I'd earned myself," the boy said. He was a little angry with his father for being so angry with whoever had stolen the bike, and with people in general. He knew his father was sympathetic and *did* want him to have a bike, but he didn't like to see his father so angry about people and things in general. The angrier his father got with people, the kinder he became with his family.

"Perhaps it's just as well," his mother said to his father. "So few boys nowadays ride bikes to school, and motorists are so careless. Perhaps it's just as well he's had it stolen. It's always made me worry. Must you have another bike?"

"Of course he must," his father said.

"No," the boy said, "I think I'd rather not have one."

"I'm sure he doesn't want a new bike," his mother said.

"Oh, *are* you?" his father said. He turned to the boy and said: "I leave it to you. Think about it and let me know."

He rode the bus to school after that. It wasn't half as much fun as riding his bike, but it was all right. He couldn't move as freely as he'd moved for a year—for the year he'd had the bike. And every now and then he forgot that the bike had been stolen, so that when he stepped out of his house or out of school he believed he was on his way to his bike and a quick ride to wherever he was going.

Five days after the bike had been stolen, he took the bus after school and rode to town and went to the public library.

He took the place shelf by shelf, forgetting the bike and his father's anger. He read parts of plays, short stories, novels, travel books, histories, biographies, and philosophy. Everything he read seemed fresh and good and new, but not quite what he wanted, not what he was searching for. He was in the public library for hours, sitting down at last to read a story, not knowing the name of the story or who the writer was, and not stopping until the story came to a description of a meal, making him hungry. He looked at the clock and saw that it was twenty-past six. His father would be getting home in a few minutes, and supper would start in half an hour. He left the book open on the table and hurried out of the library to the street. The sky was clear and the air seemed clean and fresh, as if nobody had ever breathed it. If he waited for a bus, he might not get home any sooner than if he walked, so he decided to cut through town and enjoy a swift glance at anything he came to, and then get on home. It was a walk of about a mile and a half, but he felt like walking.

When he heard the chicken under the parked car on Van Ness Avenue, he couldn't imagine what it was that was making such a sorrowful appeal for help. Every day the paper was full of stories about strange things that had happened during the storm, so he felt the noise had something to do with it, too. But he didn't expect it to be a chicken, and he didn't expect it to be under a car.

He was some time finding out what it was and where it was, and when he saw that it *was* a chicken under a car he didn't feel that he ought to try to do something for it. It might belong to the people who owned the car, and they might think he was stealing it. But when he came to the whimpering dog, he knew it belonged to no one, and he was sure he couldn't just leave it there. He called to the dog, but the dog was afraid of him. It took a good three or four minutes to stop the dog from being afraid. The dog crawled out from under the car, still struggling with its fear. The boy was very gentle with the dog, speaking softly and not touching it for some time. At last he began to stroke the dog's head. The dog got to its feet and barked, but all it could manage was one little sound that was more like a cough than a bark.

He picked it up and walked back to where the chicken was.

He set the dog down on the pavement and said: "Now, you just stand there. I'm going to take you home and give you some food and a warm place to sleep, but I've got to get this chicken, too."

The dog watched him and listened to his voice, but couldn't stand still and couldn't understand. It managed to bark again once. It ran off a little, whimpering, and then came back and asked if the boy wanted it to go away.

"Now, will you just stand there a minute while I see about the chicken?" the boy said. "There's a lost chicken under the car here that I've got to take home and take care of, too."

The dog seemed to understand a little, so the boy went around to the back of the car where the hen was sitting as if it were hatching. He began to talk to it, but a bird is a bird, even if it's a hen, and a bird, even if it's lost and sick, has *got* to be afraid of a human being. The hen got to its feet, but not all the way up: not because there wasn't room enough under the car, but because in fear all creatures, even men, do not rise to their full height: only in pride or exultation do they stand very tall, as men do when they are glad about themselves or as roosters do when they are overwhelmed about themselves and must push themselves to the limits of themselves, and then, half dying with joy, crow about who they are and what they can do. The lost hen wobbled to the next car, and then to the third car, the boy going after it slowly and speaking to it softly. He had to crawl under the third car to reach the hen and bring it out.

When the dog saw the hen it began to dance, growling softly— partly, perhaps, because it was a dog and the bird was a bird, and partly, perhaps, because another lost creature had been rescued.

"All right," the boy said to both of them. "Now we're going home."

The dog stayed close to the boy's heels, barking now and then, and the hen stopped being frightened. When the boy got home he picked up the dog and went in through the back door.

He stepped into the dining-room, the dog under one arm, the chicken under the other, the eyes of both creatures open and unsure. Everybody at the table stared at the boy, the dog, and the hen.

"I found them," the boy said. "They were hiding under cars on Van Ness. They were both crying. I thought I'd better bring them home."

"Orphans of the storm, is that it?" the father said. "That's not a bad-looking dog."

"Can I keep them?" the boy said.

"A dog and a chicken?" the mother said.

"They won't be any trouble," the boy said. "I'll fix up a small coop with a nest and a perch for the hen, and the dog can sleep in a box in the garage. Can I keep them?"

"Can he?" his father asked his mother.

"Can he?" the boy's kid brothers asked.

"Well," his mother said, "are you sure you *want* to? I mean, nobody keeps chickens in their yards any more, and dogs—*some* dogs—have a way of getting the people who own them into a lot of trouble."

"I'd like to keep them," the boy said. "They were lost. Nobody wanted them. I found them. They were afraid of me. I had to talk to them. It wasn't easy, especially the hen. I didn't buy them, but I do feel they are mine, and I'd like to keep them."

"Well," his mother said. She turned to his father. "Are you sure it's all right?"

"I don't know why not," his father said.

"All right," his mother said. She got up. "I'll help you put them away until after you've had your supper."

"No," the boy said, "you go ahead. They're both hungry. I'll give the dog a little warm milk to start, and the hen maybe a little rice or something. I won't be a minute."

All the same, his mother went with him to the kitchen and warmed milk for the dog. The boy set the chicken on the floor, and his mother sprinkled rice in front of it, and soon both creatures began to eat and come alive in earnest.

After supper the boy went to the garage with his younger brothers, and they fixed the hen a small coop with a perch and a nest, and the dog a little house, made out of a small box, with rags on the bottom for a bed.

While they were out in the garage, the boy's father and mother sat in the living-room and talked.

"Well, so far he's said nothing about a new bike," the man said. "That bike meant everything in the world to him. You know it did."

"Yes," the woman said, "but *that* bike only. *His* bike. The bike bought with his own money. No other bike can take its place. Something else has got to."

"A stray dog and a tired old hen?" the man said.

"Well, yes," the woman said. "They're *his*. I don't think he'll ever have another bike. I don't think he'll ever want another one. The next time he saves up some money, he'll buy something else. But he did love his bike. It became part of him. He knows it's gone for ever, though."

"Then I shouldn't surprise him and bring home a new one?" the man said.

"No," the woman said. "He wouldn't like it. Not *really*. Oh, he'd like it, of course, but it couldn't possibly be what his own bike was."

"Yes, I suppose so," the man said. "Well, it was quite a storm at that, wasn't it?"

"Yes," the woman said. "Everybody's talked of nothing else."

"I can't imagine," the man said, "why you allowed him to ride his bike all the way to Skaggs Bridge in the first place."

"Can you imagine my asking him *not* to?" the woman said. "He *wanted* to. It seemed silly, of course, but it wasn't silly to him, and he *did* help. I mean he did actually do the same work as everybody else."

The man saw the whole thing very clearly: he saw a boy on a bike riding to the rescue of the world, and he laughed, perhaps because it can't be done, perhaps because it must, perhaps because only a small boy can believe it's worth trying to do.

The woman laughed, too, and then both of them stopped quickly, to resume their expressions of earnestness, for they heard him down the hall with his kid brothers, all of them on their way to the living-room, to report on what they had done in the brave business of rescuing the perishing.

The Whole Voyald and Other Stories, 1956

The Inventor
and the Actress

There was a boy, and the boy's two older sisters, in the house across the alley. Sometimes he liked them and sometimes he thought they were the worst thing that had ever happened to him, for they were always coming into the yard that was his own as if it were theirs, too.

They had the family name of Shehady and the boy was called Paddy by his sisters. Paddy called the biggest sister Bellie, which she hated because her name was Belle, and he called the other one Daze, although of course the name was properly Daisy.

Belle was always dolling up in her mother's old clothes and asking if she looked at all like Ava Gardner or Marilyn Monroe or any of the other women she had seen lately in a movie, and of course she never did. She always looked like Belle, who looked like nothing at all on God's green earth a fellow could half think of as being a girl. And yet that's all she thought about: to be a girl, a big girl, a great big girl like Marilyn Monroe.

One day when Paddy came over into the yard he said: "Guess what Bellie's going to be, Jim?"

"How should I know what she's going to be?" Jim said. He was always a little surprised and annoyed by the way Paddy came up on a fellow all of a sudden and asked some fool question in his shrill, nervous voice. Once or twice when Jim had been thinking about something to invent he had jumped when he'd heard Paddy's voice, but lately, about a year now, he wasn't jumping any more, and not getting especially annoyed, either.

"Actress," Paddy said. "She's going on the stage. Daze ain't going with her."

Jim was removing the dry black casings from walnuts that had fallen off the tree in the back yard. After you got the casings off they were ready to break with a hammer. They were hard walnuts, but once you ever got through the thick shell the meat in there, arranged in a way that was so perfect a fellow never could figure out how it was done or whoever thought of such a thing, was the best-tasting thing in the whole world. That was what made it worth Jim's while to go to all the trouble, getting his hands stained black from the casings. The tree was old. It grew a great many walnuts every year. There were some in the garage from two or three years ago. His mother spoke once of using them for fuel, there were so many of them and nobody eating them, but Jim told her he wanted them. He was going to clean them and eat them, but of course he never got around to it, and every now and then his mother probably burned some. They made a great fire, but he didn't like them to be burned. He kept the casings and empty shells in a box, and set them aside for his mother to burn, but he didn't want the whole walnuts burned. You just don't burn things like that.

"What are you doing?" Paddy said.

"Cleaning these walnuts," Jim said.

Paddy had seen Jim dozens of times cleaning them, but he asked the question every time, as if Jim was actually finding out from the way they were made how to invent something that would make him one of the richest men in the world. Jim always answered the question as if it were brand-new.

"Can I help you?" Paddy said.

"Sure, but you'll get your hands dirty."

"I don't care."

So Paddy Shehady sat down under the tree in Jim's back yard and began to take the casing off one of the walnuts.

"How many of 'em have you got?" Paddy wanted to know.

"The garage is half full of them, almost," Jim said.

"Are you going to clean 'em all?"

"Well, I clean some and put 'em away," Jim said, "and then when I want to break them they're clean and ready. If you break them when they're not clean you can't break them right and you spoil most of the nut inside."

"Can I break this one and eat the nut in there?" Paddy said.

"Sure," Jim said. "But don't hurt your hand."

Paddy had hurt his hand twice already, once badly enough to have Mrs. Shehady herself come over into the yard—not enough the two girls and the boy coming over all the time, the mother, too—and she'd wanted Jim to tell her exactly what Paddy had done to hurt his hand so. Jim had told her, and then she had asked if Jim's mother was home, and he'd told her she wasn't, and then she'd asked how Jim's father had been killed in the war, the mother standing there by the hour and not letting him go about his business. She was a big woman, almost as big as the wrestlers he'd seen at the side-show during the county fair last summer, but it was fat mostly. At the same time she was nervous and she was always wondering when the cost of living was going to come down where it used to be.

One day Jim heard Mrs. Shehady ask his mother about that, and his mother said she didn't know, which didn't help Mrs. Shehady very much, and Mrs. Shehady couldn't think of anything else to say for a long time. The time she came about Paddy's hurt hand Jim told her Paddy had hurt his hand breaking walnuts. She then wanted to know if Jim had pushed Paddy or anything like that and Jim got annoyed and said he not only *hadn't* pushed Paddy, he had demonstrated to Paddy a dozen times how to break walnuts without hurting his hand.

But Paddy always hurt his hand, at least a little. The time he hurt it badly he jumped up, howling and stamping his feet and saying: "I've smashed my hand! I've smashed my *whole* hand!" He kept shaking it and jumping up and down and running around in circles, and finally he broke down and cried bitterly, swearing at last, accusing Jim, saying it was Jim's fault, and then ran home. He didn't have far to run, and Jim could hear him wailing to his mother, and his mother saying all sorts of silly things to ease the pain and make him forget.

"I won't hurt my hand," Paddy said now. "She's going to be like Ava Gardner, she says. You know? All done up that way, lying there on tiger skins, and all that? She's lying on the linoleum now."

"What linoleum?"

"In the kitchen," Paddy said. "Practising. She's not allowed in the parlour, so she's practising on the linoleum. She's got an empty Quaker Oats box that she's using for a pillow. She's got Daze saying things to her, so she can practise saying things back the way Ava Gardner does."

Paddy placed the walnut he'd cleaned—but he hadn't cleaned it right—on the boulder that was as big as a big eggplant and he held it carefully with two fingers. He then picked up the hammer, and Jim watched every move he made to stop him from hurting his hand again if it looked as if he were going to. Paddy brought the hammer down on the nut and broke it, but not in half, not along the line where it was sealed together, as Jim had told him so many times was the place to strike it with the hammer. The nut was smashed, and Paddy's fingers were hurt a little, but not much, not enough to make him jump up and cry. Paddy just dropped the hammer, grabbed the crushed nut into his right hand, and shook the other until the pain was gone. Then he transferred what he had to his left hand and began to pick through the debris for anything there that might be fit to eat.

Jim broke one, too, to be eating with him, and Paddy said: "Bellie don't want to be somebody that ain't famous and beautiful. She wants to be rich and refined, too. She says if she practises a little every day she can do it. She's got Daze coming in and out of the kitchen saying things to her, like servants, like the men who go to visit Ava Gardner, like her old father, like her poor sister, and everybody else, so Bellie can lie there on the linoleum and say things back to her."

"What's Daze *say* to her?" Jim said.

"Well, you know," Paddy said. "There was one time there where Ava or one of the others said to her own mother, 'I don't ever want to see you again,' and all the old mother had gone to her about was to ask her to come home. They were lonesome or something. Well, Daze comes in and says, 'Oh, my daughter, come home. We need you!' And then Bellie says back to her, 'Three years ago you drove me out into the world. I don't ever want to see you again.' and stuff like that."

"I'll break this one for you," Jim said. He broke the nut clean in half, then cracked each half so that most of what was in there could be picked out clean and whole. He handed the stuff to Paddy, then broke one for himself.

"She's going on the stage," Paddy said. "She sent me over to ask can she use the garage for a stage."

"What garage?" Jim said.

"*This* garage," Paddy said. "We haven't got a garage, just the tool shed that's full of junk. Can she use your garage for a stage?"

"When?" Jim said.

"Well," Paddy said, "now, I guess. She's in the way there in the kitchen, and my mother don't like it. She's got to step around her, and sometimes she stands and listens to the two of them saying things back and forth. Bellie says she can't practise with Mamma standing there all the time, not liking any of it. Shall I go and tell her all right?"

"Sure," Jim said.

Paddy got up and ran back to the house across the alley.

It was all right having them for neighbors most of the time, but once in a while it seemed like the worst thing that had ever happened to him, because he just couldn't refuse them anything, or ask them not to come around so much, and that meant he had to stop so often thinking about the other things he was always thinking about, especially his inventions. Now, though, he looked forward to seeing Paddy's sisters, especially Bellie practising to go on the stage.

He want into the garage, to give the place a new glance, to see if he could figure how it would serve as a stage. At one end were a dozen or more apple boxes full of black walnuts. At the other end were some old and broken furniture, some pots and pans, and some boxes with magazines and books and other stuff in them.

He was in the garage when Paddy put his head in and said: "She wants to know can we come in, Jim."

"Sure," Jim said.

Then Paddy, Bellie, and Daze one by one stepped into the garage. Bellie was all done up in black, and she was trying to act big-eyed and sad and dreamy like Ava Gardner or one of the others, and Daze was standing near her, half admiring her and half not knowing what to make of her.

"Well," Bellie said, "about *here,* I thought, Jim. This is my room, you see. I'm lying here on a tiger skin, rich. But I'm sad because I've got so much money and no children. Now, when I lie down here, somebody's going to knock at the door. It's going to be a man who's heard about me. I say, 'Yes?' Then you, Jim, come in."

"*Me?*" Jim said. "Let Paddy do it. I'll sit over here and clean some more walnuts and watch."

"It would be ever so much better if you did it, Jim," Bellie said. "Daisy will be my maid. If I want to see my tigers she'll bring them in, or if I want to eat a few litchi nuts she'll bring them to me on a gold plate."

"I'll sit over here and watch," Jim said.

"Can I lie on this old sofa?" Bellie said.

"Sure," Jim said.

Bellie stretched out on the sofa and grew sad. Without giving up her sadness she said: "You stand over there, Daisy, and wait for me to ask for the tigers. You go out, Paddy, and after a minute knock at the door."

"What do I say when I come in?" Paddy said.

"Are you the famous Madame Antoinette de la Tour?" Bellie told him to say.

"Madame *who?*" Paddy said.

"Antoinette," Bellie said sadly.

"Antoinette."

"De la Tour," Bellie said.

"De la Tour," Paddy repeated. "Madame Antoinette de la Tour."

Paddy went out and Bellie got ready to practise, but Paddy came right back in again without knocking.

"What do I say after *that,* Bellie?"

"Paddy!" Bellie said bitterly, "I won't have you calling me Bellie. I'm going on the stage. My name's Isabelle Shehady, but of course I'm going to change it to Belle Shade. I think that's awful attractive, don't you, Jim?"

"Belle Shade?" Jim said. "I guess so."

"Well, anyway," Paddy said, "what do I say after I say what you told me to say?" He tried to remember what she'd told him to say. "What *did* you tell me to say?" he said.

"Listen carefully, Paddy," Bellie said. "Are you Madame Antoinette de la Tour?"

"All right," Paddy said. "Then what do I say?"

"Well," Bellie said, "you say that, and then when I say what I say, you say whatever what I say *makes* you say. You know the way they do. All right now, let's start."

Paddy Shehady went out of the garage. Belle Shade, as she preferred to be called, got herself into the mood, and Daze stood behind the sofa trying to be earnest about the whole thing.

Paddy knocked at the door.

"Yes?" Belle Shade said.

Paddy stepped in. "Are you Madame Antoinette de la Tour?" he said.

Belle Shade looked at him sadly a moment, and then, growing more sorrowful than ever, she said: "I am."

Paddy looked at Jim, but Jim didn't help him any. Jim was just looking at Bellie, so Paddy looked at Daze, but Daze didn't help him any, either. Daze looked as if she were at a small child's funeral, so Paddy looked at Bellie again.

"I have come from Arabia to see you," Belle Shade told her brother Paddy to say.

"I have come from Arabia to see you," Paddy said.

"What part of Arabia?" Belle Shade said sadly.

Now, you couldn't very well blame Paddy for not knowing what to say next, but here he was feeling miserable because he didn't know what part of Arabia he'd come from, and at the same time not daring to break the mood.

"Baghdad," Belle Shade whispered.

"Baghdad," Paddy said.

"That's very far away," Belle Shade said with terrible grief, "for, as you know, this is Paris, and Paris and Baghdad are very far apart."

"Yes, they are," Paddy said. He was getting into the spirit of the thing now, and chances were about fifty-fifty he'd do all right as the man from Baghdad. "But I got here all right," he went on.

"Did you have a pleasant voyage?" Belle Shade said.

"I came by train," Paddy said.

"I trust you slept well *en route*," Belle said.

"I slept all right," Paddy said. "I trust you slept all right *en route*, too."

"I have been here the whole time," Belle said. "I have not travelled since Chuck fought the duel. I have been in Paris the whole time, here in this lonely castle with my memories."

"Oh," Paddy said. He thought fast, then hit on something. "How *is* Chuck?" he said.

"Dead," Belle said.

"How is his father?"

"Dead."

"Has he got a brother?"

"Yes, he has a small brother," Belle said.

"How's *he?*"

"He's dying," Belle said. She let her hand fall backward toward Daze.

"Marie," she said, "please bring me my tigers. I'm lonely."

"Yes, Madame," Daze said.

Daze got on her hands and knees and crawled around the sofa to Belle Shade, who looked sadly at her tigers. Her hand fell on Daze's head.

"My poor, lonely tigers," Belle said.

"Well," Paddy said, "I guess I'll go back to Baghdad."

Belle Shade sat up suddenly, almost terrified. "Wait!" she cried.

"I'm a little late," Paddy said. "It takes a lot of time to get back to Baghdad."

"Wait, wait!" Belle cried. "Don't leave me!"

"Why not?" Paddy said.

"I'm dying, too."

"Is it anything contagious?" Paddy said.

"No, no!" Belle said. "You're safe. It's sanitary."

"What have you got?" Paddy said.

"A broken heart," Belle said.

"You better call a doctor," Paddy said.

He went out quickly. Daze stopped being two tigers, and got up and went to Jim.

"Belle wants to be famous," she said. "She's very good, don't you think?"

Belle Shade was still acting, still dying of a broken heart. Paddy came back in and looked at her a minute. "Who's Chuck, Bellie?" he said.

"*Belle Shade*, Paddy! Will you please stop calling me Bellie?"

"Well, anyway, who's Chuck?"

"*Anybody*," Belle said. "A man. In the play."

"Oh," Paddy said.

They all went out into the yard now under the old walnut tree. Jim sat down and began to take the casing off a walnut. Paddy sat beside him, and then Belle and Daze. They spent the rest of the afternoon cleaning and breaking walnuts, eating them, and talking about the stage, and life itself. It was almost dark when Mrs. Shehady came across the alley to get them and stop a moment to chat with Jim.

"How's your mama?" she said.

"She's fine, thanks," Jim said.

"*Where* is she?" Mrs. Shehady said.

"Well, she's not home from work yet," Jim said.

"At the store?"

"In the *office* at the store," Jim said.

"I always forget," Mrs. Shehady said. "Walpole's. It's the best store in town, too. You tell her I was asking for her."

"Yes, ma'am," Jim said.

Then they all went off in the dark.

Jim got all the casings and shells together, put them in a box, and took the box to the fireplace in the livingroom, trying all the while to think of something useful to invent. It was only five, and dark already. His mother wouldn't be home until around half-past six. He started a fire in the fireplace and sat at the window, looking out at the house across the alley, at the people in the house.

Mr. Shehady was home from his job at the Southern Pacific, and Mrs. Shehady had them all at the table in the dining-room. She was pouring soup into bowls and putting the bowls down one by one in front of them.

They were a good family and he liked them—the small sensible father, the big nervous mother, the simple son, and the two daughters, the one who wanted to go on the stage and be famous, and the one who didn't know what she wanted to do.

Most of the time it was fine having them in the house across the alley, but sometimes when he was thinking, when he was trying to figure out something complicated and wonderful to invent, and they surrounded him with their strange ways, he believed their getting into his life was just about the worst thing that had ever happened to him.

"I've just *got* to invent something," Jim thought, but he couldn't get Belle Shade out of his mind long enough to think of something.

"Whoever invented *her*," he thought, "sure must have got a big surprise."

The Whole Voyald and Other Stories, 1956

Paris and
Philadelphia

*A*ndré Salamat, the actor, after he had exchanged a few words with Laura Slade, turned to the girl's aunt and remarked: "But she's not *real*—of course she's not."

"Why do you say *that?*" the woman asked.

"Because she's too wonderful to be real," the actor said.

He enjoyed listening to his own words, many of which were from plays he had appeared in at one time or another, even though he was not an insincere man.

He was along in his fifties, but he managed to stay young inside, as he frequently put it, and the handsomeness which had started him on his career as a very young man in Paris was still with him. He knew his rather long nose had dropped a bit at the end, but it was still the nose of an actor, and his Cyrano played in French at the age of twenty-two without putty on his nose was the first of a long series of triumphs. He also knew that he was not, strictly speaking, a tall man. On stage or in public he went to quite a little trouble to keep himself up to his full height of almost five feet eleven, but once he was alone he relaxed with relief and was scarcely more than five feet eight.

But acting was his profession, his bread and butter, his art, his fun, his life, and it didn't stop just because he happened to step off stage. If anything, his fame as André Salamat was even greater than his fame as an actor, but of course he had seen to it that one was inseparable from the other.

He had cultivated a clever actor's trick of speech which frequently made very commonplace remarks seem brilliant, and he did not care at all that they were not actually so. *He* certainly was, and that was all that mattered. This trick had to do with stance, manner of looking upon another person or staring into space, the volume and texture of his voice, the pronunciation of words, which he preferred to keep slightly foreign, and the rhythm with which he uttered these words.

He was very nearly a phony, but no more so, he was sure, than anybody else he had ever met, for his intention, like their own, was to get as much as possible out of being alive. He was not by any means an imbecile: he was devoted to the theatre; he read old and new plays all the time; and he had a flair for confessing earnestly that he was a religious man, loved God, and frequently found peace by kneeling in prayer. He loved churches, too, he said, but only as buildings. He had never been received officially into any church and he had no intention of seeking to be, for in religion as in amour, as he said, he liked to play the field, and he did not feel that he required an agent to intercede for him in either area. He was a good deal less despised than many actors equally famous, and, as a matter of fact, enjoyed a great deal of popularity in three or four levels of New York society.

When he met Laura Slade he was moving in what he felt was the top level of that society, for the girl's aunt, Mrs. Boake-Rehan Adams, had been famous for more than three decades for her activities in connection with the opera and a wide variety of charities. She had insisted that he appear at her CARE party, for his own country was receiving benefits every day through that charity, and he had been eager to accept.

He knew that a great many people he liked to see now and then, and be seen by, would be at the party, and, weary or not weary of standing straighter than was comfortable, he hurried along by taxi to the house on Fifth Avenue immediately after his Saturday-night performance in the sensational hit *There Goes the Devil*, in which he played the part of a man not above any kind of base behaviour, a role he profoundly enjoyed.

The play was written by a newcomer of only mediocre talent, but the central idea had appealed to André Salamat and he'd agreed to accept the part on one condition: that he be permitted to enlarge the role. It was thus that a rather slight but fairly well-organized play became little more than a vehicle for André Salamat and, as he himself frequently said, the kind of success that would make so much money for the unknown playwright that he would never write another play.

The party was well along when he joined it, and in the hall adjoining the enormous salon, even as he chatted with Mrs. Boake-Rehan Adams about how well she looked, his eye wandered among the famous guests and he made plans to exchange words with this one and that. Then he saw Laura Slade and unconsciously pushed his height to its limit. She certainly was no more than twenty-two or twenty-three, her hair was golden, her skin luminous, her figure gorgeous, and she was as excited as she could be. Fortunately, she was chatting with a man old enough to be her father, and of course it did not occur to André Salamat that he himself was that old, although not quite as old as her companion, who was every bit of sixty-five and looked it. As a matter of fact, André Salamat's only daughter, Yvonne, was twenty-five, married to a Communist intellectual in Paris, the mother of two sons, and in her own right something of a revolutionist, which was extremely tiresome as far as he was concerned. And one of his sons, Henri, was more than thirty, while the youngest, Jean, was eighteen, born in America, a student of cinematography at the University of California at Los Angeles, and living with his mother, Eve Gayley, who had been well known in silent films.

The actor, when he had seen the most important person at the party, began immediately to draw up a campaign whereby to have her notice and perhaps be enchanted by him. If she was what most American girls were, he was quite confident that this would not be too difficult, although he had once or twice been giggled at by young ladies when they had finally found a moment in which to be alone with him at a party and he had spoken to them tenderly. But of course these young ladies had been not yet out of school and were, as it turned out to his amazement, only sixteen. American girls had a way of seeming sometimes almost as old as their mothers, and it was not altogether his fault that he had not known how profoundly immature and undeveloped they actually were. To the actor, a girl who responded to his tender notice by giggling was undeveloped, and there is undoubtedly something to his theory.

Salamat, still chatting with Mrs. Boake-Rehan Adams, was about to ask who the young lady was who looked like a Renior girl and gave one the feeling of having been created out of rose petals and champagne when the girl herself came leaping and laughing through the excited people to her aunt to ask whether she might not stay with her an extra day before going home to Philadelphia. And so it came to pass that Laura Slade was introduced to André Salamat.

"You should never, never say Philadelphia," he said to the young woman.

"I live there," the girl laughed.

"No doubt," Salamat said, working on the part he had just invented—the mystic poet, so to say.

"Yes, I am sure you live there," he went on, "but you must never say it, for it is not good enough for you to say. You must say only Paris."

"Paris," the girl laughed. "Paris. Paris. Are you satisfied?"

"I am absolutely at your mercy," the actor said. "When you say Paris I am at your feet: I adore you: I believe in angels again, in love again, in little children again. When you say Paris," he went on, lowering his voice now in order to give an impression of profound sadness, "I believe in life again."

He was not sure how these words in that sad tone of voice would be received by the girl, but he prayed—he did not kneel for this prayer, of course—that she would not giggle. They were not by any means alone, but at least no one was listening, for the girl's aunt had gone to greet Tallulah Bankhead, who had just arrived.

"You sound very sad, Mr. Salamat," the girl said in a satisfactory tone of voice, so that the actor was encouraged to go a little farther along this line.

"I *am* a sad man," he said so earnestly that he himself believed it, and in fact it was not entirely untrue, for there is no man who cannot say the same thing and believe it, and if need be actually *prove* that he is telling the truth. Every man *is* a sad man: it is simply that most men have not discovered that it is frequently useful to point this out to a beautiful young girl from Philadelphia.

"But in the play," the girl said, "you seem so *above* sadness. I saw it only this afternoon at the matinée because Aunt told me you might drop by tonight."

"You saw *me* this afternoon?" the actor exclaimed.

"Yes, and I thought you were wonderful," the girl said.

"Had I only known you were in the theatre," he went on, working fast and feeling confident that he was doing all right, "I would have played the entire performance for you alone, and somewhere in the course of the action I would have spoken your name. Let me see where I might have done that. Oh, yes. As the devil is exposed and driven out of the world I would have stopped, turned to where you sat, and I would have said: 'I say farewell to none here but the one Laura.' Had I only known you were there."

He had gone on swiftly in order, he hoped, to take away some of the lameness of the line he had invented for her, which, apart from having been nonsense to begin with, had been poorly read. Still, it did not seem as if Laura Slade had noticed, and all was still well.

"I have never had any actor say a line to me from a stage in my life," she said.

"I will do it for you every time you come to the theatre," the actor said. "But now, if you will give me your ticket stub, I will have your seat located and I will go there and embrace it and have the management remove it and place it in my dressing-room, so that henceforth only you may sit in it. It would break my heart for another to sit in it."

"It was in the gallery," the girl said. "I threw away my ticket stub."

"My dear," the actor said.

"I simply couldn't get anything else."

"But of course you didn't *see* me, then."

"Oh, I saw you all right," Laura Slade said. "I took Aunt's opera glasses. It's the fourth seat from the right looking toward the stage in the next to the last row in the gallery."

"I will have it removed immediately," the actor said, "and placed in my dressing-room."

"Not really?"

"But of course."

"I don't believe it, Mr. Salamat," the girl said, "but I think you're charming."

"There will be a seat in the first row in your name at the box office for Monday night's performance," the actor went on. "I shall play the entire performance for you, and after the performance you will find your gallery seat in my dressing-room."

"I don't believe you."

"I swear it."

He himself was almost surprised at what he was saying.

His look was piercing and tender now, and he was satisfied that the girl would be there. Miss Bankhead and the girl's aunt came up and stopped only a moment for greetings, and then for another moment he had her almost to himself. There was something more to be said, he felt, but for the life of him he couldn't think what it might be and his height began to fall just a little. Finally, he resorted to repetition, hoping that it would prove effective. "The entire performance for you."

Fortunately, the girl's aunt was back, saying to him: "But get along into the party, André. What in the world are you doing here in the hall? And you, too, Laura. And if it will make you as happy as all that, you may stay until Tuesday morning."

The girl leaped and kissed her aunt, laughing, and with only the merest of glances at the actor, as if to let him know they shared a secret, she skipped and ran back into the enormous room. It was then that the actor, beside himself, if such a thing could be, remarked: "But she's not real—of course she's not."

"Why do you say *that?*" the aunt asked.

"Because she's too wonderful to be real," the actor said.

The woman took the actor's hand as kind friends sometimes do when their thoughts are impossible to put into words that will not hurt. She squeezed his hand five times in a manner that was terribly annoying, for André Salamat knew that these five squeezes were for the number of his wives, and that furthermore they meant certain things potentially more rude than blunt words could ever mean. Still, he was able to conceal his annoyance, or at any rate he hoped he had. He was a gifted actor, but this was one of those occasions when he was not sure of the impression he might have made. That, too, was annoying and had to be concealed. This he tried to do by lifting the aunt's hand with which she had squeezed his hand five times and kissing it, once on the outside and twice on the inside. As he did so, he hoped this might have some special meaning for the aunt which might prove annoying to her, and thus square matters. And he brought to mind that she had, in fact, had three husbands. Actually, all she had wanted to tell him was that her niece was engaged to a very nice boy from a very good family in Philadelphia.

"My dear André," the woman said with what he hoped was not sympathy. After a moment she went on less meaningfully: "Now you must get along into the party and let some of your other friends enjoy you."

He went straight to Leonard Lyons, standing with a man and his wife who turned out to be from Washington, the man being in the State Department. Immediately after introductions the actor began to tell anecdotes about himself which he had been saving up for over a month on a chance he would see Leonard Lyons. He mentioned what he had said to the aspiring actress who had stopped him in front of Sardi's and asked quite bluntly if she should persist in her ambition to go on the stage or give up and go home. He felt that his answer had been brilliant, but only Leonard Lyons laughed at his reply, and the wife of the State Department man asked sincerely: "Where *did* she live?" Instead of saying something brilliant in reply to this annoying question, the actor merely told her that he hadn't the faintest idea, and then he told the anecdote about the Negro woman who cleaned his apartment and how by all sorts of little ways of arranging things she revealed her passion for him, but again only Leonard Lyons was able to or willing to laugh, so that he felt quite sure his anecdotes were not apt to appear in the column.

He found an excuse for going off, and hurried to Dorothy Kilgallen, to whom he complained instantly about the State Department. He told Dorothy Kilgallen two other anecdotes about himself and added that he had been invited by the French Government to return to Paris after an absence of twenty-five years to appear in three of Molière's plays. This was not absolutely the truth, although he had recently chatted with a visiting French playwright who had urged him to return to Paris to appear in one of *his* plays, and during their conversation they had discussed the French Government and the plays of Molière.

He was careful to present to every newspaper columnist the latest news about himself, but even while he was busy with these rather tiresome, although necessary, chores he was elated by the impression he had made on Laura Slade. He watched her as long as he remained at the party, and now and then their eyes met and they handed the secret back and forth to one another.

By two in the morning everyone who had been invited to the party had arrived, and no one had gone home, so the girl's aunt obtained everyone's attention and made a rather touching speech about the necessity for everyone at the party to donate as much as possible to CARE, and to urge their friends to do so. She read the names of her guests in alphabetical order from a sheet of paper and as each person's name was called that person stated the amount of his pledge. Some of the wealthiest people at the party pledged rather small sums in order not to appear to be showing off, and it was understood by everyone present that they would donate a good deal more later in private, but when the woman read the actor's name he pledged more than anyone else had pledged. If the truth were known, he expected applause, but fortunately no one knew that, and no one applauded. He instantly changed the expression on his face from that of Hero of France to that of just another guy in the world of culture who was always ready to help those less fortunate than himself.

He did not speak intimately again that night to Laura Slade, for he knew her aunt would send her back to Philadelphia immediately if she knew their secret, but when he came on stage at Monday night's performance and acknowledged the applause that greeted him he saw that she was in the seat he'd had the management put aside for her and he was able quite unobtrusively, as he bowed very low, to look her straight in the eye, and to throw her a kiss, as if to the entire audience.

His performance that night was the best of his career, he felt, and he did in fact give it for her alone. He also said her name when he was banished from the world, but the line was better than it had been the first time, and of course it was better read.

During the first intermission he suddenly remembered that he had not had a seat removed from the theatre and placed in his dressing-room, so he called the stage manager and told him to see that such a seat was instantly found somewhere and placed in his dressing-room. The stage manager protested, but the actor was firm, and the harassed stage manager went to work on the assignment, sending the assistant stage manager into the gallery during the second act, with flashlight and screwdriver. During the second intermission André Salamat saw the seat in his dressing-room. He thanked the stage manager and handed him five dollars.

"For roses," he said. "Have them in my dressing-room before the end of the show."

This also was attended to by the assistant stage manager, who had studied playwriting at Yale and had written two and a half acts of a play in six years. On the way back from the florist's he stepped into the small bar at Sardi's, holding the bunch of roses, and had three Scotches over ice because instead of being a playwright he was turning out to be a handy man and an errand boy for a ham actor.

Laura Slade went to André Salamat's dressing-room after the performance and fell in love with him, or at any rate with the idea of being his sixth wife, but she had to keep to herself the thought at the back of her mind that no matter what people thought about a girl of twenty-two marrying a man of fifty-seven, or as some people said, sixty-one, she knew what she was doing, and she was sure it was going to be worth doing. First of all, she might very possibly actually *be* in love with him, but if it turned out that she wasn't, that was certainly beside the point, for he was charming and handsome and famous and rich enough to give them both an exciting and comfortable life. Second, she felt quite confident that in a reasonable amount of time she might safely make known to him that she wanted more than anything else in the world to be famous, and even if she didn't have any real talent for the stage, she was willing to study under him and work hard, and start with very small parts in his plays. And third, if he proved difficult in any way, as she knew he might, or if he went right on leering at every girl he happened to see, who was to stop her from getting a divorce and being none the worse for having been for a while Mrs. André Salamat? And finally, just in case he turned out to be *madly* in love with her and wouldn't think of letting her go on the stage, or wouldn't think of letting her get a divorce, or was insanely jealous, or got her pregnant and they had a child or two, what of all these things? There was surely such a thing as dying, and he certainly might not last more than five years, and she would be his widow and have his wealth, and perhaps a small son. What did she care about Joseph Daly in Philadelphia? He'd just have to marry somebody else, that's all.

Thus, she was well prepared for *anything*.

The actor was quite astonished when she accepted his invitation to go to his apartment for some tea and music, for he had expected her automatically to refuse at least once.

Still, if he was to be cheated out of the joys of courtship, no matter. It was unfortunate, however, that he was more tired than usual and actually longed for bed and sleep. The strain of standing up into the limits of his height was beginning to bother him just a little, and the back of his neck felt hot and tender.

In the taxi something she said about married people she knew rather annoyed him, for he was not sure it did not reveal a more calculating nature than he enjoyed in a young lady, but he was willing to put his annoyance down as having been the consequence of general weariness.

Laura Slade, on the other hand, was more alive than she had been when he had first met her. She was delighted with his having performed for her alone, with his having had her seat removed from the gallery and placed in his dressing-room, with the roses he had bought for her, and with being so near him.

All this excitement, he found, was also a little annoying, for if the truth were told, he was in fact a sad man, and a lonely one. His comfort was God, though few might ever suspect it.

He became sadder and lonelier than ever when it developed that she knew nothing about arranging for water to come to a boil in a kettle, about preparing tea, or about setting a small table with cups and saucers and spoons—all of which he himself did while she watched, apparently adoring him.

Finally, she tried to be of help and dropped a cup which broke into a great many pieces which he had a little difficulty gathering together. It was extremely difficult to conceal his annoyance as he did this work, but he managed to say something not quite worked out about treasuring all the lovely broken pieces because *she* had dropped the cup. Something essential had been absent from his voice when he had made the remark, for the girl replied by saying she wished she had taken homemaking and cooking at Briarcliff instead of English, math, and zoology.

This remark very nearly destroyed his soul, and he found himself saying over and over again: English, math, and zoology.

At last tea was on the table and it was time to sit down and be refreshed. After the first cup a little of his sadness and loneliness began to leave him, and he told her about his dream of finding somewhere in the world the girl who was Woman herself restored to her true beauty, dignity, and wisdom.

Laura Slade for a short time was under the impression that he was describing her, but she soon understood that he was not, that he was, if anything, only very tired, and older than he liked to believe, and not especially handsome, either. Still, she was willing to believe any one of a number of exciting things might still develop, largely along the miscellaneous lines she had been thinking about ever since he had told her all those wonderful things when she had said Paris three times.

The actor went on and on about his ideal until she was not quite sure he wasn't ill, but she knew it would not do to fuss over him as if he were actually a tired old man, so she went right on being enchanted by his remarks, which by now were beginning to be difficult to hear and were more than half in French, a language she had studied a little but could not understand at all. Once, she mistook something serious he said for something amusing, and hoping to have him find her enchanting and forget for a moment his ideal, she burst into what she believed was joyous and contagious laughter.

The actor stopped talking and smiled faintly, for she had actually giggled.

That did it.

The girl was a gorgeous idiot.

He poured for her in silence, and then for himself, and they sipped silently.

At last he said: "I did not know you were so young."

His voice was dry and old and tired.

"But I'm not," Laura said. "I'm twenty-two. A woman. My mother had three children when she was twenty-two and my grandmother five."

"So many?" the actor said dryly.

"Yes. Life was so much more exciting in the old days, I suppose."

It is incredible, the actor thought in French, that a girl so old should be so stupid.

He closed his eyes to rest a moment, and while he was resting he heard her say: "Paris. Paris. Paris."

He opened his eyes wearily, and said: "I beg your pardon?"

"Paris," the girl said. "Remember?"

"Of course I remember," André Salamat said. "I was born there." He got to his feet.

"Let me take you home now," he said in a new tone of voice. It was the tone of voice that said unmistakably that a great deal of fuss had been avoided in the nick of time, and all was now officially ended. His voice was quite cheerful as he went on. "I promised your aunt at her lovely party that I would get you home at a proper hour."

"You did?" Laura said. "I thought it was a secret."

"A secret?" he said. "But why? I adore American girls. They are so refreshing in their—*enthusiasms.* In Paris the French girls meet a famous actor and they are so *indifferent.*"

At the door of her aunt's house he lifted her hand and kissed it.

"Give my love to your aunt," he said.

"Philadelphia," Laura Slade said.

She was angry now, and she didn't care who happened to know she was.

"Philadelphia?" André Salamat said.

"Yes," the girl said. "When I say Philadelphia I believe in love again."

She stepped into the house and closed the door behind her.

The actor looked up into the heavens and felt how sad he was, how *glad* he was to be so sad again.

The Whole Voyald and Other Stories, 1956

Confessions of
a Playwright

There are a good many writers who make no bones about the fact that they write for money. These writers generally fall into two categories: (1) those who actually write for money and have very little money to show for it, and (2) those who do not know how to write for money and have a great deal of money to show for it, but enjoy saying they write for money. George Bernard Shaw enjoys saying he writes for money. It is easy for him to say that. He is a rich man and most of his wealth appears to have come to him from his writing. It is out of the question, though, that he ever wrote anything because he hoped or believed it would bring him a great deal of money. On the other hand, it is inconceivable that he ever wrote anything which he did not try his best to make so irresistible in itself as to bring him an income.

In short, after the fact, a writer may truthfully say anything he pleases about why he writes.

There are two American writers whose fame in recent years has grown in a small and not especially significant area who betrayed (when I first met them) an intense preoccupation with the problem of writing in a way that would bring them riches. Both of them tried to write moving picture scenarios, and one of them tried to invent a comic strip, but these efforts failed. They then acquired the view that they did not write for money because doing so was beneath them, and it was after the cultivation of this view that their fame began to grow. They are now fairly famous, so to speak, and they do not have very much money. They have learned to write what they must, they have discovered that this writing does not bring them wealth, and they are resigned to it. These writers, in my opinion, are no better than the writers who actually write for money and never get very much of it. That is to say, their writing is not any freer than the writing of professional hacks, and they are, as a matter of fact, nothing more than professional failures themselves. The subject of their writing is failure, and the tone of their writing is a tone of failure.

On the other hand, there are fairly good writers who are terrified of failure and consequently go about their work in a safe and sane manner, consistently turning out fairly good work which almost always brings them a fair amount of ordinary notice and a reasonable amount of money. These writers have yet to produce anything more spectacular than a best seller or a Broadway hit.

To sum up the point here, we must acknowledge that it is not impossible to write well and earn money; it is not impossible to write poorly and not earn money; and finally, it is not impossible to fail to earn money by writing either poorly or well. If this seems complicated, it is so because the matter is in fact complicated.

Some writers are ashamed of their reasons for writing. They do not want to admit, for instance, that they write so that they will become better known and thereby meet a great many more people than they would be apt to meet otherwise; or, on the other hand, that they write in order not to be required to meet anybody they don't want to meet. There are writers who are ashamed to come right out and acknowledge that, insofar as they know, they write because they suffer from inferiority complexes, or that they are chronically sick and write for therapy. Some writers are even ashamed to admit that they write to show off.

Now, let us acknowledge at the outset that in one degree or another every writer in the world writes for one or another or all of the foregoing reasons, as well as for many others. Let us accept that it is possible that a man writes for the most astonishing reasons imaginable, and let us not be astonished, for it would not seem to make the slightest difference why any writer writes. All that any of us cares about is what he writes. Now, let us say for purposes of timesaving that there is a writer who writes for the noblest of reasons—whatever they may be—and that his writing is noble. Let us say that he is a truly good man, truly eager and faithful, and let us say that his writing is of a like order. Let us say that this writer achieves truth gracefully and creates beauty meaningfully. Let us say that his work is simultaneously art and a demonstration of his personal acceptance of a profound moral obligation to society. Let us say, in short, that his intention is consistently good and that his effort to achieve his intention is invariably industrious and thorough. And then let us say that he is a playwright, and then let us look into his problems, and hear his confessions.

A writer of plays intends and expects his plays to be performed.

Let us see what this means in our time, in our society.

A playwright in order to have a play produced in New York must be a member of the Dramatists Guild whether he will or no, as the saying is. What does this Guild do for the playwright? It deducts money from his earnings, and it receives money that is due him, and it sends him this money, after deductions. Sometimes the Guild takes a little time doing this, and sometimes members of the executive department of the Guild are on vacation when the playwright needs his money badly. The Guild does not help the playwright write better plays or any kind of plays at all; it does not give him $10 a day when he is writing a play and does not have $10 a day; it does not care what kind of plays he writes or what effect the overproduction of inferior plays is apt to have on the future of the theatre or of playwrights. The Dramatists Guild provides him and play producers with a Minimum Basic Contract, and this contract is extremely minimum, but absolutely not basic. The contract is very infrequently revised, and when it is revised it is revised in favor of everybody but the playwright. It is revised especially in favor of the Dramatists Guild. Here is a parent no playwright ever had, and yet no American playwright is permitted to refuse this preposterous parenthood. Let us be generous-hearted and let us say that the Dramatists Guild is a fine organization and that it does all playwrights a great deal of good. The fact remains that it is also an organization whose method is threat and intimidation. In my opinion, it is, therefore, an illegal organization. It has collected a great deal of money from my earnings and I haven't the slightest idea what it does with the money. I would like to know what it does with the money and I would like to object to anything it does with the money of which I do not approve. I have not yet heard of its ever having staked a needy playwright, or of ever having financed the production of a play, or of ever having established a national theatre or a New York City theatre, or of ever having lent a helping hand to established playwrights of other countries who are in need. I would rather not be a member of the Dramatists Guild as it now exists, and yet I am a member. Early in 1948 I resigned from the Dramatists Guild but when I began to make plans for the production of a play in New York it was necessary for me to join again because I could not arrange for the production of a play unless I was a member of the Dramatists Guild. No producer is permitted to produce a play by a nonmember of the Dramatists Guild. No member of the Dramatists Guild may permit a producer who is not a member of the Producers Guild to produce a play. What is this but a monopoly? Why can't a man write a play and have it produced by anybody he pleases? Let us say such a man is offensive. Why can't he still write a play and have it produced by anybody he pleases? Is it not permissible for a man to be offensive and still have rights?

I will believe the Dramatists Guild is a fine useful sensible organization when it permits me to join or not join, as I see fit; and if I choose not to join, will not obstruct my work in the theatre. I would be willing to donate 25 percent of my earnings in the theatre to needy playwrights if I were permitted not to be a member of the Dramatists Guild, and would not be obstructed. If need be, short of denying my family shelter, food and clothing, I would be willing to donate all of my earnings in the theatre to a fund for the establishment of a Playwrights Theatre. I sometimes bet the horses for money. I write because I am opposed to threat, intimidation, monopoly, unfair business practices, violation of civil and private rights, and for miscellaneous other reasons.

So far we have glanced at an aspect of playwrighting which is supposed to be favorable. From here on in, the aspects of the problem grow more and more unfavorable.

The agent. Here is somebody whose very existence tends to establish the fact that artists are idiots and producers crooks. The agent is supposed to find a producer for the playwright's play, and when found, he is supposed to see that the playwright gets a decent deal; but no agent ever found a producer for a play unless there was a play in the first place and unless a producer happened to think the play would make him some money. Not having written the play, the agent is not hurt when a producer says he does not think the play will make him some money. The agent is not hurt when he fails to find a producer for a play, and he does not pay a playwright 10 percent of his annual income because he failed to find a producer. He just sends the play back to the playwright. Agents are absolutely unnecessary, or only necessary for minors. If a play is good enough or seems good enough, a few producers are always eager to try to make some money out of it anyway; and if it is not good enough or does not seem good enough, no producer wants to try to make some money out of it anyway. I have heard a great deal about the refinement, the culture, the depth of understanding of certain agents. These are irrelevant qualities in him, I'm afraid: his function is a business function and all he is set up for, and the only excuse for him, is to accomplish the impossible: that is, find a producer and get magnificent terms for a play that is no good at all. If an agent wants to demonstrate his refinement, culture, depth of understanding or anything else of that order in the theatre, all he has to do is write a play which leaves no room for doubt. If he wants to demonstrate his usefulness to playwrights on the other hand, all he has to do is make a good deal for a bad play. A good play by its very nature makes its own deal.

The producer. Here is perhaps the most preposterous mountebank of the lot. He takes a lot of time picking out a play he thinks is a cinch to make a lot of money, and then, instead of respecting his own judgment and putting his own money into the production of the play, he rounds up a group of people called backers and convinces them to put up the money for him. He gets 50 percent of the production for being the producer, and the backers split the other 50 percent among themselves for putting up the money. If the play makes no money he has earned a couple of months of excellent pay, and the backers have items for deduction from their taxes. This man frequently poses as an artist. He sometimes goes so far as to affect concern about social reform, eradication of injustice from the affairs of men, and the political education of the masses; but he never puts his own money into a production. He just doesn't believe in anything that much. The producer (especially if he has had a prestige success) frequently believes in himself to the point of fantasy—but of course he does not believe in fantasy in the theatre. (Can't understand it.) He is quick to notice that the last act of a play is "hopeless" and must be rewritten, and he can tell the playwright precisely how it must be rewritten. I have on occasion accepted the theory that the third act is hopeless and that the producer has precisely the right scheme to salvage it and thereby transform the play from a nothing to a smasheroo, as Variety puts it; and then I have had to explain that I myself could not possibly write the new third act, but since the producer is so clear about it, and since his financial interest in the property is so great, perhaps he would do us both a favor and write it, and invariably the producer has declined to do so. He has remarked modestly that he is a businessman; he has been in business twenty-five years; he helped Knut Hamsun get a job running a streetcar when he came to America in 1910; he discovered Maggie McIntyre of silent film fame; he made a quarter of a million dollars in one year alone from the musical Hot Ziggety; he knows show business; only last night he was reading around in Hamlet, and there's a play for you; but he is not a playwright, he is a businessman, and the third act is hopeless and must be rewritten. Even a bad play by a man who is a playwright is better than any play rewritten for a man who is not a playwright. If O'Casey or Shaw or O'Neill wanted to tell me how to rewrite the third act, I know I would be deeply moved by their generosity, but I also know I would not rewrite it that way; and I know they would never take the liberty of trying to tell me how to rewrite it any more than I would take the liberty of trying to tell them how to rewrite the third act of one of their plays. Any producer would take that liberty, though, and then feel hurt if a playwright did not leap at the opportunity to pick up a little free education for himself. The producer takes his instruction from the backers, it would seem, and they take theirs apparently from the latest hit, however great a failure it may be in reality.

The producer is forever trying to camouflage what he is doing— that is, trying to make money—by trying to pass for an artist. But in a showdown he will reveal his contempt for that breed. He is frequently eager for the artist to write for him because he cannot write for himself. If the playwright is so independent that even with the promise of a hit and a lot of money, he refuses to make a business deal unless it is a business deal—that is, a deal in which the playwright, all flushed with the excitement of all that money, tries to get himself a very reasonable share of the whole production—the producer swiftly and effectively switches the discussion from the realm of business to the realm of art, and remarks delicately, "Now, I want to tell you my wife read this play last night, and I have a lot of respect for her common sense, and she said to me, 'What does this play mean?' She's a well-read woman and if she had to ask that question you can be sure other people—the public, in fact—are going to ask it, too." Pause. "What does this play mean?" The playwright's goose is cooked anyway, so if he's smart he will reply, "I don't know." That is a stock question of businessmen when they discover a playwright who wants to talk business. They never want to talk business. They're not interested in money. They want to know what a play means. As a playwright, as a member of the Dramatists Guild, though an unwilling one, I offer to all playwrights this stock answer to that stock question: "If you will tell me how much money you have in the bank and what it means, I will tell you what this play means."

The director. He is frequently a playwright, and I have little fault to find with him, although a good many of the mannerisms of the producer exist also in a good many directors, especially those who are not playwrights. The director is a conductor, not a composer, but there are few directors who are willing to accept this fact. Sometimes it is possible for a director who is not a playwright to stage a play as it was written to be staged, but that must be very rare indeed. I have never had such a director connected with any of my plays. I sympathize with the earnest director's problem, for he has no choice but to create, and it is not very likely that he may perfectly create that which the playwright intended. That is why I believe that whenever possible a playwright should either direct his own plays or be on hand at all times to help the director.

I know I have found a lot of fault with the procedure of getting a play produced, but there has been a lot of fault to find. The situation is in fact a good deal worse than I have so far pointed out. A new development—without a doubt the most offensive of all—is the tryout in a private home before an audience of potential backers, men and women who have money to invest. As I write, on the last day of September, 1948, this procedure has brought to New York over one million dollars worth of plays: revues, musicals, farces, light comedies, fantasies, and serious dramas. So far only one of these productions appears to be scheduled for anything like a reasonable run. This procedure is in monstrous taste, besides being impractical. It makes a beggar of art, and if the custom continues we will certainly see more and more expensive productions whose sole object being to earn profits for backers must do one of two things: drive the backers back to stocks and bonds or remove forever from the presentation of plays all ease, all freedom, and all fun. To my mind it is much more reasonable for a playwright to enquire of a potential backer where he got his money, how he got it, how much he has, what he has done with it so far, what his purpose has been in accumulating it, and so on, than for the backer to ask the playwright to put over his play in the parlor. In short, it is more reasonable for money to go on trial before art than the other way around.

The Critics. There is little to be gained for the theatre in complaining that the drama critics exert a great deal of influence: they do, and that's the end of it. Few of the drama critics of the daily papers are, as a matter of fact, critics; they are reporters, and they are pretty good reporters. They tell their readers that a certain play has opened, and they say a few things about the event. Sometimes they talk about the plot of the play, if it has a plot, but almost invariably they comment on outstanding or inferior performances of certain players; the scenery is frequently described; the direction is discussed; and the effect of the play on the audience, and its effect on the reviewer himself. Rarely is the play itself, as a play, as an entry in the playwriting sweepstakes, discussed. This is understandable. Readers of newspapers are not students of drama, they are people who expect to find out if a play is apt to appeal to them, or they are people who somehow enjoy reading about an opening, just as many people who are not in society like to read about the goings on in the social world. The newspaper reviewer's job is to write a review that will attract and keep daily readers. I have seldom had a haircut in New York during which the barber has not included among other topics the current theatre and remarked, "I see where another flop opened last night." Few critics need to be taken seriously. Their standards are properly Broadway, or success, standards. They cannot be blamed for this. It would be silly for a morning tabloid reviewer to discuss drama seriously. But it is impossible not to take them seriously as judges, and, for good or bad, we must understand that every opening is a court trial. It does not matter that the decision of the judges is only the equivalent of yes or no, thumbs up or thumbs down. In the event that the greater number of the decisions are yes, everyone specifically involved is pleased and proud and does not complain that the decisions were reached haphazardly and came to pass in a most mysterious and accidental manner; but if the greater part of the decisions are no, then, of course, everyone specifically involved believes it is time to clean up on the critics.

I believe I am the only American playwright and producer who complained when a play was praised. Of course, I was willing to complain only by word of mouth, as the saying is. I did not write a protest, but I wasn't fooled for a moment. Just as easily as the critics had for the most part said yes, they might have said no, and they said yes most haphazardly and for the least pertinent reasons. The play was *The Beautiful People*, which I produced with my own money—$11,000, as I remember it. I personally guaranteed the play, and I had money gladly refunded to any who wished to have their money back—for any reason—no questions asked.

Is there anything sensible to be done about the power of the drama critics? It would appear to be in order to have the first performance of a play—the opening—reviewed by every practicing critic. As it is, the magazine reviewers see the second performance, and certain reviewers for certain periodicals with limited audiences see later performances, if there are any. This is a foolish procedure. The same performance should be reviewed by all reviewers, so that a reasonable consensus of opinion may be immediately available to the management of the play; and for the purpose of having the more serious critics in the auditorium along with the newspaper reviewers. The management should arrange with the weekly reviewers to have copies of their reviews as soon as the reviews are written. In addition to this, certain individuals who attend the opening should be encouraged to write short reviews of the plays, for use by the management if the comments are favorable. Who should the management approach for such reviews? I would go about the matter thus: every person at an opening would be handed, with his program, a card on which to write his opinion in one word, two, three, or as many more as space might permit. This should be followed by the person's name, age, address, profession, religion, political party, financial status, health, and opinion on the theatre in general. These cards would be deposited in one of many boxes placed in the theatre. The man who pays his way deserves to have his say. He is supposed to be the great critic anyway, and it would do no harm to make it possible for him to speak out at last. As the matter now stands, the theatregoer is a sheep which hangs its head and follows the goats anywhere they happen to go.

Under the foregoing circumstances, how may the playwright do his work, maintain his integrity, and manage to survive economically? I have already remarked that I sometimes bet on the horses. I should like to enlarge a little on this. Horse bettors as such are generally regarded as fools, and it is proper to accept this view without embarrassment. They are especially foolish if they lose, and more often than not they do. But the virtue to the playwright of seeking to exempt himself from the urgent need of money by studying the races and occasionally making a bet is this: that it establishes more swiftly then any other activity the essential irrelevance and worthlessness of money, whether the sums involved are enormous or insignificant. This, in turn, re-establishes emphatically the profound relevance and worth of art, of integrity, of pride, of indifference toward material success or failure. In short, it permits the playwright to work as hard as he is able to work on a play for its own sake. For he knows that while it is not easy, it is nevertheless true that money as such, as money, may be abundantly obtained by so simple a process as believing one horse among eight or nine will run faster than the others, and backing up his belief with a bet. By the same token, he knows that much needed money may disappear that easily, too. Consequently, money by itself is seen to be so nearly meaningless as to be unworthy of any broader identification.

In other words, betting on the horse races gives the playwright the contempt for money which money must have in order for him to go about his work of writing plays in a free, proud, independent and sensible manner. It does not matter if he loses or wins, or loses more than he wins, or always loses and never wins. What matters is that he discovers, as he could discover by no other activity, that money is simultaneously phony and irrelevant, however profoundly it conditions the behavior of man, distorts his real character, and upsets his life. This discovery is a basic requirement for the playwright, and for that matter for all men who are concerned about the achievement of meaning and right in the affairs of populations, nations, governments, and cultural systems. The one world will obviously be one world only geographically until the horse bettor's discovery that money is irrelevant becomes an accepted basic fact to those whose end in life seems to be to gather together as much of it as possible, whether individuals, corporations, or governments. Why, for instance, is it acceptable for a government to maintain a Department of War and not maintain a Department of Art? The Army and the Navy do not have to bother their heads, so to speak, about the cost in money (or for that matter in lives) of any project, however experimental or even impractical: they just naturally get the money, which again brings home clearly the horse bettor's intelligence of the irrelevance of money. No one, of course, has ever been able to understand or explain clearly why a government does anything.

The playwright, to continue and conclude, who expects to do his work with a free heart even though he has little money must simply arrange his life in a way that will permit him to survive pleasantly without very much money. He must cut down expenses and still live as extravagantly as the richest man in the world, or as extravagantly as he likes. He must do without but at the same time never want. If he does not even have the very small amount of money he requires, then of course he must think about the matter very carefully and perhaps do something about it. To beg in the street anonymously, as a man who is in need, I regard as more honorable than to beg in a parlor as a playwright. To borrow (from anybody) is also all right, for there is no man in the world who may not someday be able to pay all his debts. To gamble, however, is the best procedure of all, for it simultaneously reveals his contempt for the unsound and foolish economic system, and provides him with either a clearer picture than ever of the fierce role of money in the affairs on men, or with enough of the stuff itself to keep him going for a while.

Tomorrow (Magazine), 1949

Hal Francis and Thomas Wolfe

*A*t Stanley Rose's bookstore in Hollywood about twenty-five years ago there was a fellow who had worked in the Pittsburgh steel mills and had written a number of short stories about Polacks and the Bohunks. He was a big, hearty, loud-voiced, happy fellow by the name of Owen Francis, called Hal by his friends. The stories he had written had appeared in such magazines as *Atlantic Monthly*, and the *Saturday Evening Post*. But Hal hadn't had a book published when he reached Hollywood and began to look around for a movie producer who might want to put him to work writing a movie about life in the steel mills. As last he found a producer, but he was asked to write about the intelligentsia of New York, which wasn't his territory, as he put it. All the same he worked for twelve weeks, and every week picked up a check for more money than he had ever before seen at one time in his life, a man in his middle twenties, eager for better food, better booze, better broads, and better fun, all of which were readily available if you had money, if you had a little importance, and if you were in the movie business. Like all of the writers who were going out to Hollywood from all over the country in those days, his declared purpose was to pick up some of the big money, hurry back to his proper place in the world, and write his first novel, which he expected to be something good. It is well known that few of the writers did what they said they were going to do, so it isn't necessary for me to dwell on that aspect of the matter. Very nearly all of the writers who went to Hollywood talked about the novels they were going to write as soon as they had saved up five thousand dollars, or ten, which soon became twenty, or even fifty. The more money you get, if you are a hungry writer, fresh from poverty, fresh from the cold of the grubby neighborhoods of the big cities of America, the more you believe you must have before you can write the great novel you believe you want to write. At first these writers talked about these unwritten novels, but after a year or two, after they had put away ten thousand, and then twenty, and a number of them fifty, and after they had run through half a dozen beautiful girls from all over the country with aspirations to be movie stars, and after they had bought homes with gardens, and after they had staffed their homes with Filipino or Chinese houseboys and cooks, and with gardeners, and chauffeurs, they not only talked about these unwritten first novels, they cried about them, and they blamed Capitalism for their failure to write these great books. It was a joy to visit the fine home of one of these writers, and to meet three or four of his friends, also writers, and to hear them all crying together about this outrageous situation into which they they had been dragged against their wills. Stanley Rose himself was frequently on hand, and even while the writers wept he drank brandy and said, "They never had it so good, and they know it."

All it was was fun: the champion writers of the Hollywood studios, the writers of the screenplays of hundreds of the worst movies ever made, enjoyed gathering together and pretending they were martyrs.

But that wasn't how it was with this fellow from Pittsburgh. He was very happy to have the big money, to write the stuff the producers wanted, about intelligent people in New York, or about stupid people in Nebraska, it was all the same to him, and he was proud of the fact that he had gotten his first job on the strength of five short stories that his employer hadn't even read. Somewhere along the line, though, he had met Thomas Wolfe, and they had become friends. And all Owen Francis wanted to talk about was Thomas Wolfe and his writing, especially *Look Homeward, Angel*. Now, there *was* a writer—that Tom Wolfe, that giant of a man who sometimes wrote for three days and three nights steadily, in a kind of ferocious trance. There was a real writer, not a writer like these Hollywood cream puffs, not a phony, not a crybaby on his way to the bank with another week's paycheck for three thousand dollars, his gorgeous girl on his arm, keeping him from dying of loneliness.

"Hell," he used to say, "let's face it, I'm not a writer, and this easy work out here is just what the doctor ordered. I like to *read* good writing, but I know I can't write it, all I can write is a simple story about the poor slaves I worked with for so long, and the only reason the stuff I write is interesting is that I know it from the inside out. The background stuff is all true, and nobody else who knows that background can write at all, or wants to. My subject matter has a certain authenticity and appeal, but my writing itself is just plain routine and ordinary."

All the same, after about a year and a half of work in the movie studios, and a lot of fun, Hal found himself out of work, and his agent just couldn't find him a new job. And so Hal decided that, like it or not, he had better get the hell to work on his first novel. He had a little money stashed, but he knew it wasn't going to last very long at the rate he was going, so he put his typewriter on a table in his hotel room and he began to write the novel. The going was tough, first because writing had always been hard work for him, and second because he had gotten so far away from where his life had been hard and real that he couldn't get the feel of it again. All of his Bohunks and Polacks had become members of the Intelligentsia, or worse. They were all soft and glib instead of hard and inarticulate, as they had been when he had worked with them, as they still were, and as he himself no longer was. He kept after his work just the same, fighting a desperate fight, throwing away one false start after another, working from noon until dark, and then hurrying over to Stanley Rose's bookstore, and then going next door with Stanley and whoever else was around at the time, myself, for instance, to Musso & Frank's, first for three or four drinks at the bar, and then for a big supper, and all during the drinking and eating, Hal would say, "Man, I'm trying, nobody can say I ain't trying, but I just ain't making it, that's all. And I've *got* to make it. It isn't that I have got to write a *good* first novel, it isn't that at all, I don't need to be a writer at all, but unless I write and publish a novel, I just won't be able to get another job in Hollywood, and I don't want to leave."

Every now and then he would say, "Well, it's going a little better at last. I got out three pages this afternoon that I think are the beginning of something halfway worth the bother. It's the first chapter, and I call it *Don't Laugh at Me, Mr. Boss.* You see, Bohunks and Polacks hate to be laughed at. Being laughed at, especially by the boss, is something like the supreme insult; it's like calling a man's father and mother dirty names. And I never knew a Bohunk or a Polack who had been laughed at who didn't go a little mad. Inside, at first. But from one day to another that dirty laughter grew in the poor man's heart and then you could *see* his madness, and you knew he might just kill somebody, not necessarily the boss. It might be his wife instead—not the wife of the boss, his own wife, who had been taking a lot of beatings since the poor man had been laughed at, as if she were responsible for the whole thing. And he would beat his oldest kid, too, and the kid would believe that this was the way it was, that's all. He wouldn't believe this was wrong or different. His father was beating him lately, that's all. Well, that's the stuff I have got in the first chapter, and now all I have got to do is keep this stuff going until I have got a book written. In the last chapter I am going to have to decide if the poor man kills somebody—his wife or his oldest boy—or gets over his madness. So far it looks as if he's going to kill somebody, but at the last minute I may have him get over it. I saw it happen half a dozen times, and it's the gospel truth, but I'm not sure it's right for a novel, that's all."

Do you want to know how he gets over his madness? Well, the boss notices that the man has worked harder and better than ever since the boss laughed at him, but he also notices that the man is ready to go berserk, and so the boss goes to him while the man is busy with his work, and the boss says to him, 'Nick, you are the best God-damn worker I got in this whole God-damn mill.' That's all the boss has got to do. The man is healed. His madness is gone. He gets drunk after work, he goes home with a new dress for his wife, a new shirt for his son, and he puts his arms around his wife and his son and all the rest of his kids, and they don't know what the hell's happened to him—but I know, I saw it happen. Have I got a good story here?"

Stanley would say, "Sure you have. I got a man coming out from Scribner's tomorrow and I'll tell him about it. You write it and Scribner's will publish it, and then you can go back to work at a studio for big money. The book will make you five hundred dollars, but it *will* be a book, and I'll take it around to every producer in town and show it to him, along with the other books I'll be showing at the same time, and you'll be in again."

Well, Hal Francis worked on, and the going never stopped being tough, but little by little he got about half the book on paper. The man from Scribner's sat with Hal and Stanley and a few of the rest of us who were loafing around the bookstore in those days, and he said he liked the idea and would speak about the book to Mr. Scribner himself. The minute it was finished, he was sure Scribner's would publish it.

I went back to San Francisco for three months, and then I got a ride to Hollywood again, and I began to loaf around in the bookstore again.

One evening Hal Francis came in and I asked him about the novel.

"What novel?" he said. "I can't write. Tom Wolfe can write. He's the only writer in the whole country. When a guy like that is writing, all the rest of us can put away our typewriters. Just take a look at his new book. It's right here on the table." And he picked up a book and handed it to me. "Stanley just ordered a hundred copies more of the book. He sold a hundred in three days, and it's not even a novel; it's a collection of short stories, and you know short stories don't sell at all. *From Death to Morning*—well, take it, read it. Tom Wolfe is saying everything worth saying, and nobody else is saying anything. What's more, Tom's saying it the only way it ought to be said. He's bawling it out, shouting it out, roaring it out. He's got one sentence that goes on for three pages because he's a writer and he's got something to say, and you don't even notice how long the sentence is. It's that simple and that right, and the more you read, the more you know he's the only writer in the country, and maybe in the whole world. The rest of us nibble at little edges of life, but Tom sits down and eats the whole human race in two big bites, that's all. Ever since I read this new book, I just haven't had the heart to sit at my typewriter and try to write my silly little story about a Bohunk who has been laughed at by an idiot boss. About the poor man's wife, and his poor son, and the rest of his poor kids, and his poor madness. But Tom writes about the whole dirty human race and he transforms the sons of bitches into angels, all of them, even his dirty villains are angels, even they are immortal in Tom's writing."

Stanley told Hal to forget Tom Wolfe and write his own novel. It wasn't necessary for one writer to write like another. There was no reason for a fair writer to quit because there happened to be a better writer writing at the same time. What Stanley wanted was to have Hal Francis in town, a nightly visitor at his store, because when he wasn't knocking his own writing Hal was one of the best guys in town to have around. In the end, though, Hal never finished the novel. He got a job with a producer again, but his pay-check was very small, and the job lasted only six weeks, and that was the way matters stood for the next two or three years.

Hal Francis and Stanley Rose met and drank and ate good food every night, going next door to Musso & Frank's, where they could afford to eat and drink, and Stanley tried to get his friend to finish his novel. Years after Hal had put the thing aside, despising it, Stanley was still up late at night, both of them drunk, urging Hal to finish the thing—he only had three or four more chapters to do—finish it, and get back into the big money. But one night Hal didn't show up, and Stanley went out to his place and found him sick in bed, and the next night Hal died.

"He died in my arms," Stanley said. "I buried the kid."

Well, now, Owen Francis was only one of the writers out there in those days, and what happened to him didn't happen to the others, or at any rate not to many of them, and certainly not in the same way, but the thing that killed the man, or helped do it, apart from the weight he had put on, and apart from the drinking he had done for years, was the fact that he didn't believe in his writing, *couldn't* believe in it. He believed that as long as Thomas Wolfe was writing there was no reason in the world for him to write, too. Tom Wolfe was saying it all. He loved and admired Wolfe as a giant of a man, voracious and insatiable, a compulsive writer who was also inexhaustible, or very nearly so, and he loved and admired him as a writer, a working writer, a man who stayed in a dump of an apartment in Brooklyn, who worked with such intensity that he forgot time, forgot food and drink, and then after long hours of fierce and trance-like concentration and the swiftest writing in the world, and sometimes after a whole day and night of it, and sometimes even more, he staggered out of his hovel, his huge body purified by the fiery labor, his heavy body made light, almost weightless, by the passing of the hours, and he began to fly over the streets, crossing the bridge to Manhattan at three or four in the morning, finding men at work on the docks, joining them in their work for an hour or two, then flying on. Tom Wolfe was a soul, he was a spirit, an angel in a huge human body, and his old friend Hal Francis believed that he himself, equally big and almost equally voracious, was nothing and nobody, and had nothing to say. Well, of course Hal was mistaken, at least a little, about Tom, and he was mistaken about himself, too. He *had* something to say, and he said it often enough, but not in writing. He said it at the bar, drinking. He needed somebody to listen to him *now*, and not later, and the best ear he had was the ear of Stanley Rose, a new friend in a new part of the world.

Not Dying, 1963

Joe Gould
and "The
Oral History
of the World"

I was pruning vines on a vineyard in the San Joaquin Valley of California when I was sixteen years old, after I had been kicked out of school so many times I decided not to go back. Heavy rain began to fall and all of the workers had to quit work for the rest of the day. I went to a bookstore in Fresno, to the back room were the old books were, and I began to look around for something priceless that I could buy for a nickel or a dime. I found a stack of old magazines, but *good* old magazines, not junk magazines, and the name of one of them was the *Dial*, which I had heard about. There was only one copy of the *Dial* in the whole store. I asked the old man and he said it was the only copy he had, the only copy he had ever had, he had had it for a year, he didn't even remember how he'd got it. I paid him a dime and I rode my bike home in the heavy rain, the magazine inside my shirt. I read the magazine from cover to cover because it was raining anyway, there was nowhere to go, I couldn't be bothered about going to a movie, there was nothing to do, I had quit school forever, I was going to be a writer or nothing at all, I didn't know how I was going to be a writer, or how (if need be) I was going to be nothing at all, so I sat at the round table on the screen porch and started to read. Christ, what stuff. How did they do it? How did they write that way? Every word just right, every word clearly printed on heavy white paper, every word full of meaning, all of the words together making one short story after another, or one poem after another, or one essay after another, and there I was sixteen and stupid, a lousy reader instead of a great writer. Even so, being a reader was better than nothing, especially if the stuff you were reading was good, as it was, although I knew it was writing I could never do. Those guys knew how, and I didn't. And I probably never would find out how. I would have to learn how to write in a way that would compel editors and publishers to publish my stuff in spite of the fact that I didn't know how to write. And I didn't believe this was impossible, although I didn't believe it was inevitable. I wasn't sure. No writer at sixteen is. I knew I couldn't write as these writers were writing, though, because I could see they had been to school. In order to write as they were writing I would have to become like them, and how could I do that? It was out of the question. I didn't know them, except one or two by name, but I could almost see them, and it seemed to me they looked like writers, and I knew I didn't look like a writer. They had learning, and I didn't. I had wisdom, though, or at any rate I believed I did, or else how was I to account for the arrogance I had for everything and everybody in the whole world, including these writers, whose writing on the one hand I admired, whose learning on the other I resented? They had picked up a lot of information about other writers, other periods of writing, and all kinds of theories about what this particular writer had done, how he had in fact started a whole new school of writing, as they said, and all sorts of other things like that. And what did I know about stuff like that? Almost nothing, although I knew the *last words* of two or three hundred men, as reported in an old almanac, one of my favorite books. Before I reached the end of the magazine, though, I came upon four or five pages of writing that made me jump for joy. The stuff had been lifted out of a large, unfinished work entitled *The Oral History of the World*, and the name of the writer was Joe Gould. Well, now, when a writer calls himself Joe instead of Joseph, you stop and wonder. Whose little pal is *he* trying to be? Before I began to read what Joe Gould had written, I figured him for a phony, and I came near skipping what he had written. I found that I couldn't skip it, though. I read it and jumped, because this was plain, this was straight, this was the real thing, and all it was, was people talking. And they weren't great people saying great things, they were ordinary people saying ordinary things.

I went back to the vineyard the next morning and I began to listen to the ordinary things the other workers said to one another, and to me, and there it was: I had something, Joe Gould had put me wise to something: listen and you shall hear. And I listened.

We talk, we talk all the time, and when we write we don't stop talking, we go right on, it is all talk. I kept looking around for more stuff by Joe Gould, but there just wasn't any more of it. I kept waiting for the book to be published, to arrive at the Public Library, so I could read the whole thing, because I didn't buy books in those days, except a dictionary, and I did that only once, because once is enough. But the book didn't come out. I kept remembering Joe Gould and his big book, and I went right on looking forward to the happy day when I would see it, and read it from cover to cover, which I knew I would do, because there just wasn't any such thing as getting too much of that kind of writing. The years went by, but still there was no book by Joe Gould in the world. Well, where the hell was the man? What had happened to him? Had he died, or what? Where was his book? Another year went by, and then another, but still no book, and now I myself had published two books, and a third was about to be published.

I was in New York, and I knew Joe Gould was in New York, too, if he was anywhere at all. But I've got it all wrong, so I've got to go back and get it right.

What actually happened was that I read the fragment from his book in the *Dial* and went back to work the next morning, and one day when I was in New York, thirteen or fourteen years later—wrong again.

One of the greatest men in this whole world, who made drawings of plays in rehearsal for *The New York Times* and the *Herald Tribune*, a man who loved New York and made drawings of the windy streets and the hurrying people in them, moving in and with the wind, a man named Don Freeman, came along one day in New York and opened his sketchbook and showed me the drawings he had made that day. They were great, and I said I wished I had a book for him to illustrate. A year or so later I had such a book and he illustrated it, and he wrote to me in San Francisco from New York. He sent me a magazine he himself got out every now and then called *Newsstand*, full of his drawings. In one of them was a drawing of a full-bearded man with twinkling eyes, and the name of the man was Joe Gould. The minute I got back to New York I telephoned Don Freeman and asked him if he could tell me something about Joe Gould.

"Hell," he said, "I'll take you to him, or bring him to you."

Well, Joe Gould was a little bit of a fellow with a kind of birdlike voice. I told him how I had found his piece in the *Dial*, and had never been able to forget it, where was the whole book? He said he was still writing it. Well, why not publish parts of it in the magazines? Well, he didn't know. Well, how much of it had he written so far? Well, a million words of it. Well, that's the equivalent of four or five novels—long ones, not short ones. Why not publish the book in three or four, or even five or six volumes? Why wait any longer? Well, he didn't know. For one thing, he didn't know where most of the manuscript was. He hadn't quite lost it, although he may have. He had forgotten it in one or another of the many rooming houses in New York where he had lived for a while. Well, did h.. have *some* of the manuscript? Yes, he had quite a lot of it. Well, did he want to publish what he had? Well, maybe. He hadn't looked at the stuff, he was busy writing new stuff. Well, did he have any of the new stuff. Yes, he had some of it in his back pocket. He brought some stuff out of his back pocket, six or seven kinds of paper, folded together, on which he had written more of the book, and he read a couple of pages of the stuff, and it was great. What you read at sixteen may not mean very much to you when you're twenty-eight or twenty-nine, but Joe Gould's new stuff was just as good as his old stuff, if in fact it wasn't better, as I believe it was. Well, it's no good having stuff like that all over the place, some of it lost, all of it likely to become lost, since Joe Gould had no permanent address, had no money, lived from one day to the next, a man in his middle fifties at that time. Stuff like that ought to be published, so that others might know about it, read it, have it, so that I, for instance, might. So how about it? Well, everybody *knew* he was writing the book, Joe said. Everybody in the publishing world knew he had been writing it for twenty years or more, but nobody had invited him to offer the stuff for publication. Well, this was just plain silly, so I had to say, "Now, Joe, please tell me, is it possible you *prefer* not to have this book published, for some reason?" Joe said he didn't prefer not to have the stuff published, but at the same time he didn't especially mind that it hadn't been. I had to drink a little more and I had to think a little more about this. Joe had become a kind of legend, to begin with. He was famous in the little saloons of Greenwich Village. He had a lot of friends, most of them writers and painters, and most of them without money, too, although none of them were so steadily and consistently without it. Also, was it possible that he had in reality written very little during the years since the *Dial* had published a little of his writing, and he was only pretending that he had written a lot, had lost a lot, had misplaced a lot? What was the truth? He had certainly produced some of the work, brought it out of his back pocket, and from the looks of it, the writing was new, it had been done earlier that day, or yesterday, or the day before, he seemed to be at work on the book all the time, the talk was about new stuff in the world, very recent stuff, the big names discussed by the talkers were new big names, so what was going on? It seemed to me that while I did not want to intrude, I owed it to writing itself, and I owed it to myself, if not to Joe himself, to do something about having some of his great work published.

Joe said, "O.K., but I don't think any publisher will be willing to publish any of the stuff."

I wanted to know why not, and he said, "Well, *you* liked it, and I *believe* in it, and Don likes it, and a lot of other people I have read some of it to like it, but it isn't the kind of stuff publishers like, the kind of stuff they are used to, the kind they believe will make a lot of money, but go ahead if you want to."

I visited my publisher and we talked about it and he said he would be very happy to see the stuff if Joe would take it up to his office. I told Joe, and I believed he would actually go up there with some of the manuscript, but at the same time I couldn't help noticing that he wasn't excited about the idea, and again I felt I just didn't understand what was going on. In the end, over a period of six or seven years, I spoke first to Joe about the book and then to a publisher, a new one each time, six or seven of them, and I always believed, or hoped, Joe would take some of his manuscript to one of the publishers and the publisher would bring it out in the form of a book, under Joe's title for it, *The Oral History of the World*. But it didn't happen, and Joe died.

At first Joe disappeared, or at any rate nobody saw him around, although one or two must have known what had happened to him. I heard about it later: Joe had spent the last three years of his life in a kind of lunatic asylum, but you have got to bear in mind that if Joe needed a place where he could rest a little at last it would more than likely be his preference to go to a place reserved for people who are so alive as to seem mad. He was close to seventy by then, and he had been homeless for the better part of his life, one of the most erudite men of the world, a member of the famed family which he had long since forsaken, which in turn had long since forsaken him, a character in the Village, a laughing little fellow whose false teeth now and then fell out of his mouth, and were once stepped upon and crushed accidentally, who smoked incessantly, placing his cigarettes into a long holder from Woolworth's, whose grey beard was stained brown all around his mouth, who lived in his clothes, who was dirty and dynamic all his life.

A rich New Yorker once asked me if I might be able to get Joe to take a bath and put on new clothes supplied by the New Yorker and then go to dinner at the New Yorker's house. I said no. And nothing more. I was willing to try to get Joe interested in the idea of having his great book published, but I'd be damned if I would ask him to become a bathed and neatly dressed freak for the amusement of a millionaire.

But we talk, don't we? We talk all the time, and Joe Gould was the only man in the world who hit upon the idea that our history and our meaning might be best revealed *through* our talk. But the book was never published. We don't have it. The manuscript was written and lost, or it wasn't written. Or it was written, and ignored. Certainly nobody in our world was able to get Joe Gould either to show what he had written or to settle down and start writing what he had said he had written, whichever is nearest the truth. Nobody, including myself.

Not Dying, 1963

The Poem

I had fought everybody for so long at school, at home, and everywhere else that I was sick of it, and sick of myself. I believed the way to become healed was to get out of town.

It was July, 1926.

Soon I'd be eighteen years old, but still I was in Fresno, which I now hated.

I went up to Aram's office to see about getting paid for the occasional office work I had done for a year or more, which I can't pretend I had especially *minded* doing, which in fact I had enjoyed doing. It had been better than nothing, so to say, but at the same time I had actually written a great many letters for him on the typewriter. I had run errands for him, I had announced his clients, I had asked them to wait when he was busy, and in general I had made myself useful.

Still, he hadn't ever handed me any money, except when he had sent me out for a cold watermelon from Long John, or a pound of pistachio nuts, or a leg of lamb for him to take home. Even when I had handed him the change he had invariably accepted all of it.

He was alone in his office when he looked up and saw me. I couldn't help noticing that he knew my visit was not a routine one. And I knew he was ready for me.

"Sit down," he said. "What's on your mind?"

"I want to get out of town."

"I think that's a good idea. You've been giving my sister a bad time long enough. Get out and stay out. When are you leaving?"

"Right away, but I haven't got any money."

"You don't need any money. Bums don't need any money. Go out to the S.P. and grab a freight, the way all the bums do."

"I thought you might pay me."

"For what?"

"For the work I did for you."

"Work *you* did for *me?* This place has been a college for you. You should pay me."

"Well, maybe, then, you'd *lend* me five dollars."

Well, here, for some reason, he went a little berserk, shouting first in English, then in Armenian, and finally in Turkish and Kurdish.

His voice was being heard all over the Rowell Building. The dentist next door stuck his head into the office expecting to say he had a very delicate piece of work to do and Aram was disturbing his patient, but Aram shouted at him before he could open his mouth, which soon enough fell open with astonishment.

"Get out, you dentist. Don't come into this office. This is a place of business. Get back where you belong, and drill your rotten teeth."

And now he felt required to imitate the sound of the drill, saying, "Bzzzz, bzzzz, bzzzz, all day long. Open wider, please. Wider, please. Bzzzz, bzzzz, bzzzz. Get out of here with your dainty little washed hands."

The instant the dentist's face disappeared, before the door was even fully shut, he came right back at me.

Inside, in spite of the anger I felt, I was laughing, because the man was crazy, but very funny.

Now, though, when he renewed the attack, I couldn't take it in silence any more, and I began to shout back at him, only louder than he was shouting.

"For God's sake, what kind of a man are you, anyway? You made a fortune last year and you're going to make a bigger fortune this year. I worked for you. Every penny I've ever earned I gave to my mother. I can't go to her and ask her for money. What are you shouting at me for?"

Now, after I said each of these things, he shouted a nullifying reply, making a kind of ridiculous duet.

All of the windows on the court of the Rowell Building were being lifted by typists, bookkeepers, dentists, lawyers, fruit shippers, and others, and everybody knew who was shouting: the Armenians, the Saroyans, Aram and his nephew Willie.

When I said, "For God's sake, what kind of a man are you?" Aram said, "A great man, you jackass, not a jackass like you."

"You made a fortune last year."

"Bet your life I did, more than you or anybody else will ever know."

"And you're going to make a bigger fortune this year."

"The biggest yet in every way, shape, manner and form."

"I worked for you."

"You *shit—that's* what you did."

"Every penny I've ever earned I gave to my mother."

"That poor girl has been driven mad by your foolishness. You want to be a writer. Get money in a bank and write *checks,* that's the way to be a writer. That's the kind of writer *I* am, not a stupid poem writer. *The moon is sinking in the sea.* The moon is sinking in your empty head, that's where the moon is sinking. (This of course was his swiftest idea of poetry, and of course there's no telling where he had gotten it from.) You gave her a few pennies, so you could eat six or seven times a day, and sleep in a warm bed in your own room, and get free hotel service. Don't talk to me about giving my sister money. Your *pennies?*"

"I can't go to her and ask her for money."

"Bet your life you can't. You've got to go to the bank for money, the way I do. Tell them what you want it for—to be a bum—and they'll give it to you. But if they don't, they'll give you a blotter. You can always use a blotter, can't you?"

"What are you shouting at me for?"

"Because you're a disgrace to my family. To my sister. To the Saroyan family. Now, get out of here."

For some reason all of a sudden I thought of my father. Surely nobody had ever spoken to him that way if in fact anybody had ever shouted at him, but I got the feeling that they had actually. Who wanted *The moon is sinking in the sea?* Who wanted any part of such nonsense? This was America. This was California. This was Fresno. This was the real world, not the world of the moon and the sea.

I knew I wasn't going to get any money, so there was no point in shouting any more. I just didn't know how to get money, even money I had earned, or at any rate *believed* I had earned, but perhaps I was mistaken, perhaps he was right, perhaps I owed him money for having gone to college in his office, and so the first thing I must do is earn some money and pay him. It didn't help at all that he was famous all over town as the most open-handed man of wealth among the Armenians. He donated, officially, to everything that came along, and he made generous hand-outs to all kinds of needy Armenians because they knew how to get money from him. They knew how to get him to write a check, and they always cried out with feigned astonishment, "A hundred dollars, Aram? Really, I had hoped for no more than ten."

Hushed, earnest, a little astonished, but still respectful, I left his office and sneaked out of the building, taking the stairs so I wouldn't have to face the elevator operator or anybody who might be in the elevator.

I went to the garage of the Californian Hotel and asked the man there if he knew of anybody driving out of town. He said somebody at the hotel had asked to have his car ready at nine, but it wasn't six yet.

I said I'd wait, and I did, which is never much fun and at that time was none at all. At last a bellboy brought the man's bags across the street from the hotel to the garage, and there was the man himself. He was just fine, but all of a sudden I didn't think I ought to speak to him, even. If I didn't, though, what then? I couldn't go home again. But if I asked for a ride, he might turn me down, and I'd been turned down enough for one day.

He was a well-dressed, successful-looking man of forty or so who was smoking a nickel cigar, a salesman of some kind, and he was all right, but I just didn't want to risk another humiliation.

In any case, he'd *seen* me, and he knew perfectly well I wanted a ride out of town, wherever he was going, so why didn't he say something?

I was hungry, I felt desperate and cut off from everything I had ever been related to, but I wanted to be snappy and smart like so many guys in the movies I had seen, a maker of laughter, somebody anybody would be glad to have along for a ten-hour drive somewhere. I *wanted* to, but I couldn't. This just wasn't a movie, it was me.

At last I decided I'd have to risk it, that's all. By three or four or five in the morning I'd be out of town at last, and on my own.

I went around to where I'd be able to see the man, and he'd be able to see me, and with the driest mouth I have ever had I said, "I'm looking for a ride. Anywhere."

But before I had finished speaking I knew it had happened again. I'd been turned down. The man didn't even answer me. I wanted to walk away quickly, but that would have been too humiliating. It would be better to just hang around, not facing him any more, until he drove off.

I'd have to try the S.P., after all. I turned away and pretended to be interested in the hood of the parked car directly in front of me. I heard the motor start and felt deeply relieved. The motor was raced a couple of times, and then I heard the man call out, "O.K., kid. Hop in. It's a long way to San Francisco."

I was about to run, but suddenly I had to check it.

"I'm going to Los Angeles," I said.

The man puffed at his cigar. "You said anywhere."

"Anywhere *south.*"

He puffed again, and drove off.

I was about to start walking to the S.P. when the same bellboy came along with some more bags, and with him this time was a little old man who came straight up to me and said, "You want a ride, I'm going to Los Angeles."

He stopped in Bakersfield and asked me to have a sandwich and a cup of coffee with him.

"I haven't got any money."

"I know that. You'll have a dollar in your pocket when we get to Los Angeles, too, and forget it."

We reached Los Angeles a little before daybreak. I got out of the car in the heart of town and said, "I'll never forget this."

"Forget it, I said." And he was gone.

And there all around me was this strange silent city that I hadn't had in mind at all. I had had San Francisco in mind. I was awfully tired, but keyed up, too. I walked around and saw some coffee shops that were open, but I didn't go in because I didn't want to break the silver dollar until I had to. I found a water fountain and had a long drink, and a half hour later went back and had another one. I felt beat and mean, but at the same time exhilarated and glad. At least I'd *started*, thanks to the good luck of running into the little old man.

He's been dead for years, most likely, but even if he weren't, he wouldn't know what he did for me, although we talked all the way from Fresno to Los Angeles. I must have told him quite a lot about myself, from which, I mean, he *might* have gathered that he had done me a great, an unexpected, an incredible kindness.

Here Comes, There Goes, You Know Who, 1961

The Eaters

*E*ddie Jabulian was a messenger at Postal Telegraph after having shined shoes at an alley stand for a year after graduating from high school. Eddie was nineteen to my fourteen, but he learned telegraphy, and after the telegraph companies brought in teletype machines, Eddie got work in little railroad depots.

He used to come in from a long delivery and say, "Here, let me show you what I had."

And he would smooth out the wrapper of a nickel candy bar with a name like Golden Jubilee, or Forever Yours, or Jungle Jive. What he meant was that he had eaten. This would always be at night, when we worked the night shift, from four to one.

One time he came in but didn't ask me to see what he had had, so I said, "Eddie, didn't you have anything on this long delivery?"

"I had something all right, don't worry about me, I take good care of myself, candy for quick energy, but I know you, I been watching you out of the corner of my eye, you been laughing at me, you been acting like you admire the candy I been eating, Diamonds and Pearls, and all those, but what you really been doing is laughing at me, I know you guys from Bitlis, you always make fun of a fellow, and all the time he thinks you're a pal, you ain't no pal of mine, Willie, as long as you're going to laugh behind my back."

"*No*, Eddie. I been jealous."

"You been a *little* jealous, I know, but I never notice you buying two, three candy bars a night, sometimes four, you guys from Bitlis don't throw away money on luxuries, you're famous for being tight, while us jackasses from Harpoot, we spend the stuff as fast as it comes in, and the hell with you from now on, Willie, I'm not going to show the wrappers any more."

"Ah, come on, Eddie, I know you had a real good one on that delivery, let me see the wrapper, I won't tell anybody you been eating up your pay."

Sure enough he reaches into the inside pocket of his blue coat and comes out with a carefully folded wrapper, unfolds it, all crazy blue with flashes of red charging through it, and he keeps looking at me out of the corner of his eye, but the dazzling thing is just a little too much for him to care if I *am* laughing, inside of course, where he can never see it and know for sure. He just stands there and admires the wrapper: Iceland Fire.

"It's the best yet, Eddie. Thanks a lot."

"I had it from just a little past Stanislaus all the way to Maroa."

"Boy, I bet it was good."

"Hot and cold, just like it says, hot and cold, one of the best. Damn you, Willie, you're laughing at me, I know you are, I can't *see* you, but that's the way you guys from Bitlis are, you keep it inside."

"*Laughing*, Eddie? I'm crying because I can't afford to eat that kind of stuff."

But the kind of stuff I *could* afford to eat wasn't so bad, either. Food, that is. It's the stuff you have *got* to have, of course. You can't get through one little old day without it, let alone a week, although one time when I was an old man of forty I only drank for a month, but than I *did* drink, and the fact is I sneaked in a steak now and then, too.

At the orphanage the best was meat pie. Tapioca was poison. We hated it, everybody in the place hated it, I actually didn't like the flavor of it, or rather the flat pointless *lack* of flavor of it, but I ate it every time, I emptied my bowl, and if there had been more I would have had more, too, hating every bit of it.

Well, we were growing, you see, and they knew it, and they knew we'd eat anything they put in front of us, because we had to have something, and we would take whatever we could get. The orphanage people had a tight budget to keep, so of course we couldn't expect anything fancy, it had to be basic, it had to have bulk, it had to cost little, it had to take up space. But don't get the idea some of the stuff wasn't great, because that would be a lie, and as far as possible I don't want to lie about the people at the orphanage.

The Irish cook, for instance. It would be impossible for me to do anything but honor her memory, for she loved us, she loved every one of us, every big hungry mouth and big empty stomach. At every meal she stood in the doorway of the kitchen and just watched us put the stuff away, which *she* had cooked for us. She did baked macaroni real good, too.

Breakfast had to be some kind of hot cereal of course, with milk, and nobody could knock that, and cocoa, as we called it, and fresh bread and butter. The way you did it was to spread butter on the bread and dunk it into the hot cocoa and then slop it quickly into the mouth, for the mixing of the mushy bread, the melting butter, and the hot chocolate flavor, all of which blended together in a very satisfying way. Sometimes she baked a million biscuits and that was something we loved, too: again with all kinds of melting butter in there, and honey if there was honey set out on the table, and if not, whatever it was, excepting catsup. She made great cornbread, too, for breakfast, lunch, and sometimes for supper, too. She was great on pork and beans, too, and this was always a favorite. Her hash was better than any hash I have ever found anywhere, and so was her meat loaf. You may have noticed that the things were made out of stuff that is never expensive, but she transformed that stuff into great steaming pots and pans full of what we wanted. Nobody ever asked anybody to eat in that place, because it made you grow, a little for mamma, a little for papa, a little for Jesus, or anything like that. God help us if the word was out that there would be seconds as long as it lasted, because that meant the fastest eating anybody ever saw. The stuff disappeared almost before everybody was seated, or rather before the starting bell had stopped ringing, and I mean, specifically, the stuff on my own plate, whereupon the plate shot out for more, and more was put there. Now, for some preposterous reason, poultry wasn't on the table very often, most likely because it was too expensive for the budget, and so the eating of chicken came to be associated with the dining of the rich, with what we used to call society people. We got chicken or turkey, by official vote or decree, on Thanksgiving Day, Christmas Day, and possibly on Easter, although I'm not sure. I know that if we got it, it was a special occasion. In my first play, *My Heart's in the Highlands,* the poet's little son Johnny is talking to the boy who delivers newspapers in that part of town every morning. Johnny brags that he has eaten chicken, and so the paper boy takes pride in the fact that *he* has, too—*twice.* Old George Jean Nathan got a big kick out of that.

"Why chicken?" he said with his high-pitched voice. "Why not something *fit* to eat?"

He hated chicken.

"What's more," he said one day, "I hate people who *don't* hate chicken."

Now, what else did that great Irish lady prepare that I had better remember with tender reverence and deep and everlasting admiration and gratitude? She's gone, dear woman, let this be for Ireland, for all Irish cooks, for the cooks in all institutions, Irish or otherwise, who do not hate the inmates, who love them, children, criminals, the sick, the mad, or the aged. To all captured and imprisoned, in all of the institutions, greetings, and a sincere prayer for a decent cook.

Rhubarb—she stewed rhubarb real nicely, cooked but not mushy, the color a magnificent red and white, the juice transparent but sweet and tart at once. Well, that was pretty much what it was at the orphanage.

Then came Fresno, the home cooking, the food of Armenia, the famous dishes of Bitlis. Well, of course you know there are several basic foods among the Armenians, as well as among the Turks, Kurds, Arabs, Persians, Greeks, Georgians, Roumanians, Bulgarians, and two or three dozen other tribes, all the way from the Black Sea to the Siberian shores of the Pacific: yogurt and pilaf, or sour milk and rice, for instance. There are small differences in how the stuff is made, but these two items are basic. If you make the yogurt out of goat's milk, you get a different yogurt than the more common yogurt of cow's milk. And so it is with the milk of other animals. Also common to all of these people is lamb roasted on skewers over a no-longer flaming fire, or shish-kebab. *Shish* is Turkish for spear, and *kebab* is Turkish for cut-up lamb. *Tass-kebab* would therefore be cut-up lamb cooked in a tass, or pan. And so on. On a spear it would go like this, more or less, for flavor and variety: a piece of meat, a piece of bell pepper, onion, tomato, and then another piece of meat, and so on, depending on what you had plentiest of. And so that sort of eating was routine for me in Fresno, excepting the shish-kebab, which has to wait for a family picnic, or a whole big Armenian picnic, because you had to prepare it right if you really wanted it to be what it ought to be.

Now, there is something the Armenians and the Turks and Kurds, and surely the Arabs and a few other people, consider basic, too: the Armenians call it bulghour. This is a brown cereal. It's boiled cracked wheat dried brown in the sun. If the wheat is cracked into a fairly large size, it is used for pilaf. I like it far better than I like rice, which I like quite well. You can do anything with bulghour, mix anything with it, that is, but the usual procedure is to fry a couple of cups of it in butter, pour over a couple of cups of clear broth of any kind, or if there is no broth, boiling water, and cut up two or three big brown onions into it, and eat it steaming hot with yogurt. This is the favorite dish of the peasants everywhere, who generally have at least seven or eight kids, and there is said to be a relationship between the eating of this dish and the number of kids in the family.

My mother used to send me to Chinatown, to the famous Japanese fish dealer over there, Takamura, who every Saturday got in a good supply of a small fish that my mother fried and ate with bulghour. For a dime there was enough fish for the whole family, two pounds, a couple of hundred little fish, to be eaten without taking out their insides or removing their heads.

The wheat that was cracked small was mixed with ground meat to make meatballs of all kinds, solid, or with a stuffing made of pomegranate seeds, or to stuff into tomatoes, bell peppers, squash, zucchini, pumpkin, eggplant, and to wrap grape leaves around. In Armenia they stuff apples and quince, too, but that wasn't anything that was done in my house. Dried apricots and peaches went into thick meaty stews to cut the heavy flavor of the meat and garlic and dried eggplant and okra and whatever else might be in there, but apples and quince were not used in that way. They *could* be, of course. The best cooking comes from necessity. You use what you have and you find out how to use it well.

The favorite dish at my house was what the people of Bitlis call Tut-too. Perhaps that isn't the spelling likeliest to help you get the pronunciation of it, but it's said swiftly, with the accent on the last syllable. There is almost no first syllable, actually. The word means sour, or tart. Take a big cabbage, cut it up big or small or both, put it in a crock, throw some salt in there, a piece of bread, or a little dry yeast, pour warm water over the stuff until the water is near the top of the crock, then place a dish over the stuff, and place a weight on the dish to press the solid stuff down. We always used a rock about the size of a big eggplant. After seven, eight, or nine days the stuff is sharp, it has gone sour, but nothing like sauerkraut, something else, in my opinion something much better. The juice deeply satisfies thirst, and is considered an invigorating tonic. Now, if you have other stuff, put other stuff in there with the cut-up cabbage, too: turnip greens especially, celery, green tomatoes, and all like that. It's good raw, the juice is always good cold, but the stuff is prepared pretty much with the intention of cooking this great dish I am speaking of: Tut-too.

In my family there are only five of us, but two of us were very good eaters, that is, my brother and myself, so my mother used a large pot, three gallons or more.

First, she put a gallon of the sour juice in there, and half a gallon of water because that much of the liquid would boil away in the cooking. Into the juice she dumped three or four pounds of cut-up shoulder of lamb, big chunks, bone and all. When the lamb had cooked for half an hour or so, or a little less, she added three or four pounds of the sour cabbage, and a cup of washed *gorgote:* well, *gorgote* might be barley, but I'm not sure. It cooks in there, opens up, and is a very important part of the dish. It *ought* to be in there. Then six or seven big tomatoes are cut up and put in there, and after the whole thing has stewed for an hour or more you have got it. If there is any left over, it is always better the second day. It is eaten steaming hot. In the winter it is great.

Sherwood Anderson in *A Story-Teller's Story* spoke of eating cabbage soup at his house almost every day because hoodlums in his neighborhood used to throw cabbages at his front door, onto his porch, and his mother, instead of being offended by the intended insult, gathered the cabbages and cooked them. I liked that.

Lamb's head was cooked in a lot of water, but my brother wouldn't eat it, because he couldn't stand the head looking at him that way. This also was a favorite of the peasants in Bitlis, called Pah-chah. In addition to the garlic in which the head is cooked, mashed garlic in water is added to the dish at the time of eating, and so you've got a strong dish on two accounts: the strong broth and the strong garlic. The peasants generally ate it on Sunday morning so that by evening it would be digested and they would be sure to sleep well.

Armenian bread was baked all the time at my house, in all of its forms: the rolled out flat bread, thinner than cardboard, the loaves, called Bahgh-arch, and the various breads with a great deal of oil or fat of one kind or another in them, called Gah-tah.

Now, when it was a day for the baking of bread, my mother would be up very early to get to it. She could easily have gotten up three hours later in the wintertime when there was no work at the fruit-packing houses, but she didn't feel bread was being baked unless she got up in the dark, at five, summer or winter, and went to work. By the time the rest of us were up and ready for breakfast her work was finished and the house was full of the smell of freshly baked bread, and the whole pleasant warmth of it, as it had been for several hours, while we slept. When we sat down to eat, though, we got the real treat of Bread Baking Day. This is called Tazhah-hotz, or new-bread, and this is how it is made. Take a handful of the bread dough, flatten it to a thickness of a little under an inch, and drop it into a frying pan in which any kind of fat you use, or butter, is very hot. In a few minutes one side will be a handsome golden brown. Turn it over until the other side is the same, about six minutes all told. Now, break the thing, open up a pretty good-sized piece, and into the opening stuff white Armenian cheese. Drink tea with it. *Only* tea. Cocoa or coffee or anything else would make a mess of it. Hot, sharp, brisk, weak tea, after the manner of all of the tea-drinking peoples, excepting the British, who regard tea as coffee, to which they add milk.

The roasts were all lamb: shoulder, leg, and stuffed breast, which is a truly great dish, very hot, or cold, generally hot first, and the left-over portion cold, because certain roasts, if in fact not all of them, are nullified by a second roasting. The stuffing is a basic rice, with whatever you fancy: dried apricots, raisins, dry or fresh mint, chopped heart and liver, chopped meat, whatever you've got that wouldn't be half so good by itself and shouldn't be wasted. To be on the safe side the rice might be boiled for ten minutes before making the stuffing, so it will be a fine cooked part of the roast.

Well, that's a *little* of what we used to eat. Even so, my brother and I sometimes imagined the food we were eating wasn't high-class. We never suspected it was the greatest food in the world, and of course you must understand I have mentioned only the basic stuff. There was a lot of special-occasion stuff, but the hell with it. We ate, we ate good, but we wanted to eat differently, like the Americans did, and so one summer when my mother was working at Guggenheim's, packing figs, and there was a lot of overtime work, with extra pay for it, and she wasn't getting home until late, sometimes at ten, sometimes even later, she gave us permission to eat supper together in a restaurant in town. Within reason, you understand. And we understood. It had been our own idea to keep it within reason, not hers.

We didn't expect to eat in a fancy restaurant where the six-course meal cost anywhere from twenty-five to forty cents. They wouldn't let us sit down in a restaurant like that, most likely, so we scouted the various inexpensive restaurants, and settled for The O.K. on Kern Street, between Jay and Van Ness. This was Chinese-owned-and-operated, but American food exclusively, five courses, ten cents, the favorite supper restaurant of day-laborers with no money to throw away. All counter, no tables.

Well, who will ever forget the first time we went in there and found two free places and sat on the stools and waited to have our first meal in a restaurant?

My brother was all for examining a menu, like he had seen in the movies, but before he could find one the Chinese waiter came trotting up with two bowls of soup. Dish-water, but my brother said it was great, and after the third spoonful I didn't mind it too much, either. Next came a plate of some kind of stew, cat stew apparently, but we were in a restaurant at any rate, we were being served, and we were hungry, so we ate the cat stew, and the three slices of beets for salad, and then came the dessert: bread-pudding, the bread not quite transformed from bread into pudding. Well, we had had a lot of experience with bread-pudding at the orphanage, and this just *wasn't* bread-pudding. There was a little dab of something red over it, not quite liquid, not quite solid, something out of cornstarch probably, but with sugar in it. We ate that, too, the same as all the day-laborers in there, and finally came a chance to choose: coffee or tea? I think I said milk, and the Chinese said very quickly, "No milk, no milk—coffee or tea?"

So we took tea, got up, paid our dime apiece, put a toothpick apiece in our mouths, and walked out to Kern Street like a couple of characters in a Paramount Picture.

We said it was good, we said it was great, we wondered how the Chinese could afford to dish out a meal like that for a dime. And the next night after we had sold all our papers, around half-past eight or nine, we went in there again and ate the same meal, except that instead of cat stew, it was some other kind of stew, possibly dog stew. Again we said it was great, and we walked home like millionaires, men of the world, diners in restaurants.

After the fourth night, though, I said, "Henry, let's not eat that dime dinner, let's go home and make something ourselves."

Well, he was crazy about the idea, because that food was killing him, too.

And so we gave up that premature venture into lordliness and went home. The place was loaded with the makings of anything we might care to eat.

Henry made bulghour pilaf, and I made a salad, and we sat down and ate the stuff, and my sisters hung around telling us they could have done it much better, and from now on if we weren't going to eat in town they would have stuff waiting for us, but we told them to keep out of it, we wanted to make our own stuff. They were both working, too: the oldest at Gottschalk's as a secretary and the youngest at Woolworth's selling stuff, and they were pretty tired when they got home, and all we wanted them to do was take life easy in the parlor playing the piano and singing while we got our own stuff.

When my mother got home that first night at half past ten she looked at the pan that Henry had cooked the bulghour in. There was a little left in there, so she sat down and put some yogurt on it, and she said, "Who cooked this bulghour?"

Henry said, "I did."

"Where you find out how to cook such good bulghour, Henry?"

"Right here. It's very simple."

And of course it is. All you've got to be is good and hungry.

We paid a dollar ninety-five one time for an ice-cream machine, but it was a flop. Too much trouble, and the stuff *wasn't* ice cream. We went back to lemonade, and good old plain cold watermelon.

For me, though, the greatest meal in the whole world for a summer night was cold grapes, flat bread, white cheese, mint, bell peppers, green onions, tomatoes, cucumbers, and cold water.

Here Comes, There Goes, You Know Who, 1961

The Trick of
Truth and the
Truth Itself

George Bernard Shaw over a period of fifty good long years of adult work as a writer earned for himself perhaps the greatest fortune any writer of our day has ever earned, but in comparison with the fortunes earned during the same time by hundreds of thousands of ordinary businessmen Shaw's fortune was small potatoes. Somerset Maugham, now ninety, has also earned a fortune, but again it is a small one. And six or seven dozen popular writers since the turn of the century have known prosperity of one degree or another, but the majority of writers, and especially the better ones, have had a financial struggle from the beginning to the end, and this struggle has been made all the more difficult by the demand of the government that every writer must also be a businessman, which he simply isn't and doesn't know how to become.

It is a headache. It may be unavoidable, but that doesn't make it any less a headache.

Mr. Edmund Wilson has rightly made a protest about all of this in a small book that most reviewers have ridiculed, perhaps because everybody wants everybody else to accept the rules of the game: never to protest, that is, but to find out how to make the most of the rules and to keep the large mouth tightly shut. True businessmen, millionaires and multimillionaires, meticulously abide by the rules of the game, and quietly find and exploit perfectly legal loopholes by means of which to become richer, and to hold onto that which they have accumulated. They use a great deal of energy, which in a writer may be called creative energy but in a businessman is something else, in order to appear to be patriotic and law-abiding, but they are quite simply dishonest. This dishonesty is actually a kind of basic contemporary intelligence, which is morally crooked, but only to somebody who has a feeling for morality and honesty, which businessmen do not have, because it is not required, by law. They have only what the law asks them *literally* to have, and this always begins and ends with a complicated and badly written law which actually has no real meaning, and must be interpreted by a lawyer or a court, although even this interpretation is subject to rejection and reinterpretation.

Well, what are we going to do about it?

What are we going to do about the law, the lawyers, the courts, and the judges? Mahatma Gandhi in India *joined* them, the new statesmen of the new states of Africa are joining them, the Negroes of America are joining them, but what about us, each of us, one at a time?

The theory is that the right thing cannot be made to happen except by law, and the discovery and exploitation of loopholes in it. The acceptance of this theory is an insult to the human race, if there is such a thing as the human race, and if it is possible for such a thing to be insulted. The theory is certainly an insult to any individual who lives honorably, or by the moral law, as Tolstoi and Dostoevski would have put it. The law, the courts, and any clever lawyer can make a fool of such a man.

I know, because they have been making a fool of me all of my life.

Something of the system and instruction of the law, something of its deviousness moves out and into everything an individual becomes involved in, in his society, in his world: in the public-education system, in the colleges and universities, in business, in employment, in wages, in hospitals and asylums, in the army, and the hell with the rest of the long list. You name it, some of the misuse, misunderstanding, and mischief that is in the law is in it.

The human experience is *forced* to become a legal experience.

One of the most legal things is death, and before the legalities of my own death come up, I owe it to myself, and to yourself, and to all not overly patriotic citizens of any country, to all who simply by accident happened to find themselves there, under the law, surrounded by it, to tell my legal story, or at any rate that aspect of the story that made a fool of me, or impelled me to make more of a fool of myself than I am ordinarily able to do without any help.

Now, of course everybody knows that the law is the same for everybody, except that everybody also knows that it isn't. Only the moral law is the same for everybody, except that again it is the same only for everybody who *lives* by it, by those who place honor, truth, and right above a number of other and lesser laws which are easier to live by— easier, that is, to exploit for a profit.

My luck with the law, the law of the land, so to put it, has always been lousy. Perhaps this is so because I have never quite managed to conceal my contempt for those who are experts in it. I can think of no group more despicable than the hundreds and thousands of small men who sit in judgment, by law, on the unfortunate human race in petty aberration: judges all over the country in small courts, most of them formerly lawyers. I long ago imagined that these men, walking about in the streets of Fresno, for instance, and called Judge by everybody, and nodded to, were in fact men of great humanity, but by the time I was sixteen and had gone to court six or seven times as an observer, I knew that they were actually criminals. And not helplessly, as the criminals they judged were. The judges were criminals by profession. The fact that they hadn't the wit, imagination, or intelligence even to suspect the truth about themselves does not diminish their stupid guilt. And the supreme aspiration of almost every lawyer in America is to become a judge, and to commit crime officially, in the name of the people, entirely without risk, criticism, guilt, or punishment, even though a few who have actually gone into more conventional crime have been brought to trial, or have resigned in order to avoid trial, or have disappeared, or have killed themselves.

But the real reason my luck with the law has always been lousy is simply that I have never been interested in the trick of truth but have been interested in the truth itself, and the law lives in truth's trick, the law *is* a trick. Right isn't right to the law, the trick is. If right happens to have the trick of right, too, all the better. But if wrong happens to have the trick of right, it thereby becomes right, although everybody knows it is still wrong. One reads with amazement, amusement, and disgust of the multimillionaire who beats off the greedy government because there was a flaw in the wording of the claim made by the government against the multimillionaire for sixty million dollars. Well, between the government and the multimillionaire it doesn't matter who gets the loot, in any case, but we know from the power of the flaw how absurd and difficult the achievement of equity in any legal dimension is.

In 1934 I was a writer, but without a published book. In 1964 I am a businessman, but without a business. In 1934 I had never been taken to the law, but in 1964 I am being taken to it all the time, as I have been ever since the law took me to the army.

"Good morning, Judge," they used to say, but I think the judge knows how I would put it. I think he knows precisely how I would put it.

After Thirty Years: The Daring Young Man on the Flying Trapeze, 1964

No Defense of
the Story

*T*he story is an infinite thing. It is astonishing how little its infinitude is demonstrated by writers, and how few kinds of it are achieved by any given writer, myself included, myself *especially.*

There is a little variety in the subject matter of stories, but there is nowhere near enough insofar as other things are concerned. Livingness is inexhaustible, and the livingest form of writing is the story. If there is a writer, and he is willing, the story can accommodate any order, any size, any style, and any *repudiation* of these.

It is the most natural of forms, coming directly from the people talking to one another, from gossip, from jokes, from mimicry, from improvisation, from the telling of stories by skilled storytellers, long before writing, long before print and paper and the printing press, long before literature. Every family had at least one good storyteller, many had several, and in a few families everybody was good at it.

What is a story for? It is for telling, and for hearing. After that it is for as many things as there are, and for as many that need to become. For fun, for entertainment, for zest, for diversion, for instruction, for anything, for everything. A story can be to celebrate the living, to mourn the dead, and frequently both at the same time. It can be a grand curse, or a joyous prayer.

I felt all this strongly in 1934, I feel it even more strongly in 1964, but I felt then and I feel now the enormity of my own neglect to demonstrate all this, my own incredible, unaccountable failure. What the devil happened? What could I have been thinking?

There are no excuses for me, or for any of the other writers. We goofed.

There may be an explanation, however. This oldest of forms, this truest, certainly came to be considered a lesser order of writing, hardly possible, for instance, to be considered a big form, a major form, as the saying is. The novel was that form. Many a good writer of stories was bullied into believing that nothing he might ever do in that form could be considered major. Unless he wrote a good novel, he didn't really count as a writer. Publishers sponsored this bogus and unfortunate theory, and literary critics supported it.

The fact remains just the same that the long novels, the dozens of them, by the most honored novelists, rather suddenly become unreadable, and at best patches are removed from them for study—patches that are in essence short stories.

On the other hand a good short story tends to remain forever readable, and frequently becomes more and more readable as time goes by, more enjoyable, more significantly itself.

My own theory is that the story should have no limitations of any kind, provided only that it lives, however unaccountably.

Form as such impels much too much comfort in the writer. It gives him a feeling of being safe at home, and this has got to make for repetitiousness, at the very least. It both permits and compels the writer to know what he is doing, and it prevents the accidental, which almost always turns out to be the inevitable, too long postponed.

But doesn't this apply to all writing? It *could* perhaps, except for the element of time that is involved, in the listener to a told story, or in the reader of a written one. An hour is just about enough for anybody who is himself busy being alive, an hour at a time now and then, possibly daily, possibly weekly, possibly every once in a while. The reading of a long novel is a great comfort to many people, as if in the reading they were recuperating from themselves, and this is a rather valuable thing for people always to have. It's not unlike always having sleep to sleep.

Having life to live, however, makes the story. It is *for* that, and moves with it, to it, through it, and away.

But this is no defense of the story, and no attack upon the novel. The story needs no defense, the novel cannot be attacked. Each lives, at its best, in the livingness of the race itself.

Both of my grandmothers were great storytellers. Both were illiterate, although each spoke three languages fluently. The banishment of illiteracy does not make a better order of livingness inevitable, and it frequently makes growing into livingness impossible.

During the thirty years since the publication of my first book I know all too well what happened. I was so busy living I almost forgot how *not* to write. The trouble is that if you are skilled at it, even when you write as you ought not to write, when you keep to the forms, the stuff is all right, it seems to be more than all right now and then, except that in your heart, then and years later, you know you could have done it better, you could have refused to be bullied, by your experience, your skill, your love of comfort, your laziness, or by the theories of readers, critics, editors, and publishers. You didn't because you didn't.

And the hell with it. One good story about somebody with large ears or a bad cough, who barks when he talks, makes all the theorizing about stories only a big laugh. One great story makes a lifetime memorable, even if the story appears to be about a mouse, a hat, a demented mother of a dentist, or a Presbyterian vice-president of a bank.

After Thirty Years: The Daring Young Man on the Flying Trapeze, 1964

Pebbles on
the Beach

Pebbles on the Beach *tells something more about my life on the beach at Malibu. I was unavoidably in the general vicinity of Holly-wood, with its preposterous people and values, and I had to see about not letting it bother me too much. Being on the beach helped. The piece was written in 1952, and under another title came out in* Art News. *The thing about the piece is that it keeps some of the truth I knew at that time on record. I have always felt that something of that sort is desirable, and as soon as I took to writing I began to write about where I was at the time and what I was doing. In one degree or another all of my writing marks passing time. Pebbles on the beach are marks of time. Each of them is also a thing of beauty and meaning for whoever happens to be there to notice. Frequently I came upon a patch of pebbles that made me feel I was in the presence of a congregation of people. A pebble is not unlike a face, and a crowd of people seems to be a sea of faces, as the saying is. I loved the pebbles. I loved getting out to them every day. But most of all I loved the sea.*

I live in a small house on the beach at Malibu, quite close to the water, if not in fact upon it: high tide certainly brings the sea under the house. It also brings miscellaneous objects.

Some of the objects are man-made and may be dismissed: bottles of various kinds, light bulbs, old shoes, brushes, brooms, parts of furniture, and so on. There is form in many of the man-made things, and frequently it is good form.

The other objects are not man-made. They are sea-made, water-made, tide-made, time-made, sun-made, wind-made: pebbles and rocks, sea-trees and plants, shells, driftwood. These objects are made accidentally, inevitably, haphazardly, without plan, without beginning or end, without intention. Nature does not strain after art. It *is* art. Everything it does, or everything that is done to it, whichever happens to be true or truest, *is* art.

I collect the objects rolled up onto the beach by the sea.

I look at them, study them, have them around, turn them over to friends, lose them, or throw them back into the sea. I do this because it is satisfying, and because it is the means by which I get the small amount of exercise I need.

Mainly, I collect pebbles, but only because there are always more of them than there are of anything else. I think it is the simultaneous general sameness and infinite variety of rocks that appeal to me. Solely in the realm of size and shape rocks are very exciting. Add to this the matter out of which a rock is made, the probable manner of its making, the weight, color, and texture of it, and a student has a very great deal to notice.

My collecting has never been systematic, but it has acquired a free and easy method based on simple principles.

Three months after I moved into this house the front porch was loaded with pebbles of all kinds. A number of people said, "What are the rocks for?"

Each person was given an answer appropriate to his character.

"They are to remind me that art should be simple."

"They give me ideas for characters and stories."

"I like them."

"They are for throwing at people who ask what they are for."

A thing that is in space, as a rock is, is sculpture, or, if you prefer, *raw* sculpture. Now, imagine the enormous variety of sculpture to examine at one's leisure or whenever it is convenient, after only half an hour on the beach.

Let us say that out of the hundreds of thousands of pebbles on the beach the thoughtful collector has brought home only three or four dozens of them. He has run water over them and placed them according to size on the counter between the kitchen and the parlor—a counter that is a daily art gallery.

Now, he noticed each rock, each piece of sculpture, when he picked it up. He noticed it again when he ran water over it. Again when he set it down on the counter. And he notices all of them together from time to time, whenever his glance happens to fall on them.

This nearness of these individual works of sculpture, and the gallery-group of them, is a source of great delight.

A natural thing has a soul, a personality, a reality, whichever you prefer. Certain rocks have souls more moving to the beholder than a good deal of man-made sculpture. Rocks do not even accidentally resemble other things. They resemble nothing. They are rocks. That is a very delightful thing. But of course there is always somebody who will pick up a rock and remark how like a fish or a seal it is. It would be a lot more nearly accurate to say of a rock that it is simultaneously preposterously simple and profoundly mysterious.

If it is possible for a rock to be a work of sculpture, an object of art, then what is an object of art? An object of art may be anything noticed in its entirety. Now, it happens that I am nearsighted. I see near things with great clarity. I must put on glasses to see far things clearly. Thus, it is quite natural for me to notice a rock clearly and in its entirety. It is this noticing of the rock that makes the rock an object of art. And the purpose of art may be said to be to impel careful and creative looking—at a given object, at anything, at everything.

Is there such a thing as creative looking?

Yes.

What constitutes such looking?

Clarity, intelligence, imagination, admiration, and love.

You make a point of looking at the object, you look steadily and clearly, you see the object, you see it again, you see it again, you notice the true nature of it in its entirety and in its parts, you relate its reality to all reality, to all time and space and action, you admire its survival, and you love its commonness and its individuality.

But the gifts of the sea are not rocks and pebbles alone. Its shells, whole or broken, are rich and rewarding. I am not thinking of the shell as the literal instructor it is to the sculptor. I am thinking of it as an object of art to observe for its own small sake. Again, the same order of shell may be collected by the dozens, and not two will be alike. This is always a delight to notice.

The fibrous trees of the sea are good to behold because by the time they are washed up onto the beach they have taken a beating from the sea, but are still beautiful. Their thick and knobby bases, which had seized upon rocks and fastened there, have been very slowly, very gradually, drawn away from the rocks by time and the gentle or violent play of water around them, and then they have been shoved and rolled around and about, perhaps for years, dislocated, dying, or dead, and then they have been rolled out of the sea.

Now, there are things from the land that are washed down hillsides in heavy rains, or in rivers, into the sea, and sooner or later some of these things find their way back to the land—driftwood, in particular. Roots of all kinds, washed and rubbed clean to the heart of their reality. Plain sticks, designed by erosion and washing. Branches, knobs, stumps. One of the best stumps I ever found must have weighed sixty pounds, and had fallen into a design which I did not expect to know fully in anything under three or four years, but somebody who came to my house when I wasn't home went off with it. There is no more unfair thief than the driftwood thief.

What about the man who doesn't live near the sea? Where is he to find nature's objects of art? Well, they are everywhere. Leaves, for instance. Leaves and twigs are not junk—they are objects of art.

Well, then is junk junk? Is man-made stuff junk? Not necessarily. Anything—anything at all—noticed particularly is not useless, it is useful. And an object of art is profoundly useful.

It reminds you that you are alive.

I Used to Believe I Had Forever, Now I'm Not So Sure, 1968

I Don't Get It

I have a jealous nature, so I don't have any trouble at all hating a great many people every day, especially when I am reminded that they are being mistakenly considered greater than I am, when they get too successful, too rich, too important, too big for their britches. I see photographs of them on the covers of magazines or on the inside pages, or in newspapers, and dozens of long paragraphs about them, and I flip. What the devil's the matter with this country? Here I am, the greatest, and these second raters, these counterfeiters, these phonies, grab all of the attention, and sometimes all of the girls, too.

Now it's Arthur Miller, now Edward Albee, now Arthur Kopit, Jack Kerouac, Jack Gelber, Paddy Chayefsky, where did all these guys come from? And these aren't the only ones who make the wig flip: What about Allen Ginsberg, Gregory Corso, Lawrence Ferlinghetti and a lot of other guys writing poetry and making a lot of noise? And then there are the geniuses of the movie business—what was that guy's name who always talked fast and made at least five thousand dollars a week every week of his life—every time I think of him, even without being able to remember his name, just remembering his jumping personality, I feel this country is nuts, this culture we've got isn't a real culture. And then there are the geniuses of television—not the actors, the hell with the actors, everybody makes allowances for actors, it's part of their good luck for actors to be unconscious, and the more they try to acquire intelligence, the more hopeless the situation becomes like that poor bastard who was born feebleminded but nevertheless worked hard at acting and finally got a fairly good part, about a strong simple man, or at any rate that's how it came across in the movie—well, this poor man began to go on television in all kinds of interviews, and he worked at being so humble that anybody could see he actually believed he was *that* big, that it was permissible for him to be humble, and it wasn't, he was only entitled to be arrogant and stupid, by birth, by nature, just as by birth and by nature I am jealous and suspicious—of everybody who gets noticed more than I do, and for 30 years almost nobody in the whole country has been noticed less.

I hate these kids. They gripe me. Give me men like D.H. Lawrence, H.G. Wells, H.L. Mencken and H. Rider Haggard—dead. Such men, such superior men, I like, I love, I cherish. They don't go hogging all the attention, all the magazine and newspaper space, all the money, all the fun. And what about Henry Miller—an older man, entirely without a lovable nickname, no palsy-walsy side to him at all, but still a grabber— *Tropic* of this, *Tropic* of that, he knew some sloppy girls, that's all, so everybody says he's surely one of the great writers of our time, and nobody says anything about me. That's not right.

I don't begrudge Alexander Pope his fame, he's entitled to it, but these other kids, where do they keep coming from, most of them irreligious, too, many of 'them blasphemous, several unbathing. I respect William Blake his fame—he worked hard for it, and honestly. Besides, while he was alive he must have felt a little like I have always felt—lousy, because William Blake wasn't considered the great man during his lifetime that he was. I think Bill Blake is entitled to every bit of his belated fame, and the thing that burns me up about Bill is that he didn't get rich, all kinds of other people got rich, but Bill didn't, he started poor and he stayed poor his whole life. And I'll be damned if I want that sort of thing to happen to me, too, having the same first name, but so far not having encouraged a lovable nickname. I could long ago have encouraged everybody to call me Bill. In fact, long ago I was called *Wild* Bill ten or eleven times by newspaper reviewers of books, but I soon enough noticed that they called anybody whose first name was William the same lovable Wild Bill, and God knows *all* of us Williams weren't wild or certainly not equally wild. The reviewers weren't sincere, and one thing a suspicious man is everlastingly concerned about is the sincerity of his admirers. Are they sincere, the nonentities? I am an entity. I have been an entity all of my life. It hurts an entity to find all kinds of nonentities, or only recently graduated entities, getting all of the attention.

It isn't easy for me to be comfortable about never having been on the cover of *Time*, for instance. What does *Time* mean by by-passing me year after year? Do they mean to imply that these other kids who are getting on the cover are more important that I am? I'll be damned if they are. I'll be damned if anybody who has ever been on the cover of *Time* is more important than I am. I happen to understand about importance. I'm an expert at it. I know who is important and who isn't. And towering over and above everything I know is the proud and lonely fact that I am the most important of all, so what's *Time* trying to do, confuse me? Well, brother, just remember one thing. I can get hot, but I'm awfully difficult to confuse.

Nobody, but nobody, is going to tell me I'm not the most. I am. I was the most when everybody else was struggling bitterly to become a little. Peter Ustinov, all bearded that way and brilliant, unable to open his mouth except to say something bright and true, where does he get off trying to make a fool of me that way, by comparison? I don't happen to want to wear a beard, I find a beard like that an unnecessary calling of attention to oneself. And I keep my weight within bounds—*large* bounds, but still bounds. I don't believe it is nice for any man to have more than an average of 20 pounds of blubber to carry around and laugh with whenever he is embarrassed about his bad jokes. I carry a proper average of only 20 pounds of blubber, which in itself is superiority. But not just Ustinov, all of these guys from London, from England, from Wales, from Scotland, from Ireland. What was it with Brendan Behan, singing those irrelevant ballads all the time? Talking all the time, not letting anybody else get in a few quick words, and then when they did, refusing to listen. That isn't the way. That's a very impolite way to be an entity. I always give the other kid a chance to say his say, stupid as I always know it is going to be, and as it always *is*. Kenneth Tynan, or Ken as so many of his admirers prefer to call him, where did he ever come from, with all that fancy writing about the theater? I've got more theater in my little finger than Kenneth Tynan has got in his opposable thumb, which I have just lately learned is the difference between us and apes. He's got his opposable thumb and I've got mine, but I swear it isn't arrogance that impels me to point out that mine is the superior opposable thumb, it is simple devotion to the truth. These kids won't stop. They keep coming at you from everywhere, from all directions, and some of them seem to drop out of the sky or come up out of holes in the ground, all eager and swift, and none of them aware, as I am, of the difficulty and enormity of the present human predicament. They get the publicity, just the same, even Irving Lazar, and he's not even a writer, he's just an *agent* for writers, he can't even write a letter, he telephones, so he's in *The Saturday Evening Post* with a great big feature story— Irving Lazar. Is Irving Lazar as great a man as Sam Spiegel, who made the movie of Lawrence of Arabia and is a greater man than Lawrence of Arabia, and has a yacht? And pays taxes? And could buy a whole fleet of London taxis if he felt like it? Well, I'm bigger than Sam, everybody knows that, and I'm not referring to height alone, although I'm bigger there, too. I'm referring to size in ineffables, but, if that's not good enough, in *effables*, too. I don't begrudge Irving and Sam having what they have. I'm all for it, if that's the sort of thing they want, all I'm saying is what the hell is the yacht *for?* From the four corners of the world year after year fourflushers keep arriving on the scene and grabbing all the attention and the money. It's not right. It's wrong. It hurts. Makes me stop and wonder if all of my noble work has been worth the while. Or did

I throw the pearls rights smack into the kissers of the pigs? It's not nice even to suspect that I may have.

Put it this way, or as nearly this way as you can possibly manage: A hundred years from now, in 2064, where are all of these kids going to be, and then honestly guess or estimate or compute on a machine where I will be, and then I think you'll understand some of my annoyance, because, frankly, it isn't possible for any outsider to understand *all* of it. Even an insider, and I am very nearly the only insider there is, can't understand all of it. Or *don't* plunge a hundred years forward, make it a smaller portion of time, make it day after tomorrow, because tomorrow is just a little too near—well, where are these kids going to be the day after tomorrow? Pretty much nowhere, wouldn't you say? While I am going to be right where I always have been, at the tippy-tip top, alone, aloof, supreme, and still in need of a haircut.

Norman Mailer—why should so many people feel, especially the young, that Norman Mailer is the man who has got something to say to them, and not I? I can't account for it. It simply has got to be the consequence of some sort of unfortunate misunderstanding of something or other. So far he doesn't seem to have encouraged anybody to refer to him by the lovable nickname of Norm, but that in itself doesn't justify the belief so many kids have that Mailer has the message they want to hear. He can write, nobody in his right mind, nobody in anybody's right mind, wants to pretend he can't write, but let's face up to asking the key question at this point: Can he write, can he even begin to write, as I can write, as I have written? Let's just ask that key question, and then let's just try to answer it honestly. He keeps getting all kinds of complicated things straighter than all of the other kids, but the complicated things I write about are even more complicated than the ones he writes about, and I get mine straighter than he gets his. I get mine so straight I have to guard against their moving back over on the other side. And Nelson Algren—what is this wild stuff about Chicago, is Chicago some kind of zoo, or what? And going around the world, and meeting different people—that's a matter of travel, that isn't preaching the gospel. I preach the gospel. And yet these kids are getting all the gravy. And they keep coming—Heller, I can't even remember his first name, *Catch 22*. I never even read it, although there is a kid in there by the name of Yossarian, but the kid's not even an Armenian, let alone me. It just isn't possible for anybody who isn't an Armenian to have the name of Yossarian. One of the hottest writers going, and all on the strength of one novel about how a kid in the Army discovered that an Army is made up of a lot of frightened phonies, each of whom is slyly fighting off accident and death with every ounce of his animal cunning. Something Heller, a name before Heller, but not a nickname, a straight name of some kind. I was in London one time and every newspaper in town had a piece about him, and not a lousy word about me, stopping at the Savoy. J.D. Salinger aching with love for his classy, glassy people, whose family name *is* Glass, but loathing everybody else, as if everybody else were in fact in another race entirely—crooks, charlatans, killers. There's another kid who keeps grabbing—space, fame, money, and all he does is hide, all he does is refuse to see anybody, so everybody keeps trying to get a big story about him just the same. Burns me up. What am I supposed to be, a has-been? A never-was? A second-rater? I don't get it. How can anything so plain as my incomparable superiority go so unnoticed? I have never been cheap. I have always had a cheerful word for just about anybody, children who tend to turn away in terror from most people run to me, even though I look like hell most of the time. And I think about big things earnestly. I worry about the world. I seriously question the wisdom of having a lot of high explosives stockpiled all over the place and ready at a moment's notice. Kids in the Government get a lot of notice, too. They go on television, on *Meet the Press*, on *Open End*, on the Jackie Gleason show, on *Open Mind*, on *Open Window*, and they casually, playing it down, let everybody know it is only a matter of a small mistake, a nervous accident, until everything will be shot. A lot of high explosives stockpiled all over the place makes me worry as much as it makes anybody else worry. I mean, it isn't all poetry with me, as it is with Ezra Pound, for instance, some of it is anxiety about the whole mother human race. I don't want that race to be blown to smithereens, because a thing like that could make a lot of trouble for me personally and for all I know forever prevent the true greatness of the human race from emerging from the junk pile where it's been for so long. If everything and everybody becomes part of that junk pile, how the hell will I ever make it clear once and for all that I got entangled in the junk by unhappy accident, and by rights should be out in the light, standing straight on a pedestal plainly marked The Greatest. I worry about that, too. And I hate all these kids who don't worry about big things at all. It isn't right. I'm jealous of all these kids, because if anybody deserves to be lucky, I deserve to be. And I'm suspicious of everybody who seriously imagines that these kids are possibly as important as I am, which on the face of it is fantastic. I am the greatest. Let's just understand that. Let's just accept it, so that we won't become neurotic, and then let's all pitch in together and be nice. Let's all be nice to one another, for as much as ye are nice to one another, ye are nice to me, and ye know me. I'm the nicest. I love everybody.

Playboy, 1966

A Soft Word
to the
Gravedigger

A Soft Word to the Gravedigger appeared in Cavalier *in September
1965. A year or two later it came out in the Weekend Magazine of* The
London Telegraph. *It speaks for itself, of course, as in fact all of the
pieces in this book do. About ten years ago in one of the big fat
magazines dentists keep in their waiting rooms a long article appeared
in which the theory was put forward that I had started out to be a good
writer in 1934 but had steadily declined year by year. This was nothing
new to me. Nor is it unusual for any writer to read that he is steadily
declining. One might say it is unavoidable, because nothing is so
convenient to the inept critic than to point out that the writer under
consideration started out fairly well but quickly went to pot. This
particular essay was accompanied by five or six drawings that purported
to be of myself: in which the literary decline was revealed in the face, as
sketched by a hired artist. The final drawing seemed to suggest that the
writer really ought to be buried. All the same it continues to be my own
theory that I am alive, able, willing, and compelled to write. And I know
that the only money that has come to me since the year 1934 has come
from writing, excepting for the three years I was in the Army, when my
wages were something well under $100 a month.*

Nobody is interested in what success does to American lawyers
or thieves, but everybody wants to know how success
destroyed every American writer who ever succeeded: Mark

Twain, Sinclair Lewis, and Scott Fitzgerald, for instance, to name only a few.

There are specialists on this subject, and of course they prefer the writer to be dead, to have been knifed in the back by fate, or America, or money, or success, because then it is an open-and-shut case, as the saying is, and the specialist can get right in there and be very bright—and important, too.

He can say how he read Mark Twain when he was 11 years old, and again when he was 21, and still later when he was 31. He can say how he once spoke to Sinclair Lewis and called him Red, because calling him Red meant they were pals. He can say how he once wrote to Theodore Dreiser, asking him if he really believed his novels were as effective as action in the matter of social reform. And, in reporting that Mr. Dreiser didn't answer his letter, he can indicate how success had begun its deadly work on yet another writer. And he can do just about anything he likes with Scott Fitzgerald, who published a book called *The Crack-up*, in which he made it quite clear that he had had a lot of success but a lot of failure, too.

As long as his boys are dead, the specialist is just fine. His theory is proved, for what is better proof of failure than death? But let the writer still be hanging on, and it makes trouble for the specialist. He can dig a grave, but he can't put a live man in it. He can hope that by the time his writing appears in a magazine or in a book, the writer will have obliged him by dying or by killing himself, and then of course the specialist will have a scoop, and he will appear to be a prophet, too.

Now, all I'm doing is dying, and success isn't killing me, failure is, or at any rate failure and catarrh. It isn't easy to make an autopsy on a writer who doesn't know enough to lie down and die, who doesn't even suspect that success is slowly but surely killing him or driving him mad, or both, whichever is first or most, as the lawyers like to say.

Well, now, the simple fact is that I have always been just about equally successful and unsuccessful, both in my writing and in the spending of the money it has brought me. There is no doubt that on six or seven occasions I made more than enough money, but then my idea of enough is not very much like anybody else's. I have always had the feeling that being out of debt is enough, and on six or seven occasions I actually got out of debt.

Now, it doesn't matter that I hadn't gotten myself into debt on behalf of writing, or in a good cause of any kind. I hadn't had a bad time as a writer and I hadn't gotten into debt in order to buy a ready-made suit, a pair of shoes, or a beret.

I had gotten into debt from the old and well-established limitations and flaws of my character. I had always been both willing and compelled to use money as if I had a machine that made the stuff, as in a sense I did. I got into debt, I sat down at the typewriter, I wrote, and on six or seven occasions I earned enough to pay my debts again.

But I can't pretend that I have ever been as successful as three or four dozen other American writers, or perhaps as many as 300, including those who write for films and television. I have never needed to open an office, hire a business manager, call in a tax expert, sit down with lawyers, incorporate, reincorporate, double incorporate, and triple incorporate, and I have never gone to lunch with investment experts and discussed how to put my half-a-million dollars to work so that in a matter of five years, which would be passing in any case, the half-a-million would become two or three million, net, after taxes. I just haven't been interested in the stuff.

Every now and then I've overheard the really successful writers discussing their various financial coups and achievements, and I have almost admired and envied them, but I soon got over it, because they sounded like businessmen, and their writing, although enormously profitable, was no good. And of course the writing of any number of them *seemed* to be first-rate, but actually wasn't. I have tried to read it, to find out about it for myself, and the stuff just wasn't any good at all.

I've done well enough, I suppose, if you take into account that I used to sell papers and don't sell papers any more. And I have seen older men than myself selling papers, and they appeared to be as real and interesting as any writer I have ever met, successful or half-successful or not successful at all.

My success has been different.

You might even say I have been successful in spite of the fact that I have always failed. I have always written what I *had* to write, such as this. What is it? It's not a story, it's not even a proper autobiographical fragment. It hasn't got a plot, and there aren't any big parts in it for any of the stars of stage or screen. For all I know, it doesn't have a chance of being published, even.

Publishing is getting to be something else, too, just as writing long ago began to be something else, too. A publisher isn't any more interested in writing for its own sake than a produce merchant is interested in potatoes for their own sake, or a manufacturer of cars is interested in cars for their own sake. What everybody wants is something he can sell, fast. And there's nothing wrong with that, either. I'll be very glad, for instance, if my next book sells a million copies in all editions, as they say, but on the other hand I won't kill myself if it sells only a thousand copies. Why should I? I'm a writer. There's plenty more where that came from. Now, if I won't kill myself from failure, I don't see why I'd be likely to from success.

But the gravedigger seems to look at it another way. His attitude seems to be that success is actually killing me (or any other writer he might find useful), and I just don't happen to know that it's killing me, perhaps from not having gone to Harvard, or from never having had any real intelligence; just an innocent slob being pushed steadily into the grave.

Well, I don't agree, that's all. I like writers. I like the successful ones, the rich ones, the incorporated ones, the good ones, the bad ones, the real ones, and the phony ones. I'm interested in the whole thing. I like especially the ones who can really write because they have got somebody to write out of, namely themselves, but there just aren't many of them anywhere in the world, let alone in America. Time and trouble catch up with writers, time starts to run out on them, they get confused, they get scared, they goof, they run away, they hide, they curse it all. I like them. They're fighting something.

The point is: I'm trying to remember what success actually did to me, and of course by success it must be understood that I refer to the success that the specialists mean when they speak about it: acceptance, fame, money.

By the end of 1939 I had all of these things, but I also had a gimp, and from having had to salvage a totally wrecked play, against a lot of expert opposition, I had become irritable, and frequently seemed arrogant and rude. But I did salvage the play, called *The Time of Your Life*.

It was the first American play to win both the prizes, and it did bring me enough money to pay all my debts, so I paid them. But there was still enough money left over for anything I might care to buy, so of course the question is what did I buy? I didn't buy anything. I only wanted that play to be the play I had written, and that's the play it became.

I could have turned that triumph into an industry, there's no doubt about it. I could have made deals with Kewpie-doll manufacturers, and sweat-shirt manufacturers, and distillers, and nightclub owners, and just about any money-hustling outfit in the world, but I didn't do it, and I'll tell you why I didn't do it. It wasn't my work. What's more, I was bored with the whole thing. There was other writing to do. There were other plays to write.

I didn't consider it a miracle that the play was all right. I went to saloons and drank and had fun, but I would have done that if the play had been a flop. So it was a success, so what? Was everything else everywhere else also a success? Everything was precisely the same as ever, so I went right on being the same cheerful psychotic I had always been.

But just imagine how much more cheerful and how much more psychotic I would have been if I had not been a writer at all. And that appears to be the little thing that the gravedigger seems to forget.

The only success that means anything happens when a writer becomes a writer at all. The rest is beside the point. Would any of the writers the gravedigger keeps writing about *not* have died? Would any of them have been something more or better had they not become writers? Who knows? I don't. I should imagine, though, that they would have died in any case, and would have lived their lives out in pretty much the same manner, only worse, most likely.

I am not a success, and success isn't killing me. I am a writer, and I am dying, but I would be dying in any case, and had I not become a writer it is possible I would have died long ago, so there's a big fat profit right there, and not taxable, either.

I Used to Believe I Had Forever, Now I'm Not So Sure, 1968

Applause

Applause appeared in Theatre Arts *magazine, April 1955. I don't know of anybody else who has written about applause, although I'm sure many people have, especially psychiatrists.*

Yesterday Hal X. phoned to ask if I'd write a play for him, in memory of the days when he was looking for work in New York and came to the rehearsals of *Across the Board on Tomorrow Morning*, ran errands and was generally helpful and amusing, without having a part in the play, or pay, or promise of a part.

"What does a world-famous movie star want with a play by me?" I said. "I write failures."

"Never mind the world-famous stuff," he said. "I want to spend a lot of time rehearsing and opening a play that hasn't got a chance."

"I might just accidentally write a play that *has* got a chance."

"Have you got an idea for a play like that?"

"No."

"Well," Hal said, "I've got an idea for one that hasn't got a chance, and if you'll write it, I'll do it."

"What is the idea?"

"Applause," Hal said. "Do you know what I mean?"

"I've got an idea."

We talked a minute and I said I'd think about it. I remembered the applause Hitler created and came to count on, to enjoy and believe in. But what's the good of thinking about a man like that? I considered next the applause of audiences at concerts. Why did certain conductors insist upon having a great deal of it, by various tricks? I then considered the applause given to political candidates, baseball players, actors and actresses in plays, in radio, on television.

What is applause? When it is valid, and when isn't it? Was there ever a first-rate man who was able to enjoy applause?

I thought of Darrow at the Mecca many years ago in New York, and his unmistakable annoyance at being applauded. The applause started and stopped almost at the same time. He just wanted no part of it, and the audience understood and respected his wish instantly. Had he been critical of the audience, or of himself? Neither, I think. He had been critical of emotionality. He was an intellectual, and a lonely one, and if he was to appear before a group of people, it was to be solely as himself, not as a creation of the audience. He didn't care for mobs, and the audience knew it. If they wanted him to maintain integrity and to respect each of them, they would have to put aside any herdlike rampaging. He had been nervous while he had waited for his turn. He had been miserable while someone had taken too long to introduce him. He had insisted upon no applause. He had spoken clearly, unemotionally, intelligently, quickly, and he had sat down. There was little applause at the end of his talk, but I doubt very much if this signified that he was not respected by the audience.

The next speaker, however, permitted applause, and at the end of his speech enjoyed something like an ovation. The same audience.

I consider the second man a fool, but in my thinking I employed the phrase which I find more accurate. I considered him a deliberate mischief-maker, a prolonger of herdish idiocies and hysteria, a fraud.

Is it ever in order for any man to accept applause from any group at all? In my opinion, it is not. And this immediately establishes a problem that deserves to be carefully considered—by others more systematic and more expert at this sort of thing than I am. The problem is this: If it is desirable for the human being to be both a sentient and an intelligent creature, how can he become such a creature if the herd habits which operate in his mass-life, which belittle his sentience and prevent his achievement of even the hope of intelligence, are permitted to persist?

To put it another way, if the most effective art is hysterical, if the achievement of its effectiveness is by means of emotionality, how can common life be serene, reflective, poised, intelligent?

I have heard, by way of a biographer and by way of a playwright, that Lincoln was bewildered by applause. Surely now and then, though, he must have been thankful for it. In short, he must have felt on occasion that he was entitled to it, for reasons he alone knew. They may have been excellent reasons, too. And he may not have been thinking at all about the reasons the applauders may have had to applaud him, or to seem to applaud him. For whom does anybody ever applaud but himself?

The church, which is so frequently inept in so many other things, begins and ends all of its performances without applause—with applause prohibited, in fact. My son once applauded at a rather hushed moment in a church in New York. The wave of astonishment and silence stopped him quickly.

In the street I asked him what had impelled him to clap his hands. "Well, when the man came out," he said, "didn't you *see* him?" I had indeed. Well, wasn't he dressed that way? Yes, he was. Perhaps. Then why was it wrong for him to applaud? And so on.

The fact is, applause does belong to children. The clapping of hands with joy is rather inevitable for them, as when my daughter was taken to the biggest and brightest department store during Christmas week in San Francisco. The minute she was beyond the revolving doors and inside the magnificent and enormous room, she clapped her hands and cried out, "Oh, Papa, look at that!" I had almost forgotten what a special and wonderful place it was, in fact, and how deserving of a large glance.

I shall never forget the producer of a play in New York at the end of a preview performance before an invited audience. He stood in the aisle, applauded wildly, and then began to stamp down the aisle toward the stage, shouting bravos and applauding as he went. The play had been far from flawless or meaningful. I had been the producer's guest. With what I felt was friendship, I said, "But you can't do that, can you?" The producer was deaf, however. But a producer—after all, what is a producer? What may one ever expect of a producer? Alas, he was a leading figure, if not the leading figure, in a kind of dynamic campaign to revitalize the American theatre. He was not a money-man, he was a man of high cultural aspirations. Had his applause been helpless? I doubt it, but if it had, all the worse. Had it been deliberate, almost part of the play itself, a kind of valid element in the potential wholeness and effectiveness of the play? Most likely, but again all the worse. You cannot in fact applaud (literally) that of which you yourself are part. You can for the fun of it, if you happen to be young and a little rambunctious, or even a little scornful of both the play and the audience. Otherwise, you can't.

Now, it is easy to slide this whole subject over to an area of insignificance. Why, it might be said, we applaud solely because we are civil and polite. The whole business is nothing more than common civility. Applause does not need to be sincere, any more than saying good morning to a neighbor needs to be sincere. It is routine. There is no reason not to applaud, no reason not to greet a neighbor.

It is easy to say that applause, at its best, is a good and necessary thing, and it does not matter that most applause is for nothing and useless.

In reply to that I say it's noisy.

Will the good psychiatrist say applause is a safety valve? If he will, I will say, open the valve for sunrise and sunset, seashores, skies, mountains, meadows, rivers, lakes, forests, birds, insects, weeds, whatever. If disaster in drama impels or requires applause, why does disaster in the real world prohibit it?

But what is applause for a play? I presume it is intended to be thanks—to the playwright, to the players, to Heaven, to life, to art itself, if I may run a lot of things together quickly. Anonymous thanks, and what's wrong with that?

If the play is good, I suppose there's nothing wrong with it, although I don't like it on general principles.

But everything is applauded. A man on a television giveaway program is asked if he is married. He says he is. Applause. He says he isn't. Applause. He says he loves his wife and sounds as if he means it. Applause. He says he loves his wife and sounds as if he is only trying to get along with her. Applause. The next man on the program is a celebrated guest. He is one of the biggest men in the government. He signs the currency, for instance. He is asked if American currency is sound. He says it is. Applause. The following week on the same program, a dazzling, middle-aged woman with an accent is asked how she manages to be so pretty-looking all the time. She says, "Bot I vaz alvays very pretty—since leaddle goil." Applause.

What is this? In short, has applause—the device of it—nullified the hope of decent discrimination in all areas?

A girl has a round figure. A camera is turned on her. She is watched putting on a dress, pulling up her stockings, walking half a block. Applause. What for? Is it astonishing or miraculous that a girl with a round figure, knows how to put on a dress and is able to walk half a block? The movie ends and the newsreel comes on. The cabinet is in session before television cameras for the first time. A man says something that sounds as if it means something but doesn't, or certainly doesn't mean what the man implies it means. Applause. A captured bank robber walks to a train handcuffed to a plainclothes police officer. For a minute you don't know which is which. Then the smaller man turns and waves. Applause. The plainclothesman looks on shyly. After all, who is he?

What about the play for Hal X., fifteen short years ago a young man from a poor New York family looking for easy work (a part in a play), for the past ten years a name, face and figure known all over the world wherever American movies are shown?

Three years ago when we met by accident in New York, I said I was on my way to Pasha's on Allen Street because of the Near Eastern music and dancing there. Would he care to go along?

"Ah, they'll mob me," he said. "I haven't been able to go to places I like for years. I've got to go to 21, the Stork, Sardi's and all the rest of the places that are safe for celebrities."

I insisted that he wouldn't be mobbed at Pasha's. He was, however. The whole place was jammed with young Syrians, Greeks, Armenians, Turks, Jews, Spaniards and others in less than half an hour. We took a taxi back uptown and drank in peace, surrounded by other celebrities scared to death of the public, and its affection and applause.

He asked for it, though, didn't he?

Well, *did* he?

Hal X. is now thirty-six years old. He is not much unlike other men in their middle thirties. The mob at Pasha's included not one man who was not as interesting as Hal X. himself. The trouble with Hal is that he knows that. I don't think he especially dislikes what's happened to him. I can understand, however, that he might be a little fed-up with the unnecessary fuss that is made over him—for nothing. Now if I could write a play about a man who doesn't enjoy applause, he feels sure he could go to work and really perform that part. No doubt, but it wouldn't help. He'd be applauded just the same. If the play failed, as it would, as he himself would prefer it to, he would be applauded, the good drama critics would only remark that he need not have wasted himself in such a part, and they would criticize the playwright for writing another bad play.

Still, the subject of applause deserves a play, no doubt. If I write it, Hal X. can have it, and good luck. He'll never have to put up with the public's affection and applause for the Vice-President, for instance, but at the same time he'll never again know the freedom and chance to grow in integrity that he knew when he was unknown and truly famous.

I Used to Believe I Had Forever, Now I'm Not So Sure, 1968

Armenak
of Bitlis

W ell, I visited your grave in the cemetery by the railroad tracks in San Jose, California, earlier this year, and standing there on the numbered plot I remembered the first time I went there.

It was with your kid brother Mihran when I was seventeen or eighteen and he was thirty-seven or thirty-eight, forty years ago. Your brother wept standing there, and I with my big mouth, which I got from the other side of the family, from your wife, your widow, my mother, from the loud side of the family, I said, "What are you crying for, he's not here."

And I laughed, with the simple pleasure of being in a place like that, on a grand day of summertime, because it was so good to be alive and because I didn't believe in death, couldn't believe in it, didn't believe you were dead, for instance, or that *anybody* had ever died.

Your brother was shocked by my remark and by my laughter, and not being able to speak clearly for the sobbing he was trying to control, he said, "Where is he, then?"

Well, this only made it worse, because Mihran always had a kind of earnestness and simplicity that put him to asking questions that were very funny to others.

"Oh, many places," I said. "No man ends in his grave, only his bones or his dust go there. A man stays forever where he had been. Where he was born, where he had his childhood and boyhood. He stays where he traveled, too, on the trains and ships, and he stays in the books he read. I have my father's books, he's all over the place in his books. I came here only to see where they put his bones. My father isn't dead. I'm here, so he's here, too." Well, of course, such theories are open to dispute, but that's beside the point.

For a long time I only remembered that little space in the grass, under the trees there, beside the road and (beyond the road) the railroad tracks. I didn't think or feel, "That's where my father is" or "That's where my father's bones lie" or anything like that. I only remembered that I had been there.

Now, as a small boy beginning to try to understand things, I believed that one day soon you would come walking up a street to me and know I was your son, aged three, four, five, six, seven, or eight. I went right on believing you would come walking until I was eleven or twelve, and then I forgot all about that idea. I didn't *disbelieve* it, I forgot about it, I let it go, and it stayed gone for a long time; and then all of a sudden it began to come back, and by that time I was a grown man.

I knew nothing but laughter, wild health, unquestioned confidence, ideas of all kinds day and night, and all kinds of interior and exterior movement, all kinds of going and coming. I started to travel as soon as I had the money for it, but the first big jaunt was financed by your kid brother Mihran, who loaned me $200 in 1928 just before I turned twenty, so I could go to New York by Greyhound bus. I paid him back of course, but he was always lending me new money even after I had earned twenty or thirty times as much as he ever did, and I was always paying him back, except once or twice when it took a number of years, and in the end I am afraid he may have loaned me more than I paid back.

I was all too well along in years, almost as old as you were when you died in 1911, when I began to believe *again* that you would come walking up a street and find me.

Or rather than *believe* this would happen, I began to remember how I had long ago believed it would. "My father," I had thought, "he'll do that, because he's my father; he won't stay gone just because he's dead, he'll find a way to get back on his feet and come walking up a street and find me somewhere, because he's my father, and the way we are, we'll do a thing like that, we know it can't be done, it's against the law, but my father, he'll do that, and then what will the world think? What will people say? They'll say, 'He was dead for ten years, and then he came back, just like that, not a ghost, not somebody who looked like him, but himself, he came back, he came back to say his son's name,' that's what they'll say." And so it went, even when I was all over the place being myself so loudly and swiftly that total strangers in public places drew back in astonishment and sometimes even in fear, as if I myself were more than just one loud-mouthed laughing man.

And then one thing leading to another I forgot again for a long time. I remembered, but didn't pay very much attention to the remembering, because it was either not working or I hadn't grown with it to a new understanding of how it would happen, would *still* happen, after more than thirty years. All of a sudden in 1939 I became no longer tireless, no longer inexhaustible, and something happened to the laughter, the jokes, the noise, the going and coming, the travel, the eating, the drinking, the fun and the work and the fame and the money. I was thirty-one years old when I noticed a terrible sorrow in me wherever I went. Perhaps it was because the War was upon us again. I thought, "The streets are too cluttered for my father to come back now, he'd be lost in the hysteria, if we came face to face he wouldn't know me, he'd be terrified of everybody, and he'd be scared to death of me, too."

I found a little girl and married her and she gave birth to a son, and I looked at him and smelled him and listened to him and spoke to him, and something quite simple happened in my thinking, and this is what it was: "Here he is, and soon enough I'll see him walking up a street, and he'll stop and speak to me, just as I knew he would. This old man, already eight hours old, is my father."

But I let it go, I didn't think it would do, it wasn't quite the same thing, although there was in fact something to it that couldn't be totally dismissed.

After the War, when I saw my son again, he was two years old, but he didn't seem to know me, and I can't say I really knew him, either. In his earliest months his crying had troubled me, because it wasn't the way I had heard other small children cry.

When I got back from Europe, angry, confused, sick, desperate, as dead as I was alive, my son looked at me and burst into tears. The first thing I thought was, "It's my poor father, dead at age thirty-six, but back again, and all outraged. Is he mad at me for bringing him back? Have I been at fault in this? Has a crime been committed against him, by me?"

We broke up, but by that time there was a daughter to stand and walk beside the son, only they were with their mother, and I began to think, "Well, how are they, what's happening to them, how are they getting along, are they all right, will they be all right?"

By that time I was older than you ever were. The year was 1949. I was forty-one, and shot. I was *all* shot, all over the place, but that's all right, it happens all the time, it can happen to anybody, for all I know it has *got* to happen to everybody, but when it happens, and it's yourself, it's something else again, not something you can just talk about, it's what's going on, and it's killing, you've got to be very tough and very lucky to survive it.

For years I didn't go back to the little place in the San Jose graveyard, although I drove down the highway alongside the place and remembered the grave and now and then looked in that direction. I didn't think about any of it in that old way anymore, I just drove by, being followed by the broken pieces which were trying to catch up and get back together again.

And so it went for a long time. I sometimes woke with a start, as if from death, and tried to piece it all together, asking, "Now, wait a minute, where am I, where are my people, where's my father, where's my son?" And then little by little it would all come back and I would know what every man still alive knows, and I would get up and light a cigarette and pour whiskey into a glass and inhale smoke and swallow whiskey, and try to think.

I saw my son now and then, and his sister, and I spoke with him, and with her; but we were strangers, I really didn't know him, didn't know her, didn't know you, and didn't know myself.

And then one day in New York I was walking up Fifth Avenue from 44th Street. I had made a point of not writing to let my son know I would be in New York, because he so infrequently answered my letters, and when he did, his letters seemed strange. In one letter he even said my letters were a nuisance to him, so I didn't write anymore.

When I saw him coming down Fifth Avenue I knew he was my son, but it didn't matter, and I decided to walk by and let it go at that. It was all right, it happens all the time. Who's whose father? Is anybody anybody's father, isn't some crazy idea of the world itself every man's father? "He's fifteen years old now, he's as tall as I am now, he's coming toward me down Fifth Avenue, but I'll walk by, I'll see him, but he won't see me."

And then I thought, "It is in fact as if it were my father coming down a street as I always believed he would, only now I see him but he doesn't see me, so it'll be as if somebody in a crowd of people passed by, that's all, that's all it will be, and that's all right, too."

I kept looking at him as I walked, and when there was not more than four feet between us, among dozens of people, I saw him and he saw me, and I went on up Fifth Avenue, and he went on down. I didn't smile and he didn't smile. I didn't nod and he didn't nod. And I didn't care and I didn't care that he didn't care.

And then it happened, but not quite the way I had imagined for so long that it would.

I was walking straight ahead when somebody came running through the people to walk beside me, and when he reached me he almost shouted, "Pop."

I stopped, and he looked at me and said, "For God's sake, Pop, you passed me in the street. You saw me, but you didn't stop. I must have been dreaming or something, because I wasn't sure it was you, I thought it must be somebody else. Why didn't you stop, Pop? Why didn't you speak to me? Why didn't you say my name?"

I said, "Listen, my boy. Yes, I saw you, but you were going somewhere, and I didn't think I ought to stop you, I didn't think I ought to say your name. Now, I know you *are* going somewhere, so go ahead, because I am, too, and I've got to go."

I wasn't angry, and he knew I wasn't angry, and he understood.

"Can I call you at your hotel?"

"Any time."

He went on down Fifth Avenue and I went up.

I had been going to the same hotel for years, and he knew I always stopped there, and many hours later that day, it was around eleven at night, he called and we talked, and an hour later he came by and we went out and walked and talked.

Soon afterwards I went to Europe, and back and forth every year, and then one day when I went back to San Francisco I found a letter from somebody at the State College in San Jose in which I was invited to go there soon and talk. And all of a sudden I remembered the little place in the graveyard in San Jose, and I answered the letter and said yes, I would go there for two or three days. When I got there I went straight out to the graveyard and into the office, and a lady got out the records and gave me the number of the place and told me how to get there, and I went there, I went to your grave, and I stood there looking down at the weedy grass.

I just wanted to stand there.

I remembered the first time I went there, with your kid brother Mihran, when he had stood there and had wept and I had laughed.

My father, standing there I was fifty-eight years old, my son was twenty-three, your kid brother had died the year before, aged seventy-seven, and your bones were still thirty-six years old. I'm not sure, I wouldn't care to swear to it, but I believe I said to myself, or thought, or felt, "Yes, my father is dead here."

I have an idea I was mistaken, but something like that is what I thought or said or felt or believed, but there was no sorrow in my heart. I guess it was because there hadn't been any when I was a little kid and believed you would come walking up a street someday and find me and say my name. Nothing exactly like that ever happened, but *something* happened. Nothing much can be made of it, most likely, but I thought I'd better mention it before I forget again.

Letters from 74 rue Taitbout, or, Don't Go But If You Must Say Hello to Everybody, 1971

Hovagim
Saroyan

I remember staying overnight at your vineyard on the north side of
Fresno, to which my brother Henry and I traveled with you in a
carriage drawn by an old horse. I know the distance from our house
at 2226 San Benito Avenue to your vineyard was only four miles, as I have
made the journey recently several times, but it seemed to us a far greater
distance.

Henry and I sat in the back like passengers, and you sat on the
higher seat up front, none of us speaking, perhaps because your
language was Armenian and ours was English, although we *could* speak
Armenian, too. But mainly we were not speaking because we were glad
to be together, traveling. It was late in the afternoon of a hot day, and you
came to our house and said to our mother, "Takoohi, let me take the boys
to the ranch, I will take them jackrabbit shooting, we will have supper,
we will listen to old country records, and I will bring them back
tomorrow in time for church. I don't want to ride home alone." And my
mother said, "Hovagim, if you want them to go with you, take them."
And so we went.

It was 1917, exactly fifty years ago, perhaps this very same month,
July, and you were alone out there on the vineyard. Your wife and two
sons were in Bitlis or near there or far from there, if they weren't dead, if
they hadn't been killed, or hadn't died of hunger and thirst on the long
march from Bitlis to the desert which so many others made and in which
so many died. But even if they were alive, you hadn't heard from them or
from anybody who had seen them. Perhaps the boys were alive, but
didn't know who they were, having been too little to remember, having
been taken to an orphanage and given new names.

I used to know you were alone, even before I heard about what had
happened, heard my mother telling somebody.

You came to America, to work, to send money to your wife, so she and your sons could come too, but it didn't work out that way. You sent money and letters, and your wife replied, and then she didn't reply, and a whole year went by, and then another whole year went by, and you didn't know what had happened. You had an idea, but you didn't know for sure. You were alone everywhere I ever saw you, even in the Arax Coffee House full of card players. I knew you were alone the first time I saw you sitting in our parlor sipping a cup of coffee, so when you said, "I don't want to go home alone," I knew what you were talking about, the way a small boy will know such a thing and never be able to talk about it.

Riding in the back of your carriage, on our way to your vineyard and your little house there, I kept wondering what it was that had *most* made you alone, and I thought it must be from not having your father with you, because that's how we think, I guess, out of what is true for each of us, out of whatever each of us knows that makes us alone. Your father and my mother's father were brothers, and I knew my mother's father had died in Bitlis and, dying, had said to my mother's mother, "Get the family out of here, leave this place, go anywhere else, but do not stay here any longer, go to America if you can manage."

And of course she *did* manage, although it wasn't easy: the people who control the papers and the rubber stamps had to be bribed with gold one by one, and then transportation had to be paid for, first by donkey train over high mountains along narrow roads from Bitlis to Erzeroum, where my brother Henry was born in 1905, and from Erzeroum to Trabizon, where a ship carried them to Constantinople, and then to Marseilles, where they all had to work to raise money for the train ride across France to Le Havre, where again they had to work until there was enough money to put everybody on the ship that sailed to New York—a long crossing, far below in the ship, in steerage, where hundreds of families prepared their own meals and made sleeping places on the floor, followed at last by the fear and terror of Ellis Island. Everybody was "bono" except Lucy, my mother's mother herself, and somebody with a rubber stamp said she would have to go back to Bitlis. The whole family went mad. The situation was unbelievable for hours, in which the heart died in everybody, and the old woman, then scarcely forty years of age, said, "Do not despair. God will put forth his hand." And the next day her eyes were examined again, and almost as if it meant nothing, nothing at all, somebody else with a rubber stamp stamped her papers and said, "Bono." And thus the family was not deprived of its force, authority, intelligence, wisdom, and faith.

What had made you so alone? I kept wondering what had made us all so alone, even when many of us were together, and what it was, I felt, was at least partly the people with the power, with the paper, with the rubber stamps, the enforcers of the rules and regulations, a whole world full of such people. They scare a man. They are killers.

After we finally arrived at your vineyard you took us to your cow and milked her and invited us to drink fresh milk. It was warm and seemed all right, but an hour later, while we were out jackrabbit hunting, we both threw up. We saw a couple of the big loping jackrabbits but they were too far away to shoot, and then we came back to your little shack house, and you served us a good dinner of stuffed tomatoes, bell peppers, and cucumbers, with flat bread and yogurt. And then we sat down in your parlor while you played Armenian records on the wind-up phonograph. The music was proud, beautiful, and lonely. And then we both began to fall asleep and you got us to our beds.

Hovagim, sleeping in your house was something I couldn't understand when I woke up in the morning. There was a smell of sorrow and loneliness in my nostrils, and I couldn't remember where I was, but I knew I wasn't in my own bed in my own home. And then I remembered. I was at Hovagim's house. I got dressed and went out and ate figs straight from the big tree, and then my brother Henry came out, and he ate some figs, too. And he said, "It feels funny sleeping in somebody else's house, doesn't it?" And I said, "Did you feel it, too?"

Pretty soon we saw you coming from your ditch where you had been guiding water to your vines, and you said in English, "All right, boys, now we eat." And you fixed us tea and fried dough, or new bread, into which we stuffed white cheese, and we ate boiled eggs and slices of dried beef, and lots of parsley and mint and fresh tomatoes and cucumbers sliced lengthwise.

And then you harnessed the old horse to the carriage and we set out for home. That's all, Hovagim. But it was one of the great experiences of my life, don't ask me why. It just was. I guess it was your kindness and aloneness. It certainly wasn't the milk fresh from the cow—that stuff's poison.

I saw you around town for a couple more years, and then all it was was a matter of remembering.

I hope both of the boys got out of it alive, even if they lost their names, because under any name I think they would be O.K.

Letters from 74 rue Taitbout, or, Don't Go But If You Must Say Hello to Everybody, 1971

Calouste
Gulbenkian

When I arrived at the Avis Hotel in Lisbon, in May of 1949 I was surprised to learn that you occupied all of the mezzanine floor.

"Gulbenkian?" I said to the manager of the hotel. "Do you mean the man who is rich?"

"The richest man in the world," the manager of the hotel said. "He is Armenian, as I believe you are."

I was forty-one years old at the time, and in a bad way, having just left my wife, small son, and smaller daughter, for reasons that were grave enough to make my leaving imperative.

I was in a state of spiritual shock. I missed something. I could say it was my wife, my son, and my daughter, but I'm afraid it was something else—I missed the truth. I was suddenly without home, continuity, and meaning. I was without myself, my own ghost. I was not only lost, I was cut down. I was in fact dead. But I *seemed* to be alive. If anything, more alive than ever, from not knowing what to do next, or where to go, in order to start being alive in the truth again.

You were almost twice my age, and in vigorous good health. You mentioned during lunch that your father had lived to be ninety-eight and that you believed you would live at least that long, too. The money that came to you daily from oil leases which you had negotiated on behalf of countries having the oil and countries wanting to buy it did not stop four years later when you did, however. Money flows in secret rivers in many different places, from somewhere to somebody, and the river that had flowed to you for so long continued to flow after your death at eighty-four to the Foundation you established in Lisbon.

At that time Russia was putting pressure on Iran and Irak, and there appeared to be a chance that these countries would be taken into the Soviet Socialistic body of nations, whereupon the flow of the rivers would be diverted from you to the Soviet government or to the people of Iran and Irak.

I tend to ask anybody I am with simple questions, not in rudeness but in the interest of truth, and so I asked if such a condition would come to you as a blow, or a sorrow, and you replied, "Oh no, if it happens, I shall not mind at all. It will be all right, not so much because in any event I am not a poor man, but rather because change of one sort or another is always happening and unavoidable, and there is no reason for me to regret any change that affects my interests. It may even be a good thing—for me, even. I might find time to concern myself more with art—I love great paintings, for instance. And the money involved might be put to better use than I might ever manage, although I have great numbers of skilled people working on the problem of how best to put to work the money that has come to me."

The richest man in the world, or at any rate one of the richest men in the world, speaking to me in this manner, in the Armenian language as well as now and then in English, pleased me, for I have always believed that money ought not to go to a few lucky people in the world as long as there is poverty of any kind among the majority of the people. In short, you were speaking both truthfully and honorably about your good luck in having had the skill of negotiation which had started the making of your great fortune.

Because of my own particular astonishment and anxiety at that time I listened carefully to everything you said. You had no idea how things were with me, although you may have suspected that something was wrong. I know I do when I am in the company of somebody in some kind of trouble. On the one hand, it really didn't matter that you happened to be Armenian, and on the other, it pleased me deeply that you were, for I needed to see somebody in the family, so to put it. I needed to talk to somebody who might very well be almost a relative, and while I didn't think of you as a father, or somebody who was something like a father, I did feel that there was a real connection between us. We had almost nothing in common, and yet we were instantly related: it happened when you surprised and pleased me by speaking a dialect of Armenian that was no trouble at all for me to understand, and I was delighted to notice that you instantly understood my replies in the dialect of Bitlis.

In a sense, we were both homeless, we had no geographical country of our own as we had once had and as we had ever since *wanted* to have, excepting the very small portion of what was once our country, which had become a part of Soviet Russia in 1921.

By nature, neither of us could make a life there, if in fact we would *want* to, even had we had our own independent nation. You had made your way in Istanbul, in Tehran, in Mosul, in Baghdad, in London, in Paris, in Lisbon, and in many of the other cities of the world. And in a sense I was making my way in much the same manner, starting in California, moving on to New York, and from there to Europe, and to Soviet Armenia in 1935.

We simply did not belong to a geographical and political country that was our own. We lived and worked here and there, but it was known that you were Armenian and that I was Armenian, and at lunch we acknowledged to each other instantly that we were. We spoke our language, and enjoyed doing so.

I was pleased when you said, "The waiters who are paid to pass along things I say in English, French, Portuguese, and other languages shall be very puzzled today. Very few people in the world make a point of learning the Armenian language. In a moment you will observe the headwaiter as he comes to this table to move a fork or pour wine, but actually to listen to our speech, and to wonder what language it is. I speak Turkish and Arabic as well, of course, and he has heard me do so, but he has never heard me speak Armenian. I shall enjoy his bewilderment."

And sure enough, the headwaiter did in fact come to our table and very slowly pour wine, as you said in Armenian, "Let us please keep talking, I want him to hear the Armenian language being spoken."

And simply to comply with your request I said, "But he knows you are Armenian, and he will presume that we are speaking that language, won't he?" And you said, "Well, it is one thing to know we are speaking the Armenian language, but another to know what we are saying. He is paid to pass along information about anything I happen to say that he hears and understands, but what information can he sell this time?"

I said, "He can certainly say an Armenian from America had lunch with you today, but no business of any kind was discussed or transacted—they just ate and drank and spoke Armenian."

And then the waiter was obliged to go back to his watchful place, and you said, "I am glad you have come to Lisbon, but how did you happen to come to this hotel? People reserve rooms a year in advance, and there are very few rooms to be had."

"At the airport I asked the taxi driver to take me to the best hotel in Lisbon," I said. "And the taxi driver said in Portuguese, which I neither speak nor understand but nevertheless understood when he spoke it: 'Well, the best is the Avis, but it is very expensive.' And so I came here. Ribeira, the manager, at first told me there was no room, but after a glance at my passport, he asked me to wait five or ten minutes. And then he said, 'Room 404,' and I must say I like the room very much, especially the tile floor and walls and halls, tile everywhere."

We had lunch the following day, too, and dinner several times, and you began to suspect that something was the matter for I was hungover every day, and went by taxi every afternoon and again every evening to the casino at Estoril and gambled—winning and losing, and losing, and winning, and drinking all the time, and of course there were pretty women there to be taken somewhere, so that between the gambling, drinking, and women I decided it didn't matter any more: it was all right, I really didn't care that I was dead, homeless, lost, and forty-one years old. I don't know how you found out, but one day at lunch you said, "In all the years I have been in Lisbon, I have never set foot in the casino at Estoril. If it happens that you need money, please let me know." I must say I was dumbfounded, both that you knew I was spending so much time at the casino and that you nevertheless wanted to help me—even with money. But I am the Saroyan I am. I pay my own way. I make mistakes and pay for them. I am not permitted to accept money from others for any purpose or reason. I said, "Thank you very much, I am all right. I have everything." But that very night my luck (if there is in fact such a thing when a man is drowning) was incredible, both when it was good and when it was bad, so that in the end I didn't even have money enough to leave the casino with one of the women there. And almost nothing in Room 404, only a few dollars, and one gold coin worth abut fifty dollars, and there was still the hotel bill to pay. The next day at the casino I exchanged the gold coin for enough chips to at least begin to play carefully, but sooner or later I cannot do anything carefully, and I began to bet everything I had in one play, and to win, too. And so it went for the next two or three hours. And then I had enough money both for the hotel and to take a train to Biarritz. I didn't want to fly, I wanted to sit in a train and try to think.

I won't say anything about gambling, except that it has been a part of my life from the beginning. In money I have been a winner many times, but in money I am a heavy loser over the years. In other things, happening at the same time as the gambling, I have been a winner, including writing. During our meetings at lunch and dinner we talked about many things, a hundred times more than the few things I have here remembered, and during our last lunch we touched upon the future, knowing I was taking a train the following morning and we might not meet again for a long time, if ever. Again you said, "If you need anything, anything at all, please tell me." And again I thanked you and said I was just fine.

At Biarritz I gambled again, but the rampage was over and if I won, it was money of the kind that one counts and puts against things one can pay for as one goes along, and if I lost, it was only a small part of what I had, so I knew the worst was over.

I didn't like Biarritz, but I didn't dislike it, either. It was not at all like Lisbon and Estoril, both of which I loved. I may say I instantly liked the Portuguese people, who are mainly poor, but stand and walk with a kind of elegance and pride that I was deeply moved by, children, men, women, and even very old men and women. And they had faces upon which were engraved the lines of deep sorrow, gentility, honor, and courtesy. For instance, when the taxi arrived at the Avis, not knowing the value of the Portugese money, I made a guess and put quite a variety of coins into the hand of the taxi driver. He protested, or at any rate (having lately come from Rome) I imagined that he had protested and I began to bring out more money, but his protest had been that I had put *too much* money into his hand. He picked out a number of the more valuable coins and handed them back to me. I was deeply moved, for in Rome, no matter how much I gave a taxi driver, he immediately cried that he could not live unless people were more generous, he had a wife and many children, and so on and so forth. And of course I found myself frequently at Machado's for food and drink, and to listen to the men and women who sang fado, which so suited my own condition at the time.

In Biarritz it was another story entirely: the casino was a boring place, the players were cautious and pompous, and there didn't seem to be any women I cared to look at twice.

I went on to Paris and stopped at the Scribe. One of the reasons I did so was that Scribe to me means "to write," and I felt my best chance of getting myself back together again was to write, and I went there because during my first visit to Paris, in 1935, I had gone into the hotel just to have a look at it, and finally in 1945, when I had been in the American Army, the Scribe had been a popular hangout for foreign correspondents, photographers, and writers. Almost every night at the Scribe there had been a poker game in which I took a seat, finally losing three thousand dollars to my friend Robert Capa.

I had an outside room, and it seemed to me to be just right for going to work—a top-floor room with a sloping ceiling, like an attic.

I hoped to do a novel, for I needed money—not immediately, but in the future: a divorce coming up, two small kids to support, and so on and so forth. I didn't wait, I brought out the portable typewriter, I put paper beside it, a sheet of paper upon the rubber roller, and I began to write, simultaneously glad that I was at least *trying* to get back together and *disbelieving* in the possibility of it, even. (What could I write?) The going was rough, but I kept at it, and then after five or six days I stopped, I had had enough.

What I had written was not a novel, but it was a long short story, and it was about you, and it was about me, and the name of it was "The Assyrian."

My mother's kid brother had a son who was living in Paris at that time with his bride, and he had read in the *Herald* that I had come to town and was stopping at the Scribe, so one afternoon he came up to the room to talk. I had known him from the time of his birth, when I had been ten or eleven years old. I was glad to see him again, to hear about his adventures during four years in the Navy.

And then he said, "How come you're traveling alone?"

I told him I had left my wife and kids, and then he said, "Tell me all about it, will you?"

But I couldn't, and then he said, "What do you think of *my* marriage?" I didn't understand, and told him so.

He then said, "I mean, I'm here in Paris with my wife, I'm trying to write, and she's trying to write, too."

I told him that that sounded all right to me.

We went down to the street and walked to where he was living in an attic somewhere on the Left Bank, and I sat and chatted with his wife.

And then the three of us went to dinner nearby, and after dinner he brought a manuscript out of his back pocket, a rather thick manuscript, folded as if for slipping into an envelope and mailing, and he said, "Will you read this, please, right now, right here, and tell me honestly if I can write, if I ought to go on, or if I ought to forget it?"

Well, it was a kind of short novel, but it wasn't easy to read because he hadn't cleaned the type on his machine, and all the vowels looked alike. All the same, I read the story very carefully, and although it was badly written, it *was* a story—of confusion, sorrow, ignorance, doubt, and the state of being lost. As I read I tried to think how I would speak to him about what he had written, and he smoked one cigarette after another, compelling me to say, "I read very slowly, please be patient, I don't want to miss any of it," and then at last I came to the last word, and he very nearly leaped at me, saying, "Tell me, tell me the truth, don't tell me any lies."

I don't think I told him any lies when I said, "Well, the writing *does* lack skill, it has no real style, but that's all right, don't worry about that, skill and style will come if you write enough, the important thing is that the story is a very good one, a very important one, but don't write it again, study it, revise it carefully, perhaps salvage it, but at the same time move on to a new work."

"Am I a writer?" he said, and of course the proper answer to that question would be, "If you can ask such a question, you are not a writer," but I didn't say that. I said, "I think you are. I would like to ask you to find it in yourself to believe you are, because if you don't believe that, your writing will show it."

We walked about a mile to a vaudeville theater and went in, and after the show we sat at a sidewalk table and drank whiskey and smoked cigarettes and talked.

Now, the point about my cousin is this: his story had things in it that were also in the story I had just finished writing, "The Assyrian," about yourself and myself, and at the same time about other people, and other things, so that I was impelled to think, "My cousin's in trouble, too, he's in a lot of trouble. What's eating *him?*"

After having lived in Paris with his wife for two years, they returned to the United States, because she was pregnant and she wanted the child to be born in California. One day when I ran into him in Fresno, he said, "I just read your new book, *The Assyrian and Other Stories,* and the best thing in it is the title story, but why did you call Gulbenkian an Assyrian? Why didn't you call the story 'The Armenian'?"

I said, "It comes to the same thing. The Assyrians have always been close to us, and lately almost the same thing."

"I don't understand," he said. "Everything in the story is so true, and then it turns out the writer has made the two main characters Assyrian, and they're not Assyrian, they're Armenian."

But he was saying something else, only I wasn't sure I knew what it was. But I knew he was in trouble, *still* in trouble, his son was two years old, and his wife had just given birth to a daughter, and these things didn't seem to have done anything for him that all of us, Armenians, Assyrians, and everybody else, have always believed would do *everything* for us.

"It's one of your best stories," he said. "Maybe it's the best one you've ever written or ever will write, why call them Assyrians?"

"Well, all right," I said at last. "I guess I goofed. I won't do it again."

He roared with laughter, shouting, "No, no, that's not what I mean, God damn it, I'm not giving you a lecture, I just wish you had called them what they are, that's all." But he didn't say anything about his own writing, and I had heard he had tried operating a vineyard but hadn't liked it and had gotten out of it, and then had taken a kind of unbelievable job for a while in a big department store, selling shoes. But he had given that up, too.

Well, what's he got to do with us? This. He was, he is, he always will be, one of us. Shall I say homeless? No, the hell with that. Lost? No, he was no more lost than anybody else in the world. I really don't know what I should say, except that he was in so much trouble that for ten years he kept going to places for all kinds of treatments—shock and pills and whatever else the confused doctors and psychiatrists happened to believe in at the time—and finally he started trying another way out, and then at last he made it, the hard way: divorced by that time, his kids out of sight for years by that time, the car that he was forever washing and waxing and rubbing until it looked like a little blue jewel fell slowly over a small cliff near Piedra upon an abandoned railroad track in gasoline flames, himself a jumping and running torch. And then lying upon thick grass, asking for water, saying with annoyance to the girl who had seen his car go over the cliff, "What are these people here for?"

And then to the highway patrol cop who pushed his way through the people, "Are you going to kill me?" And hours later at the Veterans Hospital, when he was no longer anything anybody ought to look at, he kept saying, "I'm not going to die, am I?" And early in the morning he did, he died, forty-four years old, God have mercy on his soul.

I probably goofed saying we were Assyrians, but not really, because in a sense everybody in the world is an Assyrian, a remnant of a once-mighty race, now all but extinct.

Letters from 74 rue Taitbout, or, Don't Go But If You Must Say Hello to Everybody, 1971

Carl Sandburg

I remember our first meeting, in San Francisco, at the bookstore owned and operated by Leon Gelber and Theodore Lilienthal, on Sutter Street, in 1937, exactly thirty years ago, when you were fifty-nine, which is my present age, and I was twenty-nine.

Gelber, Lilienthal's was one of several bookstores I liked to go to in San Francisco in those days. Jack Newbegin's on Post Street was another. Paul Elder's was a third. As a new writer I liked to step into the stores and find out how my books were doing, and look at the new books that had come out, and chat with the owners and the clerks, and sometimes even meet a writer, although this was never something either to impel me to go to a bookstore or to keep me away.

One day, for instance, when I walked into Newbegin's, big cheerful loud-speaking Jack said, "You just missed Richard Halliburton."

I didn't know how to tell him it was all right.

Leon Gelber was one of my favorite people in San Francisco: keyed-up, enthusiastic, courteous, generous-hearted, and a good listener. There was more to him than met the eye, for he was one day found hanging by his neck, and everybody who had met him was surprised.

It was Leon who told me one summer afternoon when I walked into the store on Sutter Street, "Carl Sandburg's in the back room, do you want to meet him?"

And so we met. I suggested we go to a bar on Turk Street for a drink, because John Garfield was going to join me there. With John was somebody else, also a writer, and quite famous at the time, at least in Hollywood, but for the life of me I can't remember his name.

After two drinks at Joe Bailey's, where I used to play stud, you asked about the Cliff House, so we left the saloon and got into a taxi and drove out Geary to the Cliff House for a couple more drinks, all the while watching the seals on Seal Rock, and the ebb and flow of the ocean around the Rock.

Then, we took a taxi back to town, to Joe Vanessi's on Broadway near Pacific for some good Italian food. You were older than the rest of us, but you did just fine—talking, drinking, eating, and looking exactly the way you do in your photographs, exactly the way a poet ought to look—that is, simultaneously special, different, unique, but at the same time also casual, commonplace, and one of the people. The straw-colored hair of your head always stayed just a little awry, uncombed, apparently ignored.

Around eleven, after the Italian food and wine, we broke up, having all of us had a rather nice time. That is to say, you went home somewhere, to a hotel or to somebody's house where you were staying, and the writer whose name I can't remember said he had a big day tomorrow, and he began to walk home, and Garfield and I went up to Izzy's on Pacific Street.

"Imagine it," Garfield said, "a great man like that, a famous poet, an old guy, loafing around with a couple of kids from the slums, talking with us, drinking with us, eating with us, as if he were a kid from the slums, too. When I get to be his age I only hope I can be that young."

I was impressed, too. When I had been a telegraph messenger in Fresno, aged thirteen, working the nightshift after school, from four to midnight, I used to write poems on the company typewriters, because I had read everything on the poetry shelf at the public library—Walt Whitman, Vachel Lindsay, Edgar Lee Masters, and Carl Sandburg, among others, and I believed I ought to write stuff like that, too, but in the end it turned out that my first book was a collection of short stories, and after that I wrote fewer and fewer poems and hardly ever offered them to an editor, because for one thing there weren't many magazines to send poems to, and for another even if a magazine liked a poem they could pay only very little or nothing, and the very first thing I had to do was find out how to make a living at writing, so I wouldn't have to do other work.

Well, John Garfield died at the age of forty or so, at the height of a sensationally successful career as a movie star, and the writer whose name I can't remember, who was also a little under thirty when we all met, has faded away, which is either the same as dying or worse. And a lot of new poets and actors and story-writers have come along and taken their places among their kind, the new poets moving in the direction of Ezra Pound, T.S. Eliot, William Carlos Williams, and Wallace Stevens; the new actors taking their places beside Clark Gable, Humphrey Bogart, James Cagney, Paul Muni, Spencer Tracy, and Cary Grant; and the new story-writers moving in the direction of Ernest Hemingway, Scott Fitzgerald, William Faulkner, Morley Callaghan, and Stephen Vincent Benét.

That *was* America, in short. That was innocent America, or ignorant America, or confused America. And always, no matter how the history of the nation changed, or what happened in Europe and Asia, or who arrived or who departed, there was news in the press about Carl Sandburg, and a photograph, so that I was reminded of our happy hours one summer day and night in San Francisco long ago.

You played the guitar, you sang "The Blue-Tail Fly," you made records, you went to New York, you went to Hollywood, you gave interviews to newspaper and magazine writers, and at the same time you finished the biggest biography of Abraham Lincoln ever written.

In fact, I visited you overnight once at your home in Harbert, Michigan, on the lake, not far from Chicago, when you had just finished that enormous work. We went for a walk in the evening to the house of a neighbor where a party was going on—about thirty people of all ages, everybody having a good time, drinking, talking, laughing, listening to loud music on records, and there you were, very tired after perhaps ten years of hard work on the biography of one of the most complicated Americans of all time. And you were still just another plain ordinary man, with two mops of unruly hair hanging over your forehead.

A young high-school girl brought her copy of *The People, Yes,* and asked if you would autograph it for her. And you did, working at it, so that it would mean as much as possible to her.

And then you opened the book to the first page and began to read out loud.

The girl listened, I listened, somebody turned off the phonograph, everybody looked at you, everybody listened, everybody was delighted, everybody thought it was very kind of you not only to go to the party but to read one of your poems. They were dying to give you an ovation, their hands all ready to make loud applause the minute you stopped reading.

Now, here, they thought, was a good place to stop after five minutes of reading, but you didn't stop, you started reading another page.

You read well, in a deep earnest voice, saying the simple words as an actor would say them. The people at the party continued to be deeply impressed and grateful, and more than ever ready to give you the ovation you deserved for writing such powerful things about the people—the common people, the poor people, not people like themselves, upper middle class and even well-to-do.

One or two boys and girls, under fifteen, tip-toed away, but kids are kids and life comes before art with them, as of course it should.

Then, one or two of the younger adult couples quietly moved out of that great room, and very likely out of the house itself to where their own talk and laughter would not be a disturbance.

Then, two or three of the middle-aged couples found a way of leaving the room unobtrusively, until at last it was yourself, the girl you had signed the book for, and myself.

When you finished reading the whole book, it was only myself.

The People, Yes—but not the people at that party. You put the book down and we walked back to your house.

You met several Presidents, and you told me that somebody had approached you about accepting the nomination for the office of President—don't pass it along. Well, you certainly knew more about Lincoln than any other potential Presidential candidate. You met Marilyn Monroe and she loved you like a father. You were a consultant during the filming of the life of Jesus.

Yesterday when I read that you had died at your home in Flat Rock, North Carolina, I felt great sorrow, even though you had lived almost nine full decades, had had no failure or frustration, had never been accused of treason, never committed to a hospital for the insane, never been hated, despised, held in contempt, abandoned, hounded, misunderstood, misinterpreted, scorned, belittled, dishonored.

I felt sorry because somewhere along the line the easy careless fall of the hair on your head, in two mops, right and left, had come to mean to the *people*, to use your term, poetry itself, American poetry, so that you yourself and your poetry and your other writing were taken to be great by the people who do not read poetry, prose, or anything else.

You lived and died famous, but actually unrecognized and unknown. The President himself issued a formal tribute to you which was written by somebody who had made a careful study of your verse. It sounded awfully important but didn't mean anything. You were probably a great man of some sort, but *that* couldn't have been the sort. Not that poets die young, although they do, no matter how long they live. They die real, and contrary to the misconception involved, not once, at the end, but many times right up to the end.

Letters from 74 rue Taitbout, or, Don't Go But If You Must Say Hello to Everybody, 1971

Days of Life
and Death
and Escape
to the Moon
(extracts)

I have now lived long enough to have noticed the arrival and departure of everybody. They came forward shining, and went away faded or invisible. That's the thing about staying alive—you see *that*.

As for myself, the whole thing is a joke. I look like an old man. One would think I had gone to a lot of trouble about getting ready to play an unsuitable part in an absurd Sunday School morality play.

But I'm still alive, and everybody else keeps dying.

The last Krupp died yesterday. His first year was 1907, mine 1908.

During the past forty years I have read many obituaries. The death of D.H. Lawrence saddened me. The death of Thomas Wolfe surprised me. I felt nothing at all when J.P. Morgan died, or John D. Rockefeller, and many others, although it was interesting to read what was said about each of them.

Nobody died, nobody went to his death, with any real style, and this seems strange, or even sneaky. Nobody gathered his family and friends together for a big celebration, and then killed himself—but killed is the wrong word: and then stopped his life where he wanted it to stop.

The body I inhabit has grown round and heavy, the head thick. The face has a badly banged-around nose, a great gray moustache drooping about the corners of the mouth, but the hair of the head is still full and black.

The trouble is I used to be a young man and I haven't forgotten it.

But it's all right. I still have an idea or two in my head. I don't know what they are, but I know they're there, and I know I'll get to them when it's the right time. I don't mean suicide. I'm not interested in suicide, although I *am* interested in death. But then who isn't? Who could possibly not be, all his life?

ꗢ

I couldn't even read *The Murders in the Rue Morgue*, although I finally forced myself at the Fresno Public Library to fight through the dismal story, about which I had heard so much—for I wanted to find out what was so wonderful about it, and how a new writer might learn to write something like that, and not write something dull and stupid. Well, Poe wrote something dull and stupid but it was taken by many people to be wonderful, and that was something more puzzling to think about than who committed the murder in the Rue Morgue. (I believe it turned out to be an ape, which in itself is irrelevant.)

ꗢ

If it can't be for everybody, what good is it? That's the way I felt as a kid, even before I decided that writing would be the way I would get to the business of being of help, and that's really still the way I feel, the only way I feel. And yet I know the folly of believing anything can be of much use to anybody—short of money for everybody, which in itself is absurd because if money went to everybody it wouldn't be money. Money is money in that it is withheld from the many and handed to the few. (Those poor people, the rich say of the poor, they wouldn't know what to do with money.)

But the poor people are really the only people, and they keep coming, hungering and laboring, procreating and dying, maintaining the great ecology of nature. The rich are out of it, they really don't belong to the human race. The race they *do* belong to is not a superior race, as they like to imagine. It is a degenerate race, belonging to the world, not to nature.

From a swift young man delighting in new clothes, moving everywhere with noise and laughter, I became a sloppy old man in old clothes with a careless posture and a lazy walk, going nowhere. What did I expect? Well, the fact is everything of an external kind that I expected I got, such as fame and money, but it always turned out to be only for myself, and that had never really been the idea.

ꗢ

I walked the streets twice this morning, once in heavy rain, the second time in a drizzle. I was a kind of ghost, a kind of freak with an enormous moustache, absurdly trimmed at the ends, in the expectation of an improved appearance, only it didn't work. A foolish appearance became absurd, that's all.

And there I went, marching along in heavy cordovan shoes bought by mistake ten years ago in New York, scarcely ever worn, but worn enough to know that such shoes are not for human feet. They are for water buffalo. In the wet, however, they seemed sensible, but of course by that time I *was* a water buffalo.

꙰

What can a man do to move along in some kind of grace through his days and years? Well, there are a million ways of putting it, but it always comes to pretty much the one way—he can do his best, in accordance with his laws, and in keeping with his truth, in favor of himself, and on behalf of his expectation to see it all through in the best possible style, with some meaning, and without harm to anybody else.

꙰

The wisest thing any writer can do who is getting along in years and feeling it enough to know he can't do what he used to do is not to blow his brains out but to take it slow and easy, not feeling obliged to be a kind of hero of the world, and not being miserable about the fact that he has changed, as all things must, in time.

That is the wise thing to do, but it isn't easy, and many a writer has had long years of terrible unhappiness about the fading of himself in himself, and of his name in the world, and of his meaning among the millions of newcomers, long after he himself was a newcomer. It is strange that a writer, who has considered so carefully the varieties of human vanity, should himself be so vulnerable. A writer has a right to be pleased that he has found his work and is able to do it, but to get this simple fact entangled in all kinds of alien and irrelevant matters is a mistake. Other workers have no such miconception about themselves and the work they do. The farmer does not weep because his crops are eaten and forgotten. The manufacturer of shoes has no regret that his shoes are bought, worn, and discarded—except when I buy them, because I *keep* them. (I have this thing about shoes, and perhaps about everything else.)

꙰

And then I walked down Strasbourg to the grand boulevards, feeling fine. Feeling good, for no particular reason, certainly nothing new, nothing suddenly come to me, nothing suddenly achieved, nothing discovered or revealed.

And yet I was absolutely delighted. Why? Well, perhaps for no better reason than this: that I was there, I myself, not a fantasy, not an illusion, not a movie. Me, on the last day of August, the last day of my fifty-ninth year, still walking, still free.

)C

I have always been fascinated by disputation, as much in nature among animals and plants as in the human family. There are people who thrive on it, asking one another clever questions intended to expose the other person as a fraud. These disputes go on and on.

What is it that human beings want to get right? Who gets the loaf, who gets the stone? Well, yes, that's certainly the *essence* of all disputation.

Plays and movies on television, in which people are engaged in these disputes, are not only boring, they are unbearable.

Snarl and bark, growl and roar, maul and bite, leap and seize, fight and kill, are central to life among the animals.

Even so, man's disputes, even those chronicled by Shakespeare, are boring, because they are stupid, no matter what lyric language they are put into.

)C

And when I think of the people who talk big, I am delighted. I myself have talked big almost every time I've opened my mouth.

And then I've wondered if it hasn't been in order for everybody to talk big whenever possible. Why shouldn't talking big be an acceptable order of talk? Doesn't it mean quite simply that the talker is out of pain, and therefore able to believe he *knows?*

)C

Turnips. There comes a time when turnips must be considered, along with literary style, personal integrity, and universal meaning. The greens of turnips stewed in the broth of lamb—fifteen minutes is long enough—have a flavor that is so deeply satisfying that one is at a loss to understand how such a simple member of the vegetable family can mean so much to the soul in the body, but there it is—every time I have some turnip greens in this manner, by themselves, alone, pure and simple, I wonder how it is that I have gone so long without them. Once again I feel rare salts and minerals of mystic power charging through the liquids of the body and making everything else stand up and cheer. Is this possible? Can a matter of eating, of getting stuff down the gullet into the gut, mean so much? Well, it seems to, that's all I know. It is necessary to consider to the end of time and life, the other things, the big things, but now and then one must remember at least for a moment or two turnips and their greens.

Long ago, certainly before I was twenty, whenever I sat down to write, I was overwhelmed by the great number of directions I might take, the endless styles I might employ, the ever-increasing events of human experience I might isolate for careful examination, and the many attitudes I was free to impose upon the whole collective action of making a new work of writing.

All this freedom made the going difficult, although once I had jumped in and had made a choice or had found myself following a course without actually being *aware* of having made a choice, the going was reasonably easy, and I could believe in the likelihood of making the *whole* thing, whatever it turned out to be.

If I didn't start somewhere, I soon noticed, as the earliest years of apprenticeship went by, I simply sat there and rejected one choice after another, and got up feeling stupid and tired after an hour or two, with nothing at all made, nothing brought into being, nothing written.

I learned from these engagements with potential: do not wait for the perfect choice, for if you do you may very well be obliged to wait forever. There may be no such thing as a perfect choice, any choice will do. After you begin to work, the usage of all of your energy will move the poor choice nearer to the illusion of being perfect, if not in fact to the reality.

By the time I was twenty-two I knew that if I sat down and didn't write, I was being foolish and lazy; it was not because I was holding out for the best possible beginning of a new work.

I was goofing, that's all. And this was a sin, for I knew that every man is allotted only so much time, and he must decide how it is to be used. If he doesn't use it well, that is his own doing.

Thus, it became traditional for me to go straight to work the minute I sat down.

After each job I was tired, because during the making of the new thing all fire and machinery was engaged full force, at top speed, moving like a train. I kept a rhythm, reached a destination, and stopped—glad to be there, and even a little proud of it.

꒰꒱

The human experience is personal, private, and in every instance unique. That which each man *knows* he alone knows, however nearly like the next man's knowing it may be. It is his, and it remains his all through his life, right up to the last minute of it, whereupon before he lapses into the coma that is his transfer to the next thing, he perhaps says to himself, or himself says to his fantasy, "Nobody, nobody will ever know how it went with me, and now it's too late to tell. Nobody will ever know what happened."

Well, what *did* happen? Nothing, by God. If you survive, if you're not killed at an early age, if you don't kill yourself, whatever it was that did in fact happen must be noticed as having been nothing, but with a lot of flourishes.

"I got it wrong," the man says. "I thought I was getting it right, or I believed I soon would, another year perhaps, and then it would all be clear. But it turned out that every day's confusion *is* the truth. There is no dispelling of yesterday's confusion, and no seeing through today's."

)C

More and more the professional writer is giving up the hard work of writing out of himself. He is going out to the named people of the world, talking to them, and writing down how they looked and what they said. Is this a good thing? Is it a new thing? Of course it's a good thing, although it can confuse a writer about who he himself is. Of course it's not a new thing. The disciples of Jesus did it and made their names.

What are we to think of the people of the world, intellectuals and other people alike, who become excited about a long piece of writing about actual people and events, when in fact the book is made out of bad writing?

Well, I do believe the people of the world may be forgiven for being so easily deceived and taken in by the spurious. It is our *way*. We prefer it.

)C

Nobody is able to do anybody any good.

Is that what bugs us? Is that what's at the bottom of our annoyance with things all our lives?

After we make the small discovery that anybody can do anybody else a little *insignificant* good now and then, we make the large discovery that not only is it not possible for anybody to do anybody else any *real* good, it is almost impossible for everybody not to do everybody else a great deal of harm.

We also discover that religion, philosophy, science, art, education, and everything else can do nobody and nothing any real good. Or if we don't make the discovery, we sense it, and go about our lives hoping matters will improve, so why don't they?

Days of Life and Death and Escape to the Moon, 1973

Guggenheim's Water Tank, Fresno, 1921

T he tank was at the top of a timber derrick among the Santa Fe Railroad tracks, at the end of San Benito Avenue. The timber was old and rickety. The ladder rungs had been nailed to the frame long ago. The nails had rusted, and some were loose. In one place, midway, a rung was missing. The climber going up had to put some muscle into it, and coming down he had to see that he didn't slip. The water tank had had a sign saying that it was against the law to climb the tower, but somebody had sensibly removed the sign.

One summer I climbed the tower a couple of times a week, once to drop a cat, which landed on its feet, bounced, and ran away at full speed. I was never mean to animals, and on this occasion I was more stupid than mean. I really believed the cat would not be injured in the fall. Perhaps it wasn't. All the same I have always felt a little guilty about having dropped the cat. And ashamed.

The railroad tracks and the eucalyptus trees among the tracks, in the Jungle, where the hoboes rested and cooked their stew and smoked cigarettes and talked, black and white alike, but never immigrants, never people who came to America to make good, the railroad tracks had cat packs, old toms, females, and half-grown young cats, all lean, all tough, all dirty. The cat I had taken up with me and had dropped from the top of the tower was one of these—a cat which had been trusting, unlike most of the others in the pack, which were suspicious of human beings, and afraid of them. This cat considered me a friend, and there it was—I betrayed the cat. I dropped it to hard ground from a height of at least a hundred feet.

And I had to be clever to do it, for the cat clung to my arm, and spoke, not piteously but rather bravely, as if to say, "You're not going to do something stupid, are you?"

I had to turn quickly and let the cat go. Even while it was tumbling head over heels and the boys who were with me, watching, cheered and laughed, I thought, "Please spare the poor animal, and I will never do such a stupid thing again."

I was thrilled when the cat struck the hard ground *lightly*, feet first, and bounced so swiftly that it was almost as if it had not in fact had a real impact with the ground, and then raced away. The escape and survival of the cat thrilled me deeply, because it made my mischief something less than a criminal act upon life.

The climbing to the top of the tower, then walking around the tank and looking around at the whole small town in all directions, and the climbing down, required concentration and care. It was all very definitely very dangerous. Why did I do it, then?

Because I believed in my ability to do it. After having done it, I actually was able to feel I had accomplished something of some importance to me

Places Where I've Done Time, 1972

Fresno, 1926

The first purpose of my life after I reached the age of ten or eleven was to get away from Fresno as soon as possible. It was a great place to look back on and remember perhaps, but of course no man knows such a thing when he's there in the middle of it. The fact is the only reason it was ever a great place was myself, my *saying* so. In itself it was a lively if poor and stupid place, although there were some people who were not exactly poor in possessions and some others who were not exactly backward in the dimension of cleverness. Otherwise it was a place to avoid, and if that was not possible, to get away from as soon as possible.

Going away has something to do with the search in general—for love, for the beautiful girl or woman who is to fulfill a man's truth and reality, for recognition, for acceptance, for work, for enthusiasm about the whole human experience, but most of all going away is a search for one's best self. It is not just simply getting up and going. It is also the beginning of the embracing of the whole world, of putting one's arms around it and holding it in a tight and loving embrace. It is a moving out to all of the human race, not just that portion of it that happens to be where a man happens to be—held prisoner, as he sometimes feels. Mainly, in spite of the terrible boredom and stupidity and meanness of Fresno, my life there was full of drama and swift growth. Being in the streets from the beginning and going to all of the places of the city and seeing all of the members of the human race there, I found more than enough to keep my mind and soul fully occupied.

Everything was all right, one might say, except that there was more wrong with every part of everything than right. Much more.

I began to leave in 1926, when I was pretty well along in years, almost eighteen, after having had a full decade of important growth in the busy town. I was gone for good (or at any rate almost for good) by the time I was nineteen. Thereafter I went back for a visit now and then, but these visits were very brief, and their purpose was to check various places and people, and to confirm certain facts or truths.

San Francisco was the place that followed Fresno, and it was a whole new world, with a far better location, climate, culture, and humanity. But I traveled from San Francisco, too. I had to see everything, or as much of everything as I could possibly manage with the money I earned, or won at gambling, or acquired from the faithful cultivation of my skill as a writer—and from the hard work of writing.

Going away, going to a new place, was beautiful. It pleased me in a way that very nearly nothing else could please me. It was a large act of pure love.

Places Where I've Done Time, 1972

The YMCA
at 23rd Street
and 7th Avenue,
New York, 1928

The Young Men's Christian Association in Fresno was on Broadway above the Public Library. It was a place both ridiculed and exploited. One Saturday morning in 1922 there was an unforgettable illustrated talk on veneral diseases, followed up by a free visit to the gym and pool, and that was enough for me.

When the Greyhound bus finally arrived in New York, and I got off, to make my way to fame and fortune late in August, 1928, the hour was almost midnight, everything was closed, I had been traveling for ten days, I was excited, tired, angry, and I didn't know what to do or where to go. I knew nobody. I had no letter of introduction to anybody. Cash on hand came to a dollar and a few coins. The rest of my money, almost a hundred dollars, was in my suitcase, and the suitcase was lost, stolen, or misdirected—that's what the baggage clerk in New York said. It would be tracked down, he said. The number of the baggage check was written down, and I went out into the midnight streets of New York.

First I ran two New York blocks. Maybe it was from having sat so long. Maybe it was from having no money. Maybe it was from feeling lousy. But the running stopped that, and made me feel good. I was light. And I had no luggage. I didn't know where I was going, but I was going swiftly. At each corner I looked to see what was around. At 23rd Street I saw the big YMCA sign in lights. I said to myself, "That's it. I'll go there."

The room was a dollar in advance, and that left very little, but even a little is something. The cafeteria was closed, but the clerk said if I hurried back the man might make me a sandwich. He made a big one—ham and cheese both—and he took only a dime instead of fifteen cents, because it had been his idea to throw in the ham. I took the sandwich up to the room, and saw a bed, a wash basin, and a drinking glass. I ran the water out of the tap until it was cool, filled the glass, sat down at the rickety desk, and began to eat the sandwich and drink the cold water. I drank four glasses of the cold water before I finished the sandwich—it was so good I kept saying to myself, "I'll make it, lost suitcase or not. I'll make it."

There was a shower down the hall, so I went there and had a great shower and walked back to the room and got in bed and went to sleep.

Places Where I've Done Time, 1972

Blood of the Lamb Gospel Church, Turk Street off Fillmore, San Francisco, 1929

*I*n 1929, after my return from failure in New York, I used to seek free diversion wherever I might be able to find it, for the simple reason that I did not have the price of any other kind, and so I learned to find restoration of the soul in walking, looking at people and houses and animals and trees, or in visiting the places to which admission was both free and eagerly sought: the Public Library, the museums, the art galleries, the department stores, and the churches.

The Blood of the Lamb Gospel Church was actually an empty store on Turk Street. The plate-glass windows were whitened with Bon Ami, so that the services might be conducted in private. From the third-floor flat at 2378 Sutter Street the little store-church was a leisurely evening's walk of under fifteen minutes. After supper I frequently set out for a walk of restoration, thought, and peace, having in mind that I might just go into the little church and take a chair in the last row, and look and listen for a while. It was a church founded by several black people, and one frequently heard grateful references to Brother Hutchins, Elder Montgomery, Gospel Singer Sister Ellison, and Sexton Graves. There was no preacher, as such, or rather there was no official or ordained minister. But everybody seemed to be equal to giving either a testimonial about his life and transformation, a reading with asides from the Good Book, a loud prayer, a very lively dance, or a recitation in Tongues.

It was this last, which I heard and witnessed by good luck on my very first visit in January of 1929, that sent me back, in the hope that I might see and hear another version of it. The man who had been Talking in Tongues before my arrival was standing, his fists clenched, his eyes shut, sweat rolling down his tan face. It took me two or three minutes to understand that he was not preaching, not praying, and not testifying—and furthermore that he was not speaking English, Spanish, (which I imagined he *was* speaking, from the sound and rhythm and usage of the words): French, Italian, German, or any other language spoken by mortals. He was speaking in the language of the angels. He was possessed. I found that I did not consider that he was sick or mad. On the contrary, although he looked pretty wrought up, I felt that he was a kind of genius, a little freakish but no less authentic on that account. He talked and the congregation listened and cried "Yes," "Hallelujah," "Glory," "That's right," and other expressions of appreciation, as if they understood perfectly what he was saying.

I can't pretend that I didn't understand, for it seemed to me that he was simply demonstrating a little more of the mystery of the human being and the human soul. I studied his language, the rhythm and the words, hoping to type them out and to see if I could track them down. They seemed to be rooted in very real languages. From memory I will put down something like what he said: Esposa conta falla almahada appalappa dablu. Said of course with expression, emphasis, and all of the vocal shadings by which spoken words in a sentence take on form. And his own emotional involvement in what he was saying or thinking or communicating rose and fell, so that he was frequently highly excited, that is even more than he was at the outset, even more than anybody in a trance is, and then subsided to more controlled, unemotional, rather intelligent gibberish.

Best of all, though, I went to this church to hear the songs, and to join in the singing: "There is power in the power house." I loved this song because of its proud and loud happiness. And of course there were several songs about being washed in the blood of the lamb.

Places Where I've Done Time, 1972

The Great Northern Hotel, 118 West 57th Street, New York, 1935

I arrived in New York for the first time in August of 1928, a few days before my 20th birthday, and I walked in many parts of Manhattan, and in a number in Brooklyn. I took the subway to Coney Island, and to many other places, and went up the subway stairs to a new world, to look around.

During my walks up or down 57th Street, I passed the narrow entrance to The Great Northern Hotel many times and several times noticed the name and liked it, but I did not take a room there until 1935, after my first book was published, and I was famous, or people believed I was, or I was able to imagine that I was, if not famous, then at least well-known. I went to The Great Northern Hotel after I had tried staying at The New Yorker Hotel on 34th and 8th Avenue where the rooms are very small.

I was delighted to be at The Great Northern, for the rooms were large, the bath was large, the ceilings were high, and (this may be difficult to believe) the rent was $12 a week. From a room on the fifth floor, number 512 I believe, an inside room with a poor view, I did the planning for my first trip to Europe, and I did some writing.

For instance, I read in *The New York Times* that I had recently arrived in New York, and that I was writing a play which I expected to finish before sailing to Europe. How or where the *Times* had gotten this mis-information I can't imagine, but I decided, "Well, if *The New York Times* says I'm writing a play, why not? Why make a liar out of *The New York Times?* Write a play."

In 1928 I made many notes about the writing of what I believed was to be my first novel, and perhaps one of the best things I would ever write, to be called, simply, *The Subway.* Meaning of course the New York subway, but also meaning the concealed way, the inside way, the hidden truth, the hidden life, the hidden meaning of people, of passengers, not of the subway alone, but of time, riding to the end of the line. But alas, this great book was never written.

Why?

I don't know. How could I know? It just wasn't. And I have always regretted that it wasn't.

So now, in 1935, seven years later, seven incredibly difficult, swift, dangerous, great, sorrowful, and laughing years later, back in New York, I remembered the book I failed to write, and I decided to see if I could do something or other with the subway in the form of a play, and so in the matter of three days I wrote *Subway Circus.* It has been published, it has been produced by amateurs, but I have never seen a production. And so the report on the theatre page of *The New York Times* turned out not to be, not to have been, inaccurate, after all.

I loved being at The Great Northern Hotel, and I went back to the hotel again and again when I was in New York—until at last it just wouldn't do any more: the hotel had changed, I had grown more worldly, I had become wealthy, and the world itself had changed, so I moved on and up, as the saying is.

Places Where I've Done Time, 1972

Governors Island, New York Harbor, 1943

*I*t is a big joke to many people when somebody talks with annoyance about the dirty tricks of the Army, because the feeling is, "Big deal, thousands have been killed, so tell us all about your hard times with the Army."

The fact is that one is bored by the Army even while one is putting up with its treachery. The worst kind of officer was the Medical. He was a clever, calculating son of a bitch. Play ball and you would be O.K. He would write an exemption that would prevent anybody from giving you dirty or hard work. Play better ball and he'd write you a medical discharge—a little gift of some sort, say one thousand dollars under the table, to a confederate, no strings attached, or if the drafted man happened to be loaded, a sum two or three times as large.

I was drafted with a bad upper-leg or low-back condition, which when it was acute was the most painful thing in my limited experience of pain—it was as violent and intense as the pain of a bad tooth, but this pain was in an area a hundred times larger. General tiredness, anxiety, frustration, anger, and all of the other negative states of the human mind and spirit tended to bring on an acute phase of the condition, whereupon I would be in serious trouble. I couldn't stand, let alone march, or work, or run.

Like a great many drafted men who were in the Army in the New York area, I was permitted to live off the Post in my own apartment, which happened to be at 2 Sutton Place South, not far from the Queensboro Bridge, which I crossed early every morning in a taxi—whereupon my little bride, pregnant, went back to sleep until noon.

I stood in the six o'clock Roll Call Formation, answered to my name, and had half an hour to go get breakfast. I did not eat in the Army mess, the smell made me want to vomit, it did not smell like the world, it smelled like a loathesome sore on a great sick body. I hurried two blocks to a little all-night place run by a Jewish family and had a bagel and coffee while I looked through the *Times.* Then I went to the day's labor.

One morning at five I couldn't get out of bed: the slipped disk of the lower spine was out of place, and I was in terrible trouble. I telephoned the Sergeant at the Astoria Army Post, and after a little chat he said, "Well, come in when you can." Around noon I was able to move a little, and by two I went out to the Post, and checked in. The Sergeant, who confessed that before he got into the Army he sold shoes in a department store, wanted to know if I appreciated what he had done. I said I did, but he didn't mean that kind of appreciation. A month later I couldn't get out of bed again, so again I phoned, and I believed the situation was the same as last time, but around eleven two Military Police, two Medical Corps Sergeants, and two privates all came up to the penthouse at 2 Sutton Place South.

They were only following orders. I was to be taken to Governors Island. This was plainly a dirty trick. It was retaliation, because I had not rewarded anybody for letting me get to the Post half a day late. I was invited to lie upon the stretcher, but I forced myself to walk, and I was deposited in the hospital on Governors Island. A ratty place, with a great round stockade, or Army jail. And for all practical purposes I was in jail—apparently for desertion. I spent a week there, and was then transferred to another, bigger, Army hospital on Staten Island, and after a month of more chickenshit I was sent back to the same place in the Army. I wasn't playing the game. So I was being given the business.

Places Where I've Done Time, 1972

24848 Malibu Road, Malibu, California, 1951

Suicide was suicide, divorce was divorce. I flipped a coin, and it came up divorce. The *second* divorce, that is, from the same little bride. I was bankrupt, in debt to the Tax Collector for about fifty thousand dollars, about half that much to others, most of them merchants who had sold her stuff. During the short second marriage I had bought her diamond rings, fancy dentistry, expensive furs, shoes and clothes. This hungry little girl with the pudgy, spongy flesh at which she worked better than half the day in order to be ready in the evening for her public at another party talked and laughed, talked and laughed, talked and laughed, and consulted her lawyer. She was a real Broadway musical comedy. Everybody loved her, men and women alike.

Her lawyer was the most famous in Beverly Hills, who imagined he was among the immortals of law. My lawyer had been recommended by a man I had considered a friend. In going over the papers, however, I noticed that the little woman had agreed to find an apartment to rent somewhere, for herself and the two kids, with a rent not to exceed a hundred dollars a month. Well, there just wasn't any such apartment unless you went to the slums. I didn't like the idea of the kids being in such a place.

I said, "No, I don't want that. I'll find a new house somewhere, I'll make the down payment, and I'll make the monthly payments."

My lawyer protested and said if I insisted on such a thing he would leave the case immediately.

This annoyed me, so I told him to leave.

He did, and sued me and collected a couple of thousand dollars for his fee.

In the end I got them into a fine house in Pacific Palisades, and I looked around for a place for myself. At last on the Beach at Malibu I found a little house on top of piling, and I bought some basic furniture and moved in. It was 1951. I was forty-three years old. I was very tired. I was very broke. I was very mad, but in that house on the Beach I had the feeling that I was home, I was back in the world of the spirit, the world of truth, and I began to get back my soul.

But how could I, how could I *ever*, how could I *permit* myself to actually get up and leave such a joyous, luminous treasure of a girl? Well, I really don't know how. Just more of my stupidity, I guess. Just more of the same unfortunate behavior that put me to marrying her in the first place—taking her away from the world, to have all to myself. That's not right. I was punished for doing such a selfish thing. My punishment was the divorce and my arrival in the house on the Beach.

Places Where I've Done Time, 1972

Raphael Hotel,
Paris, 1959

The big movie man complained over coffee in October of 1959 that his last girl just wasn't a star, to which I replied, "That can't possibly be so, since there is nobody who is not a star—the fault is either bad directing or bad writing."

I had written a play for the girl. Then, I had taken a Crime-and-Court story owned by the producer, upon which he had spent a quarter of a million dollars, and for twenty thousand dollars (twenty cents?) I had transformed that absurd and boring story into something at least here and there amusing, which the producer six months later sold to another producer for a good net profit.

The big man was pleased and his stooges said so, but they said he would be much happier if I would do an extra ten days of work on the story, because he felt certain things in it could still be improved. I had just come back from a visit to Portugal and Spain, after the departure of my two kids, who had spend the summer with me, and their going had left me rather sharply alone.

There was nothing for it, and although the idea of working on the absurd story again was distasteful, it seemed to me that it might just impel me to forget the sense of isolation in which I now moved and dwelt, until I might get my bearings and be all right again.

Consequently, I told the giant and his hirelings to find me a place to live and work in and I would see what I could do—free of charge. There was nothing in my deal to compel me to do this extra work.

There happened to be an Automobile Show in Paris at the time, and so there were no rooms at the hotels. The only thing the movie hirelings were able to find was a suite at the Raphael, on Avenue Kleber near the Étoile—very expensive. Even a small room at that hotel, sought out by famous people who did not wish to be disturbed by the press or anybody else, was very expensive.

I said, "Well, it's up to you—if you want me to go to work and that's the only place available, you decide. The La Perouse wants the room I'm presently in, because they let me have it with the understanding that I would leave in two days and it is now six."

After an hour, during which the hirelings tried other hotels, and explained the situation to the big man, they called back, and told me to present myself at the desk at the Raphael—everything was in order. And so I moved the few items I carried around with me out of the small attic room at the La Perouse and traveled a mere two short blocks on foot, and was taken by the assistant manager of the Raphael to a very large suite of rooms on the second floor.

"Who has occupied this place in the past?" I asked.

"Well, actually," the man said, "royalty and such—people with servants."

I went to work in a very small part of the apartment, and in a short time I had it—the work was done, but there was nowhere to go, and the isolation I felt was still overpowering, so I took the story and improved it even further, beyond the expectations of the little man who was the big man. He was thrilled by what I had done, and thanked me. But when I left the hotel I was presented with a bill for $668 for ten days.

Months later the hotel informed me that the bill had not been paid by the producer, who insisted that I must pay it.

I paid it. I'll never be a millionaire, that's all.

Places Where I've Done Time, 1972

The Bahai
Temple
Haifa, 1961

*A*t a party in London in 1944 Mr. Ernest Hemingway ridiculed the man whose guest he was, saying, "He pretends that that's his girl, so nobody will know he's a fairy." And Mr. Arthur Koestler, virtually resting his head on Mr. Hemingway's shoulder and looking up into his eyes with unfeigned adoration, did not speak up for his friend, with whom at a Greek Restaurant a month earlier he had dominated, bullied, and bored a group of six or seven writers, mostly American, vollying back and forth between them sarcastic words about the others.

"The writer must know everything," the little man had said, by which he meant that *he* did, he knew everything, and that the others were stupid bums.

And the host, with his thick head and weary confusion, had added, "It is not enough merely to write."

So a month later here was the big bearded American calling him a fag, and here was the belittled man's best buddy (in snobbism) adoring the big boy. As for myself, I was amazed. What was the matter with these men, these writers, heterosexual, homosexual, bisexual, non-sexual, or whatever the hell they might be? Why were they such horse's asses?

Well, the scene changed, the world changed, everybody went home, I went home, it wasn't home, I didn't know whether I was going or coming, I couldn't write, I couldn't think, the telephone was busy all day and all night, somebody was calling the little woman, or she was calling somebody, every half-hour.

And then in a London Sunday paper one day I read a big essay by Arthur Koestler about his recent visit to the newly formed nation called

Israel. And I remembered him, both at the Greek Restaurant in London and at the party given by his friend, a far better writer than himself.

Apparently unintentionally, he made Israel seem to be the scene of the hope of the world.

And so one year, by that time divorced, broke, up the creek, damaged beyond repair by the war, the Army, an unfortunate marriage, desperation, impulsiveness, gambling, drinking, I decided to visit Israel, too. A ship stopped at Haifa, and I was told the best hotel in town was the Dan, up the hill. After I was settled, I walked down the hill and came to a place with fine gardens inside a high metal picket fence, and as the gate was open I went in.

It was the Bahai Temple. It was the Main Office of International Bahai, a very nice religion without much of an image, with no hero, or at any rate no hysterical hero, no big show-biz trial, no fancy parables, no crucifixion, just a man who sincerely believed there *was* a nice way for *everybody* to live.

I met a number of the people who either ran the office or helped run it, and a number of visitors, or pilgrims. It was all nice, if lonely. But the grounds were beautiful and the building was beautiful, and the people were gentle losers.

I've always remembered that place. It was put there long ago, when the area was not called Israel.

I even went up to Acre, to the shrine of the founder of the cult. The caretakers were a retired professor from Berkeley and his wife. There were roses in the garden, and rather lovely butterflies, as well as several long lizards. It was all hopeless and sad, while Israel was all business, but probably not quite the hope of the world.

Places Where I've Done Time, 1972

74 Rue
Taitbout,
Paris, 1969

Yesterday, Friday, August 8th, I decided that after having had a moustache for almost a full year, growing freely, never trimmed, and after having not had a haircut in three full months, I would take the barber shears I keep on my desk and reduce the moustache to a brush, and cut the hair of the head.

Does this seem impossible? It is no such thing. Does it seem foolish, in the sense that one is bound to make such a shambles of one's head that a barber will be required to straighten the matter out, after all, and that the barber will be impelled to ask, "What happened?"

Again no such thing. With only the shears and a small comb, I trimmed an enormous moustache to a very sensible, full, neat moustache, and I removed an enormous amount of black hair mixed with gray at the temples and in the sideburns from the head. I then shaved and used the safety razor to tidy up the back of the head at the neck. And then I got into a tub to have a shampoo and a shower.

The result was amazing. I was suddenly not so much somebody else as myself long ago, as in fact I had *seen* my face and head long ago, when I was thirty, for instance. Something had been lost in the all-around shearing, but I could well afford the loss, it was midsummer and very hot, and in a matter of three weeks I would have finished the 61st year of my time, so I rather enjoyed the giving of a general lightness to the face and head, and therefore also to the body and spirit.

And suddenly there he was, the writer, far from Bitlis where his people had lived until the turn of the century, and all of the men had worn moustaches precisely like the one he had just trimmed. And there he was far from Fresno where 61 years ago he had arrived in total forgetfulness, and had immediately begun to fight his way to the World and the Word. There he was, himself again, as he had been thirty years ago, the well-known total stranger.

Yesterday was a good day in Paris and the World, and very hot, with a wild glare. I moseyed along through two one-hour walks, drank gallons of cold water, and really didn't mind anything at all.

Places Where I've Done Time, 1972

The Light
Fantastic of
George Jean
Nathan

*I*t is understandable that Henry Louis Mencken would be pleased to
have as his best friend for half a century or more George Jean
Nathan. They were altogether unalike, and therefore precisely
suitable for friendship. A rough-and-tumble newspaperman and an
elegant dandy drama critic, one a German, the other a Jew. The theory
persists that H.L. Mencken was anti-Semitic, but I never saw any
evidence of it either in his writing or in his conversation.

In his contribution to a series entitled *Living Philosophies*, first
published in a national magazine, perhaps *The Bookman*, and then in a
book, George Jean Nathan said that he had no impulse at all to love the
Armenians, and H.L. Mencken wrote somewhere that any begger who
approached an Armenian for a handout was a fool and a dreamer,
because no Armenian ever gives money to beggars. Even so, I never felt
that either of these remarks demonstrated that these men were anti-
Armenian. And when both of these editors ignored the young writer in
Fresno who now and then sent an essay to *The American Mercury*, I did
not feel that this was because they had recognized the writer's name as
Armenian, I presumed that they didn't like my writing. Furthermore,
had they indeed *been* out-and-out anti-Armenian, I really doubt that
their attitude would have cancelled out for me the rest of the character of
each of them.

I had always liked the writing of the two friends, Mencken and
Nathan, and so early in 1939 when I arrived in New York by Grace Line
ship from Vera Cruz, and went to the Guild Theatre on 52nd Street and
saw the fourth performance of my first play, *My Heart's in the*

Highlands, and the next day read George Jean Nathan's review in one or another of the national weeklies, I was delighted that he liked the play.

I didn't mind at all that Burns Mantle writing for the *News* and Sidney Whipple for the *Telegram* considered the play a hoax. They were not drama critics in any case, notwithstanding that Burns Mantle appeared to be the founder and editor of the *Best Plays of the Year,* a worthy project that continues to this day.

If George Jean Nathan liked *My Heart's in the Highlands,* I didn't care who didn't like it. What's more, he voted for the play at the Drama Critics' Circle, which convened at the Algonquin Hotel, and one day out of the blue telephoned me at the Great Northern Hotel. For the first time in my life in April of 1939 I heard his elegant, slightly quavering voice. He told me that he was inviting me on behalf of the Drama Critics' Circle to the annual Awards Dinner, would I be able to make it?

Well, I was never a snappy dresser, and I went where I liked, and I probably really couldn't be counted on to behave as drama critics preferred their honored guests to behave.

Thinking of all this, I nevertheless replied, "Yes, sir, I'll be there, and I'll be neat."

I think it was this demonstration of a willingness to meet convention halfway that made George Jean Nathan believe we ought to meet for a drink at his corner table at the famous 21 Club.

In any case, it was probably his campaigning on my behalf that got me up to the Awards Dinner, and put me across the table from Eddie Dowling, who told me that he would produce sight unseen any play I might care to write. And *that,* in turn, sent me to work the following Monday morning on the writing of *The Light Fantastic,* which George Jean Nathan read in manuscript and thought might be better called *The Sunset Sonata,* thinking somewhat of August Strindberg. In the end, however, the play was called *The Time of Your Life.* It was written in six days, by a rube who didn't know the first thing about dramaturgy, a rustic who was not in the Group Theatre, and did not consider Harold Clurman an oracle of art, the first authority of the modern American theatre, and the all-around curator of culture for the masses.

The fact is I found him bumbling in thought and speech, with a tendency to hysteria. There was a miscalculation in his mind about the connection between himself, theatre, culture, politics, women, and the human race. He loved to gather the faithful around him and to pontificate in the most indulgent manner for hours, delighting in the admiration of ambitious actors and actresses, an order of society excessively vulnerable to even spurious articulation of ideas and theories related to their problems of identity, function, and effectiveness.

The night I saw *My Heart's in the Highlands* I went on to a party that included most of the cast and a great many of Harold Clurman's friends, including his wife at that time, Miss Stella Adler. He talked continuously, and now and then almost but not quite said something. *Rubber mouth* is the way I thought of him quite spontaneously and helplessly.

As a gesture, and indeed as a requirement of courtesy and gratitude for the fact that Group Theatre had produced *My Heart's in the Highlands,* I offered him *The Time of Your Life,* which I felt sure he *would* accept, making it necessary for me to write another play for Eddie Dowling—which would have been just fine, too, keeping me busy at new writing in a new form, or at any rate an old form which I was now at last beginning to manage with a certain native virtuosity. (The first thing I wrote, on lined tablet paper, and then on the first typewriter I ever owned, was in fact a play.) But Harold Clurman did not even reply to my note, attached to the play. I expected him to reply in a matter of forty-eight hours at the most. After quite a long time, perhaps two weeks, he telephoned and asked me to meet him in his office. When I got there, he picked up the manuscript and said, "I'm not going to produce this play, and I want to tell you why."

"I'm not interested in why," I said. And I took the play and left his office.

He would have talked for two hours, and for all I know he might have talked himself into producing the play, after all—and ruining it forever. Or he might have made me understand that you just don't write a play, you think about it, you discuss it with your girl, with your friends, with your mother, with Harold Clurman, and then perhaps if *they* feel you are really ready, you take at least a whole year to give it a go, and then and only then you deliver the first draft. How dare you just write a play?

George Jean Nathan never had anything *instructive* to say about the *writing* of plays, but he knew more about the theatre than anybody else I have ever talked with. He passed along what he knew in a way that was easy for me to take or leave. And his talk both invited and compelled participation on my part, and on the part of anybody else who happened to be at the table.

Once it was two Chinese girls, who were actually Japanese, but on account of Pearl Harbor had to watch it: they were delightful, in any case, and so one drink became two, then eight drinks, dinner, brandy, the Cub Room, and finally around four in the morning George Jean Nathan climbed very carefully out of a taxi at the Royalton and I took the girls on to the Victoria. But when I reached the Great Northern there were six messages from one of the girls, so I went up there, because she said on the phone, "I want to know more about the source of drama."

There were many great evenings with George Jean Nathan both before and after the War, when I disappeared from Broadway for the three years I was in the Army, and for all practical purposes forever after. During my absence all sorts of hustlers with sharp agents got busy and got rich. And after the War all I had was a condition of simple madness, the consequence of having been for three years subjected to unremitting chicken. I also had a wife and a son. I also had a theory that now I would get back to the proper founding of the family, and return to my proper work stronger than ever.

I was dreaming. My major work turned out to be to keep the bride, now the mother also of a daughter, not quite so desperately unhappy, and this meant moving a lot: from San Francisco to Oyster Bay, back to San Francisco, and then to Manhattan, where one day I ran into George Jean Nathan at 21. He said, "Well, where are you, what are you up to?"

"I'm looking for an apartment," I said. "There are four of us now, you know."

"Why don't you go to Poland?" he said, and I knew one man remained in a silly world who still made sense—he *laughed*, at any rate.

And then all of a sudden he was sick, and it was terrible.

By that time I was no longer able to deceive myself into any theory of being married, of having a wife, of being involved in the bringing up of two kids. It just wasn't so. I had spent half a million dollars trying to insist that it *was* so, and that there would be more children.

I had begun to stop at the Royalton Hotel for a number of reasons, not the least of which was the lower rates, the bigger rooms, the high ceilings, the central location, and the tradition of the place. Also I had come to dislike the Algonquin, just across the street, and the ever-lastingly gushy crowd there. As far as I was concerned, for half a century the real writers had gone to the Royalton while the dilettantes had gone to the Algonquin. At any rate, Robert Benchley, to mention only one other besides George Jean Nathan, had lived at the Royalton.

I liked it there, and I began slowly to get back to work. Three years in the Army and a stupid marriage had all but knocked me out of the picture, and, if the truth is told, out of life itself.

But now it was George Jean Nathan who was in terminal illness during one of my prolonged visits at the Royalton.

Julie Hayden, who had become his wife, telephoned now and then to let me know the situation, and I would drop by and find the magnificent fellow in a robe, almost totally nullified by illness, sitting in virtual darkness listening to a Catholic priest. He became a convert and quite a few people were shocked, as if at the last minute he had let them down.

To me his conversion seemed altogether personal and therefore beyond my understanding, and none of my business, precisely as T.S. Eliot's had been. You live and die according to what goes on in yourself, which no one else can ever begin to know, not even father, mother, wife, son, or daughter.

One evening the phone rang and his voice from just two floors below and midway down the hall, directly across from the elevators, was young and alive, and he said, "Not tonight, but this coming Saturday, let's get out on the town, keep Saturday open, I'll call you." Oh boy, I thought. He can't move, he has to be helped out of bed to get to a chair at the card table where he sits and chats softly with the priest for hours, so we're going out on the town Saturday night. And of course there would be no call at all on Saturday. A week or two later he would phone again and say pretty much the same thing.

Brooks Atkinson visited him faithfully for surely longer than a year. And there were others, but not many.

And then he died, and Broadway was diminished enough not to be thought of seriously again.

Did he really do anything for Broadway, for New York, for America, for the theatre, for art, for life?

Yes, he did. He dressed neatly and he went out among the thieves and assassins. And in his quavering voice he greeted beautiful girls and berated and scorned frauds of all categories. And he wrote. He was always writing. And everything he wrote had laughter in it. He was one of the most serious men in the living world, certainly as serious as his old friend, H.L. Mencken, but he refused to burden his writing, or his readers, with the agony of his unconverted and apparently indestructable soul. And then it *was* destructible, and being held fast to one small place, a small suite at the Royalton, he didn't know what to do, what to do. There can't ever be anybody like him again.

Sons Come & Go, Mothers Hang in Forever, 1976

One of the
Great
Mothers of
the World

*T*here are many mothers in the world, and every man runs into his share of them. L.B. Mayer, who pretty much owned and operated what I used to call the Laundry, Metro-Goldwyn-Mayer, when that place was in its prime, is one of the great mothers of all time.

He had a potbelly and a direct line into the current President, from Calvin Coolidge to Franklin Delano Roosevelt. And he even stayed in touch with the candidates who lost, such as Alf Landon and Wendell Willkie.

What for? Well, he had stars, like Clark Gable and Carole Lombard, for instance, and they could always be useful to the government when it had a piece of political propaganda to put over on the people.

L.B. Mayer had a good thick face with a kind of round quality to it and a sharp nose. And he had a reputation that was enormous, and evil.

All of his slaveys, especially in the writing department, told stories about him every day, and pretty much every night. He could make or break movie people, in all departments, and he did so whenever desirable or necessary. He was faithful to the faithful and ruthless with the smart alecks, as he put it. Anybody who got sarcastic with old L.B., even only in the eyes, giving him only a sarcastic *look*, would soon enough learn that L.B. would take it slow and easy, and then at an unexpected moment take his revenge. Like death itself.

When L.B. Mayer wanted to con me about movie rights to *The Human Comedy*, he called in Eddie Mannix, Sam Katz, Benny Thau, and the best man of the lot, Bernie Hyman. These men gave him moral and legal support, and he gave them another lesson in motherhood.

Eddie Mannix arrived with a big smile on his face. Sam Katz came less cheerfully, more warily. He was physically a much smaller man than Mannix and apparently much more aware of the realities of power maneuvering among the top half dozen executives at M.G.M. They were all at work for the company and the owners, a certain Mr. Nick Schenk, and a certain Mr. Lowe, who was never referred to by his first name. But they were also at work for number one, as they liked to put it in private.

Benny Thau was a slim swift lawyer who was there primarily to keep L.B. Mayer informed about the legalities or illegalities of any given situation, and to draw up an agreement on the spot.

"This is the best agreement I have ever handed to anybody," L.B. Mayer said to me, looking at Benny Thau. "I want the very best deal for this boy who has written this amazing story about life in wartime America. Lillian Messenger read the story to me while I sat at this very desk three weeks ago and listened to every word she read for almost two hours, and I cried—yes, gentlemen, tears poured out of my eyes, and I want this boy to have our very best contract, do you understand, Mr Thau?"

And of course Mr. Thau understood perfectly. Not so, my agent, however. He wasn't even there.

There are several reasons why Stanley Rose was my agent. In the first place, he had informed me while I was rolling dice in Las Vegas that he could get me a job at M.G.M. for big weekly money in case I wanted a job. In the second place, he was bankrupt, owing to the fact that almost all of his Hollywood customers owed him great sums of money but refused to pay, or paid only in very small installments. His bookshop was in danger of being closed. He said that if he could get ten thousand dollars soon, he could save the shop.

Well, *somebody* had to be the agent in any case, why not Stanley Rose?

But he was deliberately kept out of these earliest meetings. Vic Orsatti, L.B. Mayer's *private* agent, as it were, poured good whiskey for Stanley Rose on his daily arrival at the studio, and kept him pleasant company, far from where business was being transacted.

But when things began to be super-clever, and the bull-shit was flying fast, and L.B. Mayer was performing the part of the great benefactor of American writing, I said, "Shouldn't my agent be here?"

L.B. Mayer got to his feet, almost in a rage: "Why isn't this boy's agent here?" he said. "Who is responsible for this?"

His associates didn't even look at one another, for they *knew* who was responsible. Thereupon, the guilty party said, "All right, all right,

Mr. Thau, go out and find this boy's agent. Who is he? William Morris? Charles Feldman? Irving Lazar? Vic Orsatti?"

The rhetorical question permitted me to remark, "My agent is Stanley Rose."

L.B. Mayer pretended to be confused.

"But isn't he a *bookseller?* Don't I see him going down the hall of the Writer's Building carrying a satchel of books every now and then? How could *he* be your agent?"

Even so, Stanley Rose was quickly brought into the meeting in L.B. Mayer's enormous private office. Stanley tried his best to keep his equilibrium, and L.B. Mayer said, "Mr. Rose, I want this boy here who has written this patriotic story of simple Americans in a simple American town living simple American lives to have the best deal that I have ever given any writer. And I want this deal to have his approval, and the approval of his agent. He tells me *you're* his agent. Is that true?"

"Yes, sir, I am his agent," Stanley Rose said, "and I want him to have the best deal, too. What *is* the deal?"

Everybody then looked at one another, for hardly were the words out of his mouth than Stanley Rose shut his eyes and appeared to be fast asleep.

L.B. Mayer spoke almost directly to Eddie Mannix.

"Let's have some coffee, gentlemen."

Eddie Mannix go to his feet.

"What's coffee got to do with the deal?" Stanley Rose said. He also go to his feet.

Soon we were all standing around, sipping coffee and talking, and believing in America, the home of mothers, and the hope of fathers.

Stanley Rose got his ten thousand dollars, kept his shop open, and visited his mother Kate in Matador, Texas.

I got cheated, but legally, the motherly way.

L.B. Mayer died, and everybody who was anybody loved his funeral.

Sons Come & Go, Mothers Hang in Forever, 1976

Life, Art,
Politics, and
Lunch at
Hyde Park

*T*he luncheon took place in the garden of the President's summer residence at Hyde Park. I'm not sure the tables were assigned, but I found myself at a table for four just to the left of where Franklin Delano Roosevelt was to sit, at the head of a very long table, at which already were seated Hendrik Willem van Loon, a writer of popular history, and F.P.A., or Franklin P. Adams, a man who for a hundred and eighty-four years had been getting out a daily newspaper column entitled *The Conning Tower* (or at any rate something like that), to which a wide (but not really terribly wide) variety of people had been sending little tidbits of writing in both doggerel and straight language. And gathered around this main table were dozens of men and women waiting for the arrival of the President, who was to greet the people of the arts, the writers, the newspaper columnists, the actors, the actresses, and similar fish easily schooled into a net. It was the eve of the campaign for an unprecedented third term, and the President and his people were determined not to lose the election.

On the other hand, the upstart Wendell Willkie seemed determined to keep the great aristocrat of American democracy from breaking with tradition. Wendell Willkie had recently returned from a nonhazardous trip around the world, and had come out with a small book aptly entitled *One World,* and he seemed to be swiftly winning the affection and respect of the voting people.

Hence, this lunch at Hyde Park: stop Willkie. Invite writers to lunch, and stop him cold. And of course a President *can* round up very nearly anybody he likes.

My invitation was both unaccountable and informal, if not

irregular. I received nothing in the mail. Nobody phoned. Nobody, that is, except the playwright Sidney Kingsley, who called from somewhere in New Jersey to say that he and his wife Madge Evans were driving to Manhattan tomorrow, Sunday, and then they were going on to Hyde Park, for lunch with the Roosevelts, how about going with them?

I seem to have an insatiable curiosity, and I certainly like rides out of Manhattan into the country, so I said, "Sure, I'll be ready."

Madge Evans drove, and years later, she and Sidney Kingsley at Leonard and Sylvia Lyons' one night asked if I remembered how our car was stopped for speeding and how I argued with the cop—and won, or was it that I had argued in vain?

In any event, I forgot all about *that* episode, although I did not forget about being put down by Miss Katharine Hepburn for opening my big mouth about her participation in a political program that everybody seemed to believe would improve everything everywhere instantly. She was carrying under her arm a stationary box, the contents of which rattled as she bound about, and so I was unable not to ask, "Are they in that box, Miss Hepburn—all the answers?"

The elegant lady gave me a very icy look and said, "It's none of your business what's in the box, Mr. Saroyan."

That was a very nice reply, with flawless diction, and timing, as if in a Philip Barry play, perfectly spoken and timed.

And I don't consider it odd that in the intervening years I have come to take pride in not having said anything more, for whatever *had* been in the box, it very probably hadn't been answers.

The President was lugged in by two secret service men and placed in his chair at the head of the long table, and everybody quickly sat down, because he had other plans for the afternoon. He wanted to get his part in this New England chowder lunch with the arty crowd over with as soon as possible, so that Eleanor could carry on in her usual thorough and efficient manner, while his elegant mother, Mrs. James Roosevelt, observed Eleanor, and now and then chatted with a guest: "Does Franklin seem a little tired to you, Mr. Saroyan? He does, to me."

So there I sat, and across the table for four was James Thurber, and beside him sat his wife.

After lunch, I said to James Thurber that I would not be going up to shake the hand of the President, as everybody else was doing. James Thurber also declined to honor, or to bother, the President, or himself.

Thus, only a political anarchist, who voted once at the age of twenty-one and never again; and a humorous writer and cartoonist, who could no longer see—only these two, unrelated and unrelatable, did not that fine Sunday afternoon, shake the hand of Franklin Delano Roosevelt.

Sons Come & Go, Mothers Hang in Forever, 1976

Greta Garbo at the Little Woman's Big Party on North Rodeo Drive

S he came into the house on North Rodeo Drive in Beverly Hills, full of people drinking and eating, and with her was her friend John Gunther, and his wife Jean, who had indeed won her over to the idea of going out to a private *party*, and she was precisely the lady the rest of the world had seen only in films: Greta Garbo.

She seemed even more exciting in person than in film. She went straight to Charlie Chaplin, who was sitting demurely beside his recent bride, Oona, and she said, "Oh, Charlie Chaplin, Charlie Chaplin," and nobody ever heard anything more astonishing or right, or more simply spoken.

But what did it mean? Well, of course it meant that in the fable of the human race in the human world, there were these unaccountable luminaries who in saying nothing to one another nevertheless say everything, and understand perfectly.

She was then perhaps forty-eight years of age, and had long since done her last movie, which hadn't meant very much to her, or to the producers of the movie, or to the bankers, or to the exhibitors of movies, and worst of all to the buyers of tickets.

Greta Garbo, in her last three or four movies, had still been Greta Garbo, but this truth had begun to signify less and less to the human race of the Western World at large, and almost nothing to the Eastern World.

It was my house, but I never gave a party in my life. The party was the production of the wife, just lately married to me a second time, in 1950, no longer trying to make a life on Taraval Street in San Francisco, or on West 59th Street in New York, just up from the Plaza, but apparently trying to make a splash in Hollywood with a big party costing me a couple of thousand dollars.

She knew she could count on her old pal Oona from girlhood days in New York to bring her husband Charlie Chaplin, and if John Gunther could bring Greta Garbo, then that would really make it a triumph, wouldn't it?

Well, there were at least a hundred people in the house, and overflowing onto the front lawn, and out into the back garden, and the tennis court—after the lease ran out the owner of the house, Jan Kiepura's father-in-law, sued me and was given a judgment of a couple of thousand dollars over and above the high rent, because somebody had spilled champagne on his wallpaper here and there, and some kids had made crayon marks in other places.

It was a noisy party, and nobody was noisier than the host—myself. I was drunk before the first guest arrived, but I can drink and go right on being polite better than anybody I know, or anybody I have seen in action.

I had heard that Greta Garbo might come, just might at the last minute decide to come, although she had told John Gunther, "Oh, no, no, I do not go to parties, I can't stand parties, it is bad enough trying to speak to people one at a time, to dear friends, even."

And so there she was suddenly speaking to Charlie Chaplin.

Were they old friends? Lovers? Had they worked together in a movie? Well, little by little it became clear that no, really, all it was was her own recognition of the fabulous reality of Charlie Chaplin in the human story of the brave little man in the hard big world. And she simply had to let him know.

Later, in New York, and in Paris, I saw her at similar private parties, and she was always the person who looked at everything and everybody, as she always had at lovers in movies, with a pity that was ravishing, and said, "Oh, you poor poor poor soul, will you never stop being pathetic and stupid?" That was the secret of her love scenes, and her success.

Sons Come & Go, Mothers Hang in Forever, 1976

Orphan in Tears

S he was in the bathroom after a bath, and I was in the parlor of a tiny bungalow in back of somebody's Hollywood house, the sort of thing put up to accommodate a sudden guest. I could hear her breathing, or so I thought, and I wondered why she wasn't humming or singing or laughing, and how long would she be.

After ten minutes I began to get ideas—the girl is getting herself delicious for me, that's all.

But after twenty minutes I decided, The girl is either mean or sick to expect anybody to sit in a dismal parlor waiting for her, what's the matter with her?

After thirty minutes of hearing her breathing, or thinking I heard it, fighting off irritation, annoyance, anger, outrage, a feeling of being deliberately belittled by a silly ambitious girl, I thought, Well, now, it's too late, I've got to find out what goes on here, who this is, and what this is about.

A friend of mine had interviewed her for a movie magazine, and she had told him to please arrange for me to meet her.

And then about a month later I was at a summer evening outdoor picnic at the home of a friend, and there she was, accompanied by a famous director who invited me to ride back to town in his car, and between us sat this girl.

By that time I had discovered that she was very eager to get into the finer world, as somebody must have put it to her, the world of literature, for instance, and as a matter of fact she spoke about Dostoyevsky, and from the odd silence of the director I gathered that he had put her in touch with that mighty writer.

The director was returning to New York in a day or two, and in bringing us together I got the impression that he would like me and this ambitious young lady to go on meeting, now that we had spent forty minutes chatting in a car, but of course that was speculation and in any case irrelevant, and I didn't think I would be very likely to see her again.

To begin with, my second marriage to the same woman, on behalf of a small son and a smaller daughter, and indeed on behalf of the woman herself, and also on behalf of myself, and on behalf of the revived fantasy of founding a family, had again become impossible, I knew she was seeing the world-famous divorce lawyer Jerry Geisler, and that only rotten times were ahead. I lived at a hotel, and I missed the boy and the girl, and I worried about them, and I owed the Tax Collector so much money I didn't see how I'd ever be able to pay him off, and my writing wasn't bringing me any money, and I was drinking a lot because I wanted to, and every morning when I got up to start a day I was more like a dead man than a live man. I wasn't really in any proper shape to take on a strange girl who wanted a number of things known or knowable and a number that were surely as unknown, as unknowable, as things wanted might ever be.

So there I was in the little parlor waiting for her to emerge from the bathroom, going a little berserk because she *wasn't* emerging and wasn't speaking and *was* apparently just barely breathing.

When she came out she was fully clothed and spoke in a sorrowful whisper, asking me to please not mind the time she had needed to take—and I knew instantly that it wasn't meanness at all, it was something more complicated, and something not for me to try to help her with.

The director was supposed to be good at that sort of thing, at least when it came up in plays, so if he hadn't been able to help her, it wasn't likely that I would.

And of course any illusion of having been compelled to wait in order to behold a ravishing sex-bomb was totally dispelled.

I took her to a circus, but after only half an hour of finding the stuff unbearable I asked if she would mind if we left. We went to the Hot Dog Show for hot-dogs and soda-pop, and we talked, and a month later I took her home and got in bed with her to find her sobbing like a small abandoned child, and a week later she said she was going to meet Joe DiMaggio, and I said, "He just might do it."

Sons Come & Go, Mothers Hang in Forever, 1976

Benjamin
Kubelsky of
Waukegan,
Rich and
Famous at a
Hollywood
Party

I first met Jack Benny at a Hollywood party, which is where almost
everybody in Hollywood first meets.

Claudette Colbert was also there, straight out of *It Happened
One Night,* but now she was not with Clark Gable, she was with her
husband, who was some kind of doctor of noses and had done the nose of
a cousin of mine.

George Burns was also there, making Jack Benny laugh by not
saying anything, by only looking as if he *might* say something.

And at the party there was this woman, and that man, and that
woman, and this man, and everybody was glittering, everybody had
prepared for the party. Every wife wanted to be the star of the party, and
every husband had been thrilled to spare no expense to help his woman
in her ambition.

The paintings on the walls of the house were worth at least three
million dollars, and the glassware *was* glassware, so that when a drink
was fixed for you, and you accepted it, and you took a sip, you tasted
wealth right there at the rim of the sparkling glass with the glass-clean
ice in it, and the super-smooth Scotch, and you let it go, you let the
absurdity of it all go, the only right thing in human reality was the
Hollywood party, and in between was only rehearsal time. Be smart, join

the Hollywood famous and the Hollywood rich and the Hollywood wise and the Hollywood wonderful. Just lift the best glassware ever fired, just sip the best Scotch ever aged, just look and listen, just tell them one and all how great they are, see what they think. They thought it was fascinating that this writer in person was actually not unlike everybody else at all of the Hollywood parties forever and forever.

About a year later an editor of a national magazine telephoned and said he had heard that I had met Jack Benny at a party and had told Jack Benny what his comedy really was, a kind of contemporary American folklore involving the vast astonishment of everybody about the crude and dishonest behavior of everybody else.

"We want to do a big important interview with Jack Benny," the man said, "but he told us to talk to you, so can you come in tomorrow at our office in Beverly Hills, so we can go to lunch and talk about this?"

By that time I lived in a house on the beach at Malibu, I was bankrupt, deep in debt, and needed money desperately.

I hung up and sat down and wrote a piece about Jack Benny, but also about myself of course, perhaps more about myself than about Jack Benny, and the next day went to lunch with the three editors at a very expensive restaurant.

After lunch the editor who had telephoned said, "Will you write a piece about Jack Benny for us? We'll pay our top fee, twenty-five hundred dollars."

I brought the folded manuscript out of my back pocket, and handed it to the man.

"Here it is," I said. "Just mail the check, please."

This scared the man half to death, but in the end the piece was published in *Look* precisely as I had written it.

Sons Come & Go, Mothers Hang in Forever, 1976

From Fortnum & Mason in Piccadilly to Shaw & Shaw at Ayot Saint Lawrence

There is an Armenian tailor whose home and place of work is less than two hundred yards as the crow flies from my fifth-floor flat in Paris, where I am writing this book. He is soon going to Soviet Armenia, not to visit but to live, and when he gets there he wants to write a book called *My Neighbor Saroyan*, so he keeps inviting me to his place for a cup of tea. And while I am at his house he asks questions, and writes on a lined tablet in Armenian, because he wants to get my answers just right, he says.

"Well," I tell him, "it really isn't necessary to get any of this just right, these really aren't the things about myself, or about yourself, or about anybody at all, that make a difference."

"What is, then?" he says, and I say, "Well, the *living* thing of course, that's what takes noticing and is likely to be worth writing about."

"The living thing?" the tailor says. "What's that? What do you mean? I want to get everything you say just right, what *is* the living thing?"

And then suddenly he goes right on and says, "How did you meet Shaw?"

"If you mean George Bernard Shaw," I say, "I met him through an Australian newspaperwoman in London in 1944. She insisted that I must meet the old man. I told her I didn't want to bother him. I told her I was also supposed to meet Sean O'Casey, another Irishman, who lived down in Devon, but I didn't want to bother him, either. But this lady from Australia went to work and all of a sudden I had a long handwritten letter from Mr. Shaw asking me to take a train three days later at eleven in the morning and to arrive at Ayot Saint Lawrence where his chauffeur would pick me up and drive me to his house, and so that happened, That's how I met him."

"Well," the tailor says, "please tell me about *that*, because Shaw is a great writer, is he not?"

"Yes, of course he is," I say, "but I didn't care about that so much as about the fact that he was alive at all, well along into his eighties, and still saying outrageous things to the English. At the height of the bombing of London, for instance, he piped up to a number of visiting newspaper reporters that Hitler was one of the greatest men in the history of the world, and that everything he was trying to do made sense if you studied such a simple thing as cause and effect, and of course everybody in England, not to mention everybody in France, and America, felt that George Bernard Shaw was a senile, sick old fool. But that was none of my business, either. It was the living thing about him that interested me, and that is why I went to the trouble of going to Fortnum & Mason in Piccadilly to buy him some hothouse grapes, a sweet-smelling golden melon, some figs, some peaches, and a few other things like that."

"What did he say?" the tailor said.

"I'll tell you," I said, "but first you must know that he looked something like a contemporary saint, a white-bearded skinny old geezer in knickers. Second, he sounded like a choirboy. He had a chirpy high-pitched voice. Third, he wanted me to understand that he was a performer, and would soon begin his performance. He did this by saying: 'Armenian? But didn't the Turks *kill* all of the Armenians?' This was said in order to give me fair warning about the working of his mind. Perhaps also to diminish any high regard I might have for his character. I think he suspected that I considered him a kind of saint, and he didn't want to be a saint. But he couldn't fool me, and he remained the gentlest, kindest, the most decent fellow in England, and possibly in the world. And so we sat in the parlor of his house, and this woman, not his wife, brought tea and spice cake for me—he didn't have anything—and I smoked one cigarette after another, even as I gulped down many cups of hot tea and finished all the slices of spice cake. The woman suddenly discovered the basket of fruit I had left in the hall upon arrival and she said, 'Mr. Shaw, I thought you might like to see what this young American soldier has brought you.'

" 'This is not a young American soldier,' George Bernard Shaw replied. 'This is the last Armenian in the world, and what's more, he writes plays. Why did you bring me all this food? Why do Americans think I'm hungry? I'll give it to the neighbors.'

"Oh, he was a card," I said to the tailor, "but he couldn't fool me for a second. I had paid more than twenty-five dollars for the stuff in the basket, and he really enjoyed seeing so much beauty, he just wanted to go right on being a performer, because *that* is the living thing. *Performing.* He was a liar on behalf of style and truth, or at any rate on behalf of a new variation of truth."

"I don't understand," the tailor said, "but let me write that down just as you said it, maybe I will understand it later on, or somebody else will."

Sons Come & Go, Mothers Hang in Forever, 1976

Chance Meetings

*C*hance acquaintances are sometimes the most memorable, for brief friendships have such definite starting and stopping points that they take on a quality of art, of a *whole* thing, which cannot be broken or spoiled. And of course a sort of spoiling is the one thing that seems to be inevitable in an enduring friendship—new aspects of the person become revealed, and that which one had believed to be the truth about a person must be revised. The whole reality of the person must be frequently reconsidered, and so instead of having the stability of art or anything like art there is a constant flux, a continuous procedure of change and surprise, which at its best, if both people are lucky, is far more appealing than art, for this is the stuff from which art is to be made, from which art is to be continuously enlarged and renewed.

An acquaintanceship, if all goes well, can linger in the memory like an appealing chord of music, while a friendship, or even a friendship that deteriorates into an enemyship, so to put it, is like a whole symphony, even if the music is frequently unacceptable, broken, loud, and in other ways painful to hear.

One encounters acquaintances endlessly, especially on one's travels.

There is always somebody on the train, ship, bus, or airplane, who wants to tell you his story, and in turn is willing to let you tell yours, and so you exchange roles as you listen and tell. If the duet works well, you say so long at the end of the ride, and you remember the occasion with a pleasant satisfaction with yourself and with this other person who was suddenly a part of your story and of yourself.

Now, if you play your cards right, and this acquaintance is a pretty girl or a handsome woman, you can risk trying to extend the chance meeting to a non-chance meeting, but the rules of this sort of thing, although unwritten and unstated, do not tend to even permit either party to *think* in terms of anything less than absolute purity, absolute impersonality, total awareness that each represents the whole human race at its courteous best.

You have been thrown together accidentally, total strangers, in order to pass along as if to Truth itself, or to God, or to Memory, or even to Yourself and to Your Family, the essence of your own story and reality. You are not there to acquire more story, to have more material to carry with the rest of the material that still hasn't been really understood, or certainly hasn't been used, and you are there anonymously.

The game does not work if you let the other acquaintance know your name or who the people are in your inner life.

What you share is a kind of gentility, sympathy, and charity, not so much for one another, not so much each of you for the other, but rather for the unnamed people in your lives who have been stupid, wrong, unfair, cruel, and altogether human.

And so while the carrier moves steadily toward where you are going, you speak to one another, and you say things you wouldn't say to any other people, and you know everything you say is understood and will not be used against you, and then when the carrier arrives you look at each other and smile, and say good-bye, good luck, and you move along, and that's it, and you aren't sorry that that's it, you are pleased that it is.

I have had many such acquaintances—literally hundreds, but I remember best going back to San Francisco from New York in January of the year 1929, after I had failed to take the big city by storm, after I had *not* started my career as a writer just twenty years old. I traveled chair car the whole distance and the whole time, about eight days, I believe it was, it might have been even longer. And then all of a sudden during the last two hours of that long train ride a little girl joined me in a sip of coffee from the Candy Butcher's urn in the corner of the parlor car, and we got to talking. She was married, she was pregnant, her husband was an office worker in Denver, they had no money, she was on her way home to her mother in San Francisco until he could get a proper one-room apartment, with bath and kitchenette, but she was in love with everything, especially the baby, and her husband, and life. And with me, as well, as I was in love with her. And I may say passionately if also totally impersonally.

Chance Meetings, 1978.

The Cabinetmaker

On Ninth Avenue in San Francisco between Irving and Judah Streets there used to be a cabinetmaker who lived above his shop. He was called in the old country manner, Barone Gapriel, or Mr. Gapriel. His family name was Jivarian, and he, also, was from Bitlis. He wrote poems.

I asked him how it happened that he took to the writing of poems, since he was a cabinetmaker, and a very good one.

He said, "Well, now, my boy, Mr. William, when I am standing here at my bench, doing my work, my mind does not have very much to do, it is a matter of hand, and eye, so my mind speaks to me, saying things, and pretty soon I listen to my mind. I hear my mind say one word, two words, one line, another line, and so in the evening after work I write down what my mind has told me. That is how it happened."

He was a man of medium height, heavy set, with something about him that suggested the trunk of a large tree. His shoulders were broad, his hands large, his fingers well shaped and very strong. His eyes had in them a mixture of terrible sorrow and continous dancing amusement.

His kids were away at college, for that was the one thing he believed was his responsibility to them, to see that they were as well prepared for sensible living as anybody might be: two sons, one daughter. His wife he had found in America, but again she was from the city of Bitlis. Every afternoon around three she took him a brass tray, upon which rested a small cup of Turkish coffee, one piece of lokhoum, and a glass of cold water.

She smiled and said softly, "A moment of refreshment for you, sir."

She left the tray on a clear place of his workbench and went back upstairs, for she knew that when he was in his shop he was an artist, a thinker, and did not want any kind of small talk to intrude on his own cabinetmaking and poetry-thinking.

Now, in those days there was a famine in the land, one might say in the manner of the writers of the Old Testament. There was certainly a shortage of money, and many poor families became poorer. All the same, they managed to sit down to hearty meals of very simple and very inexpensive fare, including my own family, in the second floor flat at 348 Carl Street, about eight blocks from the shop of Barone Gapriel Jivarian. I was twenty-two years old and felt just slightly desperate about not having a steady job. Also, about not having become a published writer, although I worked at writing every day, and pretty much also every night.

Thus, being without income and therefore also without cash, I did a lot of walking, and a lot of water drinking, until suppertime, when great mounds of bulghour pilaf cooked with cut-up brown onions was heaped upon plates, so that my brother and I could eat heartily if not elegantly, so to put it.

I loved the stuff, and I still do. And long after I was rich, I frequently asked somebody to cook a big pot of it for me, or I asked a chef at a restaurant to make a special big pot of it for the following day. And finally I myself learned how to fix the dish, and so I have it whenever I want it, wherever I happen to be.

On my walks I frequently passed the cabinetmaker's shop, and once or twice he saw me and waved at me to come in, whereupon he would say, "Well, now, you're just the man I want to see, Mr. William. You are a writer, although not yet famous. You use the English language. I, also, am a writer—well, perhaps not quite a writer, but at any rate I write my poems. And I use the Armenian language. This is the poem I wrote last night."

And then he would read a poem that I thought was wise and human, and incredible, not for a cabinetmaker to have written, but for any man to have written.

And I thanked him and went on to the beach where I walked and picked up pebbles, as if they were words, or coins of money.

Four years later, I broke through at last, and my first book was published, let me even now, almost forty years later, say praise heaven, praise God, praise Jesus, praise the sun, praise everything and everybody. While the poems of the good cabinetmaker were never published, heaven help us one and all.

Chance Meetings, 1978

The Owl and
the Shoemaker

*U*p at Number 4 bis Rue Chateaudun four blocks from my four-room flat on Rue Taitbout, is a small square room on the street, which is a shoemaker's shop, not far from the entrance to a hotel with a name like Baltic. This hotel, according to a conscientious objector who did a little time in a pen somewhere in the United States for that private bravery, during the year 1944 was also a whorehouse, because he and his bride on their honeymoon took a room there, and the first thing they noticed was that there were a lot of men coming in and going out of the place, especially from 10 p.m. to 2 a.m., especially to and from the first and second floors, which in America would be the second and third floors.

In this little shoemaker's shop, which has a high ceiling and a steep corkscrew metal stairway that goes to a basement precisely the same size and shape as the shop, there is a large brown owl.

This bird has the freedom of the shop, the door of which is sometimes kept open on the street, and yet the owl has never ventured out of the shop.

There is no telling (by me) why *this* is so, but I do know the story, however sketchily, of the owl and its adjustment to life in the shoeshop.

A nice lady back from the country, whose apartment is two doors from the shoemaker's shop, brought into the shop one morning eight years ago two helpless infant owl chicks, both apparently near death.

She asked the shoemaker if he understood such birds.

He didn't, he said, but he suggested that she improvise a system of feeding them and keeping them warm. She in turn insisted that he keep one of the chicks for himself.

He did.

And that's how he has had the owl these eight years. And that's why the owl loves him, and he loves the owl.

His wife died recently, and his son and his daughter are adults, and well along into their own lives.

The shoemaker is a year or two younger than myself, he's sixty-one or sixty-two years old. He is an Armenian, born in Gultik, down from the highlands of Bitlis, but he was taken early in life to Antakya, which is the modern name for Antioch, where St. Paul stopped now and then on his missionary excursions.

Well, now, this man, Hovaness Shoghikian by name, is perhaps an inch or two under five feet in height, but powerfully built. As a matter of fact he was once a champion weight lifter and wrestler, and has many old photographs to prove it.

In short, he is not simply a shoemaker, although he actually *makes,* shoes, *entire* shoes, and for forty years has never worn a pair of shoes he hasn't made.

First, it is his trade, and he likes to work at his trade, but nowadays almost nobody wants a pair of shoes made to order, to fit the feet, to fit a cast of the foot's precise shape. Second, his own feet are small and broad, and the best he has ever been able to do in finding a ready-made pair of shoes (before he began to make his own shoes) was not very good. Ready-made shoes were always something his feet could barely tolerate. But in his own shoes his feet are at home, and standing on his feet in his shop he himself is at home. Naturalists have visited his shop to speak with him about the owl, and about a green bird the shoemaker has had almost thirty years. "She can't grip with her claws properly," he says of the green bird. "But she will live most likely another thirty years, they sometimes live to be eighty."

Where he found out such a thing I can't imagine, for he does not look into books for information.

Without any outside help, or instructions, he long ago discovered that the owl has to have in its diet fur or feathers, otherwise its digestive procedure becomes impaired. And so all these years the owl has been fed thin strips of raw beef, chicken hearts, and live mice, which he buys from people who telephone to let him know there is a mouse in their trap.

And so of course the shoemaker loves the owl and the owl loves him.

The owl certainly permits itself to be held by the shoemaker. The two of them have a simple ritual of displaying trust and affection, which involves his saying, in Armenian, "Well, a kiss, then." Whereupon the owl puts its beak to his upper lip.

Chance Meetings, 1978

The Macaroni
Review

*P*apulius was the publisher of the *Macaroni Review.*
His office was on the second floor of a rattletrap building
on Howard Street, where the winos lived the philosophic life,
and still do, between Fourth and Fifth Streets in San Francisco.

Overlooking the street was one large room in which he had a desk
with a telephone on it, a few copies of the *Macaroni Review,* and three
wire baskets containing a great variety of pieces of paper, letters,
pamphlets, clippings, and anything else that had come to him in the
mail, or by handout.

At the top of one basket, for instance, was a religious pamphlet
entitled, "Do You Want to Live Forever?" (I gather that he was giving the
question his best attention.)

He was a slim keyed-up man with a strong Greek accent. (Many
years later when I listened to Spyrous Skouras I immediately remembered Papulius. But then you might well ask, Who is Spyrous Skouras?)

Papulius was about thirty-eight to my twenty-four in 1932. He had
put a short ad in the classified section of the *Examiner,* which I
examined every morning free of charge in the display frame at the Hearst
Building at Third and Market Streets.

The ad said something along the lines of "Writer wanted. Papulius.
848 Howard." This meant that he had got the ad into the paper at the
lowest possible cost, but I couldn't be bothered about a detail like that,
the thing that got me was that straight-out statement about what he
wanted. Writer.

Well, that was me all right, and it didn't matter that there was no
word about wages. Were the wages to be by the hour, by the day, by the
week, month, year, or perhaps by the piece? If the writer wrote an
especially good piece, would this man, this publisher, Papulius, show
his appreciation by paying a little something extra? And in those days a

little something extra was highly cherished, for the reason that a little something without anything extra was just about the highest achievement any young man could make.

"Papulius," I thought, as I hurried at half past nine one morning in June to 848 Howard Street. "Where have I heard that name before? Isn't it the name of one of the greatest and noblest Greek philosophers, and isn't this man at 848 Howard Street a descendant of that great Greek?"

Well, whoever he was I would soon know.

When I climbed the stairs to the second floor I saw a door marked THE MACARONI REVIEW. I knocked softly, waited, and then tried the knob. It turned, so I went in.

A very intense little woman with rather insane eyes, and taunt muscles, glanced in my direction, while a man who wore a very seedy gray Vandyke beard, standing across a table from the woman, not in anything like a game of ping-pong or anything like that, but in some kind of activity involving open books and long lists, this seedy man not only turned and glanced in my direction but actually asked, "Papulius?"

"Yes, the ad in the paper."

"Well," the man said, "he'll be in in about an hour, I suppose. Come back in an hour."

"Is the job open?"

"Oh, yes, yes, yes," the man said. "The job is open."

"The ad said writer wanted."

"Yes, yes, that's right, talk to Mr. Papulius about it."

An hour later when I went back Papulius received me with enormous cordiality, and said I was just in time to go along with him on some calls. He drove to a spaghetti factory in the North Beach, and, talking quickly, extracted not one hundred dollars, not fifty dollars, not dollars, not forty dollars but *thirty* dollars in cash money from a spaghetti manufacturer for a full-page ad in the next issue of the *Macaroni Review*.

Papulius wanted me to learn to call on such people and to get them to advertise in the magazine, six copies of which he showed me in the car.

The magazine consisted of about forty rather thick slick pages in which there were many full-page advertisements from spaghetti manufacturers.

"There are eighty-four spaghetti and macaroni manufacturers in San Francisco alone," Papulius said with a certain amount of astonishment and pleasure, "and they do not have any other magazine in which to brag, only the *Macaroni Review*. The minute I go to a new customer and open my magazine his eyes pop open, and of course you heard what I told him."

"Yes, you said you would write about his company."

"Exactly," Papulius said. "And you're the writer. On this piece of paper I jotted down his name, and a few facts. Give him a write-up, about a hundred words is enough. Just say he's got a nice clean factory on Columbus Avenue, number 142, he's been making macaroni at this location for eight years, and the family has been in the macaroni business eight generations, something like that."

"Yes, sir," I said, because he hadn't yet come to the money part, the wages, and I figured if I sounded eager and sensible he would mention wages of a certain dignity, but he didn't mention wages of any kind at all, so that I was ready to consider rather undignified wages, even.

We went four blocks in his old Overland to another prospect, and he made the same pitch, but this time the macaroni maker said, "I no need advertise, I got too much business already."

"Prestige! Prestige!" Papulius shouted, *"That's* the reason we want to advertise."

But the macaroni maker waved his arms and said, "I no want what you say," and walked away.

Papulius said, "I did it wrong, it was my fault, learn from my mistakes, I should have mentioned his mother, remember that, with certain big men speak softly of their mothers and they begin to listen, that man didn't listen."

After stopping at half a dozen more places, and after he had won two more advertisers, we went back to his office, and he quickly made a phone call.

"Hello, is that you, dentist? I got some people coming from Sacramento for dinner, I want the teeth cleaned—right away. No time to lose. I be over in five minutes."

And he hung up.

"Have you met Mr. and Mrs. Goostenhouse?" Papulius said, and I thought, "Not officially, and let's just keep it that way, too." But Papulius hollered out, "Come in here, you two."

After they arrived, almost running, he said, "I want you to meet my writer, this boy has got it. He's going to do the writing and the hustling both. Tell Mr. and Mrs. Goostenhouse your name."

I said my name quickly, and the little tense husband and the little insane wife nodded, and Papulius shouted, "All right, back to your work." And sure enough they went trotting back to their tiny space in the outer office.

"What do they do?" I said.

"They do *something,*" Papulius said. "I don't know. I give them the space, free rent, they answer the door and the phone when I'm out. They fool around with dogs, I think. They look like dogs, too. All right, this office is also your office, this desk is also your desk, that typewriter over there, that's also your typewriter, write something for the *Review,* I'll read it tomorrow."

And he went out, to get his teeth cleaned for dinner.

After he was gone Mr. Goostenhouse and his wife stayed away for about an hour, during which time I wrote what I thought was a literary essay about eating, about wheat, flour, water, salt, the discovery of new usages for flour, the meaning of Italy, and the marvel of macaroni—all in well under a thousand words.

I was revising the essay when the husband and wife came into the office and picked up pieces of paper from the wire baskets, and then stopped to chat.

They were breeders of dogs—but only of the very rarest of breeds, not popular dogs.

They showed snapshots of three of these breeds and the dogs looked strangely not unlike the husband and wife.

"May we read what you've written?" the man said, and standing together they read it.

"You *are* a writer," the man said. "But this isn't what he wants."

The following day, after reading the piece, Papulius said, "This is great—we feature it. We go hustle now."

Three days later I stopped going up there, that's all, because he didn't pay wages, and I didn't even want to *try* to earn a living from wheedling money for macaroni ads from sensible men who just couldn't quite resist the fame of having a full-page ad in a fine magazine, and for only $22.50.

Chance Meetings, 1978

The Wrestler

I worked on a vineyard with a retired Armenian wrestler named Nazaret Torosian one year, and he is one of the few people I believe I have ever learned a little something or other from, for he frequently stopped in his work to say, "If your opponent gets a headlock on you, feel out the action of his muscles, and when the pattern of tension and relaxation is known, wait for the next instant of relaxation, and then leap upward with all the force you can manage, and I think you will find that you can break free from his hold upon your head."

"Yes, sir," I used to say, "but in leaping up is it not possible that the top of my head will strike the bottom of his head, his *chin,* and be considered a foul?"

"No, sir," the retired wrestler would reply. "In making your break for freedom, the force of your movement automatically drives him out of the line of your released head, but let us say that somehow or other his chin *is* in fact directly in line with your head, and that the top of your head *does* strike him on the bottom of his chin—all the better, my boy. Don't worry about it, *you* will scarcely feel the impact, whereas he may be pushed close to unconsciousness by the force under his chin."

"Yes, sir," I used to say, "I'll remember that."

And so we might not speak again for ten minutes, or even twenty, and now and then not even for an hour, because pruning muscat vines calls for a certain amount of concentration, and at the same time in noticing the beauty of the structure of the vine one tends to fall silent.

But sooner or later the Armenian wrestler would stand up straight and say, "If you are on the mat, and he's sprawling all over you to keep your back flat on the mat so that he may win the round, God help you, that's all I can say."

"Yes, of course," I used to say, "but is there nothing I can do to stop him from keeping my back flat on the mat?"

"Yes, there is," the old wrestler would say, "but it isn't easy, it is almost impossible, everything happens very swiftly in wrestling, and when you are off balance in that manner, where is your strength to come from? You are flat, and you have nothing to hold your strength together *upon*, for a counterattack. But there *is* one thing you can do, and again it is something more in the realm of art than athletics, and I myself in a long career of professional wrestling was able to do it only perhaps half a dozen times out of at least a hundred opportunities."

"And what was that?" I would ask.

"Disappear," Nazaret Torosian would say. "And I *mean* just that. Disappear, out from under. How it happens I have never been able to understand, and I have studied the matter from every possible angle. My wrestling weight was 240 pounds, all muscle, bone, and cartilege, and so we know that this is a great deal of body to cause to disappear, and yet, that is precisely what happened at least half a dozen times. I was flat on my back and my opponent—once he was Strangler Lewis himself, another time he was Jimmy Londos, and another time he was Stanislaus Szabisco—and then suddenly I was *not* flat on my back, I was *up*, on my feet, and he was just turning to see where I had gone. So I invariably thought to myself, Now, how did that happen? And of course I went on and won the round. The matches in those days were the best two out of three, as I think you may remember."

"Yes," I would reply. "Yes, sir, I *do* remember, but after you had given the matter a great deal of thought, what did you conclude? How did it happen that you were able to disappear in that manner? What was it that permitted that impossible disappearance?"

"Well," Nazaret said, "I finally decided that it was Christianity. Jesus did it. Our blessed babe worked another miracle. It is not for nothing that we are the first nation in the world to accept Jesus. It was Christianity that did it."

"Yes, sir," I used to say, "but your opponents, they also were Christians, every one of them."

The wrestler would look up and consider what I had said, and then he would say, "What you say is true, but we are Armenian Christians, and that gives us just the edge we need. An Irish Christian, a Greek Christian, a Polish Christian—Jesus *will* help them, but only *after* he has helped an Armenian Christian."

I have never had occasion to use any of the wrestler's advice, however.

Or so I seem to believe, at any rate.

But who says I am a Christian? With me, in religion, it has got to be all or none, and none is just an edge too little and belittling. Chance meetings with living saints and sons of bitches go on and on.

Chance Meetings, 1978

The Daily Fight

*L*et me tell you how I live. I live like this. I get up in the morning after all the sleep I think I want. I put fresh water into a kettle and turn the electricity on that is rated from 0 to 10. I let it work at 4, so that by the time I am done with the morning routine the water will just be coming to a boil, and be ready. The ablutions are as follows: brush the teeth, shave, shower, do light exercises, get into the appropriate clothes for the day, and I mean in accordance with the weather which has been pretty cold this winter, even in California, in the rest of the country it was the worst winter in a century or more, the winter of 1977, that is. But all this is not how I live at all, and this is, this now is how I live: I live in the spirit, in thought, in exercise of the spirit, in work, in writing, in reading, in riding a bicycle every day, and in visiting the gardens to observe the growing things once a day. I bought two tract houses and had a young Japanese gardener set out trees in the front and back yards of the two houses: many varieties of trees, and half a dozen or more vines, not excluding a Concord grape vine which is really no good at all for Fresno, or for me, but I let it continue just the same, for I have not the heart nor the will to stop anything that is alive. Well, almost anything. The soil of the gardens is very rich because I have watered and I have permitted fallen leaves and grass to become mulch and to enrich the soil, which almost from the beginning began to be full of worms, and when worms thrive soil is rich—that is not a principle of some kind, but it is something I seem to know. My work is writing, but my real work is being. That's not kidding around, that's the truth. I like being and I am concerned about its continuance for me, myself, and I—once in a while I remember that phase of boyhood in Fresno sixty years ago, and I enjoy using the phrase, as silly as it is to do so. I breathe, and I enjoy breathing. I used to smoke cigarettes very heavily, from about the age of 18 to about the age of 60, when I quit, cold, and the reason I did was that the business was no pleasure for me at all, on the contrary, it was a pain first thing in the morning and all day and half the night. It was sickening. Before I had taken four puffs, inhaling to the bottom of my feet, and to the depths of my mind and spirit and soul, I was sick of it. My spirit didn't leap like a trout in a lake, it sank like rock, but not a fine clean smooth rock, it sank like a rotten rock. That went on for many months, and then I began to feel exhausted after I had been up only an hour into a new day, and I knew it was from the poisoning of the smoke. So I gave it up, and that slowly cleaned out the lungs and the blood and the mind and heart and soul and spirit, and ever since I have enjoyed breathing. I can smell the faintest scent of new almond blossoms, and that is a very fragile scent, and worth going after. I like to eat, too, of course, but plain stuff pretty much, which I can fix or set out for myself, as when what I eat is no more than something you need only put on a table: walnuts from my own two trees, enormous seedless raisins made by my cousin Louis Saroyan of Sanger, dried peaches from my cousin Harry Bagdasarian of Selma, cousins from paternal and maternal sides, respectively, and like as not cold water from the tap. And that's living, and something I insist upon, water from the tap, everywhere I go, for if the people are having it, I ought to have it, too. But surely there is more to living than that, and there is, and don't we know it, though, but we are here and now concerned about pretty much an outline of my way of getting through one day to another and thus through the years, which might be worth comparing with your way. I ask for a clear head, and that means that I don't drink, I don't take popular drugs like pot, or any other kind, I don't take medicine, not even for pain, like aspirin, and if I find I have got something that is loosely referred to as a cold, I give the whole man more rest and recreation than ever, and I take to hot lemonade with honey, as desired, and I spend time in bed reading trash (but glorious) books. I do not read systematically, for the acquiring of information. I find that my wisdom is sharpened and deepened by haphazard reading of all kinds, and that is the kind of reading that gets me over any cold, and the kind that either banishes discontent, depression, impatience, annoyance, anger, despair, and all of the other negative states which are continuously real, and likely to be very troublesome to a man, at home or abroad, with wife or without, surrounded by people or in the midst of solitude. How do I live? Well, very simply, and very gladly, and very much in a daily fight with death, believe me, old reader, young friend, with despair, with discontent—who? Me? Yes, me, myself, and I, so old pal just remember that one of the really joyous sons of bitches in the world, and everywhere else, for that matter, one of the perpetual songsters of the human race, one of the laughers, has to fight every day not to be undone by the damned sorrow that is in things themselves, it would seem, in matter itself, and in spirit, and in procedure, and in energy, and in action, of any kind. But Christ, what would I do if I didn't have the fight to fight? I don't think I would know, or begin to know what to do with myself. Just to avoid dying every day is the joy of my very dream of myself and my truth and my meaning. Do you think anybody would have done anything at all except for that daily fight? I feel sorry for people who for some reason do not seem to know, even, that they are in any such fight. They have got to be bereft of the best that is man's alone.

Obituaries, 1979